FIRST SIGN OF DANGER

Also by Kelley Armstrong

Haven's Rock

Murder at Haven's Rock
The Boy Who Cried Bear
Cold as Hell

Rockton

City of the Lost
A Darkness Absolute
This Fallen Prey
Watcher in the Woods
Alone in the Wild
A Stranger in Town
The Deepest of Secrets

A Rip Through Time

A Rip Through Time
The Poisoner's Ring
Disturbing the Dead
Death at a Highland Wedding

Past Series

A Stitch in Time
Cursed Luck
Cainsville
Otherworld
Nadia Stafford

Standalone Horror

Hemlock Island
I'll Be Waiting
The Haunting of Paynes Hollow

Standalone Thrillers

Wherever She Goes
Every Step She Takes
The Life She Had
Known to the Victim

Young Adult Novels

The Masked Truth

Missing

Aftermath

Someone Is Always Watching

Otherworld: Kate & Logan

Darkest Powers

Darkness Rising

Age of Legends

FIRST SIGN OF DANGER

A Haven's Rock Novel

KELLEY ARMSTRONG

MINOTAUR BOOKS
NEW YORK

This is a work of fiction. All of the names, characters, organizations, places, and events portrayed in this work are either products of the author's imagination or used fictitiously.

First published in the United States by Minotaur Books,
an imprint of St. Martin's Publishing Group

EU Representative: Macmillan Publishers Ireland Ltd, 1st Floor, The Liffey Trust Centre, 117–126 Sheriff Street Upper, Dublin 1, D01 YC43

Printed in the United States of America. For information, address St. Martin's Publishing Group, 120 Broadway, New York, NY 10271.

www.minotaurbooks.com

The Library of Congress Cataloging-in-Publication Data
is available upon request.

ISBN 978-1-250-35182-1 (hardcover)
ISBN 978-1-250-44246-8 (Canadian edition)
ISBN 978-1-250-35183-8 (ebook)

First U.S. Edition: 2026
First International Edition: 2026

10 9 8 7 6 5 4 3 2 1

INTRODUCTION

If you're new to the Haven's Rock series—or if it's been a while since you've read the last book—here's a little introduction to get you up to speed. Otherwise, if you're ready to go, just skip to chapter 1 and dive in!

Welcome to Haven's Rock. Population eighty-seven people. Located in the Yukon wilderness, we're a hidden town where people go to disappear. Residents come here under false names and false histories. Haven's Rock has been up and running for a year and a half now. Most of us previously worked in the earlier incarnation, Rockton.

Rockton was born in the 1950s as an exercise in idealism. A place for people who needed refuge, and in those earliest years, it was often their ideals that brought them there, fleeing McCarthyism and other political witch hunts. When the town struggled in the late sixties, a few wealthy former residents took over management and organized regular supply drops. That's when the town began evolving from a commune of lost souls into a for-profit institution, with a board of directors. Some, though, still believed in the philanthropical ideal of the town.

We believed in that ideal, too, which is why, when things became untenable, we started Haven's Rock. This one is ours.

Like Rockton, Haven's Rock is off the grid, with no access to the outside world. No roads. No internet. We're cut off from the world, and we need that to keep everyone safe. You won't find Haven's Rock on any map, and we stay that way with the help of camouflage, both structural and technological. That's easier than it seems when you're in the Yukon—a northern Canadian territory the size of Texas with fewer than fifty thousand people.

I'm Casey Duncan—known here as Casey Butler. At eighteen, I blew up my life in such spectacular fashion that I'd spent the next twelve years going through the motions, working as a homicide detective while—ironically—waiting for someone to arrest me for my own long-ago crime, when I'd unintentionally killed the guy whose life choices led to a beating that nearly killed *me*.

I'm the local detective. Eric Dalton is the sheriff and my husband. We also have a deputy, Will Anders, and an honorary canine officer, Storm, my Newfoundland dog. Our six-month-old daughter, Rory, has not yet been recruited to the team.

We aren't alone out here. Our favorite neighbor is Lilith, a photographer, who lives with Nero, the wolf she rescued as a pup. Then there's the mining camp that popped up after Haven's Rock was built, and they've been nothing but a source of stress and angst for us.

Others who joined us from Rockton are:

- my sister, April, our doctor
- Kenny, the local carpenter and head of the militia
- Isabel, who runs our bar, the Roc
- Phil, Isabel's partner and our town manager

- Devon and Brian, a couple who run the café—my favorite shop in town
- Sebastian, Rockton's youngest adult resident
- Mathias, the town butcher, a psychiatrist with an expertise in criminal pathology, both professionally and personally
- Raoul, Mathias and Sebastian's dog
- Eric's brother Jacob, his wife, Nicole, and their young son, Stephen, who live here part-time but are currently living on the land

We've also picked up a few staff from the construction crew:

- Yolanda, who built Haven's Rock and is the granddaughter of Émilie, the benefactor who largely financed our new town
- Kendra, social worker, town plumbing expert, and militia member
- Gunnar, our jack-of-all-trades

FIRST SIGN OF DANGER

CHAPTER ONE

Our daughter is six months old, and our dog is still clearly convinced that we have no idea what we're doing and, without her intervention, our child will crawl into the woods and be devoured by wolves. We'd been hiking for an hour, with Rory happily bouncing along in the carrier on Dalton's back. I'd walked behind him, so I can ensure she's okay . . . and make faces at her.

We've stopped in a clearing, taken her out, and put her on the ground, and Storm is in full herding mode. Despite the fact that Newfoundlands are not herding dogs. Despite the fact that Rory is crawling around gurgling gleefully. Also despite the fact that we walk this route once a week and put Rory down in the *exact same spot* every time.

When Storm's anxious growls turn to full-throated Newfie woofs, I cover my ears and shout to be heard over the noise. "One of these days, we are leaving you behind, dog."

She keeps barking. We keep wincing. And Rory grins up at her massive black-haired mop of a big sister.

I order Storm to lie down, which makes barking impossible,

so she resorts to loud grumbling as she watches Rory, ready for . . . I don't know, our baby to leap to her feet and make a run for it?

I drop to the ground beside Rory, which seems to calm Storm. Dalton roots around in my pack and pulls out the water canteen, granola bars, and one digestive cookie for our red-cheeked teething baby.

"See, Casey?" he says as he hands me the canteen. "She just needed a distraction from her teeth. Long walks always work. Now, the trick is to tire her out so she falls asleep on the way back and then we can ease her into her crib and really enjoy our day off."

I stretch out in the long grass. "I'm enjoying *this*."

His brows rise. "And that's all you want for a very rare shared day off when the baby is actually sleeping?"

I smile. "No, I'll take whatever you're offering. I just mean that I like this. And not just because she's finally quiet."

"Rory? Or Storm?"

"Both."

I lay my head on Storm's flank as I watch our daughter grabbing at a grass strand. My miracle baby. A miracle in the sense that I didn't think I'd ever be able to have children. And a miracle because I never thought I'd find someone I wanted to have them with.

Dalton and I wouldn't have dared try for a child until the town was fully functional, but nature intervened and gave us Rory. As for Haven's Rock, it's been chugging along uneventfully for six months, and *uneventful* is exactly how we like it. The town continues to fill with people seeking refuge, and we're growing confident in our ability to provide that refuge.

It's early September now. In southern Canada, it'd still be summer, with fall on the horizon. Up here, it's been autumn for a few weeks, the world turning golden and quiet as we begin the descent into another long winter.

Dalton finishes his bar, stretches out in front of Rory, and prods things for her to explore—twigs, rocks, a bug. He grew up in the wilderness and has never left, and I smile as I watch him engaging our daughter in her environment. Storm might not like seeing Rory crawling about on the ground, but this is the life she will lead, and she's already happiest here, in the sunshine watching a bug crawl up a twig.

When Storm leaps up, unceremoniously dumping me to the ground, I barely have time to recover before she resumes barking.

"Really?" I say. "What's wrong *now*? Rory hasn't moved from . . ."

I trail off as I realize Storm is looking into the forest. Of course, my husband has already realized this and is on his feet, scanning the trees, fingers resting on the butt of his gun.

Yes, Dalton carries a sidearm. So do I. In Rockton, he was the sheriff and I was his detective, and we continue those roles in Haven's Rock, mostly because we've learned it makes people feel safe, and when the majority of our residents are victims, feeling safe is critical.

We no longer wear the guns around town—that was a Wild West affectation the Rockton council insisted on. But we usually wear them when we leave Haven's Rock. Dalton doesn't take his out, though. Just rests his fingers there. We're not readying our weapons when the "danger" is almost certainly a fox or moose.

Newfoundlands aren't known to be vocal, and Storm never was . . . until we brought a baby into the house. Last week, she went into a barking frenzy at a vole that snuck into our chalet. Apparently, it wasn't only wolves that could devour our child.

As she barks, I lay my hand on her head, telling her we've got this. It's not until I scoop up Rory that Storm quiets. She moves beside Dalton, who's listening intently. Something's out there. Big enough that he can hear it moving.

Dalton surveys the clearing. He's trying to decide whether it's safe to leave me here while he investigates. If Storm's barks didn't send the animal fleeing, it's not small, and at this time of year predators may actually come closer when they hear her. Snow on the mountaintops warns that winter is coming. Sick or elderly predators can become desperate. That goes double for bears, looking to store up fat to get them through hibernation. Stories of unavoidable grizzly attacks often happen at this time of year, and that's why I'm not only carrying my sidearm—I also have a rifle on my back. We have a baby now. We are ridiculously careful.

I motion for Dalton to take the rifle and investigate. Then I hold Rory in one arm as I tug the bear spray from my pack and put it in my jacket pocket. Usually, if I saw a bear I'd go for the spray first. With Rory, I'll make that judgment call when the time comes. Bear spray is very effective under normal circumstances, but a desperate bear does not behave normally.

It's only after Storm and Dalton are gone that I realize I have too much to juggle here—baby, bear spray, gun.

Storm may have a point. As careful as we are, we're still new parents.

I look around and then back against a thick pine.

Rory fusses. She was happily on the ground, playing with Daddy, and now Mom is awkwardly holding her in one arm, and Dad and Storm are gone, and it's boring. Really boring. Which reminds her that her mouth hurts where her first tooth is breaking through.

I bounce her and put my other arm around her, while keeping it ready to grab my gun or spray. I whisper to her under my breath, singing "Itsy Bitsy Spider," which is one of three nursery songs I know, and I'm probably getting the words wrong, but she's six months old—it doesn't matter. And it really doesn't matter right now, as I try to keep her quiet—

Rory roars. She came into the world that way, and she's never stopped. It's even the joking version of how she got her name. I kiss her cheeks and her forehead and she roars in rage and the remembered pain of her teething, her round face going beet red up to the roots of her wild black hair.

"Shh, shh, shh," I say as I bounce her faster.

Crashing sounds in the bushes. A dark shape appears maybe ten feet beyond the clearing.

My hand drops to my gun. Screw the spray. I have a baby, and I am not taking chances—

"Hey!" Dalton shouts. "Back the fuck up! Now!"

It is a testament to my fear that, for a moment, I think he might actually be talking to me.

When a human voice answers, I stop, hand on my gun. It sounds like a woman. It's not Lilith, the wilderness photographer who lives out here. There's also a mining camp, but there aren't any women among the miners or staff.

Could it be one of our residents? We have thirty-three women in town now, and unless I know them well, I'm not going to recognize their voice when they're freaking out . . . which they would be if Dalton caught them on a secret hike.

Rory has stopped, too, as she turns toward the voice. Something new. Something interesting. I move in that direction slowly, listening until I can make out words.

"—husband was trying to see where we are, and he slipped and fell. His ankle's twisted. I heard the dog barking and came running. Then I heard a baby. Is there a town here? A settlement?"

I keep walking toward the voices as Dalton says no, there isn't a town for a hundred kilometers or more. When I step out onto the path, he glowers my way, but I shake my head. It's not as if she didn't hear the baby.

I also see the reason for her panic. Dalton has his gun out. His finger isn't anywhere near the trigger, but all she sees is a man with a gun and a very large dog. When she spots me, she makes a noise almost like a yelp of relief and hurries in my direction.

"Stop, please," I say calmly. "I understand you're in some trouble, but this isn't a campground. We don't expect to bump into anyone out here, so we're naturally going to be cautious."

"O-okay," she stammers. "Right. Yes. Sorry. But that's why I came running. We didn't think we had a chance of finding anyone out here. Especially this time of year. I know it's off-season for hiking, but this is when my husband had vacation time, and a friend said it was gorgeous here, and the forecast was good and—" She stops and takes a deep breath and then puts out her hand. "I'm Gretchen. We're from Whitehorse."

I don't move close enough to shake her hand. "You said your husband is hurt."

"Not badly hurt. It's just . . . We lost our GPS the other day. It was a really stupid . . ."

She trails off and catches her breath again, trying to calm herself. I use the pause to get a better look at her. She's average height, slender, white with light brown hair in a ponytail. Weathered tan skin and blue eyes. Maybe late thirties. Dressed for backcountry hiking.

"We were crossing a creek," she says. "I slipped on a rock and fell in. I was wearing the equipment belt—with our sat phone, GPS, compass, maps, wallets . . . I must not have fastened it right because it came off and went downstream. Blake—my husband—went after it, but the water was running too fast. We spent all day following the creek, which emptied into a lake. There was no sign of the belt. Everything we had to navigate with was in there."

"So you're lost."

She nods. "We still thought we could handle it. We've been doing this for decades. We met when we came to the Yukon for summer jobs as students. We fell in love with the north and moved up here after graduation. We go out every year, exploring some new corner. We know what we're doing. Blake thought if he could get some elevation, he might see where we needed to go. We climbed that mountain over there"—she points—"but when he tried to get a better vantage point, he slipped and twisted his ankle."

"Where is he now?"

"Back at camp." She waves. "Maybe a ten-minute walk? We heard the barking, and I set off running. It went quiet, so I slowed down. Then the baby started crying." She exhales. "I know I freaked you out, appearing from nowhere, but I am so glad to see you."

"He twisted his ankle?" I ask.

"Not too badly. We were able to keep moving. But if there's a settlement nearby, we could get medical attention, maybe map out a route to our pickup spot."

Map out their route? If her husband is hurt, wouldn't they be looking for an exit strategy that doesn't involve walking on a sprained ankle?

I keep my expression impassive, as does Dalton. We'd encountered a badly injured hiker once in Rockton. Turned out they *were* actually injured . . . but *not* actually a hiker.

One of the reasons we chose this region is that hikers are exceptionally rare. Placer miners and hunters and trappers are a little more common, but that still means we're only likely to see signs of one a year. This isn't the middle of the Arctic, but it's not Banff National Park either. There are no trails, much less facilities.

I've been cool because I'm suspicious, but it's time to warm up, at least seem as if I buy her story.

"We're camping ourselves," I say, waving in a direction that does *not* lead to Haven's Rock. "Running trap lines before winter sets in. We were just out hiking for the day. We can certainly look at your husband's foot, though. We're both first-aid certified, with wilderness medical experience." The certified part is a lie, but living out here means we're fully prepared for both first aid and wilderness medical emergencies.

"We can help you find your way," Dalton says. "Got a compass we can spare. But we have a sat phone back at camp. Could call for a flight out."

"Oh, I hope it doesn't come to that. We're still hoping to make it up to the ridge and camp for a few days. Our friend said it was amazing."

"Ridge?" I say.

She points to a mountain maybe ten kilometers west. "On the south side of that. If we can make it there, Blake can get a few days of rest before we rendezvous with our pickup, maybe another twenty kilometers on. That's in a week, so we have plenty of time. The pickup is prearranged. We don't need to call anyone, thankfully."

We must look skeptical, because she says, "It really is just a twisted ankle. Not a break or a sprain. We still have our route plan. We just need directions so we can get back on track."

A twisted ankle *is* a sprained ankle, but I don't say that. It isn't in our best interests to openly question this story any more than necessary.

"Wait here," Dalton says, and starts walking in the other direction.

Her brows shoot up.

"He means give us a few minutes," I say. "It's getting late, and we need to discuss how we're going to do this—whether I come along with the baby or go back to camp."

"Oh, right. Of course. Take your time."

CHAPTER TWO

Dalton leads me about five hundred feet down the narrow game trail we've been using as a path. Then he stands there, gazing back in the woman's direction and saying only one word.

"Fuck."

We're quiet for a few minutes, working it through. We don't like this scenario, and we know we'll be on the same page with that.

Is her story an obvious fabrication? No, but it waves red flags in every direction. Hiking past summer, and in an area where you'll be trail-blazing through rough terrain during hungry-bear season. A woman alone, her husband left behind, because we're liable to respond better to a woman in distress. Guy's injured, which will make him seem less of a threat. He's twisted his ankle, but they plan to keep moving even when we offered to arrange a pickup.

Here's the main reason we did not intend to have a baby right now. Because protecting Haven's Rock must be our main priority. A year ago, we wouldn't have walked away to discuss it. We'd have followed "Gretchen" with extreme caution because we need to deal with potential threats immediately.

But decent parents are not going to walk into danger with a baby. Yet what's the alternative? Send me back to town with Rory? Haven's Rock is over an hour away. Also I'd never let Dalton face this alone.

We wouldn't have brought Rory if we expected trouble. But one does not expect to encounter hikers off-season in an area where we have never even seen a single hiker since we built the town.

"Thoughts?" Dalton says finally.

"I don't want you going with her. If it's trouble, Rory and I are the weak point. Her partner could circle back for an ambush."

"Agreed."

"My best suggestion would be that you stay here with Rory while Storm and I go with her."

"Don't like that."

"I know."

He exhales and stares off into the distance, crow's feet deepening around his eyes.

The woman had seemed surprised to see me. Had she mistaken Dalton for some kind of mountain man? I can't imagine that. My own first impression of him had been "cowboy," and that's still what he looks like, slightly taller than average, rangy, tanned white skin, weathered for thirty-six, light brown hair cut short with a close-trimmed beard.

My own looks lean a little more toward "environmentally conscious tourist." I'm half white, half Asian, just skimming five foot two, stronger than I look, with clothing choices that are a little more, er, high-end than Dalton's.

If the woman was surprised to see me, is that because I don't look like anyone she'd picture roughing it in the Yukon wilderness? That would add credence to her story—if she came here for Haven's Rock, she'd know who she was looking for. We're always on the alert for someone connected to Rockton tracking us down and causing trouble. However, being a town of refugees means we are even more concerned about someone coming for one of our residents, and those people would not know who to expect running the town.

"What are the odds, you think?" I say.

"Twenty-five percent that it's legit," he says without hesitation. "Forty percent Rockton council spy, ten percent tracking down a resident, twenty-five percent unknown."

"Already worked it all through, huh?"

"Yep." He pauses. "No, I should reassess. Not twenty-five percent legit. More like ten percent, fifteen tops. The rest would be that they're looking for something other than Haven's Rock."

"Lilith or the mining camp." I shift my weight and Dalton immediately reaches for Rory, who is awake and quiet. I hand her over and stretch my shoulders. "I might put those odds a bit above that. If they're here for Haven's Rock, wouldn't they ask to come back with us?"

"Don't want to overplay their hand. That could be why she insists they'll be fine without an airlift."

"Waiting until we examine her husband, and then they'll agree that maybe he does need actual medical care. Back at our so-called camp."

Dalton only grunts, and when Rory fusses, he gives her his knuckle to chew. "I agree you should go on with Storm, and I should hang back with Rory. But I'll follow along, stay close enough to listen in."

"That would have been my suggestion."

"Can you help get Rory strapped to my back? I'd like both my hands free."

"Good idea."

If the woman—Gretchen—is surprised that I'll be coming alone with Storm, she gives no sign of it. I also watch for her to signal to anyone nearby. She doesn't. Yes, there's part of me that feels guilty suspecting her, and if it turns out that she's just a hiker with an injured spouse, I'm going to feel like a cold bitch for begrudgingly offering to help. But that doesn't mean I'd be less suspicious next time.

We have earned our paranoia, and I'll continue to embrace it, no matter how it might make me feel. Our residents deserve that paranoia. It's what they came for—to be someplace where those in charge are hypervigilant, putting their safety above all else.

Even above the safety of their own daughter? No. That's never going to happen, and Dalton and I have accepted that while our residents are our priority, we are not martyrs. No one who works in Haven's Rock is.

Dalton and I have our little family, and we have our wider family in Haven's Rock, from literal family—my sister—to friends who comprise our family of choice. They come first, along with our daughter.

As I walk, I try to relax as if I've lowered my guard. Gretchen is friendly and chatty—*very* chatty, and if her story is true, that would be the chattiness of relief at having found help. My responses land somewhere between polite and friendly, which is the territory where I live.

I act like someone who is happy enough to help but isn't tripping over herself to be sociable. Again, that's me.

I don't look back for Dalton, even surreptitiously. He'll have left the game trail to slip closer. Of course, with a teething baby, stealth might not be an option. He knows that. If Rory wails, he'll need to join me and say he changed his mind.

We go pretty much exactly as far as Gretchen said before I spot a man sitting on the ground. He's about her age, which fits the "college sweethearts" part of her story. He has brown skin, dark hair salted with silver and a beard. He's holding a hat between his hands, kneading it as if in boredom. Then he sees us and starts vaulting to his feet before stumbling a bit and wincing. An exaggerated stumble? An exaggerated wince? I can't be sure.

"Hello, there," he calls. "That must be the dog we heard. Wow. He's a big one. Newfoundland?"

I nod.

He gives a soft laugh. "Don't see many of those in the Yukon. Mostly husky crosses up here."

"True," I say. The north *is* full of various sled dogs and crosses, which could support their story of living in Whitehorse.

"This is my husband, Blake. Blake, this is—" Gretchen stops. "Oh, I didn't even get your name."

"Katie."

Blake thrusts out a hand. "Very happy to see you, Katie. I'm, uh, guessing you aren't out here alone? I thought I heard a baby."

"My husband took her back to camp. I have the first-aid kit, and I'm more experienced using it."

"Oh, you should have seen the baby," Gretchen says. "So cute. All that black hair. How old is she?"

"Almost six months."

Is my tone a little cool? I struggle to warm it, to respond like a normal proud mom, but every enthusiastic comment—the dog! the baby!—only has my hackles rising. It feels like being lured into a van with candy. What dog-and-baby mom can resist someone who flatters their darlings?

On the other hand, the problem might be the vibes I'm giving off. Coolly polite, maybe seeming as if they've interrupted my day with their emergency. The begrudging Samaritan. Faced with that, they might trip over themselves to be friendly. They're lost and injured, their navigation and communication gone. They need me, and if talking about my dog and baby helps, that's what they'll do.

"Katie's husband gave us a compass, too." Gretchen holds out the one Dalton handed her before he left with Rory. She pulls a notebook from her pocket. "And he fixed our trail map. Showed us where we are and pointed out a few errors, plus a shortcut. I told you we shouldn't have relied on Matt's memory."

"Let's take a look at that foot," I say, lowering myself to one knee.

He starts to take off his boot.

"I'll do that," I say. "Just relax and keep your weight off it. You twisted it in a fall?"

"Yeah," Blake says. "I was being stupid. Gretchen blames testosterone. I told myself if I could get out farther on this narrow ledge, I would absolutely see a landmark we needed. I couldn't see a damn thing more than I could back where Gretchen was. Then I stumbled and fell."

At least his story matches hers, with extra detail. As a former police detective, I know what to look for in corroborating stories. I also note that she's beside him, drinking from the canteen, where she can't sneak him body-language messages. His gaze is on me. She's relaxed and making no effort to interject or add to his story.

"How far did you fall?" I ask as I remove his boot.

"We were hundreds of feet up, but it was only about an eight-foot drop to the next ledge, which is why Gretchen didn't forbid me from trying for a better look. The problem was how I landed. At first, it seemed okay. The kind of thing you can just walk off. I popped a couple of painkillers, and we got down the mountain no problem. Then we decided to call it an early day, made lunch, and when I went to put on my boot again, it wouldn't fit."

I glance at the boot . . . which had been on his foot. "This boot?"

"We found a stream," Gretchen says. "Ice-cold water."

Blake nods. "I got the swelling down enough to pull on my boot. That's when we heard your pup here." He smiles and reaches to pat Storm, who tolerates it. "At first, we weren't sure what it was. That's one deep bark. I started worrying about bears."

"'Tis the season."

He makes a face. "I know. It's the wrong time of year to be hiking. But we're careful, and we have spray. We've never had a problem."

"Yes," his wife murmurs. "That's what everyone says before they have a problem with grizzlies. And once they do, it's the last problem they have."

"It's fine," Blake says firmly. "We haven't even *seen* a grizzly on this trip."

Gretchen's expression suggests she'd been nervous about a backcountry hike at this time of year. It's a dynamic I'm always grateful Dalton and I don't have—where one partner raises concerns and the other dismisses them as overreacting.

It's a common friction point, though. Suggesting they really are a couple?

My suspicion meter dips a little. Then I see Blake's ankle. There's a bit of swelling, but no more than you might see after a long day of hiking. I palpate the foot, and he jumps as if I've stabbed him.

"Tender?" I say, my tone neutral.

"Yeah."

I try pressing my fingers in, but he pulls from my grip.

"I was checking to make sure it isn't broken," I say.

"It's not."

"Blake, let her check please."

"It's not broken. I couldn't walk on it if it was."

"That's actually a common misconception," I say as I sit back on my haunches.

"Well, it's not broken. I can tell."

Huh. Interesting. Is he afraid I'll realize he's not actually hurt?

If their goal is to get into Haven's Rock, wouldn't they play it up?

You're right. It does seem broken. I really should get to a doctor.

"I would like to test it for usability," I say.

"It's fine," he says quickly.

"Blake . . ." Gretchen says.

I tense, ready for him to snap something at his wife, but he sighs and drops his head.

"I'm sorry, Katie," he says. "I know you're trying to help. I'm angry with myself, and I shouldn't be snapping at you."

Gretchen clears her throat, and he looks her way with a sheepish smile. "Or at you. Sorry, hon."

"Just let Katie do her thing, okay? You don't want to be a day's walk from here, passed out from pain."

He nods and allows me to run it through some basic usability tests. The problem with those is that they rely on self-reported pain. When he winces, is he faking it? When he doesn't react, is he suppressing it?

He'd jumped earlier when I was prodding his ankle, but now his reactions are much more muted, meaning I can't tell whether that means he's not injured or just trying to convince us he's fine enough to continue on their hike.

"May I wrap it?" I ask.

"Yes," Gretchen replies before Blake can answer. "Please."

I do that as I talk them through care. It's the basic RICE first aid. Rest. Ice. Compression. Elevation. Compression means the bindings I put on, and I show them how to replace them and give Gretchen extras. Ice will need to mean cold streams. Elevation means raising it above his heart when he's sleeping. As for resting, since they already plan a couple of days off, I only agree that this is a good strategy.

"You have pain medication?" I ask.

"Ibuprofen," Gretchen. "It'll work on the swelling, too, right?"

"It will. But the meds and the ice are short-term measures. Even if it seems better when you get back to Whitehorse, see your doctor. Don't keep on with the ice and pills past that."

"We will."

Gretchen envelops me in a hug before I can duck it. I'm not sure I would have anyway. While I'm not really the hugging type, I know she's trying to show gratitude. I survive the hug, and Storm survives the petting. They ask if there are any good spots to camp nearby, and I direct them a little farther west, where they'll find a small meadow near a stream.

"Just check for berries," I say. "You don't want to pop your tent in the middle of a cranberry patch and have bears visit."

"We won't," Gretchen says with a smile, and I motion for Storm to set out back the way we came.

CHAPTER THREE

I meet up with Dalton and fill him in as we walk back to Haven's Rock. We *are* going back, and we are aware of the risk of leading them there. But I'd stuck around long enough to see Gretchen and Blake move on, and Dalton and I walked the first twenty minutes in silence so we could listen for the sound of anyone following us. We hear nothing. Storm hears nothing. We're good. For now.

We can't lurk with a teething baby—Rory was sleeping, but now she's grumbling, ready to break into screams. Afternoon is passing into evening, and we can no longer expect sunshine until midnight. We need to get back and tell the others what we found.

Once we near town, we divert into the forest, taking a longer route on rough paths, just in case we've left too much of a trail.

Haven's Rock is bustling. Shifts are ending. People are heading to their quarters or out for dinner, and—to add confusion to the mix—the Roc doesn't seem open yet. With no prospects for a post-work cocktail hour, people mill about like automatons with their path blocked.

"What's up?" I say to one of the residents.

"Roc's closed."

"She can see that," a voice says. "She means why is it closed."

I turn as a tall woman with raked-back curls and dark brown skin walks up behind Dalton.

"Stealing your baby, Eric," she says. "Auntie Yolanda has missed her Rory time today. That was one hell of a hike you guys took."

"What's going on at the Roc?" I say. "Is Isabel okay?"

Isabel runs the Roc, as she did in Rockton. While she has help as our population grows, she's still not comfortable enough with her new staff to leave them in charge. Or maybe "comfort" isn't the right word, implying she doesn't trust them. Isabel just likes to be in control.

"Iz is fine," Yolanda says. "There's a sign on the door saying the Roc opens at seven today. You know what it's like. Everyone's so accustomed to our perfect clockwork of a town that they short-circuit when a gear breaks. I think it's a water issue. Kendra's on patrol, so they're waiting for her to get back and fix it."

I glance at Dalton, who only shakes his head. There is no water issue. Yolanda is saying that because people have shifted our way, trying to eavesdrop.

"Make way," Yolanda says as she heads for the Roc. "Teething baby coming through. She needs her whiskey gum rub."

"Uh, that's not actually done anymore," a nearby woman ventures.

"No, but it's a fine excuse to get me into the bar early."

The woman steps back, eyeing Yolanda uncertainly, as if her good mood is as suspicious as our hiking couple's story.

Yolanda's construction company built Haven's Rock, and then she decided to take a break from entrepreneurship to help us because that's the kind of woman she is, endlessly sweet and kind, like her grandmother, Émilie.

Yeah, no one who spends five minutes with Yolanda mistakes her for sweet or kind. She's here because she's fiercely loyal to Émilie. Initially she suspected we were conning an elderly billionaire. She knows better now—in the sense that she knows we're just a bunch of bleeding-heart idealists who are liable to all die of misplaced altruism if she leaves.

As for the good mood . . .

"How was your day shadowing Will?" I ask.

"I survived. Had to keep kicking his ass to get him moving. You know what he's like. Heads out to do a task and stops to talk to five people on the way."

More like five people stop him to talk, and our deputy, Will Anders, shoulders the weight of being the sociable third of our law-enforcement trio. Everyone likes Anders. Including someone who is in a remarkably chipper mood after spending the day with him.

Yolanda shoves open the Roc front door like she's about to start a brawl.

"We're closed," someone snaps, and a woman appears from the dim interior. She's in her late forties, wearing a tailored blouse, hiking boots, and jeans that perfectly hug her curves. "Ah, the calvary has arrived. There's a toll for you, though, Ms. Yolanda." Isabel scoops Rory from Yolanda's arms. "There. Paid in full."

"Hey, that was mine."

"Actually mine," I say. "And if you fight over my child, I am taking her back."

Someone emerges from the shadows and takes Rory. "Problem solved. She's with her favorite uncle."

It's Anders. Big and brawny, with close-cropped curls and

skin a shade darker than Yolanda's. He recently turned forty and has the kind of good looks that'll still turn heads at twice that age. Anders chucks Rory under the chin and, on cue, the baby smiles her biggest smile.

"Even babies fall for you," Yolanda mutters. "Unbelievable."

"They have excellent taste." Anders waves to us. "Come on in. Sit down. Have a drink. Well, you and I can have a drink, Eric. Casey's still on mocktails."

"I might actually pump and dump tonight," I say.

His brows shoot up. "Rough hike?"

"Mmm, weird and potentially concerning hike. But I'm guessing by the way Yolanda was talking about a water issue that something else has happened."

I look around and spot Phil behind the counter. Phil is Isabel's boyfriend and, unofficially, the town mayor, and the order in which I place those two roles says a lot about Haven's Rock. Or a lot about Isabel.

Phil is my age, white, handsome in a fussy, corporate way—even today, he's wearing a button-down shirt and the glasses that I won twenty bucks on when I bet Dalton they weren't prescription.

"Will, Isabel, and Phil all in one place," I murmur. "Not a town meeting if the Roc is closed. Not even a town emergency. Could be that something happened while the coffee bar was open here this afternoon, but then Brian or Devon would be here. So something happened in the interim. Or something was discovered . . ." I rock back on my heels. "Shit. Did we have another break-in?"

Anders claps me on the back with his free hand while he bounces Rory. "Took you a while, Detective. Still blaming baby brain?"

I shake my head. The last break-in at the Roc was five months ago and nothing was taken. My theory was that Carson snuck in looking for a stray beer, but wasn't about to actually break into the stockroom to steal one. We announced the so-called break-in, and no one tried again. So I wasn't exactly expecting a repeat months later.

"This time it wasn't the kid," Yolanda says. "I put a four-pack in their clubhouse. Only one was drank."

I wince. "You gave beer to a fourteen-year-old?"

"The light stuff. And I just dropped it off. Carson drank one but left the rest. A second one was opened, but then the cap was put back on—badly—after a few sips. I figure that was Max."

"The eleven-year-old. Great. Just great."

Yolanda chucks Rory under the chin. "See, this is why I will be your favorite auntie."

"This was an actual break-in." Phil walks over from behind the bar. "The last time was when the back door was left unlocked awaiting a supply run."

"And the stockroom? I presume that was their goal. Did they get in?"

"No, and I'm not sure it *was* their goal." Phil motions me to the bar. When I walk over, he points at the door leading into the stock and brewing room. "No sign of a forced entry attempt."

I examine the knob and lock, and then the door. "And the point of entry into the building itself?"

"The back door, which *was* forced open. Brian and Devon were gone, and Isabel and I hadn't arrived yet."

Anders calls over, "Back door's easy to break into."

"By design," Yolanda shoots back. "I was told that the main doors didn't require heavy security. What counted was the stockroom."

"Hey, I wasn't blaming you. I was pointing out that it's easy enough to get in the back. My guess is that they came in that way and then saw how hard it would be to get into the stockroom and left. They only had an hour max before Iz came to open up."

"But wouldn't they know that the stockroom is heavily secured?" Yolanda says as I walk to the back door. "Anyone can come into the Roc during business hours—even the kids. The stockroom is right there. They'd know they'd never break in with less than an hour, midday."

"That presumes someone thought this through," Anders says. "We have a few new residents. One could have an unreported alcohol dependency."

I examine the back door. "Someone desperate enough could have realized the Roc was temporarily empty and broken in with a crowbar, which we stock in the toolshed."

Anders nods. "They come to Haven's Rock, figuring they can hide their addiction, only to discover how tightly we regulate the alcohol."

I rise. "See, this is the kind of crime I like. No dead body. Not even missing booze. A mental puzzle with no real consequences." I look at Dalton. "Hey, boss, mind if I investigate this one? You can handle the hikers, right?"

He only shakes his head. He's been quiet during all this, as he sits at the bar. Quiet because he doesn't really give a damn about a theft-free break-in at the Roc. Not when we have . . .

"Hikers?" Anders says. "You saw someone out there?"

I tell the story. By the time I'm done, Isabel has served drinks to everyone—including me—but only Yolanda and Dalton have touched theirs.

"My money is on a Rockton council spy mission," Anders says. "They've tried restarting Rockton and, from what Émilie says, it's struggling. They've already reached out to her."

Yolanda raises her hands. "They've reached out to Gran to see what you guys are all up to. They suspect you've started your own version, but they don't know it's in the Yukon again."

"Logically, though, the Yukon is the safe bet," Phil says as he fingers his beer glass.

At one time, he'd been the council's liaison with Rockton, working in a cushy office with the very uncushy job of conveying the council's word from on high, which was usually "Whatever you are doing in that town, stop it." Then he'd been exiled to Rockton himself, where he'd put in his time, waiting to be brought home.

Phil could have gone home when Rockton closed. He also could have taken his big "retirement" package and started a new career. So why is he here? The woman standing beside him. He's even stopped insisting he's only helping until we're up and running. That's another twenty bucks Dalton owes me. If Isabel isn't leaving, Phil isn't leaving, and Isabel is never leaving.

Phil continues, "If I were still working for them, I would have said to start searching right around here. That's why I argued for settling further afield. This is where you're accustomed to being—with the landscape and the climate. You also have ties in the area. Eric's brother and his wife. Sebastian's girlfriend. Even Jen and Tyrone Cypher. Ideally, you would want to be within a day or two's hike from all of that. Which is exactly where you are."

Yolanda shrugs. "But if the council wanted you back—specifically Eric, I presume—they could just keep hassling my grandmother until she agreed to let you tell them to fuck off yourself. They're not going to track you down here for that meeting."

"No," Anders says. "They'd track us down to sabotage us so

Eric has no choice but to join their venture—or let them take over here."

Yolanda sighs. "You know you're all a bunch of paranoid freaks, right? I mean, I love you for it, but that's what you need me for. To tell you that you're seeing bogeymen in shadows."

"We probably are," I say. "But we didn't come back to discuss the possibility of murdering two potential council spies in their tent. We need to decide how hard we want to lock down."

"Completely." To my surprise, that comes not from Anders or Phil, but from Isabel. "A complete lockdown with full patrols until we are certain these alleged hikers are gone. I presume you and Eric will be heading out in the morning to check on them?"

"We will. We'll take Storm for tracking. Without Rory, she won't bark. We'll find their campsite—I suggested a spot—and make sure they stayed there and then moved on in the correct direction."

I look around at the others. "Anyone think it's not enough?" I glance at Yolanda. "Notice I don't ask if anyone thinks it's too much."

"I actually don't," Yolanda says. "While I'm certain you're all panicking over two innocent hikers, at worst, we can consider it a lockdown drill." She points to my beer. "Now drink up."

"Actually, no." I push it aside. "Any chance of getting one of your fancy mocktails, Iz? If we're going to be away from Rory all day tomorrow, I need to pump and *not* dump."

Isabel takes my beer and pulls out a glass as Yolanda pats my back. "Sorry, Case. If it's any consolation, we're all very happy for your sacrifice. We get a baby, and you get the enforced sobriety, sore boobs, sleepless nights . . ."

"Oh, just wait until we drop her off at dawn tomorrow. Don't forget, she's teething."

Anders peers at me and then Dalton. "So are there really hikers in the woods? Or are you guys just saying that to get another day off . . . this time leaving the baby behind?"

"Well, you're about to find out, since you'll be joining us tomorrow. Go home and get some sleep. We'll take the evening shift. It'll be a very early start. Ideally, we'd like to get there before they break camp—so we can watch them leave."

CHAPTER FOUR

As promised, we take the evening shift, which is me following up on the Roc break-in while Dalton makes notes about our hiker encounter and does the occasional walk through town.

These days, most of our law enforcement consists of those walks, like constables on a beat, reassuring people of our presence. Otherwise, our jobs are heavily town-management oriented. Also, the lack of actual law-enforcement issues allows us to work fewer hours and spend more time as a family. Tonight, though, since our daughter was claimed by my sister, we have a relatively quiet shift.

I don't know what to make of the break-in at the Roc. I investigate, in the sense that I take fingerprints and poke around checking for anything that could have been stolen or damaged. In the end, though, I'm not sure there's much point in doing more. Nothing was taken. Nothing was damaged. We have no idea who broke in or why, and any other time, I probably would take the excuse to solve this puzzle, but we have other things on our plate.

Partway through our shift, I check in with April to make

sure Rory isn't giving her trouble, but today's long hike has put the baby to sleep, so there's no reason for me to quit work early.

Dalton and I take advantage of the rare opportunity to enjoy dinner together at the restaurant, staying past closing, which is one of the perks of being in charge. By the time we pick up Rory and Storm, it's eleven. Perfect timing to get a good night's sleep and then hit the road at five. Except, we have a baby, who needs her nighttime feeding. She wakes up shortly after we get home and then she doesn't want to go back to sleep, being well rested and also cranky from her teeth.

I insist Dalton go to bed before I feed Rory, and I try to keep her quiet afterward, but he must have set an alarm to be sure I don't spend the entire night dealing with a fussy baby—which, yes, I have done, reasoning one of us should get a good sleep. He comes down at two and bullies me up to bed. Rory must eventually drift off in his arms, and I find them like that when the alarm wakes me at four thirty.

I decide we don't need to leave right at five. There's little chance the hikers will move on early when it's not full light until after seven.

Dalton's still up by five. I have breakfast packed, so I enjoy a coffee with Anders while Dalton runs Rory to Yolanda. By five thirty, we're on our way.

We reach the area a little over an hour later. There's no scent of campfire smoke in the air. If we were the ones heading out, we'd have started the day with a fire, hot breakfast, and hot coffee. But every hiker does things differently, and the lack of smoke doesn't necessarily mean they're still asleep.

I tell Anders where I expect to find the couple camping—in the spot I'd suggested. We split up to approach from different directions.

I take Storm, which means I get the route least likely to bring me near the actual site. Storm's not exactly a sure-footed wilderness wraith. Neither am I, to be honest. I'll try, and so will Anders, but the person who can get closest is Dalton. That means he'll circle around to come in from the opposite direction, which is also the way the couple will walk if they've already headed out.

Anders's route takes him up, where elevation will give him a bird's-eye view. He might not be a silent stalker, but he's an expert climber. I get the direct route down the faint trail to the campsite. If I'm spotted, I'm the least likely to worry Gretchen and Blake. Just "Katie" and her dog come to make sure Blake's ankle is okay.

Still, I'd rather not be spotted. Our goal is for them to never know anyone is here, so we can honestly confirm that they're heading west, as they claimed.

Storm and I hike along the path, which is really just a game trail that we've used often enough for it to remain clear, even if our scent probably means animals no longer go near it.

It's familiar enough terrain that I know where it'll curve just before the campsite. I pause there and tell Storm to stay. Then I listen and sniff again. Is that smoke? It's very faint, suggesting I'm smelling a fire long since put out. The only sound I hear is a distant raven, and it goes silent after a few croaks.

I check to make sure Storm is staying put. She's lying down, and she lifts her head in hope, only to huff a sigh when I repeat the stay signal.

I creep around the corner. The empty clearing is just ahead, maybe twenty paces, off to the right side. As I ease closer, the babble of running water whispers beneath the silence. The creek is on the other side, and it's very small, just enough to provide clean water when we overnight here.

I squint into the thick woods. In a largely coniferous forest, even autumn doesn't thin out the viewing obstacles. When I can't see a tent, I take another two steps. Then I stop. There's movement to the north of the path, right around where I'd expect to find the site.

I ease into the trees and move a little closer. There's definitely someone there. I can just make out a shadowy figure, tall—

"It's me," Dalton grunts.

I walk into the clearing. "How'd you know it was me?"

He rolls his eyes. "How'd you *not* know it was me?"

"Shadows."

He shakes his head. Then he gives a birdcall telling Anders to join us.

"Shouldn't we let him take a look around while he's on higher ground?" I say. "If they got an early start . . ."

I trail off as my detective brain kicks in, and I assimilate my surroundings. I can see the remains of a campfire that's probably been out since last night. Otherwise, the clearing is completely empty.

I check my watch. "They didn't just get an early start, did they."

"Yeah, I think they stopped here for dinner but didn't spend the night."

"Shit."

"Yep."

If they only stopped briefly, that lends credence to our fear that they weren't just hikers and Blake wasn't actually injured. They paused long enough for a meal, in case we returned, and then they moved on.

I peer around as thumps and sliding gravel from the north tell us Anders is taking the speedy way down.

Dalton sighs. "Charging bears are quieter."

"Oh, don't grumble. There's no one around to hear him." I walk a few steps and bend, my fingers moving aside short grasses. "Who used this spot recently?"

"Kendra's been out with Tish. They camp deeper in the woods, though. The overnight excursion stayed by the lake. So we'd have been the last to camp here—a few weeks ago with Rory."

"And we don't pitch our tent over here, but these peg holes look recent."

He bends and then moves at a crouch to check for the other three holes. "Fuck. I missed those."

"Someone also moved our chairs."

I motion at two pieces of trunk we use as fireside seating. When we leave, we clear everything, including covering up the campfire spot, but someone found our cut logs and brought them in, only to move them just outside the clearing before leaving.

"No sign of our alleged hikers?" Anders says as he arrives.

"Actually, they did camp here," I say. "Or, at least, they erected a tent."

"So they left really early?"

"Seems so." I hunker back on my heels. "If the guy was hurt, they might start before dawn so they can maximize break times for him."

"Or he woke in enough pain that they decided to head out."

"Could be. Okay, time to put our trackers to work. See which way they went."

The answer is "west," just as Gretchen and Blake claimed. Storm and Dalton lead us along the trail for a couple of kilometers, and we decide that's enough. As we head back, Anders groans and says, "I owe Yolanda now. I argued the strongest that this was something sketchy, and she disagreed, and I don't even want to know how she'll collect."

Oh, I could joke about how Yolanda might want to collect. I could also tease Anders that I suspect it would be a debt he wouldn't mind paying. But I say nothing. In a town this tiny, when you see two people gravitating toward each other, the worst thing you can do is give them a shove.

If Yolanda and Anders want a fling, they'll have it. God knows, Anders had enough of those in Rockton. It slowed as his drinking did, and he'd finally started to fall for someone, only to have her turn against him when she learned *why* he drank. Anders and I share pasts of screwing up, and we share years of paying the price, most of it self-inflicted.

Yolanda knows what Anders did. After it came out in Rockton, he wanted staff here to at least understand the basics. I haven't embraced that degree of openness myself, but I applaud him for it. That means, though, that Yolanda knew before she decided Anders was someone she wanted to get to know better.

I don't play matchmaker. I certainly have the urge, in that way happily paired people might. But if I've resisted pushing my sister toward Kenny—despite the fact that there's been obvious interest on both sides for *years*—then I can resist nudging along this relatively recent development.

"You're going to Dawson next month on a supply run," Dalton says. "Ask whether she wants to come along."

"Anytime Yolanda wants time off, her grandmother will send a private plane."

"Yet Yolanda only goes home for family stuff," I say. "She

never takes an actual vacation, because she doesn't *want* Émilie sending her plane."

"Good point."

"Eric's right," I say. "You know half the reason she's in Haven's Rock is to deal with her Parkinson's diagnosis—and keep her family from finding out. She'll leave for family stuff, but otherwise, I don't think she wants a solo vacation. Once I get my pilot's license, I'll suggest a few of us fly out for a girls' weekend. I've just been derailed by the unexpected arrival of a tiny creature who can't have Mom take off to do her qualifying training. You should totally ask whether Yolanda wants to go with you."

"I will, but I'm not sure that's proper payback."

"Cover her hotel room and meals."

He snorts. "Cover the small bills of a billionaire's granddaughter who's a successful business owner in her own right?"

"It's Dawson. The bills *won't* be small. Also, it's the thought that counts. Yolanda will have fun ordering ten-dollar sodas from room service just to make you regret it. You should—"

Storm whines. She's looking to the left, and the whine is her signal that she'd like to leave the path to check out something. I'd taught her this as a pup, a lesson that seemed doomed to failure, as she'd leap off after anything that caught her attention. But she'd aged into it, and now she looks from me to the left side of the path.

"Animal?" I say.

Another whine, which doesn't mean anything. This is one of the lessons that never quite worked—getting her to give us some idea *what* she smells or hears. I still try, but mostly, it's up to me to interpret her body language. She's calm and only vaguely curious. In other words, something has caught her attention but it's neither alarming nor urgent. She just knows that she'll be rewarded for alerting us to anything unusual.

Dalton and Anders stop and get out their canteens, perfectly content to let me investigate this non-emergency. I follow Storm into the trees. She alternates between sniffing the ground and the air. Following a scent?

From behind me, Anders calls, "Watch out for unexplained puddles."

Yes, there's a good chance that the scent she's following is either Gretchen or Blake cutting off the route for a pee break. So I do keep an eye out for suspiciously damp trees or foliage. But after ten paces into an open area, Storm stops at an oddly placed pine bough. Oddly placed because it's lying on open ground, as it if fell during the last windstorm . . . except the nearest pine is twenty feet away.

Also, the bough has been cut.

Dalton joins me as I'm examining the branch. "Hacked," he says.

"With a knife maybe? Something not big enough for the job. Strange." I lift a rock off the bough. "Someone cut it, placed it here and put a rock overtop to make sure it didn't blow away. Either marking a spot or covering something up."

I pick up the bough. Underneath, the soil has been disturbed.

"Please don't tell me there's a body under there," Anders says as he draws up beside us.

"If you hide a body, are you gonna mark the spot?" Dalton says.

"Fair point. Mostly, I'm just glad it's not a body. In fact, I'm so relieved, I'm going to offer to dig."

Anders takes off his pack and rifles around before pulling out a small collapsible spade. No one can dig a body-sized hole with it, but it's useful for putting out fires. It's also useful when it comes to digging out a loosely filled-in hole.

Dalton and I chill with our water canteens as Anders digs. We barely get a couple of sips in before he's dragging something out.

I push to my feet and move closer. "Is that . . . ?"

"A backpack."

I take the dirt-covered pack and shake it off. It's big—camp-sized, not hike-sized. I sniff it first, making Anders arch a brow.

"Damp but not moldy," I say. "It hasn't been down there long."

"Think it belongs to our campers?" he asks.

"I didn't take a good look at their packs, but I did notice two on the ground. One was larger, like this." I glance at Dalton. "You okay with me opening it up, boss?"

He reaches and takes it from my hands.

"The boss needs to check for a bomb," Anders says. "Or a rattlesnake."

"There are no snakes in the Yukon," Dalton says.

"I know. That's why it'd make a great trap. That or poisonous spiders. Up here, everything that can kill you is big, so you'd never expect backpack-sized danger."

Dalton already has the bag open. He peers inside.

"Snake free?" I ask.

"Random-body-part free?" Anders says.

At Dalton's look, Anders throws up his hands. "Covering all the bases, boss. Not like we haven't discovered random body parts before."

"Will's just giddy at it not being a shallow grave," I say.

"Body could still be there," Dalton says as he reaches into the backpack.

"Oooh," I say. "That'd be clever. Bury the body deep. Put

the backpack on top. Mark the spot. Then when someone digs, they'll just find the backpack, and your shallow grave will remain undetected."

Anders holds out the tiny spade. "Go for it."

I shake my head. "So what's in that backpack?"

Dalton points at the piles he's been making on the ground. "A couple changes of clothing. One sleeping bag."

"Hey, that's a nice one," Anders says as he lifts it. "Feather light. I wonder what the temperature rating is."

"Those are expensive," I say. "I've been eyeing them. I can't justify replacing ours yet, but if they accidentally rip, I'm getting two of these."

"*Accidentally* rip," Anders says.

"If you want new sleeping bags, buy them," Dalton says. "Hell, I'll buy them."

I ignore him. I have money. April and I put most of our inheritance into Haven's Rock, but we retained enough to be comfortable for a few years if the town fails. Everyone else on staff is paid a salary, courtesy of Émilie. It's modest, but in a town where all your expenses are covered that salary means—for the first time in his life—Dalton has money. We're just both very careful about how we spend it.

Dalton takes out the next item. It's a small toiletry pouch. He sets it down, and I resist the urge to get a closer look until he's done. He pulls out a set of utensils, a tin plate, and a mug. Finally, from the bottom, he unties a tent. Yes, it's a lot to carry in a backpack, but everything is high quality and lightweight, and there was actually a fair bit of extra room left in the big pack.

Neither man says anything as I unroll the clothing and examine it. Two men's shirts and two pairs of lightweight hiking pants. One women's shirt. All medium-size. Extra underwear and socks, mostly men's.

Next the toiletries. One toothbrush. One mini tube of toothpaste. Bar soap. Bar shampoo. A comb.

"You think it belongs to our hiking couple?" Anders asks.

I sit back on my heels. "Yes? Mostly because I can't think of any other answer. I only noticed two packs, meaning they travel light. Experienced campers. They'd both wear medium, so that fits. It's all expensive gear, and they struck me as people who can afford that."

"So they buried one pack and marked the spot?"

I peer down at the piles of items. "If they were spies for the council—or coming after one of our residents—and they bumped into us, then I could see them hiding something they didn't want us finding."

Anders nods. "Something they don't want to risk us seeing. Especially if they've decided to build on that accidental meeting. Just happen to stumble over Haven's Rock while looking for you guys because the husband's ankle is worse. They'd hide a sat phone or compass or anything they claimed to have lost. Which isn't here."

"And there's no point hiding the rest." I pick up the backpack and check all the pockets. "Some tissues. An empty plastic bag for wet clothing. A line for hanging clothing. That's it."

"So the bag wasn't hidden to conceal damning evidence that blows up their story."

I consider. Dalton is quiet, but from the look on his face, he knows a possible explanation. He's just waiting for us to get it. I have an idea, but I'm turning it over, considering whether it fits, when Anders beats me to it.

"Lightening the load," Anders says. "The guy's hurt his foot. He blew off help, but last night, they realized they'd spoken too hastily. They decide to hit the trail early and to divest themselves of all unnecessary gear so he's not weighed down." He points.

"Extra clothing. A second set of dishes. One sleeping bag." He nudges the tent. "Personally, I'd have kept that."

"They're cutting it too close at this time of year," I say. "It's been warm, but it'll drop below freezing any night now. Sharing a sleeping bag with no shelter is risky. But my sense was that the husband takes too many risks. If he said to leave all this, his wife might not have argued. They took the food, which is the main indication that they left the rest behind intentionally."

"And hoped to return for it?" Anders says. "Seems unlikely they'd bother."

I shrug. "They might have argued over leaving behind valuable gear, so they buried it on the pretense that they could get it later."

"I can see that. Stop the fight and get moving."

I walk back to the hole and then to the piles of supplies.

"Still don't like it, do you?" Anders says.

"I do not." I look at Dalton. "Do you have another explanation?"

"Nope. My money would have been on lightening the load. They could have hidden it to be considerate."

I frown. Then I say, "Ah, right. They bumped into us. They're lost, the husband hurt. Then, later, if we found a bag of their stuff abandoned, we might panic, thinking something happened. So they hid it. That's a possibility. Another one is that they were caching it."

Dalton nods. "Come to think of it, that's what I'd do. Not necessarily bury it, but hide and mark it in case we needed to come back. Ankle feels better after a bit of walking, come back to fetch it. Ankle gets worse, come back for the tent so they can hunker down while it mends."

"That's my favorite theory," I say. "So we put the stuff back? Cover it up in case they need it?"

"Yeah. Point is that they did keep moving west, as planned. We're good." Dalton looks at Anders. "Though you will still owe Yolanda."

Anders sighs. "I don't mind making it up with a trip to Dawson. What I won't like is admitting I was wrong."

"We all were," Dalton says. "Now let's get back, tell her, and take our lumps."

CHAPTER FIVE

We bury the backpack. We've been walking for about ten minutes when I check my watch. It's barely nine. That's the advantage to getting an early start—I'll be back in time for Rory's morning nap. I might even be able to feed her, if she hasn't fussed enough for Yolanda to do it. We've just started giving her cereal midmorning, and Dalton and I usually do it together, both for the novelty and the amusement. We can—

"Hello!" someone calls, and we all stop short. The voice is distant enough that even Storm hadn't heard anyone out there, but Dalton and Anders were talking, which meant someone heard us.

It's a male voice. Our injured hiker?

"Hello!" Anders calls back. "Who's there?"

"We are from the mining camp. Please state your location."

Anders rolls his eyes hard enough to strain them. The mining camp keeps security guards, who both watch the settlement and accompany the miners. They're all paramilitary types—well-built guys, mostly white, buzz-cut hair—and we joke about not being able to tell them apart. We also joke about the military affectations, like that "state your location." That part amuses Anders most of all. He served in the US Army and now he's serving as law enforcement, but weirdly, he doesn't go around talking like that.

"The forest!" Anders shouts back. "The Yukon? Maybe Alaska? I can't tell. But there are a lot of trees."

"You can hear our fucking voices," Dalton says. "Follow them."

"Please identify yourselves."

"Fuck you," Dalton says. "Good enough?"

"Are you alone?"

Anders puts his hand to his forehead and shakes his head. "Guys? Cut the shit, please. You know who it is. You can tell where we are. You can tell there are at least two of us. There's also a third person and a dog, both of whom are retaining their dignity by not joining this nonsense, okay? We have guns, as we always do. We are not taking them out unless you approach us with yours in hand. If you intend to do so, please warn us in advance. You know the drill by now. You really do."

We keep walking. Within twenty steps, the guards appear. Two men, both white. We recognize the older guy—he's the only guard over thirty-five. The other is maybe mid-twenties, dark-haired. Have we seen him before? Like I said, we really can't tell. They don't give us names, and they all dress in quasi-military gear. What matters is that we've finally broken their habit of approaching with their guns out.

My heart still picks up as soon as I see them. At first, the mining camp had been an inconvenience and an exposure threat. Soon, between the military bullshit and the patronizing boss, it became an annoyance. But then we had an incident last fall, and since then, we've been on high alert.

We tell ourselves that the heavy security presence is understandable, considering they're mining gold, but we're in the middle of nowhere, and no one from Haven's Rock has shown the least interest in their claim, yet they have not relaxed one bit.

Something is up with this mining camp. Maybe that seems like a mystery I should solve, but we've decided it's too dangerous. We've looked for answers online when we're in Dawson—anything about gold mining in our area. We even broke down and had Émilie's investigator check into it. But we've found nothing, which would be suspicious except, again, it's gold mining. The company isn't exactly going to be podcasting about their efforts and rewards.

For now, we've achieved an uneasy truce. They don't bother us, and we don't bother them.

"For the record," the younger one says, "we would like to state that we are on neutral ground."

"Uh, yeah," Dalton says. "Otherwise, either you'd be giving us shit for trespassing or we'd be giving you shit."

"We acknowledge this is neutral ground," I say. "Are you guys out here for something? Or just taking a hike?"

"Classified information, ma'am."

The older man gives his partner a look and then says, "Ignore him. He's new. We're following up on a report of campfire smoke out this way. We know your people sometimes pitch a tent for a night, so we were just confirming that's what it was. Can you tell us how long you'll be out here? So if we spot smoke, we know it's you guys?"

Anders and I say nothing. We might teasingly call Dalton the boss, a holdover from Rockton, when he was in charge. But both Anders and I come from backgrounds where someone *is* in charge, and we acknowledge the value of that, at least if it's someone we trust to make decisions for the group. So we really will stand down here and let Dalton make the call, which he knows also means neither of us has a strong opinion either way.

"We aren't camping," Dalton says.

"I knew it," the dark-haired one mutters, like a little kid sulking over being called out for bad behavior. "They don't have the baby."

We'd have rather the camp didn't know we had a baby, but that would mean never going anywhere near their territory—or neutral territory—with Rory. We'd decided to let it play out, and this summer, sure enough, we were hiking and passed close enough for someone to come running, wondering what dangerous animal was wailing.

"They could have left their baby in camp," the older man says.

Now his partner is giving *him* a look. "It's a baby. There are bears around. And wolves."

I clear my throat. "We actually saw smoke last night. That's why we came out. Did you say you saw it this morning?"

The older guard answers. "No, it was last night. Smelled it mostly. Boss didn't want us investigating after dark, so we went into lockdown and came out first thing. There are a few teams looking around."

"On neutral territory," the younger one says.

"That's fine." I glance at Dalton, lobbing the next decision to say more his way.

"We found traces of a camp," Dalton says. "Ash was still warm, but not hot. Signs of a tent being pitched. We had the dog follow the trail. It headed west, so we aren't too concerned."

"That's a tracking dog?" The younger one eyes Storm skeptically.

"She can track," I say. "Most dogs can with proper training.

The point is that the campers went west. We followed for maybe a kilometer and turned back."

The younger one looks at his partner. "How far's that?"

"About a half mile, I think?"

"Point six of a mile," Anders says.

We've long speculated that the camp originates in the States, and this seems to confirm it. That's also why Anders joked about us being the Yukon or Alaska. Covering all the bases.

When Yolanda's team built Haven's Rock, the crew was told they were in Alaska. It was a useful fiction for security, and we have no idea where these guys think they are. Once you get this far north, it's easy to substitute in one region for another, especially deep in the boreal forest.

"Would you mind showing us the camp?" the older guard asks.

Dalton shrugs. "Sure. You walked right past it."

He backs them up to the campsite. We don't mention that we also use it—and we probably won't after this. We also apparently aren't mentioning that we met the hikers yesterday. Dalton has been careful to leave us that wiggle room, though, in case it ever comes up. Need-to-know basis, as these guys would say.

They check out the camp and pretend to know what they're doing. We help, since they're being decent about it, having dropped the military shtick. The older guy has always been one of the few guards I'm comfortable around—an old dog long past bothering with that military nonsense, relaxed and friendly enough.

Dalton shows them how to dig in the campfire pit and find warmth, which suggests it's the one they smelled last night. I show them where the tent was pitched. We say nothing about finding the backpack, and I'm glad we reburied it and replaced that bough over it.

I'm hoping they'll drop it at that. They don't, and I have to admit I'd have been surprised if they did. Strangers were camping in the region where they're mining for gold. They're going to be just as suspicious as we are, and it doesn't help us here that we can't tell them who we saw and possibly soothe their paranoia.

I'm not sure it would help anyway. Yes, a couple in these woods is less suspicious than a group or a lone person. Yes, one of them was injured. But we'd still been suspicious, so they would, too. And one reason we aren't telling them is because we don't want them running off after what seem to be innocent hikers.

That encounter between our groups that went bad ended with them sharpshooting one of their own guards. Oh, they had their reasons, but it still means we are not putting them on Gretchen and Blake's trail.

They ask a bunch of questions, mostly about where the trail led, in which direction and where did we think they might be headed. Dalton bullshits his way through it while I sit with Storm and Anders pokes about the clearing as if checking for more clues.

Finally, Dalton sighs. "Would you like us to have the dog follow the trail farther?"

"If you don't mind," the older guard says.

"Then head back and tell Mr. Rogers that we'll swing by and update him."

"Mr. Rogers?" the younger one says.

The older one grins. "That's what they call the boss. Because he's such a friendly neighbor."

His partner frowns, as if too young to get the reference.

After a moment, the younger man says, "One other thing. Do you guys have another dog in town?"

"Yes . . ." Dalton says slowly.

"Looks like a wolf?"

Dalton makes a noncommittal noise. We do have a second dog—Raoul—and he is half wolf. But he's also half Australian shepherd, and looks like it, which is why Dalton would suspect that's not who they mean.

"See?" the younger man says to his partner. "I told you it was a dog." He looks at us. "We thought we spotted a gray wolf. Then someone whistled and it ran off."

"Ah. Yeah, that'd be ours. Half wolf."

"Cool. Okay, so we'll head back and let, uh, Mr. Rogers know."

The older man nods. "If you could track whoever it is for a couple of miles, that'll make the boss happy—as long as those miles are in the other direction. I'll call the rest of the guys in."

Dalton grunts in what could be agreement, and we watch them go before setting Storm back on the trail.

We do follow the trail farther. Dalton grumbles about that, but he doesn't actually suggest we lie about doing it, so I know he's only grumbling. On the one hand, I'm ready to get back to my baby. On the other, going farther might be wise, just so we aren't back in town wondering whether we did enough to ensure the hikers really were gone.

We don't track the full two miles. After about half that, we swing north. We agreed to speak to Mr. Rogers, but we also need to talk to someone else—the real owner of that "dog" the guards mistook for a wolf.

It was almost certainly an actual wolf, one belonging to the woman who calls herself Lilith, our resident nature photographer. Why is there a woman living with a wolf in the wilderness? Because it's the Yukon. People come here for all kinds of reasons, and unless they're living in one of the towns, you don't ask why. That's none of your damn business.

So far, Lilith has managed to avoid catching the miners' attention, but it makes us nervous, having her out here alone near a camp full of men. It makes her nervous, too, though she'd never admit it.

Her cabin is on the edge of our territory, and that's where she hunts and fishes and hikes, having self-declared everything west off-limits. I can only imagine how frustrating that must be. Two years ago, she had this endless wilderness to herself. Now she has two settlements sharing her land, and only one of them is friendly.

We need to speak to her—both about the miners seeing Nero and about the hikers. So we leave the trail and head onto a route that will take us her way, and from there, we can go south to the mining camp.

I also consider letting Dalton and Anders handle Rogers, while I go back with Storm. Yes, having a baby means my priorities are split these days, but it's a matter of splitting them the right way. Having me along on this part of the excursion—and talking to Lilith—is important, but with Rogers, I'd probably just hang back and let Dalton handle it. Anders can watch his back.

Getting to Lilith's requires a bit of mild mountaineering. We've gone north, which is where Anders had gotten some elevation earlier. It's the foothills of a mountain. Honestly, I'm never really sure what qualifies as a mountain versus a foothill up here. Mostly, if it's really tall and has snow on the top at this time of year, I call it a mountain. If we can hike to the summit without gear, it's a foothill. I'm sure the distinction would have a geologist rolling their eyes.

For the "foothill" we're on, it's about a two-hour climb to the summit and tough going but well worth it for the views. We're sticking along the edge now. We aren't talking as we walk—we don't want to alert Rogers's men again. It's a silent trek east, and when Storm slows, sniffing the air, we notice right away.

I bend beside her. "Smell something?"

She keeps sniffing, with a look I recognize as wary puzzlement. She smells something, but either it's faint or she's not sure whether it's a concern.

Dalton peers around. "High enough for grizzlies," he says. "Maybe a den? We haven't climbed this way before."

"Haven't we?" Anders says. "I thought the cave system was just up ahead."

"Over that way." Dalton points up the hillside. "That's the path we take to the caves."

"Huh. You sure?"

"Which of us has the better sense of direction?"

"Casey."

I fist-pump the air.

"So who's right?" Anders calls forward.

"Not getting involved," I say.

"Afraid to contradict your husband?" Anders says.

"No, just don't feel like dealing with the gloating from the one of you who is correct."

"Hey, at least one of us is correct."

"Me," Dalton says. "Because your sense of direction sucks. The last time we relied on your—"

Storm lunges in front of us so fast we all jerk back. She stands there, hackles raised as she growls. Before anyone can speak, a roar from below has us all reaching—Anders for his big-ass .45 and Dalton for the rifle on his back and me for my bear spray.

"That's a bear roar, right?" Anders whispers.

"Yep."

"A happy bear, miles away, romping through the fields?"

Dalton snorts. The bear is not happy—nor is it miles away—and Anders knows that.

"Tell me it's a black bear then."

"Lie to you?"

"Fuck," Anders says.

"We're fine," I say. "We have three handguns, one rifle, and three cans of spray."

"I am aware that you are ahead!" Dalton calls to the bear. "Be aware that we are here."

"I'm also aware!" Anders chimes in. "Bear aware. Taken all the training."

"Here, too," I call as I lay my hand on Storm's head.

My gesture asks her to stay quiet. Dogs can aggravate bears, and while she'd be helpful in a fight, we intend to avoid that. We keep talking so the bear knows we're here and that there are multiples of us. The roar told us that the bear is somewhere up ahead. We want it to know it still has time to retreat. That's usually all they need. An exit strategy.

The bear roars again, and that is a clear signal that it is not giving way. It also doesn't necessarily mean we're in danger. Just as we warned the bear we're here, it's extending the same courtesy.

Back the fuck up, little humans.

"Guess we aren't going this way," Dalton mutters. "Sounds like it's protecting a kill."

"Go higher or lower?" I ask.

"Higher. I'd rather be above it."

"Good call."

We back up until we see a clear way up the side of the foothill. Then we climb. Anders takes the lead. I fall into the rear with Storm—no one wants to be caught under a hundred-and-forty-pound dog if she slips. Also, Dalton wants the middle spot so he's free to watch and listen for the grizzly.

Anders finds a path, and he's walked along it for about ten paces when he whispers back to Dalton, "You win." Dalton grunts. Yes, *this* is the path we take to the cave system. It's familiar and relatively easy to traverse.

We've gone maybe fifty feet along it when Dalton says, "Hold up," his voice low.

I lean left and see what he's talking about. Movement behind bushes maybe twenty feet below. I frown. We'd climbed at least fifty feet before we found the path. That can't be the bear, which had been farther down the hillside—

A tawny rump comes into view, one with a white scar on the haunch. It's a grizzly's backside, which has my frown growing, until I see the bear's jerky movement. It's pulling something. Dragging prey to higher ground so it can eat at leisure. This time of year, it won't want to share with scavengers.

"Retreat?" Anders whispers.

"Yeah," Dalton says, obviously annoyed. "Head back to the lower path."

We turn around. Then Anders says, "Uh, guys?"

I glance back down the hillside toward the bear. It's out in the open, and I think that's what Anders means—don't turn our back on it. Which is correct, but the bear is paying us no attention. It's too busy dragging its kill, now that those pesky interlopers have left.

What it's dragging is a leg. A human leg.

Attached to a human body.

CHAPTER SIX

"Casey . . ." Dalton says slowly.

"Yes," I say. "That's Blake."

The bear is maybe fifty feet away—thirty ahead and twenty down. But even from here, I can make out the body it's dragging, and recognize it as the man I spoke to yesterday.

"And yes," I say. "He's definitely dead."

"Fuck," Dalton breathes.

He motions for us to keep backing up. That's not easy when we don't dare turn our backs. I actually do—I need to guide Storm and I can't risk tripping over her. I get her in front of the others. She's spotted the bear, and her hackles are up, but she is well-trained in this and mature enough to obey.

Retreat from the threat. Do not make a sound.

If I'm right, there's a cave entrance just past where we climbed up. We would never crawl in where a bear might trap us, but we can duck into the entrance and regroup.

I find the cave, and it's not one of the small holes we often squeeze through. This is a big opening that doesn't go far. I tuck inside with Storm. The guys arrive a few moments later, and Dalton bustles Anders in while he stands guard.

"Did it spot you?" I whisper.

Anders shakes his head. "Didn't seem to. We're downwind, too."

I move past him to Dalton. "I'm going out."

"What?" He stares at me. "Going where?"

"Oh, I thought I'd just hop out and run back to Haven's Rock. Look after the baby." I give him a look. "Going back for a better look, I mean."

"That's what I figured you meant." He points at his face. "Hence this expression."

"I won't go far. I have these." I lift a small pair of binoculars.

"You think it might not be this Blake guy? Or that he's not dead?"

I could lie. But that erodes trust, even if it would help me win this battle.

"No, it's him and he's dead. But I need to check something else." I lean from the cave. "I'll go right there, to that curve. If I even think the bear has seen or heard me, I'll come straight back."

Dalton grumbles but he knows he's not "the boss" in the sense that he can order me to stand down. This is just two peers disagreeing over safety.

I walk slowly, listening and rolling my footfalls. It's unlikely the bear will see me—they don't have great eyesight. Also unlikely it will smell me unless the wind changes direction. The biggest danger is it hearing me. But I make it to that curve, and I can see it, almost up to our level now, completely engrossed in its task of getting Blake's body to its den.

I lift the binoculars and focus on the body. I stay there long enough for Dalton to make a growl of his own behind me. My lifted finger asks for one more minute. It's not even the finger I might like to use.

When I'm sure my initial observation is correct, I retreat to the cave and slip inside, staying at the mouth where I can whisper to Dalton, while Anders can listen in.

"The bear didn't kill him," I say.

"What?" Dalton's gaze shoots my way before turning back to watch.

"No signs of blood. The bear is scavenging."

"Fuck."

"Remind me how a grizzly kills again?" Anders says.

"Not bloodlessly," Dalton mutters.

"Easiest kill would be to catch someone unawares," I say. "They usually bite either the back of the neck or the head. That's not necessarily fatal. You die from loss of blood when they, uh, start to eat you."

"Remind me why I live out here again?"

"This bear isn't eating him yet," I say. "It found a whole body and is caching it before scavengers swoop in."

"So there's no sign of how the guy died?" Anders says. "From a fall maybe? That's what supposedly happened with his ankle, right?"

"Yes, but now there are bruises around his neck."

"Sure the bear didn't do that?" Dalton drawls. "Put its big paws around his neck and squeeze. I hear grizzlies like to kill that way."

That earns him a middle finger from Anders. "Okay, so not a fall. Not a bear kill. Possible strangulation. Possible murder." He looks at Dalton. "And do not tell me that strangulation means murder. There are instances where it is intentional and not meant to kill or even hurt someone."

"So I have been informed," Dalton says. "I wasn't going to

say anything. Possible murder is correct. Not only could the neck bruises be from consensual play but they could indicate self-defense gone wrong."

I nod. "Someone puts their hands around your neck to stop you, and when you don't stop, things go south. The point is that we have a likely murder victim in the jaws of a grizzly bear."

"No problem," Anders says. "You can just wait until it falls asleep, sneak in, and do your postmortem. We'll grab April. She'll be delighted to conduct an autopsy next to a sleeping grizzly."

I look at Dalton. "I don't know what our responsibility is here."

He exhales. "Fuck."

"If Blake was killed by a bear, we'd leave it," I say. "Cruel but what else can we do? We'd tell his wife we saw him but couldn't get to him. But it seems like murder. Technically, not our problem because he's just a stranger passing through. Except . . ."

"Murder means a killer," Anders says.

"Yes, which—statistically speaking—is probably his wife. We'd decided they really must be hikers, but this changes things. Is his wife a spy partner who turned on him? Did they come for someone in Haven's Rock and that's who killed him? Did they come for someone in the mining town who killed him? Even Lilith could have been the target. If the killer isn't Gretchen, is she still alive? And in any of those scenarios, what danger does the killer pose to Haven's Rock? Or to anyone walking around out here? If Gretchen is alive and not the killer, she's still an exposure risk—running around looking for her missing husband."

"Fuck."

"We need to get that body away from a hungry grizzly, don't we," Anders says.

"Fuck!" Dalton raises his fist, like he's about to hit the cave wall, but stops short and shakes his head instead.

I take his hand and squeeze it. "If you think I'm overreacting—"

"You're not."

"If it's too dangerous—"

"It is."

"What are our options?" I ask.

"The obvious one is to kill it," Anders says. "However, beyond the fact that no one wants to shoot a bear for minding its own business, I know killing a grizzly is never easy."

"It's not. Especially when it has prey."

"Did it look healthy?" Anders asks.

"A little thin, but it's not an old and starving grizzly that we could be justified in putting down."

"Is luring it out of the den an option? Before it eats anything?"

Dalton shakes his head. "Too risky. I know Casey would like a body that's as undisturbed as possible—and April will be furious if we 'allowed' predation—but I don't think we're getting that body out whole."

Anders swallows. "So I guess we need to ask a very uncomfortable question. How much is the bear going to eat before it leaves its den?"

Dalton pinches the bridge of his nose and squeezes his eyes shut. "Fuck. I hate this."

"We can't answer that," I say. "It depends on whether the grizzly is hungry, how securely it can cache the body, et cetera."

"We can estimate," Dalton says with a sigh. "As much as I hate doing this when we're talking about letting a bear consume a human body. But I really don't want to kill it for, as you said, minding its own business. When it comes to bears, scavenging big prey is actually more common than hunting it. I've seen bear scavenging on moose and caribou. They go for the torso first."

"Easy to get at," I murmur. "Minimal work."

"Yeah. After that, they'll cache the rest. I don't think I've ever seen one dragging off prey like a wolf might. But it's fall, and this one *is* a bit thin, so it's going to act out of character. Like Casey says, it doesn't want to share. Nothing's going into a grizzly's den to feed on its prey, so the body will be safe there. I'm guessing the bear will eat the easy parts and leave the rest to go see what else it can rustle up."

"It's just stocking the larder." Anders makes a face. "I shouldn't say that about a human being."

Dalton grunts. "True, though. I suggest we see where it goes while someone stands watch. Casey? You'll want to see where the bear has been, I presume. Try to find the scene of the crime."

"Yes."

He exhales, clearly not happy, even with this best solution to our dilemma. "Okay, let's get out there before the bear disappears into its den."

We've split up three ways. That makes Dalton even less happy, but it's the best use of our resources. He will keep an eye on the den, which turns out to be not far from where I last saw the bear.

Dalton has climbed a tree, which gives him a good sight line. I insisted he keep the rifle—if the bear hears Anders,

Storm, or me and comes charging out, Dalton will see and can stop it. It's a bit of a cheat, playing on his concern for us, but it works.

I have Storm. For now, I also have Anders. The plan is that we'll follow the bear's trail and, if we locate the crime scene, Anders will head back to town and grab the ATV, which we will need for transporting the body.

Or what's left of the body.

Damn, I am really trying not to think about that.

Storm easily tracks where the bear dragged Blake's corpse. Even without her, I could track it by the swath of flattened undergrowth and disturbed soil. Where the trail leads is . . .

"Okay, that is not what I expected," Anders says as we stare at the spot.

It's near the bottom of the foothill, where there's a small cave that we've used for residents who want a taste of spelunking. Real spelunking, not the type that Anders jokingly refers to as "caverning" where tourists walk upright through caverns, occasionally needing to duck their heads. This type requires crawling and sometimes wriggling. This particular opening is larger than most, and it doesn't go far. It gives residents a taste of the sport, upon which many discover they're claustrophobic, which is good to know before you try a real cave system.

The trail ends here, and there are deep scratches in the dirt, where the grizzly had widened the hole to get at something inside it.

That "something" would have been Blake's body. Using my flashlight, I peer in to find hair caught on rock. There's also a boot, which I need to crawl inside to retrieve. I bring the boot out and turn it over in my hands.

"His?" Anders says.

"Yep. I noted what they were wearing, hoping for hints

about whether or not they were legit, and you know I always pay attention to boots."

He leans over to check the brand. "Oh, I've got a pair of those."

"Sturdy and comfortable and not too trendy, which supports their hiking story." I hunker down. "So Blake is killed, and someone—presumably his killer—drags him and stuffs him in here."

"They were up here yesterday, weren't they? When he fell?"

I nod. "They indicated this foothill."

"Meaning his partner—Gretchen—could have seen this cave and knew it'd do the job."

"Yep." I straighten. "Okay, this isn't necessarily the crime scene, but I'll need to process it. Time for you to head back to Haven's Rock. Give Rory a kiss for me and tell Yolanda she may need to pass off auntie duties to Dana. I'll be out here for hours, and she didn't sign up for all-day baby care." I take a notebook from my backpack. "Better yet, I should write a note. She'll need more milk from the icebox and probably diapers and—"

"Yolanda can handle it, Case."

"I know. I'm stressing over being gone so long, and this makes me feel a bit better."

He pats my back. "Then write it all out. And Rory is fine. If Yolanda needs a break, there's Dana, April, Isabel, Kenny . . ."

Tears prickle my eyes. "I'm lucky, aren't I? To have so much support."

"You get what you give, Casey," he says softly. "And you give a lot."

I nod, letting the tears of gratitude well as I write the note.

CHAPTER SEVEN

I could have just called April and asked her to run her sat phone to Yolanda for baby instructions. We have three phones. I have one and Anders has the other, while the third is with April. But if I called, she'd demand an explanation, and I'd rather delay the part where my big sister is furious at us for letting a grizzly eat a corpse. Not because we didn't save poor Blake's body from that fate—she'd deem getting it from the bear too risky for such a mundane concern. No, her issue will be that we're asking her to autopsy a partial body when we had a chance to get a whole one.

As for why Dalton doesn't have a phone, if he's in trouble, he wouldn't summon us anyway. I try not to think about that. The truth is that he's safe in his tree—full-grown grizzlies can't climb—and he has the rifle. He will not hesitate to shoot if he's in danger. He doesn't need the phone because we'll hear his whistle telling us the coast is clear.

After Anders leaves, I feed the ground. The joys of being a breastfeeding mom away from her baby, with no easy way to pump. My choices are to relieve some pressure or deal with discomfort and leaking. Definitely not a part of motherhood anyone warned me about.

After that I spend some time examining the cave. As for what I hope to find, I have no idea. In this situation, I'm just seeing what I *can* find. The answer, as it turns out, is "nothing."

I've taken the hair, in case it's not Blake's. It definitely appears human, which means if it's not his, it likely belongs to his killer. The boot is his and confirms his body was in here. There's a smell to the boot that reminds me of muscle creams my former detective partner used. The boot is also from the foot that he injured.

I'm guessing that they unwound the bandages, hopefully to soak it in a cold stream. Then they reapplied them with whatever cream they had, hoping that might help. While I'd told them to lace the boot as tightly as possible, from the laces, it looks as if they put the boot loosely on his bound foot, and it came off when the bear dragged his body from the cave.

Is there any chance an animal found Blake's body and dragged it into the cave? No. As Dalton said, bears will cache, but that just means pulling branches over it. Wolves don't cache. Back at Rockton, we had a local mountain lion and her grown cubs, but that was an anomaly this far north, and I can't imagine that's the answer.

No, a human put Blake in this cave. I even find an evergreen bough that seems to have been stuffed into the entrance as a half-assed cover. Half-assed because I suspect whoever did this wasn't thinking of predators finding the body—predators who could easily smell it and remove that branch. They were hiding it from passing humans, who might see something.

Is it possible that whoever put Blake in here *didn't* also kill him? Yes. Imagine Gretchen finds him dead. She can't drag him to the nearest settlement. She could hide his body in a place where they'd seen caves.

All that is postulation. What matters is what I have found—evidence that says Blake's body was hidden here by a human.

Next, I want to find the actual scene of the crime. I try to set Storm on the trail using Blake's boot, but she doesn't seem able to find it.

Does that mean someone carried him, not leaving a drag trail? Or wrapped him up and dragged him? All I know is that Storm doesn't locate Blake's trail and there's no way to say to her "Do you smell another human here? Find that person." She's not a scent hound. She's just a very eager-to-please pet who has been trained to track by an amateur. We wanted her to find missing people—residents who got lost or fled Rockton. Anything else she can manage is a bonus.

Dalton might be able to find the trail. I pick up some signs myself—trampled grasses and broken twigs—that tell me the direction someone came from. Someone who, according to Storm, was not a brown bear. But I lose the trail on open and rocky ground.

The trail seems to come from the south, which is odd. We'd walked west from Haven's Rock to get to the campsite. From there, the hikers' trail continued at least a mile west. Then we circled back east, past the campsite. If the body was brought from the south, how far was it dragged? Not a mile, I'm sure. Did Blake double back east and was killed south of here? But we'd been at their camp early enough that I can't imagine he walked a mile west and then circled back. Unless we'd been following only Gretchen's trail and . . .

"Shit," I say aloud.

I've made a critical error here. Okay, we all did, since no one else caught it, but I'll still take the blame.

We set Storm on Gretchen and Blake's trail, which headed west. Except what's another thing Storm can't do? Tell a recent trail from a brand-new one. We don't know which direction the couple came from yesterday.

They might have—

The roar of a distant engine has Storm perking up. I turn. Out here, we really do try to be quiet, but there are cases where convenience outweighs the risk of exposure. The ATV is one of those exceptions. Oh, it's been retrofitted with everything possible to decrease the noise, but once it's close enough, I can easily hear it.

I jog back to the cave, with Storm alongside me. We reach it just as Anders is preparing to call me on the sat phone.

"Anything from the boss?" he says as I walk over.

I shake my head. "Storm and I didn't go far. We'd have still heard him. Listen, I just realized something that screws up a major assumption . . ."

I tell him my theory.

He curses and shakes his head. "I never thought of that."

"Neither did I."

"We don't know that our hikers actually headed west today. They might have come that way yesterday, laying the trail Storm tracked. Then they rise early, possibly because you told them where to camp."

"I didn't think of that either," I say. "I suggested the spot, so they clear out before we can check on them. From there, they head east along another trail. At some point, Blake is killed."

"Could it have been at the campsite?"

"Good question." I mentally map it out. "That's about five hundred feet from here. Not easy if you're dragging a body, but doable. We should—"

A whistle cuts through the air. Another comes in quick succession, which was the signal we've been waiting for.

"The bear has left the building," Anders says. "Now the only question is—"

One whistle, a different bird call.

Anders exhales. "Whew. Okay, the bear is headed north, meaning we are clear to ride over."

The next tricky part is getting to that den . . . while making sure the bear doesn't return. Dalton takes up watch again, this time on the hillside, with Storm, the rifle, and the binoculars. The ATV is parked right at the base, keys in the ignition, vehicle pointed out toward open ground, in case we need to make a quick getaway.

Anders and I climb the foothill. Fortunately, given that the den is home to an eight-hundred-pound bear, it's not too difficult to get to. A critter that size isn't going to edge along a narrow path every day. However, I still give the bear credit for some unexpected agility, because even I slip getting up to its den.

The den itself has been excavated by the bear, using its long claws to dig a suitable hole in the hillside. When we reach the mouth, we signal Dalton, about fifty feet down. Then Anders stays at the den mouth with his gun out. It's a backup plan, on the very unlikely chance the bear returns without Dalton noticing.

I crouch and step into the den, and the coppery smell of blood hits me. Yet even that is almost overlaid by the stink of bear. The musk is overwhelming enough that my eyes water, and I stand just inside the cave mouth, blinking. Then I lift my flashlight and shine the beam around.

Grizzlies often line their dens with grasses and boughs. This one hasn't done much of that—at least not yet. It isn't ready for hibernation, and it seems mostly to be using this as a base camp while it bulks up.

Blake's body is pushed toward the back of the den. And it's . . . I am not unaware of what we have allowed to happen here. Logically, it's nothing more than an indignity to a dead body. That's what April would see. Blake is dead. He no longer cares what happens to his physical form. But our cultural abhorrence of man-eating—be it by predators or other humans—goes deep, and I am very uncomfortable with what we let happen. However, I would have been more uncomfortable with killing the bear.

As Dalton predicted, the bear went for the stomach. Everything between the rib cage and pelvic bone is gone, with the bear also eating what it could easily pull from both ends. It also took one bite of Blake's thigh, but seemed to decide that was enough for now.

At this point, I should examine the body. And I would . . . in any case where we did not need to worry about a grizzly coming back and finding Detective Goldilocks in its home, stealing its dinner.

I take the tarp from the kit Anders grabbed in town. Then I lay it out beside the body. As I do, I make mental notes while working as quickly as I can. Once the tarp is laid out, I call Anders in.

"It's bad," I say before he enters, bent nearly in half to fit.

He doesn't answer. When he sees Blake, he only wrinkles his nose. He's been to war. He might have mostly served in the military police, but he started as a medic, and he'd continued using those skills where possible. He's seen worse, including to people he knew. I might feel a pang, thinking of this body as the man I spoke to only yesterday, but it's not the same as what Anders went through.

"Could be tricky," Anders murmurs. "I'd suggest doing it in halves, since he's . . ."

"Almost in half already."

"Yeah." Another nose wrinkle, acknowledgment that he's suggesting committing a further indignity.

"I would agree," I say. "We need to get him out of here. It'll be easier in halves, as awful as that is. Is the hatchet in the ATV?"

"It is," he says, and grimly retreats out the cave mouth.

CHAPTER EIGHT

I'm on watch now with Storm. The plan had been for me to switch and let the guys carry the body down. Now that it's in halves, Dalton is coming out with his wrapped bundle while Anders must be finishing up. I didn't see the process of separation. Not that I'm squeamish—my parents were both doctors, as is my sister—but that's when Dalton and I switched places.

Anders insisted on doing the work, which wasn't more than separating the spine. Dalton hadn't watched that. As a lifelong hunter, he's not squeamish either, but I suggested Anders might not want anyone seeing him doing it, and Dalton accepted that as an excuse.

Dalton passes me with only a nod. By the time he's down the hillside, Anders is following, his body half wrapped in a second tarp.

"Good thing I brought two," he says as he passes me, and we exchange tight smiles.

I stand on watch with Storm and the rifle while they situate the body. The ATV is a side-by-side. It can hold four people, but the third and fourth person ride in the cargo area and face backward. That means one of us needs to sit with the body and Storm. I take that spot over Dalton's protests.

"I'm the smallest," I say.

They've tied down the tarps and their contents, so at least I won't need to hold on to them. I still check that they're secured. Then I climb in, and Storm hops up beside me. The guys sit in front, with Anders driving.

Anders takes it slow. It's open ground here, which helps, but it's also rocky. I bounce around despite the custom-installed seat belt. Typically Storm would lie in the cargo area, but that's in use, and she insists on sitting on the other seat and looking around. I'm resisting the urge to hold on to her bandana to keep her from falling over the side.

Eventually, the ground levels out, and I let myself fall into thoughts of what I saw in the cave. Not the condition of the body—I really don't want to dwell on that. I'm focusing on the parts that affect an investigation, all the data I'd noted and filed away as I laid out the tarp.

I'd been partly mistaken about the bruises around his neck. They weren't the thick ones left by manual strangulation. Instead, it'd been a thinner, more regular line, with spots where whatever had been used to strangle him had cut in. Not a wire—that would have sliced in more. A rope seems thicker than the mark I saw, and it would leave scraping. A cord or something similar.

The body had been partly in rigor. Going into it? Or coming out? That's hard to tell without checking internal temperature. Either he was killed last night and is coming out or he was killed very early this morning and is going in.

The next thing I'll want to check for is signs of defense. Healthy people don't sleep through strangulation. How hard did he fight? *Could* he fight? Was his attacker behind him? Blake is wearing a jacket and long trousers, so there was no obvious sign of injury, at least nothing I could discern at a sweeping look. Nor could I check his—

Something moves out of the corner of my eye. It's off to the north, just past the tree line. The moment I realize what it is, it bursts from the forest, leaving no doubt.

I whirl and grab Dalton by the shoulder as I shout, "Bear!"

He twists so fast his shoulder knocks into me, and I duck, making sure he can see. Then he lets out a curse and shouts "Go!" to Anders.

Anders hits the gas. The ATV lurches, and I grab for Storm's bandana, yanking her down under my feet, my legs going over her to pin her there.

It's the grizzly, and it's coming fast. We've stolen its meal, and it must have smelled it—along with hearing the ATV. It's running full out, and for a creature its size, it is blindingly fast.

Dalton is shouting at Anders to be heard over the engine. Anders yells "Hold on!" and the ATV rockets forward over the rough terrain.

Behind us, the grizzly roars, and I can finally hear it over the engine . . . because it's that close. I know the rules. Never try to outrun a grizzly. Do not look at that massive beast, rolling with fat, and think "I can beat it." You can't. Not unless you can qualify for the Olympics, and even then, you will wear out first.

Grizzlies are known for fast sprints, tiring quickly. But "quickly" only means they cannot maintain that speed for hours.

We hit even rougher terrain, and my head smacks the roll bar. Dalton reaches back to steady me, but I motion for him to just hang on, that I've got this.

I don't have this. I have a Newfoundland who is not belted in by anything except my legs. I'm wearing only a lap belt—the full restraints are up front. I'm banging back and forth, and all my focus is on Storm. I must keep her in the ATV. If she falls out, she'll be dazed, and the grizzly will attack before she can flee.

The only saving grace is that Dalton and Anders secured the body parts and secured them well, leaving one fewer thing for me to worry about.

Then I realize that having the parts so well secured might not be to our advantage. If the grizzly gets close, the obvious answer is to knock one out and hope it takes that and stops. But there's no way I can untie those straps. The ATV is bouncing so much I can barely see the grizzly. We're whipping along open ground that is not meant to be a path, much less a road, and we have got to be doing forty miles an hour.

The grizzly has stopped gaining.

It's still running, still roaring, and it is not falling back, but it is no longer gaining on us. We've hit its top speed. Now we just need to outlast it.

How far can they sprint? I struggle to remember. I know people always underestimate it. I seem to recall it's a couple of miles.

We can do this. The bear is about twenty feet behind the ATV. Okay, more like fifteen. Storm whines and trembles, but we're okay. Even if the bear finds a last burst of speed, we can do this. We're even starting to pull away. We just need—

"Fuck!" Anders's curse bellows over the engine.

"Turn!" Dalton yells.

"I know! Casey! Hold on!"

Anders makes a hard right, and I'm bent nearly in two, gripping Storm as tight as I can. She still slides and my seat belt wrenches, making me gasp. I hold her with both hands and legs as she scrabbles.

"Too tight!" Anders is shouting. "Not sure I can do it at this speed!"

I manage to twist and squint to see the forest looming ahead. Shit! We're reaching the end of the clear ground. There's an opening into the woods ahead, but he's right that it'll be tight and we can't see how far it goes. This isn't a path we've ever used. It might not be a path at all.

"I'm dumping the body!" I shout as I pull a penknife from my pocket.

They don't answer. No one is going to argue we should risk our lives to keep it.

The bear has fallen back, but it's still running, and we're about to go a whole lot slower, once we hit the forest. Hell, we might not be going anywhere at all.

I reach to start sawing at the straps.

"Left!" Dalton shouts.

"See it!" Anders says.

We hit a bump, and I fumble the knife. I manage to grab it, but the blade slices my finger. I ignore it and keep cutting the strap.

"Hold on!" Anders shouts.

I flick the knife shut and grip Storm with both hands. The body bounces and strains against the cut strap. The ATV swings right again and Storm yelps, but I have her in both hands and locked behind my feet. The belt cuts off my breath, and pain tells me I am going to have bruising, but we reach what seems to be a wider opening. It's still narrow, branches whipping the ATV and us.

"Cut?" I shout.

"Wait!" Dalton calls back.

He must twist, because his hand rests on my back for a moment. I peek. The bear has fallen farther behind.

"Be ready to cut but hold off!" Dalton shouts.

I nod, not that he can tell with the jostling of the ATV. Storm shakes so much I can only squeeze her tight and hope she's reassured. Then there's a snort, and I look up to see the back end of the bear.

"It's leaving!" I yell.

"Confirm?" Anders shouts.

"Confirmed!" Dalton replies.

Anders eases off the gas—and the strap I'd been cutting snaps. The body bags start sliding toward the back. The other end is strapped, but they'll slip free from it.

"Losing the bags!" I call. "Eric?"

It takes a moment for him to assess, and the makeshift body bags keep sliding. One reaches the end, where we'd tied the small tailgate open.

"Confirm!" Dalton says. "Slow but don't stop. Casey?"

"I can get them."

The bear is still walking away, but slowly, grudgingly. I relax my death grip on Storm and reach for the bag, but when I grab it, the tarp starts to come off, the top half of Blake's body slipping out.

"Undoing my seat belt!" I shout.

I swear I hear Dalton's grumble over the engine. He doesn't argue, though. Storm refuses to get back on the seat, but I manage to get her far enough to the right that I can undo the belt and slide only my knees.

I grab the body bag by the other side, where it can't unravel. Then I ease it away from the danger zone, with the ATV jostling me—and the body—the whole time. And I keep my eyes on the bear. I know Dalton will be twisted around doing the same, but I still keep checking.

The bear continues ambling—

The ATV strikes a rock or a rut or something. Enough to send the back end jumping. Storm leaps up, hitting my arm. The body bag wrenches from my grip. The bear . . . The bear seems to slow, as if it heard something, *sensed* something.

I lunge to grab the bag, throwing myself over it even as a voice screams to let it go, let it fall out, we can try coming back later.

It's too late, though. The inner warning comes *after* I've lunged, and then I'm lying on the tarp, gripping the body bags with both hands, my legs having nowhere to latch on to. I'm sliding, holding those damn bags, and it's too late to release them.

I'm about to shout for help. I presume Dalton had returned to looking forward when we hit that bump. The bag slides more, and I start falling over the back end—

A hand grabs my coat and wrenches me up. It's Dalton, running beside the ATV, holding me. The bear is still facing the other way, but it's standing still now, nose lifted to sniff the air.

We're traveling at maybe ten miles an hour. It's fast for Dalton to run, but not nearly fast enough to escape that bear if it turns around and charges. It's had time to rest, and it'll come at us at its full forty miles an hour, with maybe a half mile between us. Dalton will never get back into the ATV in time. What the hell have I done?

I resist the urge to shove the bags out the back end. I have them, and I heave, and Dalton gives them a push. Then he cuts the rope on the tailgate and yanks it up, even as I wildly motion for him to get back into the damn vehicle. The bear is still standing there, its back to us, sniffing the air—

"Turning left!" Anders shouts.

I brace. It's a hard left, and I fall onto Storm, but the tail gate is shut and Dalton's running alongside again, ducking the branches. He hauls my arm. He wants me back in my seat.

I do that, and I motion for him to get in, but he waits for the click of my seat belt. Then he dashes forward . . . and needs to wait again, now until the path is wide enough for him to get the door open.

I squint back, looking for the bear, but we've turned enough that I don't see it. That means it can't see us, but it also means I won't know if it charges. Dalton is finally inside, and I lean to say, "Can we go faster?"

Dalton nods, and he speaks to Anders. We pick up speed. I keep my gaze on the forest, straining to listen for a roar, to see a blur of motion.

"Don't go straight back!" Dalton shouts.

At first, I think he's talking to me—and I have no idea what that means. Then I realize it's for Anders, who says, "I know!"

Don't go straight back to Haven's Rock.

Don't risk leaving a trail that could bring the bear to town.

The ATV leaves a scent of its own, and while I don't think bears have the capacity to jump from "I smelled my dinner in that stinky metal thing" to "I need to track the stinky metal thing to find my dinner," we can't take any chances. Also, the bear is no more than a few miles from Haven's Rock now. We can't let it get close.

Anders continues on this straightaway until we're sure the bear isn't following. Then he takes—or creates—other trails, circling all the way around the lake to the south of town before coming back along the shore. A group is out fishing on the far side, and they turn to wave . . . and then stare . . . which is when I realize Blake's arm is out of the tarp, his hand hanging over the side.

I wave, as if nothing's wrong, and then say to Dalton and Anders. "Let's hope they're too far away to see what that was."

Dalton shakes his head, and Anders says, "*My* hand. I have really long arms, and I don't need to hold the wheel with two hands. Also, I'm wearing a white glove."

"On one hand?"

"It worked for Michael Jackson." He launches into an off-key rendition of "Thriller."

I groan and thump my head back against the seat. Dalton doesn't get the reference, and just ignores us, as usual.

When we near town, Storm and I jump out. I fix the dangling hand before Storm and I head into Haven's Rock. The guys will skirt around the edge so no one comes out for a look. Even without that hand, they're going to wonder what we have wrapped up, and I'd really rather no one runs over to lift the tarp, hoping for venison.

Storm and I head straight to the clinic. A few people see us and wave. I wave back and keep moving . . . until I spot Max and Gunnar, walking, deep in conversation. Max is eleven and Gunnar is twenty-nine, but we've long established that there is nothing unhealthy in the friendship. Max lost his dad before coming to Haven's Rock, and Gunnar lost his childhood in a family tragedy when he was about Max's age. They're good for each other.

I call them both over. "Max, I need to steal Gunnar. Would you mind taking Storm? She's had a bit of a scare, and I think she'd just like to hang out for a bit."

"Sure. I'll play a scenting game with her. She likes that." He looks at me. "What kind of scare?"

I make a face. "We had to go faster in the ATV than she likes."

I don't mention the bear. Max had an experience last year, where he'd been kidnapped by someone wearing a bearskin, and while he knows that wasn't a real bear, when it comes to trauma, it's the experience that counts. He'd initially thought it was a bear, so he'll always link that trauma to bears, and it'll make him anxious if I suggest there is a grizzly around. He takes Storm, and I lead Gunnar to the clinic. I head around to the back and rap on the door. April didn't have office hours today, so I expect I'll need to go hunting for her, but I'll start here.

The door cracks open two seconds after I knock, and April peers out.

"I am with a patient," she says. "Rory is safely upstairs with Kenny."

Right. Anders mentioned that Yolanda might need to swap Rory off to someone, so she could take her patrol shift. April must think I'm here to collect my daughter.

"Actually, I need the clinic," I say. "We have a body."

She opens the door another inch, but her expression doesn't change. She just keeps looking at me, waiting.

"We have a body," I say. "It'll require an autopsy."

"I presume this is a joke, and while I would find it amusing at any other time, I'm a bit busy, Casey. If you need Rory right now, I'll ask my patient to move so you can come through and retain their privacy. However, I would prefer you to return later. You have been gone half the day. Another twenty minutes won't matter."

I try not to bristle at that. It sounds like criticism—I've dumped my kid on babysitters for half the day. It's not. It's just a statement of fact, told in my sister's usual way.

I lower my voice. "We really do have a body, April. Remember I mentioned that hiker from yesterday?"

"Oh, yes, the one you attempted to treat. You are not a doctor and—"

"He didn't die of a sprained ankle," I say. "Now, if you can please finish up your appointment and let me know when it's safe to bring the body in the back here."

"You aren't joking. About the body."

"No, and if you give me shit for finding another corpse, I'm going to get very testy. We've had a hell of a morning, and I want to bring the body in and then see my daughter."

Her voice lowers. "I never give you 'shit,' Casey. I tease you."

"Yes, well, it can sound like giving me shit, and I've had a very long day *because* we found a body that I really would have been happier not finding."

"Of course. Let me wrap up here."

CHAPTER NINE

I call Anders on the sat phone and tell him to bring the body in about ten minutes. When I finish, I sigh and slump onto April's back porch.

"Did I hear that right?" a voice says. "You found a body?"

I look up. I'd forgotten Gunnar. He's leaning against a tree, patiently waiting to discover what part he'll play in this. There are many words to describe Gunnar, but the best is "unexpected." He's endless contradictions. The loudest guy in the room . . . or the one you won't even notice is there. The guy who hangs out in an unfinished storage-room loft, his "roost" for watching the town. And if that door is open, women are welcome to come up and enjoy his hospitality. If it's shut, though, he wants to be by himself—absolutely by himself, sometimes all night, maybe even showing up late for work the next day. He'll also be the hardest worker when he *does* show up, happy to do any task he's given.

The answer is probably that he needs a whole lotta therapy to deal with his childhood trauma—watching his father kill his mother and narrowly escaping with his own life. He's had counseling, and it's gotten him this far, but Haven's Rock has multiple options, too. We need to, with the isolation and the fact that probably half our residents are here post-trauma. For therapists, we have clinical psychologist Isabel and psychiatrist Mathias. While even Mathias has grudgingly agreed he'd take on Gunnar, Gunnar seems happy with the casual services—via friendship—with our third option, Kendra, a social worker.

"Too loud?" Gunnar says, when I take a moment to answer his question.

I shake my head. "We're fine. Just . . ." I walk into the woods behind the clinic, and he follows. "Yes, it's a body. A hiker. Seems to have been death by misadventure, but I want to be sure."

I'm lying. He might even realize it—I can never tell with Gunnar, though I suspect he's a lot quicker than he acts.

"You said something about a fast ATV ride back?" He leans against a tree. "If the guy's dead, there wouldn't be a hurry."

I exhale. "There was a bear. I just didn't want to say it in front of Max."

Gunnar's brows rise. "Grizzly?"

"Yep."

"Chased you in the ATV?"

"Yep."

"Damn. I've heard they're fast."

"Very fast."

He seems to be considering this, putting together what I have said with what I'm not saying, and that's when the ATV arrives. Anders parks about twenty feet from the clinic, and we meet them there.

"I brought help," I say, "and I handed Storm over to Max. Rory is with Kenny."

Gunnar stares at the tarps. "That's not two very small hikers, is it."

"Nope."

"This have something to do with why the bear was chasing you? You stole its dinner?"

"Yep." I adjust the tarps so nothing falls out. "But the bear didn't kill him. It was scavenging."

"That's what bears do mostly, right? Max told me that. From . . ." He nods toward Dalton. "They scavenge more than they kill. What's the term? Opportunistic carnivores."

"They are, and that's what we have here."

"Yeah, good call on not telling the kid." He peers at the tarps. "I'm just helping carry them inside, right? I don't need to see what's under there?"

"We won't open them until you're gone."

"Thanks."

Once the body is inside, Gunnar leaves, but not before I apologize if even that part wasn't something he'd have chosen to do. He brushes it off with a joke and only asks whether there's any concern about the grizzly tracking its dinner back to town. I explain that we lost it before taking a long route in, but I also ask him to speak to Kendra. I'd like her on patrol, as our best shot in the militia and the one who grew up in the Yukon.

Dalton and Anders leave next. They need to go to the mining camp and speak to Rogers. The longer we delay, the more suspicious he'll become. We also need to talk to Lilith, but we've agreed to do that this evening. So much to do, with the constant pluck at the back of my mind, reminding me that my daughter also needs me.

I ask April to hold off on doing more than an external examination while I look after Rory. Kenny heads down to help her. I warn him about what he'll see. He goes a little green but shrugs it off and says he'll be fine.

Kenny arrived in Rockton before me. Down south, he'd been a high-school math teacher. In Rockton . . . well, the joke was that what happened in Rockton stayed in Rockton. It was like visiting Vegas under a false name. No one there knew you. No one would ever see you again.

Haven's Rock is the same. You can be who you want. For some, it's a license to be a shitty person. For others, it's a chance to explore a new persona. The high-school math teacher took up bodybuilding and leaned into his carpentry hobby, becoming the town carpenter and lead militia. Then a bullet to the lower back meant he's walking with braces . . . and lucky to *be* walking. He's still our carpenter, though, and still head of the militia. These days, he's also resurrected those rusty teaching skills with math lessons for Max and Carson.

So, forensic medicine—or any experience with mutilated bodies—isn't part of Kenny's skill set. But if my sister needs him, he'll be there, and I know better than to argue. Kenny has mellowed from the false machismo of our early days in Rockton, but he still has his pride, and he will not appreciate me suggesting he skip this.

After Kenny heads downstairs, I pause a moment to put all that aside. Then I go in to where Rory is playing quietly in her portable crib.

I spend time with Rory, feeding her, changing her, and then just being with her until she falls into a milk coma. When she's out, I put her back into her crib, slip downstairs, and ask Kenny if he'd mind keeping an eye on her.

"So my options are watching a sleeping baby or watching an

autopsy on a bisected and half-eaten body?" he says. "Babysitting duty, here I come. Let me know if you need anything."

April has reconstructed the body on the exam table, setting the two halves together. Actually, no, on second thought, Kenny would have done that. April wouldn't have seen the point. The body's owner was long gone. Therefore, there was no reason to "pretend" the corpse was whole, and it might even be easier to work on it in pieces. Kenny would realize everyone else who worked on that body would be more comfortable seeing the pieces where they should be.

"I noted that the spine was bisected cleanly," April says as I walk in. "I presume the bear did not do that."

"We did, and yes, it added damage, but it really was the easiest way to transport it. Otherwise, the two halves were very tenuously attached."

"I would agree. It was a clean cut, and it likely kept you from losing some of the internal organs."

"I thought of that, too."

"Of course you did."

I ignore the obvious sarcasm, and I move up alongside the body. The central portion has been covered. When I glance at that covering, April says only, "Kenneth."

"Ah. Well, as ironclad as my stomach is, I think I'll leave that there for now. It'll be easier to focus on the rest without that reminder."

"Did you know his name?"

That startles me. It isn't an April question. When I say, "Blake, apparently," she nods and says, "Given the condition of the corpse, would you prefer to refer to it as a body or by his name?"

I pause and give it some thought. "It doesn't matter much for me. I didn't know him beyond a brief meeting. But maybe just stick to the generic. Even though this was postmortem, it's tough to look at, especially when that was my choice."

"Your choice?"

I glance up as I run my gloved fingers over the scalp. "We saw the bear taking the body. I noticed the marks on the neck, which meant I needed to examine it, but I decided we weren't about to try taking it from a grizzly. So we let it feed while waiting for it to leave."

"That was the correct course of action, on both counts—taking it but waiting."

"Still tough." I pause my tactile examination of the skull. "There's a contusion."

"Yes."

She would have already done a preliminary exam. She just isn't telling me what she found. That's not a test—it's a way to get separate sets of observations.

The contusion is to the back of the head. I can palpate it and feel the softness. There's a slight bump, which could mean either a light blow or that he died before it could fully swell.

April wordlessly hands me a pair of scissors. I cut the hair from the spot and take a closer look. It's definitely not a "light" blow. Someone clocked him hard in the back of the head. The lack of abrasions suggests a solid object. The angle says Blake was upright when it happened.

I move to the hands and knees. There's debris under the nails and there are abrasions, but the body was dragged, so that would be expected. I'll take scrapings from the fingernails. Both hands have abrasions on the palms, with embedded dirt, the sort of mark you get if you fall forward. Chafing on the knees suggests falling to them while wearing trousers. Of course, none of that can be conclusive, given what the body went through afterward, but it's a reasonable theory.

Club Blake in the back of the head. He falls to all fours. Get the cord around his neck while he's down.

I continue examining the hands, making notes and taking pictures. With the damage from the fall and drag, it'll be hard to tell whether he fought back, and I'm not sure how much difference it makes.

I don't see any other damage on the arms or legs. No other bumps to the head either.

I move down to his injured ankle. April has already removed the wraps and set them aside.

"Swollen," I say.

"Broken."

I look up at her sharply.

"Of course, I cannot positively diagnose that without an X-ray," she says, "but if you had brought him here, I would have said it was broken."

"I couldn't bring him here. You know that."

"I wasn't judging."

"Yes, you were. You're annoyed because you think I blithely examined his ankle, declared it okay, and refused him medical help."

"I know you didn't do that. However—"

"However *nothing*, April. I offered help. I would have brought you to examine him. If you thought it was serious, we would have made arrangements. He very obviously did not want that."

"Which suggests he was not simply a hiker."

I throw up my hands. "Maybe? It also might suggest he was a guy."

When she frowns, I say, "The sort of guy who doesn't want to make a big deal of an injury. Tough it out and all that."

"Women do that as well."

"Yes, but you know what I mean. Eric and I figured it could

go either way—refusing help because he didn't want to admit he was hurt or refusing it because he wasn't actually hurt. There was only a bit of swelling when I saw it, likely because he'd recently iced it in a stream. All I had to go by was self-reporting. But if it is broken, that suggests . . ."

I take a deep breath, pushing down my annoyance with April. "It could be further proof he was just a hiker. But, if he *isn't* just a hiker, *that* might also explain why he didn't want treatment. Make contact, but nothing more."

"It's a minor fracture," April says. "He could walk on it, but it would have been painful."

"So was he downplaying it because he's a tough guy or downplaying it because getting hurt on a mission is very inconvenient." I walk along the body again. "Any idea how old the marks on his hands are? I was thinking he fell before he died, likely after being struck, but they could be from his fall yesterday. He'd have cleaned the wounds, but there could be scabs."

"I noted no signs of scabbing. There is, however, swelling in the wrist and thumb of his left hand."

I check it. She's right. Slight swelling. "So he may have broken his fall with his hands."

"How did he say it happened?"

"He was scouting after they lost their map and GPS. He went out too far on a ledge and fell about eight feet."

"Where was his partner?"

"Gretchen?" I nod. "Okay, I see where you're going. Did he fall or was he pushed? She wasn't on the ledge with him, but I'd need more details to determine whether she could have snuck up behind and pushed. The fall could have happened quickly enough that he didn't realize he had help."

"She fails to kill him and tries again."

"But under what circumstances would that be? They go for

a hiking trip, and she decides she's had enough and kills him?" I lift the hand with his wedding band. "Or she planned it all along."

"It does happen, does it not?" April says. "Usually husbands killing wives."

"*Hey, hon, let's go on a romantic hike up this remote mountain. I don't know what happened, Officers. She just fell.*" I nod. "Yes, it's common enough that I'd investigate *any* fatal fall when a couple goes hiking. Resorting to strangulation seems an abrupt switch, but if she got frustrated, or if he got suspicious? Hell, even if she just realized no one would expect her to produce a body. Go home, say he died, get a search team out and take them to another spot. The body was hidden."

"Where is his partner?"

"I have no idea. Finding her is on our to-do list. The priority was getting the body back here." I tug off the wedding ring. "Huh."

"Huh?"

I pass it over. "How old would you say this is?"

"Relatively new, I believe. They gave me Mom and Dad's rings after the accident, and theirs were quite worn."

"Unlike this one."

"Yes."

I take off my own band. "Newer than my ring?"

"It looks like it. Did they give any indication of how long they'd been married?"

"Since right after college. So maybe twenty years?"

"Not judging by that ring, they weren't."

CHAPTER TEN

Next we move to the likely cause of death—the neck wound. I examine it and then have April take a closer look. The wound suggests a textbook case of strangulation with a cord. A smooth line around the neck. Some light abrasion—I'd removed fibers on the scene, and I find a few more now. White fibers. Petechial hemorrhaging in the eyes. Broken hyoid bone.

To be absolutely certain this was the cause of death requires an autopsy. Otherwise, Blake might have been strangled to unconsciousness and then killed another way. Extremely unlikely, but all possibilities must be considered, even if I cannot fathom a way that this was anything other than cold-blooded murder. Yes, strangulation can be used for pleasure, but not when it comes with a crack to the back of the head and a cord pulled tight enough to leave a welt.

The autopsy focuses on his neck because . . . well, there's not a lot more to autopsy. The torso has been almost emptied, including most of the lungs. From the neck, everything remains consistent with strangulation. There's just no way to check other organs because . . . if they're still there, they are not intact.

Once April has done what she can, we wrap the body and put it into the underfloor compartment. With the permafrost, it'll stay preserved enough until we figure out what to do with it.

Before April cleans the exam room, she shoos me upstairs. Rory is still sleeping, so I can discuss the grizzly with Kenny. He'll do double patrols while asking for discretion. No one needs to know about the bear . . . and no one definitely needs to know about the body.

We don't have any outings scheduled for the rest of the day. It's hunting season, but we just finished a round, and nothing else is scheduled for the next week. Otherwise, at this time of year, there's a bit of fishing, but mostly gathering, and even then, primarily the gathering of dead wood, as we prepare for winter.

By the time Dalton returns, Rory is up and I've taken her out while I eat my lunch and grab a packed meal for Dalton. Yolanda has offered to take the next shift, but I'd like her on militia duty, so Rory will be hanging out with Max and Carson and their mom, Dana.

In a town with no other babies, I have enough volunteer sitters that I don't worry about imposing on anyone too much. I sometimes imagine what that would be like if we led normal lives. My parents are gone . . . and I wouldn't have let them babysit even if they weren't. April would probably live too far away. Dalton's brother would be up here. I've never been the sort to make friends easily, so I can imagine that, down south, we'd be relying on standard day care—if we could get a spot—with few options outside of day-care operating hours. If I already feel frazzled, torn between work and my baby, despite an amazing partner and a wonderful community, I shudder to think what it would be like anywhere else.

I always remember, though, that I'm not the only one who feels torn these days, and when Dalton and Anders get back, I pass Rory off to her dad with the excuse that I need to talk to Anders about patrols. The way his face lights up—and the way hers does—makes the lie well worth it. It's late afternoon, and I figure we can delay our departure about thirty minutes and still make it back before dark.

I do discuss patrols with Anders, along with the autopsy results. He might not be a detective, but investigations include all three of us, and I appreciate having extra brains mulling over the same data.

As for their trip to the mining camp, we don't discuss that. It won't be urgent. Well, not unless Rogers said, "Hey, if you happen to find a dead man out there, we killed him." Which he did not, obviously.

I swing by our place at four thirty. Dalton has eaten and he's half dozing with Rory. Storm is on the floor, half dozing as well. As much as I'd like to leave them all to it—or collapse into a chair and join them—we have work to do.

I take Rory from Dalton and steal a few moments to cuddle her. Then Dalton and I drop Rory off with Dana and give Storm the option of staying behind. She responds by sticking right at my side, telling me she's going wherever I am.

Dalton and I head out to warn Lilith. It's still broad daylight, with twilight hours away. It's cooler, the sun having vanished, but that just makes it a pleasant walk when we're moving briskly. We're away from the town before he says, "Talking to Rogers was a waste of time. Complete bullshit."

"Did you expect anything else?"

"No, but I'll still grumble. We offered a courtesy call to update him on the situation, and he acted like I was one of his guys checking in with an overdue report."

"In other words, Rogers was being Rogers."

"Yeah. Fucking asshole."

"What did you learn?"

Dalton gives me a sidelong glance. I only shake my head. Obviously we were doing more than "checking in." The point of visiting Rogers was twofold. First, to keep him from showing up on our doorstep demanding an update. Second, to get a sense of how much he knew regarding our hiking duo. We hadn't discussed that. We didn't need to. Dalton knew what he was doing, and his look is just playing with me . . . and drawing out suspense on his answer.

"They saw smoke last night, like his guys said," Dalton says finally, as we take a fork in the path. "They figured it was us, so they didn't hurry."

"Truth?"

He waggles a hand. "Fifty-fifty. I believe they saw smoke. I'm just not sure *when* they actually saw it and whether—if they thought it was us—they'd really hold off investigating. Don't see how it matters much, though. We met their guys searching the forest. So even if they investigated earlier, they didn't find Blake and Gretchen."

"Unless they found their camp and let it slide until morning, like we did."

He grunts. "Good point. Anyway, I stuck to the story we gave the guards. We also saw smoke last night. We investigated early this morning and found the remains of a camp. Our dog confirmed that whoever it was, they headed west, away from our settlements."

"What did you say about your delay getting back to him?"

"That we aren't his minions. We decided he could go fuck himself and went home for lunch first."

I roll my eyes, knowing this is not what he said, even if he might have wanted to.

Dalton sighs. "Yeah, Will insisted on an actual story. We knew they might have heard the ATV. We had a rifle, which his guys could confirm. I said that while we were heading back, we spotted a caribou, took a shot and got lucky. That meant we needed to get the ATV. We called for that, loaded up the caribou, and attracted the attention of a damn bear, which we did not want to lead to his camp."

"Nice."

"Will's idea. Anyway, we described the bear, said it was a bit thin heading up to hibernation season so it might be desperate."

"A friendly warning from a friendly neighbor."

"That's us."

"Anything else?"

"Not really. He just wanted the report. Seemed satisfied that the hikers had moved on. I did say that we're still concerned and will be scouting, but we will avoid their territory. He appreciated that."

I nod. "That frees us to search for Gretchen. Any chance we'll meet his patrols out there?"

"Hard to say. He seemed satisfied the hikers were gone, but he's not the type to volunteer information. I said we'd leave any updates at the message spot."

We're inside Lilith's house, which is a one-room cabin that reminds me of an above-ground hobbit hole. It's tiny, cozy, and perfectly furnished for one person. Or one person and her pet wolf, but Nero is outside with Storm today. There are two chairs. I'm in one, and Lilith in the other. Dalton sits on the floor. They're drinking beers we brought in a care package, while I sip tea.

I've told Lilith the whole story. When I finish, she sighs, and I say, "I'm sorry."

I know she's getting increasingly frustrated with the situation. We grumble because we built Haven's Rock only to have a mining camp put down stakes a few miles away. But Lilith was here first. It's like building your dream home surrounded by undeveloped and unwanted land, only to have houses spring up around you. Obviously, you don't own the surrounding property, but it's still frustrating.

"There's something else," I say, and I tell her that Nero was spotted by one of the mine workers. I explain that we claimed it was Raoul, but she shakes her head.

"They're going to realize I'm here," she says. "It's been a miracle they haven't already."

"Not a miracle. Hard work. With you having to watch where you walk, where you hunt, how much noise you make. Because it's a town of men, and you're a woman on your own."

"Yep. I'm sure most wouldn't bother me, but it only takes one to decide I must be terribly lonely out here by myself. And there's guaranteed to be one." She stretches her legs. "I do believe it's time for me to move on."

"Is there anything we can do?"

She shakes her head. "It's not your fault. I'd be fine with your little hamlet as neighbors." She hoists her beer. "It even comes with perks. But I can't keep living so close to the miners. There's something wrong with that camp, and we all know it."

I shift in my chair and look at Dalton. The guard the camp shot last year claimed something was going on, and he offered to tell us, and then—seconds later—he took a bullet. That should mean we locked down until we had answers. But the guy wasn't offering us free intel. He wanted us to pay him a small fortune, and he'd been accused of killing a miner, so he seemed to be just blowing smoke, willing to lie his way into an exit strategy.

Since then, everything has been quiet. We set our territorial boundaries and both sides respect them. We are two self-sufficient communities who have had one negative interaction, and the problem was resolved. So what do we do with that? Investigate them for the sake of curiosity? We sure as hell wouldn't want them doing that to us.

"If something's going on," Dalton says, "it's not interfering with us. I know it's a problem for you, and we'd like them gone, too. We've discussed everything we might do to convince them to move on but . . ." He shrugs. "If they didn't leave for the winter, they aren't leaving for any inconvenience we might devise."

"That wasn't a plea for help," Lilith says. "It's a mining operation that is actually mining—I've seen them working. It's also heavily guarded. Best to leave them alone. I just can't trust them to leave *me* alone."

"You're always welcome in our town."

She smiles. "I know. I think I'm reaching the end of my Yukon days, though. Time to pull up stakes and relocate. It'll need to be someplace where I can pass off Nero as a husky. I've been thinking northern BC."

"We'll help in any way we can. And we'll be sad to see you go."

"It's time. Between those miners and this hiker business, it's probably *past* time. So you don't know what happened to the wife?"

"We haven't searched yet. That sounds awful but—"

"Not your problem. Neither is the dead guy. I know you'll look for her, and I'll keep an ear out. If she might have killed her husband, though, I'll probably lie low. I'm not too worried about her sneaking up while Nero's here." She sips her beer. "But you're thinking she might not be a hiker."

"We have no idea. There are several reasons why someone might be checking out our town. It could also be about the gold mine—they'd definitely attract spies." I glance at Dalton.

Dalton sits up. "Awkward question time, but we gotta ask. Any chance these people could have been looking for you?"

"Nah. It's been five years. By now, the mob will completely have forgotten that I murdered three of their guys in a shoot-out. However . . . now that I think of it, the Hell's Angels were pretty pissed off about the million bucks I stole, so maybe them? Oh, wait. I forgot the cartel."

"We don't mean you're here because you did something," I say. "While I'm sure there are people up here who fall into that category, at least as many are running from something that was done to them. That could also compel someone to track you down."

"Anyone I left behind wishes me the best, and we keep in touch." She sighs and stretches her legs again. "Do you want the story? Why I'm here?"

"We don't want to pry."

"Not much prying about it. I don't want you thinking these hikers might have been here for me. So, who was I before I became Lilith, queen of the wolves? A burned-out financial-district drone, getting ready to quit her job and move to the islands. Instead, I met a photographer who grew up in the Yukon and dreamed of going back. I fell for him and his dream. He built this place. I decorated it. I happily traded my high heels for hiking boots and learned how to live off grid. And then . . . he was gone."

"Damn. I'm sorry."

She looks at me and then bursts out laughing. "Sorry. I see how that sounded. I follow my guy to the wilderness, where he dies in a horrible tragedy, but I stay, and even take up photography, living his dream. Nah, that's the Hollywood version. In real life, the city girl starts taking pictures and starts selling pictures, and then *she's* the one making money and he decides the Yukon isn't really his dream after all. Last I heard, he was living in the Outback with some girl he met in the States." She winks. "As long as she doesn't take up photography, they'll be fine."

"His loss."

"Eh, it was over before it was over, if you know what I mean. I was just trying to figure out how to build my own place in the wilderness. Then he left, and I didn't need to. Got to keep the cabin and the wolf pup. Nero and I will move on, and we'll be fine. I'll buy an actual cabin this time, probably off grid, but running water would be nice. And a microwave. Yep, I'll splurge on appliances. God knows, after living like this, I can afford it."

I smile. "Photography pays the bills very well?"

She laughs again. "Oh, hell, no. Sure, it pays. I'm actually pulling in a very decent wage for a photographer, but that'll never be a fortune. My money comes from my corporate drone days. I made some sweet investments, and they have worked so I don't need to."

"Nice."

"Very nice. I'll be fine. I won't take off just yet, but yeah, I'll be heading out before we're snowed in. And in the meantime,

Nero and I will hunker down and wait for news that you've found this woman."

After that, we head back to Haven's Rock. It's getting dark, and there's nothing else we can do. I'm trying not to think of a scenario where Gretchen is an innocent hiker who saw her husband murdered and is now hiding in the forest, terrified and alone.

The much more likely scenario is that she killed him. The buried backpack supports that theory. Whoever buried it made sure to keep the food. That suggests Gretchen sorted everything out and kept what she needed to get back home. Hopefully, she's already heading there. The only question is whether she was a hiker who killed her husband or something more sinister. For our sake, it'd be best if she killed her husband and is already heading home, no threat to us.

But then I flash back to that brand-new wedding band, and my gut says this isn't over.

CHAPTER ELEVEN

We're up the next morning at dawn. We debate taking Rory with us, but decide that would be worse parenting than leaving her in care for another day. Sometimes, it really is a coin toss, and take-our-daughter-to-work day is best done when we aren't tracking a potential killer.

We don't get away easily. One day with babysitters was a lovely distraction for a teething infant. Now she wants Mom and Dad, which makes it all the tougher because we already hate to leave. We take a few extra minutes to settle her in and distract her with toys and then it's kisses on her head and promises to return as soon as we can, which is really more for us than Rory, already happily playing.

When we do finally leave, we have backup. This time, it's Yolanda and Anders, who'll form a second search team. We'd debated bringing Kendra instead, but if there's any chance of that bear finding Haven's Rock, I want Kendra there.

Anders knows how to search. He's done it often enough. Yolanda has not, but she's game and she's good with a gun, which is really all we need.

Our first group stop is the former campsite. I'm looking for any sign that Gretchen returned. Ditto with the spot where we found the backpack. It's still there, still buried, no sign that it's been disturbed.

From there, Yolanda and Anders start a general search of the area. We'll set Storm on Blake's trail. That won't get us to Gretchen, but it might get us to our crime scene, and that's a start.

I brought Blake's shirt. I've cut off the bloodied bits. Storm's look says that doesn't remove the stink of blood and guts and bear. But I've tried, and she sniffs it gingerly and then starts nosing around.

She wants to head west, but we already suspect that was their entry trail, so I take her back to the campsite and head east. She finds a trail and follows it . . . to a fast-running stream, where Blake would have soaked his broken ankle. We even find boot marks there.

Back to the trail. Try again.

She still wants to head toward the water, and no amount of coaxing will get her to do anything else, which suggests there is nothing else to do. There's one secondary path east of the campsite, and it leads here.

Does the trail go beyond the stream? Maybe they returned here, soaked his foot, and continued east. I try to get Storm to search for that, but she keeps looking at me like I'm daft.

That's when I see the handprint.

Along the muddy opposite edge of the stream is one perfect splayed handprint, like a child might make . . . or like someone might make if they fell.

"Eric?"

He's been back at the main trail trying to see whether it goes anywhere else.

Now, as he approaches, I tell him what I'm seeing. A single handprint, plus broken foliage. He comes closer for a look as I stand back with Storm.

"Yeah, that's a handprint," he says after a moment. "Adult. If he fell here, his other hand would have gone down on harder ground. Wouldn't leave a print."

He demonstrates. Then he looks around and crouches. "This is torn up." He pushes aside the undergrowth on our side. "Scuff marks here."

"I was going to suggest removing the broken foliage to get a look at those marks. Sound reasonable to you?"

"Yep."

He stands back while I get photos of the damage to the undergrowth. None of this will ever see a courtroom, but anything I collect helps us build our case, even if it's only to be able to show the perpetrator that we aren't pulling an accusation out of our asses.

Once I've done that, we gingerly remove the undergrowth, mostly by clipping it off close to ground level. We put all that aside and stand back to look. The ground shows scuff marks and several boot prints. I photograph them and then pull up a picture on my phone.

"They're Blake's," I say. "Helpful for proving he was here. Not helpful for catching his killer." I look around. "So he was ambushed while soaking his foot. That also explains the shitty job done retying the bandage and putting his boot back on."

"Killer puts it back on, along with the bandages, so they don't get left behind."

"And, possibly, so if his body is found we don't realize he'd been soaking his foot, giving us an obvious crime scene."

And that means our killer knows someone out here *would* be

investigating. Or that there's a settlement—ours or the mining camp—that would take an interest.

We look for any other prints. The problem is twofold. One, the ground is hard except near the water. Two, I tramped about with Storm before realizing this was the crime scene.

We find more scuffs on the hard earth. Then, near the water, there's what looks like a partial print that's been erased, as if the killer spotted it and rubbed out any identifying characteristics.

We find more broken foliage, adding to our picture of the scene.

"Ambushed from behind," I say. "He was standing in the stream or had one foot in it. Hit in the back of the head. Falls across the narrow stream and lands on all fours. Attacker gets the rope around his neck and hauls him back, where these scrabble marks are in the undergrowth. Kills him here. Probably lays him down over there." I point to flattened undergrowth. "Then the killer needs to drag him . . ."

I walk to that flattened undergrowth. There are definite drag marks. There's also a spot where a boot print has been erased. Then the ground gets harder, and the trail is only obvious by the crushed foliage. We follow for maybe twenty feet before it hits rock—smooth rock, easy to pull. Another twenty feet gets him to the cave where we found the body.

"Forty feet," I say. "How easily could I drag you that far?"

"We can try later if you like, but whoever did it wasn't dragging him across the bare ground." He points at some marks. "He was on something. A tarp probably."

"Which would make it easier. It would also explain why Storm couldn't follow that section of the trail. Tarps are also a standard part of camping gear. Okay, I can reasonably assume that Gretchen—a woman in good physical condition—could pull Blake on a tarp for forty feet."

We continue searching for any trace, but after thirty minutes, I make the call. Time to move on and look for Gretchen.

At noon, we reconvene with Anders and Yolanda. They accidentally got a little too close to where the miners are working, but they backed out before being seen. That does mean, however, that they can report that the mining operation is proceeding as usual. The camp hasn't gone into lockdown, worried about potential spies. Rogers accepted our story that Blake and Gretchen had moved on. Or, I presume, he accepted it after his security team failed to turn up any evidence to the contrary.

That's one piece of good news. The bad news is that there's still no sign of Gretchen.

Yolanda and I head back to Haven's Rock. I'm going to feed Rory and spend some time with her. Yolanda is accompanying me because Dalton doesn't want me in the woods alone right now, and Yolanda has the least search party experience. He'll continue on with Anders and Storm.

I take an hour in town, spent with my baby. Then she switches babysitters—Isabel this time—and Yolanda and I head out again with a packed late lunch.

We meet the guys at the rendezvous point, split the food, and break into pairs again. We're searching north and south of Haven's Rock now. Again, we're out there for hours. Again, we find no trace of Gretchen.

We don't meet up with Yolanda and Anders. We've agreed to head back to town for dinner, and we just do that. We do eat together, though, at our chalet, where we can discuss our findings, which are—for both parties—zilch.

"So she's gone?" Yolanda says. "Killed her husband and got the hell out."

"Presumably," I say.

"But you don't like that explanation. You think something happened to her?"

I chew as I think. Rory gurgles, bouncing on Anders's knee. I smile over at her and then turn back to Yolanda. "If something happened to her—such as also being attacked by whoever killed Blake—that complicates things in ways I don't want to consider. The tidy solution is that she killed him and left. The untidy part is that she'll need to tell the authorities."

"You're worried they'll come here?"

"Not specifically here. If she killed him, she'll lie about where he fell. But she may get searchers into the broad vicinity, and that's still an exposure threat."

"We'll need to lock down," Dalton says. "As of tonight. We'll keep looking for Gretchen and also looking for signs of a search plane."

Anders clears his throat. "I hate to mention another—and more alarming—possibility, but what if she fled and she's *not* the killer?"

I grimace. "Yep, that's an alternate solution. Someone else killed Blake, she witnesses it, and she runs for help. Eric and I discussed that. Of all the scenarios, that's probably the most dangerous."

"Because she'll bring authorities to the *correct* spot," Yolanda says. "Teams of people looking for both her dead husband *and* his killer. She'll also report that she met you two. You'll need to talk to Gran asap."

"I've already messaged saying we'd like a call tonight."

"Good." Yolanda takes a bite of venison. "She'll handle it. Whichever way this goes, she should be able to give us a heads-up when Gretchen returns to civilization. Gran has a full warning system ready for this sort of thing."

The warning system being people on Émilie's payroll who work in some capacity where they'll be notified of anything unusual in this area, including a woman reporting her husband missing or murdered. We just need to tell Émilie what's happened so she can put out the word.

To contact Émilie, we use a sat phone with texting. My call with her is scheduled for ten tonight. She's at a benefit gala on the east coast, and she doesn't expect to get away early.

Dalton and I debate what to do with our remaining couple hours of daylight. Ultimately, we overcome the urge to resume the search. It's not enough time, and we really need to organize internally. Hold a meeting with the militia and arrange patrols, while extending that meeting to include Isabel and Phil because we're about to go into lockdown.

We're already unofficially locked down, having canceled any excursions, but now it'll be complete, including a strict curfew. The restaurant will close at seven. The Roc will do the same. After that, everyone is to be home, with minimal noise and minimal light. We've drilled for this, but this will be our first live run, and I do not expect it to go smoothly.

Anders and Dalton handle the militia meeting. Dalton takes Rory to that, making up for lost baby time. My job is to inform the town of the curfew. Yolanda helps. We call a town meeting, and we explain that hikers were seen two days ago and we have reason to believe they may not have left the area.

We aren't overly concerned, we tell them, but we'd like to take the opportunity to test our curfew system. This will not be another drill. Violations will result in a warning for first offenses and penalties after that. Of course, when I give the talk, I avoid copspeak like "violations" and "offenses" and even "penalties." If someone "forgets" the curfew rules, we'll let them know and we really hope that will be enough.

I go over the rules. Then I open it up to questions. I'm braced for complaints. That was life in Rockton, where I came to regret instituting town meetings because it became a place for people to air their grievances.

But Haven's Rock is different. The staff is more relaxed, and that translates into more relaxed—and more trusting—residents. All I get are questions and clarifications, mostly from those who are concerned about accidental penalties, where they get in trouble for using a flashlight to walk to the bathroom. I answer all of those patiently, until Yolanda finally says, "Look, no one's going to give you shit for making an honest mistake. Stop stressing, get to your residences, and lock the hell down."

The questions dry up after that. I'm about to dismiss the group when someone speaks up. It's Arturo, who's been with us for about a year and works in the greenhouse.

"So those of us whose shifts start before dawn don't start until it's light out."

"That is correct," I say. "As I said, the restaurant and coffee shop won't open until ten, to give that staff time to get in. No shift will begin until nine, and we ask you not to leave your residence until eight thirty."

"Casey already went through this," Yolanda says.

Arturo says, "So what happens to those lost hours? Do workers need to make them up?"

"No," I say. "Hours lost at the beginning and ends of shifts are free time, in compensation for the inconvenience. Now, if everyone could proceed—"

"But I don't start until ten normally, and I'm done at three, which means I lose out on that free time."

"You only work a five-hour shift," Yolanda snaps. "Stop nitpicking."

"But it isn't fair. Some people will get extra time off—"

"We will work it out," I say.

"The hell we will," Yolanda says. "Who's tracking that and adjusting future shifts? The staff is already going to be working round the clock on the lockdown." She turns to the residents. "Show of hands. How many of you will *not* benefit from shortened hours?"

Half the hands go up.

"And how many of you are going to fuss about that when you know that remedying it will mean extra work for the staff, who are already working overtime?"

I wave my arms. "Ignore her. We're not putting anyone on the spot. If you have an issue with the fairness, you can speak to—"

"Eric," Yolanda says. "Or me."

"I was going to say Phil."

She shrugs. "Sure, that works. He won't call you out for whining. He'll just sigh . . . and tell you no."

"We will compensate everyone for general inconvenience with extras," I say.

"Sure," Yolanda says. "The extra perk of staying safe."

"Go home," I say. "Lock down. You have thirty minutes. After that, we'll start doing rounds and correcting errors in procedure."

We issue a few warnings. All but one seem to be genuine mistakes. Someone decided to bunk down with their lover and left their own blinds open. Someone forgot their novel at work and thought they had time to retrieve it.

Then there's Arturo, who had his light blazing and shutters open after the thirty-minute mark. I gave him ten minutes so I couldn't be accused of pouncing. Then I went over myself and politely asked him to remedy the issue. He claimed that because his blinds were closed and it wasn't fully dark, he shouldn't need to also close his shutters. He wanted the fresh air. I said he could close the shutters *or* turn off his light—the choice was his.

An hour later, Dalton and I are doing the rounds when we spot light coming from the rear of a residence.

I groan. "It's Arturo."

Dalton passes Rory to me. "I'll handle it."

I take the baby but shake my head. "Then he can just accuse me of sending you to play bad cop." I look down at Rory, awake but calm, listening to our voices. "And I'd better not show up holding her, or he'll accuse me of using my child as a prop."

Dalton puts his arms out for the baby. "Fair enough, but I'll go with you. Bad cop holding a baby. He won't know what to do with that."

I laugh softly. As we walk, I say, "I don't know what's up with Arturo. He's always been fine."

"Mmm. Kenny had a run-in with him last month. And Isabel did a few months back."

"True."

Both incidents had been the same sort I just had at the meeting, where Arturo had felt he'd been cheated. In Kenny's case, Arturo complained because a new resident got a custom chair before he did—except the new resident needed it for a back problem. In Isabel's case, Arturo had been arguing that because he was a teetotaler, he was losing out when we had special days that included free drink tickets.

I continue, "He's pissy about others getting time off. Do we hold the line—everyone will get extras of some sort for the lockdown. Or do we give him something to shut him up."

"Option one. If we start giving in to him, he'll never stop complaining."

"I suppose so. Or there's option three—see if Muriel will switch shifts. She might. It'll give her a chance to sleep in."

Muriel is the other greenhouse worker. Her shift is usually six in the morning until eleven.

I continue, "I could also just adjust both their shifts to three and a half hours. She'll go for it. She's chill."

"She's the new older woman? Gray hair? Came with her husband?"

I shake my head. "Muriel arrived in the spring. Early forties. Brunette."

His expression says he's trying to place her. That's no insult to Muriel. It'd be worse if he knew who she was right away, because that would imply she'd been trouble.

"She's quiet. A hard worker. Friendly. At the meeting, she looked ready to raise her hand at the end. I suspect she realized the problem and was ready to offer a solution. I'll have Phil rearrange their shifts, which should also resolve this problem." I wave at the lit window. "Now let's go inside and get it fixed."

CHAPTER TWELVE

Arturo has his arms crossed when he opens his door, which is really tricky to do, so I give him credit for that. Or I would, if it hadn't looked ridiculously awkward—he basically tugged the door open, caught it with his foot and then used his foot to pull it open wide while he crossed his arms.

"You're wasting your time," he says. "My blind is shut. I am complying with the requirements, and you're only harassing me because I dared to speak up against injustice."

"No, the requirements are that, in the event of a lockdown, you need to close your blind *and* your shutters *and* use only your small lantern."

"The battery is dead."

"And, as I told you, closing the shutters will be sufficient. If you'd like to step outside and see how much light is getting past your blind—"

Dalton steps from beside me. "Lights out. Shutters closed. You forgot to recharge your solar lantern. Not our fault."

"So you brought in the big guns," Arturo says. Then Rory squawks and his gaze drops to her. His brows knit. Then his eyes narrow, as if this is some kind of trick. Maybe holding a baby means Dalton can hit him and Arturo can't hit back.

"Yeah." Dalton lifts Rory and holds her out. "*This* is the big gun. Close the fucking shutters or I unleash the teething infant."

"You shouldn't swear in front of her," Arturo says. "And you're telling me to turn off my light when you have a *baby*? If she starts bawling, all the closed shutters and dimmed lights won't help. They'll *hear* the town from ten miles away."

"Let us handle Rory," I say. "Now, light off or shutters closed. We will speak to Muriel in the morning about adjusting your shifts to even them out."

His blink tells me I hit the bull's-eye. He's not protesting the general unfairness of the lockdown changes—he's thinking of himself. Something tells me that if he was the one with the short shift, he wouldn't say a peep about it.

"You will each work three and a half hours tomorrow," I say. "*If* you close those shutters."

"Is that a threat?"

"Yes."

That sets him back. Apparently, I was supposed to say no, not at all, think of it as an incentive.

I continue, "You don't need to start until one thirty. Then you'll be done at five. Acceptable?"

"No."

"For fuck's sake," Dalton says. "That's what you wanted, isn't it?"

"I want the early shift. In fact, I want the early shift permanently."

I frown. "You had the early shift, and you hated it. Muriel swapped with you."

"I've changed my mind. I've had enough of her slacking. If

I'm on the early shift, then she has to show up on time, and she has to do her damn job because I won't be coming in afterward to do it for her."

I motion him back inside. Then Dalton and I follow, and Dalton shuts the door behind us.

I lower my voice. "This really isn't the time for a labor dispute, Arturo. Can you agree, for tomorrow, that you will work the later shift, and we'll sort this with Phil?"

He crosses his arms again. "No. I want it resolved now, and since you want my shutters closed, I have your attention. I'm not giving it up."

Dalton makes a rumble that's two seconds from becoming a snarl. My look tells him to let me try resolving this.

"You're having a problem with Muriel not doing her job," I say. "You seemed fine with her last month when you switched shifts. In fact, you made a point of telling Phil what a good coworker she was."

"Because she'd agreed to take the shitty shift," he says. Then he shifts his weight. "Fine. Also because she *was* a good coworker. When I came in for my shift, everything was always done, and sometimes she'd do extra. But that changed a couple of months ago, and every time I think she's cleaned up her act, it starts again. She does a half-assed job. She says all the plants are watered, but a bunch of them are dry. If I'm lucky, she does the bare minimum. And she's not showing up at six, like she's supposed to. One of the kitchen guys came by for herbs last week and when he stopped by at nearly seven, the greenhouse was still locked tight."

I exhale. "Okay, we'll deal with this."

I'll need to inform Phil, but more importantly, I'll be telling Kendra that Muriel might be in need of counseling. This sort of thing can happen—someone comes into Haven's Rock, giddy with the relief of escaping their situation, determined to go above and beyond, but then the isolation and the cooling weather sets in, along with bouts of depression. That would explain shifting moods—from working hard to barely doing her minimum.

If that's the case, she needs counseling, not disciplinary action.

"You think she's showing up late regularly?" I say.

He shrugs. "It's not like I'm checking on her. But since I got that report about the herbs, I started walking past on my way to get coffee in the morning. Two days this week, she wasn't there. Yesterday it was past eight when she arrived. I saw her coming out of the forest, like she'd been out walking when she should have been working."

Yesterday.

I don't look over at Dalton, and I try to keep my expression neutral. "Okay, she was late a few times this past week."

"She tries to cover it up—saying all the plants were watered—but I can tell. She's slacking, and I need to cover for her, which I was doing, because I didn't want to snitch. But if she's now getting half shifts? That's too much."

I could point out the illogic of this reasoning, which makes it sound as if Muriel earned those shorter shifts, but I understand what happened here. Arturo was cutting her slack, possibly presuming she was having personal difficulties. But now that she's getting a perk, it just added to his frustration and tipped the balance.

What matters is that there's a dead body in the clinic, a man who seems to have died sometime between midnight and five A.M. two nights ago. And that's the same day Muriel was particularly late getting to her shift, after being MIA a couple of mornings earlier this week.

I get dates for every time Arturo knows she was late. There are three instances. The first was when the kitchen worker came looking for herbs earlier this week. I take the kitchen worker's name to verify. Then she was late twice more—yesterday and the day before that.

I make notes. Arturo doesn't seem to see anything odd in that. He's just relieved that I'm paying so much attention to his complaint.

When we leave, I tell him that he can take the first greenhouse shift tomorrow, and he closes his shutters while we're there and says he's going to sleep early, so his light will be off.

See how amenable he can be? He just needed us to hear his complaint and take him seriously. I cut Dalton off before he says anything about that.

We head outside and say nothing until we're inside the forest on the town's edge.

"That doesn't sound good," Dalton says. "Muriel goes from being a model employee to slacking off and coming in late . . . including the morning we found Blake."

I nod and say nothing. I'm deep in thought, working it out.

Dalton recognizes my look and waits patiently until I say, "Help me think it through. If Blake and Gretchen came for a resident—like Muriel—that wouldn't explain her being gone multiple times over the past week."

"Unless she was negotiating. They made contact. She tried to talk them out of . . ." He shrugs. "Whatever."

I nod. "If they were hired to come after her, they might be open to a counterpayment. But that's a week in the forest. Very slow negotiating in a hostile environment."

"So they didn't come to kill her. They came to communicate with her. Our first fear was that Blake and Gretchen were spies. Having someone *in* the town spying is better."

"That would explain the earlier sporadic absences. Muriel seems to have been 'slacking off' in cycles, likely because she's coming in late. Those could indicate regular meetings with her handler. Muriel is snuck into Haven's Rock, presumably by the old Rockton interests, who would know exactly what Émilie needed to grant entry, though we could be looking at an unknown party. Either way, they give Muriel time to settle in, and then they start sending her handler for regular check-ins. But a 'check-in' doesn't take a week."

"Maybe she's not holding up her end of the deal. It's happened before."

He's right. We had multiple "spies" in Rockton. Residents who were admitted on the understanding they'd report back to the council. One actually was Anders, who'd been told Dalton was a corrupt sheriff. Once he saw the truth, he flipped allegiances and gave the council meaningless intel. Mathias was also supposed to spy . . . and just never bothered. Then there was Émilie's own spy, her granddaughter Petra. In that case, the "spying" had been mostly an excuse to convince Petra to take refuge because, in another life, Petra had actually been a field agent for some branch of the American government.

"Muriel would make a good spy," Dalton muses. "At first, you'd think she's too quiet, the sort of person you barely notice in the room. I'm not sure I could pick her out."

"Which is perfect spy material. Petra had a similar vibe. Hardworking. Easy to get along with. Personable. Didn't stand out in any way."

"Fuck."

I lift my hands. "I'm not saying that's what we're dealing with. Play it through. If Muriel decided she didn't want to keep spying—and they sent Gretchen and Blake to get her back on track—why would Muriel kill Blake and then come back here?"

He shrugs. "What if Blake and Gretchen were the only link between Muriel and the council? The old Rockton council hires an outside firm to run the operation, in a double-blind."

"Muriel goes rogue and kills both of them, and the council has no idea who their spy was."

"Blake's body was hidden, and we can't find Gretchen. How long would it take for the council to even realize things had gone wrong?"

I pause, thinking it through, and then say, "Yolanda would say we're getting paranoid."

"Yeah, because she didn't live in Rockton. The council played this sort of shit and worse. Step one, we talk to Muriel. Confront her about shirking work, get a read on the sincerity level. Then take it to Émilie. I'm damned sure *she* won't think we're overreacting."

I swap out partners here. I want backup—in case Muriel is dangerous and so I have a second opinion on her sincerity. But I also want to put her at ease, make her think we are—reluctantly—following up on a complaint and trusting she has an explanation. That means my backup is Anders.

We find Muriel in her apartment. I ask her to come with us to the town hall. At first, she seems to think she's violated curfew somehow, but I assure her that's not the case. With the town locked down, I have time to follow up on some outstanding minor issues. Of course, that doesn't exactly put her at ease, but I reassure her it's nothing, really. We just want her to come to the town hall so we aren't violating curfew ourselves with a late conversation in the residence building.

As we walk, Anders puts her at ease. He saw her at the last movie night, so he asks how she liked it, what sort of films she'd want to see more of, all those little touches that make residents feel seen and heard. She's obviously flattered that he even noticed she'd been there.

Muriel is in her early forties. Pleasantly pretty, with a round face and wide-set green eyes. She's blessed with the opposite of resting bitch face—an expression that always seems open and content. I don't know what she did for a living down south. If it's not pertinent, we don't always get that information, especially if it could be connected to the *reason* a resident is here.

We could get everyone's story. After all, we're in charge. But this is how we've chosen to run Haven's Rock—with a permeable wall between us and our resident's secrets. If we need to know more, we can ask Émilie. The only thing I do know about Muriel is that she was an ardent hobby gardener who'd jumped at the chance to work in the greenhouse.

"Is everything okay?" she asks as she takes a seat in the town hall.

I wait for Anders to sit behind the desk, where he's nearby but not making Muriel uncomfortable.

"It's a work issue," I say. "We had a complaint."

"What?"

"A minor one," I say. "It came in earlier, and we didn't see any need to pursue it immediately, but since we're locked down . . ." I shrug. "We're clearing our desks."

"What was the complaint?"

"There have been a few instances where the greenhouse was unstaffed early in the morning, and we weren't aware of any request for a change in scheduled hours. It seems to have been sporadic, but a couple of people reported it, so we're following up."

"Oh."

I wait for more, but that's all I get.

"Have you been late for your shifts at all recently?" I ask.

"I made up the work," she says. "I wasn't sleeping in. I started work super early and then took a break. No one ever needs to visit the greenhouse before nine. The kitchen staff takes what they need for breakfast the day before, and then come at nine for lunch and dinner supplies. I'm always back well before then."

"You said you made up the work? You were getting everything done in the time you had?"

She frowns. "Yes. Why? Did someone say I wasn't?"

"No, I'm just confirming."

"I made sure I completed my tasks, and I put in the correct number of hours. It was just the times that changed. Is that a problem?"

"Getting your tasks done is the important thing, but you should check with Phil about any changes to your schedule. Otherwise, if people realize you aren't at your post, they presume you're cutting your shifts."

"I wasn't. I swear it. Ask Arturo. Everything was getting done."

I glance at Anders. She seems adamant, and I suspect Arturo had been exaggerating. Complaining about your coworker being late sounds like whining unless you can also say they were slacking.

When I'd pressed Arturo for details, he'd only said that some plants weren't watered and "other things" weren't done. Of course, he'd also said that Muriel used to go above and beyond, which would have meant less work for him. If she stopped doing extra, he'd have another reason to be annoyed.

"So you were arriving at what time?" I say. "If your shift starts at six, that's already early."

A slight smile. "When it comes to sleep, I'm an old lady. In bed by nine and up before five, which is one reason I offered to take the early shift. I'm awake anyway. Sometimes I go in at four thirty."

"That's . . . very early. And very dark."

She flushes and squirms in her seat. "I don't mind."

When I sit there, as if waiting for more, she says nothing.

I make a few notes. Then I say, "So you go in at four thirty, work for a while, and then leave? At what time?"

"Dawn."

"You leave at dawn and come back at . . ."

"I start ninety minutes early, so I take ninety minutes."

"It's an odd time of day for a long break."

"Is that a problem?"

I lean back in my chair. "I'd like to get this written up and move on, Muriel. I feel as if I'm pulling teeth here. You were setting your own hours. You're going to need to get Phil to sign off on that. But he's going to want to know why you're taking a ninety-minute break before anything is open. You can't grab coffee or breakfast. There isn't a morning yoga class. If you have a reason why you want a break at that time, just tell me and I'll pass it on to Phil."

She exhales and looks down at her hands, clasped in her lap. "I'm sorry if I sound defensive. I'm just . . ." She looks up and meets my gaze. "I don't want to start mental-health sessions with Kendra or Isabel and I know that's what will happen. I don't need that. I'm handling it. I'm just . . ." A long exhale. "I'm struggling a bit. With living up here."

"The isolation?"

A short laugh. "The opposite. I'm an introvert, and I'm finding it all a bit much. It's like living in a dorm. Even in college, I lived with my parents until I graduated and got a job that would allow me to pay for my own place because I knew I wouldn't do well with roommates."

"Ah."

"I brought noise-canceling headphones, but it's not enough. I just feel . . ." She shivers. "Surrounded. I've also discovered I'm slightly claustrophobic, which is a really lousy time to realize that. When I need a break, I escape to my room, and the walls start closing in, and it still isn't quiet. That's another reason why I love the morning shift. It's completely silent and the greenhouse is empty."

"Okay."

"Still, I need more. I've been going on the hikes with Kendra, and I love that . . ." A wry smile. "Except for the other people. I've been slipping out for an hour in nature. What do they call it these days? Forest bathing? I have a spot, and I go and sit there at dawn. Which I didn't want to tell you because it's against the rules."

"It is," I say gently. "I presume you go beyond the perimeter path?"

She ducks my gaze. "Yes."

"And you go to the same spot? Just sit there?"

She chews her lip. "The same spot, yes. But I . . . kind of have a little setup going. A log to sit on and a backpack of stuff that I hide. I read. I knit. I pack my breakfast and a thermos of tea." She looks at me. "I'm sorry. I know it's against the rules. That's why I was doing it at a time of day when I wouldn't get caught."

"I'm going to need you to show me the spot," I say. "You'll have to bring your backpack in."

She gives a wry smile. "No more forest bathing?"

"We can work something out," I say. "It doesn't sound as if you need counseling unless you want it."

"I'd rather not. Bad experience, you know? And I'm not depressed or anything. I just need time to myself."

"Okay, we'll see what we can do."

CHAPTER THIRTEEN

Does Muriel think it's odd that Anders and I immediately escort her—after dark—to retrieve her backpack? While we're on lockdown? She doesn't seem to. She's broken one of our few laws, and she seems to think it's perfectly reasonable that we want to get her things, giving her no excuse to go back alone for them.

What I really want to do is make sure she's telling the truth about this "forest bathing" spot. And I can't wait until morning and run the risk she'll sneak out and seed it with a backpack.

She leads us straight to the spot. It's maybe a half kilometer from town, a small clearing with a log and a backpack shoved inside that log. The backpack contains a novel and knitting supplies.

"No food," she says. "I know that would attract animals. And when I eat my breakfast here, I bring everything back with me."

I glance at Anders, who's prowling about. His shrug says he sees nothing to contradict her story.

"I really am sorry," Muriel says as I shine my flashlight beam around the clearing. "I knew it was against the rules. I just needed the time away, and I was embarrassed to admit it."

"We'll work something out." I look her way. "Also, for the lockdown, we need to make some changes to your shift. We can discuss that on the walk back."

"Am I in trouble?"

I shake my head. "Just don't do it again, please."

"Tell us when you're having difficulties," Anders says. "We'll come up with a solution, and it'll all be confidential."

"Thank you."

I get back in time to tell Dalton what I found before our call with Émilie. I do that while giving Rory her bedtime feeding. Once she's down, I come into the living room to find Dalton on the sofa, with his arms out. I drop into them and give an exhausted sigh.

"Long day, huh?"

"Long *couple* of days." I check my watch.

"We have five minutes. I've set a timer."

I exhale and cuddle against him, basking in every second of those five minutes. Then it's time to make the call.

After we first met up with Gretchen and Blake, I'd texted Émilie that we had a possible exposure threat . . . and possible spies. She'd asked me to keep her posted.

I'd messaged her again last night, saying we were following up on complications, but I hadn't said that the complication was a dead body. Mentioning that we found one of the possible spies being eaten by a grizzly wasn't something I could pop off in a quick text. She'd have expected all the details immediately, and I'd been too busy for that.

I need to remember that Émilie isn't our boss. She'd be the first to remind me of that. I'm just so accustomed to having one—on the police force and in Rockton. When I update her now, I'm braced for annoyance that I didn't tell her sooner. I get none of that. She needed to know about the threat initially, to be ready to take action, but otherwise, this is our town and she's there as a mentor and a resource only.

When I finish the update, she says only, "I don't like it."

"Neither do we. We're torn between feeling as if we aren't reacting strongly enough and feeling like we're already overreacting with the lockdown."

"Neither. This doesn't seem like an immediate breach, but it is cause for concern. As you've said, there are multiple explanations, and the most likely being that this is spousal homicide. Alarming, but not our problem."

"I agree. The business with Muriel seemed concerning at first, but she has an explanation and the evidence to support it. Will was there for the interview, and he believes her story."

"You don't?"

"I should, logically, and if there's a whisper of doubt, it makes me feel paranoid. So I need to ask whether there's anything concerning in her background. Whatever drove her here, could it have brought people after her?"

"I'm going to give you her story, Casey. I know you don't like that, but we really need to take that step in any situation where you have questions. Otherwise, I'm being asked to assess risk."

I wince. "Right. Sorry. I shouldn't put that on you."

"I understand." A pause as if she's pulling up a file. "Muriel worked for a nonprofit. A major one. She was the CFO."

I say to Dalton, "That's the executive in charge of finances."

"Yes," Émilie says. "She wasn't bringing in the sort of salary she would have received in the private sector, but she was well compensated. She won that position while still in her twenties, and it was her life. After years of not taking a vacation, her family wrangled her onto a girls-only trip—Muriel, her mom, and her two sisters. They went to a fancy resort for a midwinter tropical vacation. There, Muriel met a recent widower, whose wife had died of cancer, very fast, very unexpected. They'd planned this trip together, and she insisted he still take it. So he did."

"Then he fell for Muriel?"

"It wasn't like that. He was still far too deep in the grief process, but he needed a friend, and so did she . . . particularly the long-distance sort who didn't demand much of her time. Fast-forward two years, and the relationship becomes romantic. Still long-distance, which suits Muriel. Six months later, he's gone, and so is her money and a half million from her employer."

"Damn," I say. "Let me guess. There was no dead wife."

"There was not. Just a guy playing a very long game, with the patience to reel in a huge fish. Muriel was fired from her job and the police presumed she was in on the theft. She wasn't. During a visit, her lover had accessed her laptop, captured her keystrokes and got into her banking accounts. There was nothing to suggest she was anything except a victim. No charges were laid. The suit was dropped. She did not, however, recover her job or her life savings." She pauses. "Or her reputation."

I frown at Dalton, and then I say, carefully, "That's a terrible story. Too common, sadly. The scams seem endless, and no matter how savvy a woman is, after knowing the guy for a few years, she's not going to expect that. But how did it bring her to us?"

"That would be the death threats. From a business perspective, what the nonprofit did was an unacceptable knee-jerk reaction that I suspect originated in the PR department. When the money was stolen, they not only fired her, but they went into full-scale ass-covering by taking their accusation public."

"Ouch."

"Muriel had been with them for fifteen years. Exemplary employee. Flawless bookkeeping. Every audit passed with flying colors. She'd even argued for stricter banking controls, so that no one—herself included—could access significant funds without multiple levels of sign-off. That would be standard procedure elsewhere, but management here was lax, and her request for stricter controls had been sitting on the board's agenda for two years. Yet when something went wrong . . ."

"They threw her to the wolves. She met a guy, and he must have convinced her to steal from them and then he double-crossed her."

"Yes. She was painted as a lonely spinster, rather than a savvy business executive. When the police didn't press charges, she became the lonely spinster who got catfished. She thought the trouble would end when the police cleared her name. It did not. She had still lost charitable donations, money that should have gone to helping the less fortunate, and so some people believed she deserved to be punished."

"You said *death* threats?" I say.

"People thought she should be punished by *dying*?" Dalton says. "What the hell kind of bullshit is that?"

"The bullshit of very angry people who need something to be angry about. Most of them seemed like idle threats, but one person in particular became obsessive. When Muriel went looking for help, I found her."

I consider this, and then say, "If she was followed here by her stalker, she'd speak up. She's a former finance officer, not a seasoned spy who could murder two people and bury the bodies."

"What about the guy who conned her?" Dalton says. "Any chance it was Blake?"

I describe the dead man to Émilie. Then I hold while she pulls up her information.

"No," she says. "I have a photo here of him, and he's standing beside Muriel. He's maybe five foot six."

"Okay, well, height's one thing he couldn't fake," I say. "Her ex isn't our dead guy, then. Blake and Gretchen could be working for him, though I'm not sure why he'd come after Muriel. He wasn't caught, right? It's not a matter of stopping her from testifying."

"It's not. He escaped justice, and I agree that there's no valid reason for him to send anyone to find her. Now, if he came himself, begging forgiveness, and she killed him in a rage, I could understand that. However, all of these scenarios presume someone bypasses all our procedures and finds one of our residents. That only happened a couple of times in Rockton. Once decades ago, and once with that US marshal a few years back. Haven's Rock is even more airtight. I'll never say never, but I cannot imagine anyone following a resident there."

"So we're back to the spy theory. Any chance Muriel isn't Muriel?"

A short, humorless laugh. "That hole has been plugged. I have the newspaper photos here, and you have her photo on file, which you confirmed was the woman who arrived."

"Plus DNA," Dalton murmurs.

"Yes. We now take DNA at the initial meeting and test it against the person who shows up. It was a match. You have the correct woman."

I think it through, poking at possibilities. "Okay, one more. You said she went looking for help, right? If the Rockton council wanted to spy on us, could they find an actual potential case and set it up from that angle?"

Dalton nods. "Present us with a legitimate resident . . . whom they've bought as a spy."

"Muriel certainly could use the money," I say. "She lost everything."

When Émilie doesn't answer, I wince. "We're getting paranoid, right? Why would the council even send a spy?"

"Oh, they'd send one. If they know you opened your own Rockton, they'd certainly try to infiltrate it. They started their own, in that lodge, and it is not going well, because it lacks key ingredients."

"Eric," I say.

He makes a face. "They need more than me."

"Perhaps," Émilie says. "But you're the glue that holds the rest together. If they could convince you to join their new venture, you'd bring your wife, naturally. Will Anders would follow. So would April. A solid law-enforcement team plus a brilliant doctor would be the backbone they're lacking to prop up a new Rockton."

"They could infiltrate Haven's Rock," I say. "Monitor our progress. Either wait for us to fail or wait for us to get frustrated at being in charge. Could Muriel be that spy?"

"I don't think so. When she reached out, she was looking for help, but not necessarily the kind that came with moving to the far north. She was far more interested in just starting over, finding an organization that would help her forge a new identity. She had reservations about Haven's Rock—concerns that communal living wouldn't suit her."

"Like she said," I murmur.

"Yes. Ultimately, she agreed to come, but I don't get the sense she was looking for that. She requested the minimum one-year stay. A spy would need to be prepared for a longer term. Don't discount it but . . ."

"The bigger factor is Blake's death," I say. "Is it possible Muriel is a spy? Yes. However, how likely is it that she's a legitimate refugee who agrees to spy for money . . . and then murders someone sent to check in with her?"

"Anything like that in her background?" Dalton says. "I know we don't let in people with records of violence but was there anything to suggest she *could* kill someone? Military service maybe?"

"No. She went straight from school to her job. She didn't do any kind of military or quasi-military. If you check her form, she made it clear she didn't want to hunt. She was mostly vegetarian, and that was another factor that had her hesitating."

"We hunt," I say. "And it's hard to be a vegetarian with our food sources."

"Yes."

"Okay, so it seems Muriel is what she seems to be—a regular resident who's been slipping into the forest because she needs time alone. We'll work that out later. For now, we have a lockdown to deal with."

"Tomorrow," Dalton says. "Everyone's complying, and we can get some sleep."

"Agreed," Émilie says. "Feel free to send me any questions, but first, rest. You've earned it."

Haven's Rock is quiet the next morning. While residents may not have appreciated the early curfew, they certainly aren't complaining about being able to sleep in. It helps that the sun is bright, with the temperature promising that they might be able to shed their jackets by noon. By ten, the coffee shop is bustling, and people are making their way to work, conversing quietly, no obvious word of complaint. Even Arturo is happy—having been given a three-hour shift that allows him to sleep in *and* get the late afternoon off.

I have a bit of a lazy morning. Well, if you consider "not going to work until almost ten" being lazy, which it is for us. I went back to sleep after Rory's last feeding, and woke to find that Dalton had shut off the alarm and declared an impromptu "take your daughter to work" day. I wake to a silent house, a carafe of hot coffee, and a plate of cookies. Does it get any better than that? Well, yes, it might . . . but only if I find evidence that Gretchen is alive and well and has fled back south after killing her husband.

Fine. Someone murdering their spouse should never be a *good* outcome. But it's the best solution for this situation. Gretchen goes home and intentionally misidentifies the spot where her husband "fell," and searchers don't come within ten miles of Haven's Rock.

I don't want her getting away with murder. Yet if the alternative is exposing our entire town and destroying our safe haven? Then, I'm sorry for Blake, but he'll have to hope his wife's guilty conscience is enough punishment.

We do need to head out on another sweep for Gretchen, though. While I would love to find evidence that she's long gone, I'm not even sure what "evidence" that would be. Maybe if we saw a bush plane taking off in the distance, having picked up a passenger?

In the end, days of fruitless searching will probably need to be our answer. Or, if we're lucky, Émilie's contacts will get back to her with the news that a lone woman was picked up, claiming her husband died on their hiking trip. The Yukon is so small—population-wise—that it'd be impossible to keep that sort of thing a secret.

By ten thirty, we're off. It's just Dalton, Storm, and me for now. Anders and Yolanda will take a shift this afternoon, while we come back on baby duty before heading out again.

We start with a detailed search of the area surrounding the town. Yes, if Gretchen killed her husband—or has been killed herself—this isn't where we'd find her. But our bigger concern is an exposure threat—either because she's a spy or because she got too close to Haven's Rock. So we focus there for the next three hours, covering an increasingly wide swath around the town.

We find nothing except what we'd expect—evidence of people in spots they visit on authorized excursions. Places where they fish and gather berries and picnic, all predetermined locations that have been used multiple times.

Of course, we search all of them for fresh signs of activity, in case Gretchen camped where there is already evidence of past camping. But as Muriel said, we teach residents to leave nothing behind—not even footprints in the more remote sites. There are no signs in any of those locations to indicate that anyone has used them in the last few days.

So it's back to town for baby time and a late lunch while Yolanda and Anders search the perimeter around the lake. At four, we're dropping off Rory with April and heading back out.

We return to the region where all this started—the section to the west where we first met Gretchen and Blake, where they camped, where we found his backpack and where he'd been killed.

I start with the backpack. We remove it again and search it more thoroughly, now that we understand the purpose of it being hidden.

I am reasonably sure that Blake's killer hid that backpack

because the contents could identify their victim. The question is whether it's likely that his wife hid it . . . and therefore is also his killer.

His wife or his work partner, I remind myself as I remember that very new wedding band.

Either way, I mean Gretchen.

When we first found the backpack, we thought Blake and Gretchen had been lightening their load because it's filled with things you might jettison if one person was injured and you needed to travel light. After we discovered Blake's body, that theory still held, while pointing the finger at Gretchen. If she killed him, she'd need to get rid of his backpack. She'd go through the pack first and remove anything she might need, replacing it with things she didn't.

Now I examine the contents with that in mind. Does the theory still fit?

Yes, it does. This is mostly male clothing. She'd have no need of that. But she might need to make room in her pack for food, so there's a few items of hers here. There's one set of dishes—his. The toiletries could be for two—sharing toothpaste and soap—but there's only one toothbrush.

I sit back on my haunches. "Am I missing anything?"

Dalton shakes his head. "Nothing critical was left. Nothing immediately identifying, either. It's his stuff, plus some joint items and a few things of hers."

I exhale and rise. "Okay then. We need— Shit!"

Dalton frowns as I drop and rifle through the items from the bag. I lift the one T-shirt that belonged to Gretchen.

"This has been worn, right?" I say, holding it up.

His frown grows. "Judging by those pit stains, yeah. It was past ready for washing, which is probably why she left it behind."

"Storm?" I say.

The dog rises from where she's been resting, and she ambles over. Then she sees me on one knee, holding out the shirt, and she picks up speed.

"*Fuck*," Dalton says. "Yes."

I thought we didn't have a scent marker for Gretchen. We did. I just forgot about it.

CHAPTER FOURTEEN

It's dusk when we find that scent marker, and when dark falls, we're still tracking. It's not that Storm spends that long finding the trail. It's that there are too many trails to follow. We end up turning in for the night and then heading back out at dawn. Storm follows the scent back to where we met Gretchen, east of their camp site. Then to the camp site. Then on multiple short detours into the forest.

She also follows the trail to where Blake died. It goes to the creek, right in the spot where he'd been. From there, Storm snuffles around and then heads out. I call her back to see if she can find a trail north, where Blake's body was dragged.

She does not.

"We can't read too much into that," I say. "There's a lot going on here."

Dalton nods. "And if Gretchen did drag him, the smell of the tarp might overpower her scent."

I agree. Still, I make a mental note. Storm did follow the trail to the water, where we know Blake died. Yet . . . well, it's water. That could be why Gretchen went there.

I tuck all that in my pocket and take Storm back to the main trail. From there, she gets confused. Or maybe I get confused. It's hard to tell sometimes. She returns to the campsite, which could mean she was only retracing Gretchen's steps or could mean Gretchen went from the creek to the camp, which would also make sense. This is where they'd have been washing up and gathering water.

Storm walks around the campsite a few times . . . and then continues west to the point where we'd stopped her before.

Is she following Gretchen's exit trail or her entrance one?

We let Storm continue on that way for nearly a kilometer. At that point, we have to stop her.

Did Gretchen leave along the route we gave her? Or is that an old trail?

This is what happens when a non-scent dog is trained by someone getting their own training from books. We'll never progress beyond this state, where Storm can follow simple trails, which is all we usually need.

Blake and Gretchen had camped in this area. They'd gone back and forth on this trail. Beyond that? We don't know.

We're about to give up when Storm catches a scent on the ground. We're heading back toward Haven's Rock, still on the path Gretchen had taken. Then Storm stops and looks south for the first time. She snuffles the ground right at the spot where a thin game trail branches off this one.

Dalton moves past her and examines the undergrowth.

"Someone came this way," he says. "Broken twigs on the bushes."

He backs up to let Storm lead. It's hard going for her—the trail isn't wide enough to accommodate her bulk, and the branches keep snagging her thick fur.

"I can do this," Dalton says.

Storm and I back out to the larger trail. After a few moments, he says, "It's wider here. Bring her on through."

I'm doing that when I hear a voice. I stop, my hand lowering onto Storm's back. She waits. I carefully edge around her and then move to catch up to Dalton.

"You hear that?" I whisper.

He nods. His gaze is trained east, in the direction I heard the voice.

It comes again. All I can make out is that it's male. Another male voice answers.

I back up to Storm and ask her to stay. Then I regroup with Dalton and follow him toward the voices.

We go maybe twenty feet before they come clear. Two men, talking in that way guys sometimes do when they think no one can overhear. Loud joking and teasing about sex.

"See, the problem is that women up here have their pick of guys," one is saying. "So you can't be choosy. Find one who'll be grateful for the attention, make sure she's liquored up . . . and then turn off the lights and pretend she's hot."

That's the *least* offensive thing they say. It seems one of them is about to go on leave in Dawson City. His companion is giving him advice, which starts with getting women "liquored up" and ends with suggesting he find alcoholics and offer them money because there are "lots of boozers up here, and you wouldn't believe what they'll do for a C-note."

"Miners?" I whisper.

Dalton only grunts, and the more I listen, the more I feel as if I've been transported back to the gold rush days, guys with a pocketful of money, looking for sex in the metropolis of Dawson City.

The important thing is that they didn't hear us. They are, however, heading our way. Directly our way. I glance back toward where we left Storm.

Do we acknowledge that we're here? We're on neutral ground. We haven't met any of the miners, though, and Rogers has made it clear that he would prefer his workers not to realize there's another settlement nearby. I agree, especially after hearing that conversation. One of our fears is that the miners will discover there's a town . . . with women and a bar. From what I just heard, that worry isn't groundless paranoia.

Dalton motions for us to move north and get out of their path. From there, we can link back up to that larger trail and quietly retrieve our dog.

We start in that direction. The two men are making enough noise to scare off anything, and it easily tells us where they are. They keep talking, having now moved to stories of sex with drunk women. And, if I'm understanding correctly, sex with passed-out drunk women. I block it out. Nothing I can do except resolve even more strongly to keep our two settlements apart.

When we're about thirty feet away, the men pass perpendicular to us, and I glance back to take a look. Considering what they're saying, I'd like to commit these two faces to memory. I ease left so I can see them and, with a jolt, I realize I've met them. Both of them.

They're not miners. They're guards. I've been making a more concerted effort to distinguish them, mostly so if we have a problem with one, I can identify him. One of these two is about thirty-five, with light hair and a mole on his jaw. The other is the dark-haired one we saw just the other day.

So it's not the miners talking about getting women drunk

and having sex with them. It's the guards . . . who already know about Haven's Rock.

"Fuck," Dalton mutters beside me, and I nod in agreement.

The one saving grace here is that no one has attempted to come to Haven's Rock, despite knowing there's a nearby settlement with women. That'd be Rogers's doing. I hate to give the guy credit, but he runs a tight ship. I suppose that's one advantage to the paramilitary nonsense. Rogers uses it to keep the guards in line. I can only imagine that they've been told what the penalty is for crossing onto our territory, and it's steep enough that no one is breaking it, even for sex.

I turn to head back to Storm. While I would prefer not to bump into these guys, I'm not as concerned as I had been when I thought they were miners. We told Rogers we'd keep looking for signs that hikers hadn't left, and that's what we're doing.

I only get one step, though, before Dalton touches my arm. He's looking deeper into the woods, and when I go still, I pick up the tramp of footsteps.

"Moore!" a voice snaps. "Rico! What the hell are you doing out here?"

If it wasn't for the profanity, I'd have presumed it was Rogers. Then the man says something I don't catch, and I realize he has a British accent. Definitely not someone we've met.

I back up to where I'd been and peer through. The two guards have stopped. A third man joins them. He's maybe mid-forties, with light brown hair, tall and wiry. I frown and glance at Dalton, who shakes his head, confirming it's no one we've seen.

"Sorry, mate," the light-haired guard says, affecting an accent himself. "We were just out for a ramble. Heading over to the pub—"

"I'll ask you one more time. Where do you think you're going?"

"We're off duty, mate."

"You might be, but you passed the boundary a half mile back."

The light-haired man screws up his face. "Did we? Huh. Guess we missed the signposts."

"If you have a problem, take it up with your boss, and somehow, I get the feeling, he's going to tell you to go fuck yourself. Now turn around and go back."

The light-haired man grumbles and shoulders past the younger one, but he does as he's told. Dalton and I watch the newcomer as he stands there, peering around. Then he turns on his heel and stalks off.

"You've never seen him either, right?" I say.

"Never."

"But he seems to be management. Second-in-command, maybe? At least that encounter tells us one good thing."

"That the guards have a boundary they aren't supposed to cross."

I glance up at Dalton. "Two things, then. They have boundaries even off-duty and on neutral territory. But also they weren't looking for our hikers. They've given up that search."

"Seems so."

We return to Storm, who has lain down to wait. When we approach she rises, ready to continue. We get her to where, as Dalton said, the forest opens up, and then we let her take over tracking Gretchen. She follows the trail for another hundred feet or so before stopping in a clearing.

"Huh," Dalton says, when Storm lies down.

He starts searching the perimeter of the clearing. He's looking for signs of where Gretchen might have exited. I focus on what she was doing here. If Storm is lying down, that means Gretchen stopped here—that her scent is all over this clearing.

I look first for debris, but Gretchen seems to be a seasoned hiker, and we didn't find a single scrap of trash at the campsite.

Could she have camped here? It'd be an odd choice. Murder your husband. Hide the body. And then set up camp less than a kilometer away. You know, to rest. Moving a body is hard work.

And as I'm thinking there's no chance I'll find signs of an actual encampment, I spot one. A divot in the ground. Only it's not quite a divot. It reminds me of my very rare golfing excursions, when I had a habit of hacking the ground. That's what I'm seeing. A spot where the "turf" seems to have been lifted.

I take a stick and prod under it. There's no real sod here where the ground cover can be sparse. But what I lift is the closest approximation—a layer of hardened soil held together by root systems. I take hold, and it peels back in a square about thirty by thirty inches.

By now, Dalton has seen what I'm doing and come over. He frowns at the piece of sod. I dig around all sides of the open square, but it was just that one section.

"Something buried?" he says.

"I think so."

He takes out the collapsible shovel, but I motion for him to hold off. I bend and start clearing with my hands. I lift out handfuls of dirt. Then my fingers brush something and I stop. I take a deep breath and gently clear away dirt to reveal hair. Light brown hair.

"Gretchen," I murmur, sitting back on my heels and exhaling.

Dalton crouches at the hole. "Buried standing up?"

"Seems that way."

"Fuck. That takes some work."

"Less soil disturbance, but yes, much trickier to dig the hole." I exhale slowly. "Since she didn't put herself in there, I'm going to need to get her out. And we need to figure out how to do that."

In the end, the only real solution is to dig a bigger hole. Go in from the sides and loosen the soil enough to extract her body.

Dalton has his collapsible shovel, but that's not really meant for this kind of work. We're going to need to go back to town. Still, Dalton makes a start at it, and as he does, I kneel to brush dirt from her head. And two minutes later . . .

"Eric?" I say.

He stops, wipes sweat from his brow, and grunts. Then he looks over. "What the hell?"

I have the top of the head exposed up to the brows. Now I clear lower on the face, revealing thick brows under a heavy brow ridge.

"That is not Gretchen," Dalton says.

I keep clearing. The rest of the face comes clear. A man's face. He's maybe in his thirties. Light brown skin seems to be the result of a tan. He has dark blond wavy hair and a short beard.

Dalton stares down at the man. "Did we just . . . ?"

"Find another corpse in the forest? It seems so."

"Fuck."

CHAPTER FIFTEEN

After that, we don't bother going to Haven's Rock to get the bigger shovel. We call for it, along with a bigger guy to help dig out our dead man. We ask Anders to help my sister find someone to take Rory and then come on foot with April, and to be alert for anyone in the forest.

Dalton and I keep working for twenty minutes. Then I return to the main trail, where I meet our deputy and doctor.

"Did I hear right?" Anders says. "You found a body, and it's *not* our other hiker?"

"It's a man." I look at April. "Yes, I dug up another random corpse in the wilderness."

"I was not going to say it."

"Sure you were."

"Not yet. You are obviously distressed and so I was withholding my joke for a better moment."

I shake my head and lead them in. Dalton has the man uncovered to his shoulders.

"That's a fresh corpse," Anders says.

"No, it is several days old," April says. "Despite having been buried, there are clear signs of early decomposition—"

"I meant it's recent. Which is significant because we just found a dead man and we're looking for a missing woman, the wife who might have killed him."

"I believe this is further evidence that Gretchen is not his wife," April says.

Anders arches a brow.

April continues, "In addition to the new wedding band, which belies their story of being a long-married couple, we postulated that they might have been spying on either Haven's Rock or the mining company. The existence of a second corpse—likely a third party to their group—would seem to confirm that they were not who they claimed to be."

I lift a hand. "I would prefer not to speculate on that yet. We have the corpse of a man who likely died in the past week, which suggests he may be connected to our hikers. That's all. He could just as likely be connected to the mining camp."

"One of the miners or guards," Anders says. "If so, then I'm going to guess this isn't some guy who died of a heart attack on the job. Not with the weird way they've buried him. Unless it's some kind of religious or cultural thing?"

We all look at each other, in case someone has heard of this. No one has, which doesn't discount it.

"Wait," Anders says. "Are we sure he's standing up?"

"Excellent point," April says. "This might only be half of him. The other half might be elsewhere."

"Er, not what I meant. Only that there's a reason we dig shallow graves here, and it's not because we're lazy."

Dalton curses. "Permafrost."

"Okay," I say. "Let's find out what we have."

* * *

What we have is *not* a six-foot hole with the corpse standing upright. That wouldn't be possible with the permafrost. Instead, he's been put into a hole with his knees bent, as if compacting the body into the smallest possible shape. We'd speculated that whoever buried him was minimizing the size of the hole to better disguise it. While that could be the answer, it's just as likely they were being lazy. They dug the smallest possible hole and shoved him in.

Finally, we have the man stretched out on the ground. As April said, the burial would have slowed decomposition. He wasn't exposed to air or insects. The signs of decomposition are still there, equivalent to what I might see on a day-old exposed corpse. That suggests he was buried, as my sister also speculated, in the past week.

There are no obvious signs of trauma, though. No bullet or stab wounds. No hemorrhaging in the eyes. We check his scalp for signs of a head injury and find only an old tattoo under his hair.

"He's a fit guy," Anders says, looking down at the body. "His hair's too long for a guard, but maybe a miner? Hiker is just as likely, given that tan."

I examine the hands for calluses. There are faint ones, but that could work for either mining or hiking. I check the man's feet. Some signs of chafing, including a covered hot spot. Boots would have helped decide whether he was a miner or hiker—hiking boots and steel-toed work ones—but his feet are bare. He's been stripped down to his underwear.

"The lack of clothing would suggest someone is concealing his identity," April says.

"True," I say. "But if he's a miner, his clothes would have been standard issue, and I can see Rogers saying he wants them back."

Dalton snorts. "Company property."

"There's one way to check whether he's a miner," Anders says. "See if he's chipped."

He's right. The miners—and the guards—have implants that track their whereabouts. From what I've gathered, the guards are aware of it. The miners are not. As horrified as I am at the thought of "chipping" employees, Dalton and I have actually discussed this with Émilie. Missing residents are one of our biggest problems. Would voluntary tracking help?

In the case of the mining camp, while Rogers would probably say it was for safety, I suspect it's also like removing clothing from a dead man—protecting company property. However, those tracking chips might mean their guards and miners can't sneak over to Haven's Rock.

I would love to discuss that with Rogers. Find out how he's using them, and see whether—after an incident last year—he's making sure no one comes our way. But to do that, I'd need to admit we know about the chips. We've decided that is not in our best interests. For now.

We've had access to the body of one miner, where we found the scar from the chip insertion on his shoulder. It'd been marred by an injury, so it'd taken us a while to see it. The guard who'd tried to barter with us had cut his out—also on his shoulder. So that's where we look, but the skin there on this body is smooth and unmarred.

I continue my search and find nothing.

I sit back on my heels. "There's no proof this *is* a miner—and no proof that he's not. Also no evidence he was or wasn't a hiker."

I pause. "If he were a hiker, he'd have been with Gretchen and Blake. The alternative is too much of a coincidence."

Anders points at the man's feet. "That hot spot suggests he was doing more walking than he's used to."

"So," April says. "It appears this man was with Gretchen and Blake, who were not actually hikers or a married couple, but were likely spying on either Haven's Rock or the miners. That sounds familiar. In fact, I believe it is exactly what I first theorized."

I ignore her and look up at Dalton. "Do you think there's any significance to the fact we nearly bumped into two of their guards?"

"What?" Anders says.

"Two guards from the camp were out here, allegedly just strolling around. They were heading in this direction when they were stopped by someone who seems to be management. A British guy we've never met. He said they'd gone past the boundary."

"Which he'd know if he's tracking them."

"Good point. Yes."

"So he turned them around right before they stumbled over a shallow grave?"

I consider. "I can't imagine they'd have noticed it. We only stopped in here because this is where Gretchen's trail led, and Storm indicated Gretchen had stayed here awhile. I was searching for signs of what she'd been doing when I noticed the disturbed sod."

"Gretchen was here?" Anders says. "You forgot a critical bit of evidence, Case."

"I kinda did. When we found the grave and saw the light hair, we thought it *was* Gretchen. Once we realized otherwise,

I got caught up in that. But yes, it's significant that Gretchen was here."

I rise and work out a kink in my neck as I think. "Storm was definitely following her trail. Well, no, I shouldn't say that. She was following the scent from a T-shirt we found in the discarded backpack. A women's medium, which would seem to be Gretchen's."

"Unless there's a fourth party," April says. "Gretchen, Blake, the dead man, and another woman."

"I can't rule that out, but the shirt is most likely Gretchen's. The trail went to all the places we know she's been—the campsite, the creek, and over to where she met up with us. So if that trail also says she was here, I'm going to guess there's not much chance she just happened to hang out in the same spot where a body was buried."

"What are we saying?" Anders asks. "Three people came into the forest to spy on one of the settlements. Two are dead . . . and the third is the killer?"

"We have no actual evidence they were spying on either Haven's Rock or the mining camp. The new wedding band suggests some kind of fraud, and the two bodies suggest a falling-out and double murder. Unless . . ."

I look around the clearing. "I hate to say it, guys, but I think we need to do some more digging. In case Gretchen *is* here."

We don't find Gretchen's body. I'm glad we searched, though, or I'd have leapt up in the middle of the night thinking I'd overlooked the obvious alternate solution. Why was Gretchen's scent in the clearing with a buried man? Possibility number one is that she buried him. Possibility two is that she's also buried here. She's not. Which takes us back to Gretchen as the killer.

Except, at this point, we have no evidence that the dead man was murdered. We don't know how he died, and there are zero defensive wounds. Getting more is going to require, yep, performing yet another autopsy on yet another person who isn't part of our settlement. But we can hardly leave him in the forest when we could be dealing with double homicide and a killer on the loose.

If Gretchen killed Blake, then our hope was that it was personal, and she's long gone. If she killed both men, then that's not the situation.

We return to Haven's Rock for the stretcher. Then Dalton goes back with Anders and Storm. While I wait, I get to happily do all the baby-mama stuff. Change Rory. Feed her. Play with her when she's not ready for a nap, and then rock her to sleep when she is. We're in the clinic when the body arrives, and I set to work helping April while Rory sleeps in her bassinet. Dalton offers to take her, but he needs a break himself, so I send him home. Best to not disturb a sleeping baby. He can get some rest with Storm, and if Rory wakes, I'll take her home.

Anders leaves, too. He has other duties, and he's not needed here.

We did the preliminary external exam on the scene. Now we repeat it with proper lighting and equipment, but we find nothing else. No sign of trauma. No sign of a tracking-device implant.

We are thorough. Damnably thorough, because we cannot believe this man died of natural causes.

Is it possible though? Yes, but I'd struggle to fit that into the narrative we're developing. We know Blake was murdered. We suspect Gretchen killed—or at least buried—this man. So this third confederate dies of natural causes, they bury him, argue over it, and Gretchen later kills Blake?

Yeah, that doesn't work for me.

Once we've finished the external exam, it's time for the autopsy, and that is where we get our answer. April opens him up and finds inflammation in his esophagus and stomach, along with hemorrhaging in his stomach lining.

"Poison," I say. "He was poisoned."

Rory wakes up shortly after that, and while I can't imagine she'd realize she's in the room with an autopsied body, I still don't want her there. With apologies to April, I leave the cleanup in her hands and take Rory. I'm halfway home when Dalton meets me.

"I rested," he says in greeting. "I figured I'd come see if this little one was up."

"She is, and your timing is perfect. We finished the autopsy, and I had an excuse to leave the cleanup to April."

"You want me to grab lunch and meet you at home? Presuming you can eat after that."

"I can always eat. Sure, I'll see you there and give you the results."

"Any hints?"

"Well, it wasn't natural causes."

He shakes his head. "Fuck."

CHAPTER SIXTEEN

"Poison?" Dalton says as we eat lunch with Rory at the chalet.

"Yep."

"What kind?"

I shrug. "There are a few possibilities. April will run tests, but it really only matters if he was poisoned by something we have access to here."

"Because if so, then the killer could be one of us. Except we're pretty sure it was Gretchen, right?" He lifts a dollop of mashed potato to Rory's lips, and she nearly takes off the finger with it. "Ouch!"

"Don't forget she has teeth now."

He shakes his finger. "No kidding." He gives her another piece . . . on a spoon. "If it's Gretchen, though, how the hell is she poisoning *anyone* up here?"

"She'd have brought it with her. Premeditated. Let's say the three of them are on some sort of mission. Targeting Haven's Rock or the mining camp. They get what they need, and then her orders are to kill her colleagues. It's way too James Bond for me, but if we're talking spies and assassinations, poison makes sense."

"And presumably something went wrong with Blake. The poison didn't work."

"Or Blake was in on killing the other guy. Helps her bury him, and then it's his turn to die."

I take Rory from his lap and put her on the floor. She grumbles . . . and then spots Storm and starts to crawl, crowing with delight.

"That's the problem with criminals, including spies," I say. "They can see one of their own being taken out and never think they're next."

"So Gretchen and Blake poison and bury our dead guy. Then they meet up with us, give their story, and the next morning, Gretchen kills Blake."

I nod. "Or vice versa. The other guy killed Blake and hauled him off, and then Gretchen poisons *him*. April's time of death estimate puts it anywhere between two and four days ago."

"Where does this leave us?"

"Really hoping Gretchen is long gone? If she's some kind of operative she knows what she's doing and no one will come looking for her partners."

"Fuck." He shakes his head. "Yeah, I guess that's where we're at. Lock down for a few more days. Give her plenty of time to go."

"But while that clears up the immediate issue, it doesn't solve the bigger one."

He glances at me, fork to his lips.

"What were they here for?" I say. "Us or the miners. And even if it's the miners, that's a problem for us."

* * *

I'm on a call. Rory is still crawling around the floor, while Dalton has gone in to work. Yolanda is with me, mostly because she wants to talk to the person I'm calling. Not that you'd know it by their opening exchange.

"Hey, cuz!" Petra says over the line. "I was just thinking of paying you a visit."

"Please don't."

"Oh, now I definitely will. I'm thinking of October, before it gets too cold. Maybe I'll come to celebrate Halloween. We can dress in matching costumes, just like when we were kids. I'll bring the candy."

"No."

"What's that? You'd love to have me? Excellent. I'll talk to Gran and make the arrangements."

"And I'll talk to Gran and tell her all the reasons why you shouldn't visit. You've finally started a new life, and we wouldn't want you to backslide."

Petra snorts. "That's why you don't want me up there? For my own good."

"No, that's the excuse that Gran will buy. The reality is that I don't want you here because I'd spend the next few months hearing how nice you are, how friendly and personable, and are we definitely cousins?"

"Still coming up. I'll just put on my costume early. I'll play you." Her voice goes gruff. "Halloween? What are you, twelve? Who wants candy? I don't want candy. I hate dressing up. I hate everything."

"Including you."

"You *adore* me. Casey? Mark your calendar. I will be there for Halloween with huge boxes of candy."

"I'll hold you to that, you know," I say.

Her grin shines through in her voice. "Good. It's a plan."

"And I'll be away for the week," Yolanda says.

"No, you won't. You'll be there to grumble at me, and tell me I brought the wrong kind of candy, and you'll love every minute of it."

Petra had been in Rockton when I arrived. She'd been my first good friend there. Discovering she was one of the founder's granddaughters, and a spy—both professionally and in Rockton—had been a blow.

I'd watched her take out an enemy and barely blink, and that was so far from the Petra I knew that I'd been shaken, certain the one I saw was a lie. It's not. There's the happy-go-lucky Petra, the ice-cold operative Petra, and the other one, forever grieving her young daughter's death and the aftermath that slammed the blame onto her own shoulders.

I miss her terribly, but I'm glad she's finding her footing. She'd originally planned to come with us to Haven's Rock. Then her arrival date kept being pushed back until she admitted she wasn't joining us. Being back down south for a few months helped her realize it was time to move on with her life.

"We have spy questions," Yolanda says.

Petra groans.

"Sorry," I say. "Secret-agent questions."

"That's not much better."

"Highly trained–operative questions? Oh, how about federal-agent questions. That's boring, but fitting. Unless you didn't work for the federal government."

"I'd tell you, but then . . . Well, you know the rest," Petra says, far too cheerfully. "Okay, so Gran said you're dealing with something that seems to involve espionage. Involving either Haven's Rock or that gold-mining operation."

"Yes," I say. "How much did she tell you?"

"Nothing else. She said you'd fill in what you were comfortable sharing."

It's Petra, which means I'm comfortable sharing everything, even the speculative bits that make me feel as if I've seen too many spy movies. I tell her about meeting Blake and Gretchen, finding Blake dead, and now finding a second body.

"And this second body is definitely connected to the fake hikers?"

"No. Nor are the hikers definitely fake."

I list off all the evidence that supports that theory.

"The mining camp is chipping its employees?" Petra says. "On the one hand, major privacy invasion. But on the other?"

"Maybe we should do it, too? Only we'd get permission obviously."

"Yeah, I'm guessing the miners signed some document they barely read that would allow the tracking. But if our dead man doesn't have a tracker then he's not their employee."

"Mmm. I can't say that absolutely. But yes, there is no proof he works for them and also no proof that he wasn't with Blake and Gretchen."

"So a trio of espionage agents, with orders to kill two members once the data has been retrieved. Apropos of nothing, did I hear you guys run movie nights more often?"

"Yeah, yeah. Too many James Bond movies. I've already made that joke at my own expense. So I'm way off base."

Petra exhales. "Well, it depends. Was I routinely sent on missions and ordered to kill my colleagues? No. Was I *ever* ordered to kill them? No. Did I personally know anyone who was ordered to kill their colleagues? No. But, of course, that wasn't the sort of thing you'd confess in the spy pub over brewskis."

"You never took *me* to a spy pub," Yolanda says.

"I could, but then I'd have to . . . Well, you know. But you guys understand my point. I didn't work in the sort of environment where fellow operatives were killed to shut them up. I did know people who worked in things closer to what you'd find in the movies. Private operations. I heard stories of those agents being killed when they completed a mission. Or being killed when they discovered something they shouldn't. Or when they developed a conscience. There's a lot out there, and it's not all MI6, CIA, covert-government-operations stuff."

"Okay," I say.

"Let's take that and jump to our two possible targets. Haven's Rock or this mining company. Could someone be hired to spy on you guys and then kill their colleagues? I can't see it. Sorry. Maybe in Rockton. Maybe if you were operating some nefarious and highly profitable operation."

"Which we are not."

"Correct. Haven's Rock is the opposite of profitable. On the other hand, I can see the old council spying on you for basic espionage."

"Trade secrets. Their new version of Rockton is failing."

"And Haven's Rock is thriving. Gran also mentioned they might want to lure you guys back to the fold. I can see that, too. From experience, I'd say they'd be analyzing your operation and seeing whether you're stumbling, maybe in need of help. And if not, then maybe they could change that."

"Sabotage us."

"Yep. But that would mean embedding a spy. What would they learn lurking around the forest? Nothing except that your patrols are very good and would find them if they got too close."

Yolanda says, "What if they *know* we're doing fine. Could they move straight to sabotage?"

"Yes. However, that's not the kind of operation where you kill your fellow agents to keep them quiet."

"So their target would be the mining company," I say.

"In my opinion, yes. From what Gran says, that is one hell of a secretive operation, tightly run. It's not a few guys panning for gold in the forest. It's not even some small firm running a claim." She pauses. "Are we sure they're actually mining?"

"We keep our distance," I say, "but we've been close enough to confirm that."

"Not sure what else they'd be doing," Yolanda says. "If there's money to be made up here, it's in gold."

"Maybe there's something to mine besides gold, something even more valuable. It's not a massive operation, which would make me wonder how much gold they'd be getting. Either way, considering how professional—and paranoid—these guys are, they have a serious operation there, making serious money. Which could mean serious espionage."

"So—" I begin. "Hold on. I've lost my kid."

As I hurry to find Rory, Petra calls, "Isn't she barely crawling?"

"She's fast," I call back. "Also, her mom is a little distracted."

I find Rory in the kitchen, with Storm standing right behind her, watching. The dog gives me a baleful look. I murmur an apology, pat her head, and scoop up Rory, grabbing her favorite toy—a squirrel-shaped teething rattle—as I head back to the living room.

"Storm was on duty," I say. "And giving me stink eye because I wasn't."

"Good dog," Petra says. "Hello, Rory! I didn't know you were there because your mom didn't tell me."

Rory gurgles and shakes her rattle.

"Okay," I say as I settle in with the baby on my lap. "So the mining company would be the target. That makes sense. Haven's Rock might be spyworthy to the council, but we don't have secrets valuable enough to kill for."

"Unless it's about a resident."

"Right. Do we have a resident whose secret is so valuable that someone would send spies to find them . . . and then kill their colleagues? Émilie says no."

"Also, that'd be an overly complicated operation," Petra says. "Why send three people unless you plan to kidnap the resident? But then you sure as hell wouldn't murder your colleagues first."

"Unless kidnapping was the plan," Yolanda says, "but Gretchen changed her mind. Or the plan was to *kill* a resident, and she had an attack of conscience."

"No one is sending three operatives to kill one person. That's not how assassinations work." She pauses. "Or so I've heard."

Yolanda snorts.

"Makes sense, though," I say. "While we could have a resident someone wants dead, three people aren't coming to do it. We need to look closer at the mining operation."

"That would be my advice. Now, if it's a case of corporate espionage, where the stakes are so high you'd only want one operative returning? That's not some little gold-panning operation."

"But is that any of our concern?" Yolanda says. "If it's about the miners, do we stick our head over the parapet?"

"Well, I don't know," Petra says. "Do you want this operative going back and saying she met others in the forest? A couple with a dog and a baby? Doesn't sound like she'd mistake you for miners."

"Shit," Yolanda says.

"Yep. No matter what, though, I think it's time to get a closer look at your neighbors. Find out what they're really doing up there."

CHAPTER SEVENTEEN

Last year, after the guard insinuated something was up in the mining camp, we'd asked Émilie to dig deeper, and we'd gone on spy-lite missions of our own. We confirmed that operations were underway, with several small teams working the sites.

The Yukon was the site of one of history's biggest gold rushes. People braved unimaginable conditions in the hope of making their fortune, lured up here by everyone who had a stake in selling them that dream. A hundred thousand would-be miners came north to get their share of the gold that they'd been told was just lying around, waiting to be scooped up. All they had to do was get from Alaska to Dawson City . . . on foot, often in the dead of winter.

The RCMP demanded that everyone crossing the border carry six months' worth of supplies. They thought that would discourage the miners. It did not. About a third made it to Dawson City. Some went home with the adventure of a lifetime stuffed in their back pocket, to bring out and polish when life grew dull. Most, though, left brokenhearted and disillusioned.

Did anyone get rich? Sure—those who made their fortunes from the miners themselves.

It's a story as old as time. People seduced by the promise that they, too, can be fabulously wealthy, if only they have the nerve and the willpower. Join armies and pillage your neighbors. Venture into the wilds in search of gold. Spend every penny you have on virtual investments that are sure—*sure*—to pay off. Someone always gets rich. It's never the Joe Average who did the work—fought the war, mined the gold, invested their meager capital and sold the dream to others.

How much of our local gold-mining operation is about the actual value of the gold and how much is about the value of a dream? Dalton and I discuss that over dinner, after I tell him what Petra said.

Earlier, I'd asked her to run an online search for what else is mined up here. Copper, lead, zinc, and silver are the most common for actual mining industries. Gold is the sexy one, but it's mostly for amateurs and semipros, like the prospector who sold them the claim. There's also uranium. But those, as far as we know, require actual mining, not some guys with handheld equipment.

Is there something buried here that we don't know about? Something revealed in the samples that the original prospector had provided? Something valuable that can be accessed without major machinery?

Or is someone selling a dream?

The original miner—Mark—had arrived after we started construction, and he'd struck gold, which meant he wasn't going anywhere. That had been hellishly inconvenient, especially when his wife turned up dead. In the end, Mark himself died in a fall, which had seemed to be the end of it . . . until the current mining company showed up, having apparently bought the claim before his death—or bought the information about the claim, since he never formally registered it.

"Imagine it," I say, after we put Rory to bed upstairs. "We know Mark found a rich vein. It was valuable. What if you take that data and show it to people with more money than sense? Tech bros looking for the cool new thing to make money on."

"Do I want to know what a tech bro is?"

"Probably not."

He tilts his head. "Are they all bros? Any tech sisses?"

"Oh, I'm sure there are a few, but it's ninety-five percent bros. Just think guys with a ridiculous amount of money looking for cool investments. Like Klondike gold."

Dalton sips his beer. "The theory, then, would be that the money isn't in the gold. It's in the bros."

"Fleecing the bros, who would love all the trappings—the paramilitary stuff and top-notch security."

He considers. "Or it could be more old-school Klondike. The marks aren't guys with money but guys without it."

When I frown, he continues, "We're presuming the miners are employees. What if they're investors, in a sense? Shareholders or whatever you'd call it."

"Ah. So the company offers guys the chance to work a claim and share in the profits. Except, as with the gold rush, profits are minimal and it's pay-to-play. They pay to come up here, likely an inflated travel and residency cost. Then, sadly, the profits aren't what they hoped for, but they get an adventure and a story about mining for gold in the wilderness. That could work."

"Any idea how we'd narrow down the possibilities?"

"Start by getting a closer look. Try to figure out whether

it's gold they're really mining, and if so, does it warrant all the security precautions?"

"Then I guess we know what we're doing tomorrow."

We seem to be in a new routine. Get up, spend time with Rory, take her on a quick round of town, drop her off with a sitter, and then head into the forest.

I hate being separated from Rory for so long, day after day. I also hate asking someone else to do what I consider my duty, as if I'm shirking. I returned to work not long after Rory was born, so I thought I had a sense of what it was like for working mothers. I really didn't.

Dalton and I have been splitting shifts so one of us is home with Rory most of the time. For the overlap hours when we both work, she can often come along with us. A few times a week we might need to leave her with someone.

That is nothing like what most working moms do. I knew that, but I still had the sense that I was getting a taste of it. Now I feel the full weight of the guilt, and I recognize that ninety percent of that guilt is societal. No one here makes me feel bad. But even if I'd never truly planned to be a mother, those attitudes are ingrained in me from every time I heard a mother shamed, even obliquely, for working. Or, worse, for enjoying working.

Dalton doesn't have that problem. Oh, he isn't happy about being away from Rory. He's accustomed to more dad time, and he likes his dad time. He also likes the non-dad time, when he's with me or working, with Anders and others. There's no guilt over embracing time away from our daughter, just as there'd be no guilt over embracing time on his own.

My daughter is not going to suffer irreparable harm by being with April or Yolanda or Kenny or Dana. If anything, it's good for her. I'm really glad this is temporary, but I need to set aside any shame over being eyeball-deep in an investigation.

I try to relax and enjoy the walk with Dalton. It's a few miles to where we know the miners are working. That's a solid hour's walk on a gorgeous fall day, with my guy and my dog and my thermos of coffee. Real coffee, too. While I gave up caffeine during my pregnancy, I do allow myself the treat of a cup when I won't be breastfeeding. This caffeinated milk will end up watering the local flora.

Normally, we'd be talking, but with the possibility of a killer on the loose, we've decided to keep quiet, and that's not a hardship for either of us. No one has ever accused me of being chatty. As for Dalton, he's so confident and direct in his speech that no one mistakes him for an introvert, but he really is. When we're enjoying an evening at the Roc, I can almost predict the moment when he'll declare it's time for him to turn in. That has nothing to do with needing sleep, and everything to do with him having reached his limit for socializing.

Having some time where we can be quiet only adds to the pleasure of that morning's walk. We start on a trail wide enough for us to hold hands and walk side by side, with Storm nosing around in the lead. We've been out for maybe fifteen minutes when her head jerks up and her muzzle swings to the right.

We both stop. A sound comes from up ahead, off to the right, where a trail branches north. Footsteps? They've stopped now, but Storm keeps looking in that direction. I hold my breath to listen. Silence.

Dalton's grunt vibrates with frustration. I glance over. He only scowls to the right.

Someone is there, on the trail, but they've heard us, too, and now we're locked in a standoff.

I motion for Dalton to bend and whisper in his ear. "You go."

Now I'm the one getting his scowl, but I wait it out. Give him a moment to acknowledge that one of us needs to sneak up on whoever is there, and a second moment to realize that he's the one best suited to do that silently.

Another grunt, and he motions to my gun. I sigh but take it out. I was right that he should go, and he's right that I should be armed while I wait.

He unholsters his own gun and heads out. Storm looks at me, and her expression is almost quizzical. Asking whether we should follow Dalton. I shake my head and lay my hand on her head. She chuffs in what I swear is a canine "Whatever." Clearly she doesn't like this plan. She even sits down in protest.

I turn to look for Dalton, but while I dealt with Storm, he disappeared into the trees. The wind picks up, whispering through the boughs and bringing the faint smell of campfire smoke from the west.

Gretchen? The mining camp?

Storm stands abruptly, her muzzle swinging north again. Then I catch the soft crunch of a footfall on earth.

Whoever's there has started walking again. I strain to listen. Are the footfalls getting closer?

Storm whines. I frown down at her and lay my hand on her head, but she ducks it.

She's annoyed. Anxious?

That sound could come from a person, a bear, a moose . . . Something with a relatively heavy footfall, as compared to a fox or rabbit.

I lift my gun, finger off the trigger. Whatever it is, it's approaching the intersection and—

A muzzle appears. A gray canine muzzle.

A wolf.

"Oh, thank God," a voice says, in the same second that my brain processes what I'm seeing and recognizes it as Nero and not a wild wolf.

Lilith rounds the corner with a heavy backpack over her shoulders. I lower the gun.

"I heard someone," she says. "Nero didn't seem concerned, so I was really hoping it was someone we knew."

I holster my gun and whistle for Dalton. "That's why Storm seemed annoyed that we'd stopped." I pat her head. "Sorry, girl." I look at that heavy pack. "Are you going somewhere?"

She draws closer, coming out of the shadows, and I see her face is drawn, eyes bleary.

"Lilith? What—?"

Dalton steps out behind her, and she whirls, sees it's him, and exhales.

"Lilith?" I say.

"I'm taking you up on your offer of hospitality," she says, trying for a light tone as she adjusts the pack. "Hope you've still got room for a guest."

"Absolutely. But what happened?"

"I had a nighttime visitor."

"What?"

She fusses with the straps again. "Someone spent half the night outside my cabin, which means I spent half the night sitting inside with a damn rifle."

"Oh shit. Come on then, and tell us what happened."

CHAPTER EIGHTEEN

We talk with Lilith as we return to Haven's Rock. Or I talk to her, while Dalton follows with the canines. We keep our voices down, but I want her story before we reach town, where others can overhear.

"Nero was out last night," she says. "He's not a pet, and he usually prefers to stay outside at night. Sometimes he hangs around, but other times he's off hunting or wandering or whatever wolves do. After you told me what was happening, I'd have liked him inside with me, and I would have insisted on it, but when I went to ask him to come inside, he was gone. I heard him a little while later, howling to other wolves, and I knew he was out for the night, so I battened down the hatches."

She looks at me. "There's an interior latch on the door, but no lock. I just closed everything up and made sure my rifle was out, while telling myself I was overreacting."

"Which you weren't."

"Apparently not. I wasn't worried enough to sit up all night with the rifle on my knees, though. I read by candlelight and then fell asleep around midnight. An hour later, a noise outside woke me, which proves I was calm enough to fall asleep, but not soundly. Still, I figured it was Nero, and I was going to try to entice him inside with a bone. Half asleep, I opened the door, completely forgetting what you'd said until I looked out and there was no sign of Nero. Then a twig cracked, and I got my ass back inside fast."

She's quiet as we turn a corner with care, making sure it's empty ahead. Then she continues, "I still told myself I was overreacting. It definitely wasn't Nero—he'd have come out when the door opened. But a cracking twig could be anything. I was jumpy because Nero wasn't around, and I'm also not accustomed to hearing noises at night because Nero usually *is* around."

"He keeps any critters from getting close."

"You've seen that firsthand. Whether I'm home or not, he guards the cabin, and nothing is coming near it. So I tried to settle. I sure as hell wasn't sleeping—and I didn't feel comfortable lighting a candle to read—but I tried to just lie down and relax, with the gun beside my bed."

She glances back, as if checking on Nero. He's padding along behind Storm, bringing up the rear.

"I kept hearing noises," she says. "Rustles, snaps, all the little indications that something was out there. Honestly, my biggest fear was a bear, especially that one you mentioned. You said it looked a little thin, and I'm hypervigilant in autumn. During my first fall here alone, an old bear stalked me. At first, I wasn't concerned—I had Nero and he was nearly full-grown. What animal is going to mess with a healthy young wolf?"

"A desperate bear."

"Yep. It stalked us almost back to the cabin, and then it charged. Luckily, I had my spray ready. It went after Nero, and I hit it with the spray, and it didn't give a shit until it couldn't see. Then I shot it. Took more shots than I care to admit to—my hands were shaking and I'd never killed anything that big. I learned my lesson, though. Whatever I think I know about bears, it doesn't apply when they're desperate."

"It really doesn't."

"That was my fear, then. That a hungry bear—maybe the one you dealt with—was outside the cabin, and my door isn't meant to stop a grizzly. So I got out of bed and shifted into full hillbilly-grandma mode, on a chair facing the door with a gun over my lap. I also had bear spray. If it came at me, I'd do what I did the last time. Spray first, shoot later."

"Good plan," I say.

"I thought so. I'm sitting there, listening, and I swear the motherfucker is circling the cabin. There's a crack in front of me, a rustle beside me, another crack to the rear . . . But then I realize what I'm *not* hearing. Animal noises. No snuffling. No grunts. A grizzly is never going to be that quiet for that long. If it was circling, it'd be looking for a way in, sniffing at the cabin, pushing at it, trying to figure out how to get the tasty treat inside."

"There was none of that."

"None. And after a while, the noises stopped. So I breathed a sigh of relief. I overreacted. It was a curious critter, maybe another wolf or a fox. Whatever it was, though, it was gone."

She rubs the back of her neck. "And then someone tried the door."

"Shit."

She nods. "Again, my first reaction was that I was imagining it. You've seen my door. It's a simple construction. You turn the exterior handle, and if I haven't put the inside latch on, it opens. I'd latched it, so the handle won't turn. All you get is a jiggle. That's what I heard—a jiggle of the doorknob. I walked toward it, but everything was quiet. Then it moved. I was looking right at the handle, and it moved very slowly up and down."

"Someone trying it again, but carefully."

"I pressed up against the door, and I could hear someone breathing. I don't know how long we were both standing there, on either side of that door. I kept wishing that I had a peephole." She gives a humorless chuckle. "Not something you ever imagine you needing in the wilderness."

"Did they try the door again?"

"A few times," she says. "The handle would move or the door would groan, as if someone was testing it."

"Did they know you were right on the other side?"

"I don't think so. I wasn't making any noise. They seemed to be trying to figure out how to get in without alerting me that they were there. They must have been at that door for at least fifteen minutes."

"And then?"

"And then they started circling again." She shivers. "I could hear them, just enough to know they were still there. At the front, the side, the back."

"Trying to find a way in."

"Trying, but not too hard. Maybe they only wanted to see who was inside. I thought about what you said, that woman who's missing. I was wondering if it could be her, figuring out who was in there, looking for help."

"Or looking to see if she could overpower you and steal whatever isn't nailed down."

She sighs. "That was the problem. I know she might have murdered her partner, but I couldn't help worrying that I was ignoring someone in need again. I kept thinking back to when that happened with the kid."

When Max escaped his kidnapper, he'd found Lilith's cabin. Unfortunately, he also found Nero, who ran him off.

"You didn't ignore him. He got spooked and ran."

"Still, I felt terrible. What if I was doing that again? This woman saw her husband murdered, and she doesn't have a sat phone or any way of calling for help, and she's been running through the woods trying to find help because she knows you guys are here somewhere. She finds my cabin, but she's not sure it's you, and I'm inside with a gun, ready to blow her head off."

I shake my head. "You couldn't take a chance. So what happened?"

"Nero came home."

"Ah. That must have been a shock for whoever was there."

A tight laugh. "I think someone needs a clean pair of underwear, that's for sure. You know how he is. Being a wolf, he's not going to bark a warning. He seems to have smelled an intruder and come charging from the woods. I heard a yelp and a flurry of activity, as if the person was running. I called Nero back. I couldn't tell whether that yelp was a man or a woman, and if it could be a woman in trouble, maybe hearing another woman's voice would bring her back. But whoever it was, they just kept going. I called Nero inside and waited until after breakfast. Then I packed a bag and here we are."

"Did your visitor leave anything behind?"

"Honestly, I was too spooked to check." Her jaw sets. "I'm done here. That really was the last straw. I know you guys don't pose any threat, and I've been telling myself I'm still safe, but I'm not. I'm really not."

Back in Haven's Rock, I get Lilith settled at our place for now. She'll have a room in the family quarters tonight—we have plenty of space there. But I really want to get a look at her cabin, and that means we don't have time to properly introduce her to everyone. Considering that we're on lockdown, people are going to freak out if they see a stranger in their midst, even if it's a pleasant-looking woman. Well, pleasant-looking woman with a wolf. Yeah, that's going to take some explaining.

So for now, she can rest in our chalet. While I show her around, Dalton goes into town to tell Anders and a few others that she's here. He'll also pop in to check on Rory, so I'll resist the urge to do that myself. Otherwise, it'll be an hour before I'm ready to go.

We need to get to Lilith's place, and then, if we have time, we need to spy on the miners. My baby must wait. For now, I use a few minutes to pump-and-dump and change the leak pads in my bra.

Twenty minutes after we arrived, we're off again. This time, we're moving faster, aware of both lost time and added tasks. We head straight for Lilith's little cabin.

I start by popping my head inside. I want to see whether anyone came by after she left. There's some signs of disturbance, but on closer inspection, it's just the chaos caused by a speedy packing. Her food stores are all neatly stacked, and that's the first thing an intruder would go for.

I join Dalton outside. He's pacing around the perimeter. Storm is doing the same, with her nose to the ground. We hadn't asked her to find a trail, but she can tell Dalton is in search mode, so she is, too. She seems to be following something, but she's calm and only casually focused, which I could interpret to mean it's not Gretchen—her former target.

I start my own search. When I see a footprint, I am pleased by the fact that I recognize it as my own. I've been distracted enough in the past year that it can sometimes take a minute to figure that out. I also find three more that seem as if they came from a woman's boot, but I had the foresight to take a photo of Lilith's tread, and this matches.

And then I find another print. It's in the woods, maybe ten feet from the side of her cabin. A wide boot tread a couple of inches longer than my own. I call Dalton over, and he sets his boot beside it. The mark is about a size larger.

"Likely male," I say. "When I saw Gretchen, she was wearing women's hikers. Average size. We've also seen what seems to be her footprints, and that's not it."

I hunker down. Dalton watches silently, letting me work it through. "Not Haven's Rock standard issue." I pull out my phone and search for two photos. Then I compare them to the one on the ground. "It doesn't match the footwear from the miners or the guards. Of course, we've seen that they can sometimes bring their own, so that's not proof positive this isn't one of their guys."

Dalton grumbles under his breath.

I straighten. "Yep, I don't like that answer either. We know Gretchen might be out here. We know the miners and guards definitely are. What we don't need is an unknown third party."

I look around. "I'm considering the usefulness of having someone—well, a couple of someones—stake out the cabin tonight."

He nods slowly, taking a moment to think. "In case our stalker comes back. Maybe Will and Kendra?"

"That'd be a good team."

"I'd say Will and me, and but with everything that's going on, I don't think you want me leaving you alone with Rory."

I shrug. "I might lose a little sleep, but I'd bounce back. My bigger concern would be having you awake all night, when I have a feeling we aren't resolving this today. Better to put Kendra on it. They can sleep here in shifts. We have enough militia to fill in for the lockdown."

"That's what we'll do then. Anything else you need to see here?"

I shake my head. "We still have time to get a look at the mining operation."

CHAPTER NINETEEN

Both of our settlements have a section of land that's off-limits to the other side. We get extra, having bargained for the mountain that straddles the north end of both of our areas. Everything outside those sections is neutral territory.

The mining operation is obviously on their side. We even have a very good idea where to find it. For one thing, we'd known where Mark's initial claim was. For another, we have—as I said—spied from a distance, having been up the mountain with binoculars. Also, in passing their land, we've heard noise that indicates we're right about the general vicinity of the operation.

What we're about to do now, though, is trespass. We do not want to be caught breaking that trust, because we can't afford to open ourselves up to retaliation.

I don't think the camp's guards would storm Haven's Rock. They don't need to. They just need to open some gentle inquiries about this little town that seems to have popped up on territorial land. Yes, technically, we're in violation of more laws than I care to count.

Worse, though, we aren't just walking around their backyard. We're pressing our noses to their window.

So we are careful. We'd considered leaving Storm behind. She's not exactly good at sneaking. But what's going to be more suspicious if we're caught? A couple and their dog? Or a couple who are always with their dog . . . but apparently left her behind today. We've decided that if we are spotted, we'll blame it on Storm.

She bolted after something. I don't know what happened. She's never like that. I'm so sorry. From now on, we'll leash her when we're near your territory.

Yes, I'll feel guilty about blaming her, but everyone needs to do their part to keep our town safe.

We've plotted out our spy plan with a precision that would make Petra proud. Or, more likely, make her roll her eyes at our clumsy attempts at espionage. We're taking the route with the shortest walk between neutral ground and the operation. It's on the opposite side from the camp, which minimizes the chances of being heard. We know that Mark's original operation was in a streambed. We're going to come in from the other angle. That also happens to be downwind of where we expect the miners to be. Not that they'll smell us—they don't have dogs. But any sound of our approach is less likely to carry upwind and any sound of their camp is more likely to reach us before we need to get too close.

Before we even leave the trail, we can hear them. The murmur of voices. A clang. A laugh. A thud. The sounds of people at work. When we map the trajectory, it seems to be upstream from Mark's old spot. That would make sense. Whatever they've found, they would have exhausted the vein by now and had to go searching for more.

We start making our way toward them, moving carefully

through the trees. We judge them to be about three hundred feet from the trail, which is perfect. It's just the right distance that, if we're spotted, our story about chasing after Storm will make sense. It's not as if we've gone a mile deep into their territory.

Soon we realize we're actually hearing two sets of voices. One seems to be upstream, and the other is off to the west. We pause and take out our map.

To the west of the original mining site is a canyon. We've been there, before the miners arrived. Is that where the second group is?

We spend a few minutes considering. Then we veer northeast to get closer to the stream. Once the voices come clear, I go on ahead while Dalton waits with Storm. I get another ten feet, and then I can see distant shapes. I slip behind a bush and pull out my binoculars.

When I peek, I train the binoculars on the source of the noise. It's a small group of men. Two guards are standing back, talking, and it's their voices I hear. They aren't saying anything useful—they're comparing stories of concerts they've attended.

Four men work the stream. They seem to be doing the same thing Mark was—an updated version of panning for gold. They're in hip waders and two are literally panning with screens while one watches and the fourth checks a screen set out in the water.

The men work silently. I peer at each. I don't know what I'm looking for, but they're exactly what I'd expect from guys doing manual labor. Just average men, the youngest in his early twenties, the oldest in his early forties. Two white, one Black, one brown.

I do check footwear. Both guards wear the same boots, and

there are four pairs of boots lined up on the bank for the workers, all identical steel-toed work wear.

I'm too far to get good pictures, but I snap a few anyway. Then I hunker behind the bush and listen, but nothing changes. Just the guards shooting the shit while the men work in silence.

I take a closer look, trying to assess moods. The guards are relaxed. They're armed, but the guns are holstered and they're so chill that I'd hate for a bear to come charging out of the woods.

The miners don't particularly seem to be enjoying themselves, but they're working hard, without needing the guards looming over them. It's manual labor, and I wouldn't expect too much joviality. It doesn't seem like backbreaking work, though. Just boring.

I return to Dalton, and we wordlessly head to where we can hear the other team. Again, I approach while he stays with Storm. I'm not getting so close that we need his stealth, and as the one with more "real world" experience, I'll have a better idea what I'm seeing.

That was the theory, anyway, but having only ever seen Mark's claim, I'm hardly an expert. At this second site, there are fifty percent more guards and workers. The guards are less relaxed, but they seem mostly bored, two leaning and watching, while the third is writing stuff down . . . or doing word puzzles, for all I know. Even looking through the binoculars only shows me that he's intent on writing.

Here, the miners work on the side of the cliff. A few hack with pickaxes and shovels, while others do finer work with smaller tools, digging away at the dirt. Again, I take pictures. Again, I assess moods. The miners here are in higher spirits, with some joking around. I suspect that has a lot to do with group dynamics—how well the men know each other, what kind of personalities are at play.

When I'm done, I retreat. Dalton and I head out as quietly as we can, and we don't speak until we're on our own territory. Even then, I keep my voice low as I explain what I saw.

"So they're definitely mining," he says.

"Yes."

"Gold in the stream with the original claim. Either gold or something else in the cliffside."

"Yes."

He scratches his beard. "They're doing what they say they're doing, which means everything should be fine, but it still bothers you."

"I'm not sure 'bothers' is the right word. They *are* mining, and that's good. I don't care what they're taking out of the cliff. I mean, the work could be environmentally damaging, and I care about that, but selfishly, I only care if it exposes Haven's Rock. What doesn't seem right is how slick the operation is when it's so small-scale. I counted fifteen miners. A third of them are working the stream, mostly with screens. That's penny-ante stuff." I shrug. "It seems as if it might be financially worthwhile for one guy, which makes it a very secure and well-run operation for . . ."

"Minimal gain."

"Right. And it's very low-tech. Screens and picks and . . ." I shrug again. "I don't know. Maybe I'm overthinking it."

"No, it doesn't seem as if they've hit a mother lode. So, like we speculated earlier, the value might not be in the ground."

I nod. "It's in the investors, who expect a slick operation with visible results. Which is what they'd be getting. There might be fraud happening here, and that could explain the spies."

"Yep. It's not that the gold vein is so rich people will skulk around the forest—and maybe kill each other—to get a better look. It's that investors have started to realize they're being bilked. They send some people up to get a look while posing as hikers if they're caught."

"Except they weren't caught. Gretchen came to *us*."

"Fuck. You're right."

"It could still work, if she thought they'd been spotted and needed to establish their story. I still don't see someone sending three spies to prove fraud . . . and then killing two of them. Either we're missing something, or we've got this all wrong."

"All I know is someone is definitely out here. They stalked Lilith last night. Did you get a look at the boots?"

"Yep. They were all standard issue, and we've seen the prints for them."

"So whoever was at her cabin wasn't one of the miners or guards."

"And doesn't seem to have been Gretchen either."

Someone discovered Lilith's cabin. They circled it for hours, and it doesn't take that long to realize you can't get inside easily. They knew she was in there, and they were spooking her . . . until her guard wolf came home.

Why spook Lilith? I must consider the possibility she's lying about why she's here, and all this has been about finding her. I don't think so, but I need to keep that theory on the page.

If it was a guy from the mining camp, it would make sense. Well, it would make sense in a disheartening way—a camp full of men, one discovers a woman living alone in the forest and decides to give her a scare, maybe to convince her that she needs a man in her life.

Could it have been a miner? We can't dismiss that based on the boot prints.

But what about the tracking implants? If one of the miners—not knowing he's chipped—found Lilith's cabin, wouldn't Rogers know it?

That depends on how closely they're being monitored.

I'm working through all of this as we get closer to Haven's Rock. Normally, by this point we'd hear the town. We don't, which means they are doing an excellent job of locking down. It's still midday, and work is progressing, but all loud work has ceased, and all conversation is taking place indoors.

"They really do deserve a reward when all this is over," I whisper to Dalton, after we've commented on the quiet. "Maybe—"

I stop. My voice is so low that when a twig crackles to our left, I hear it. We all stop and listen. Storm sniffs the air. We're downwind, and the scent she catches has her whining. I look over, and she whines again. It's a good whine—excitement, not fear or concern.

Someone she knows.

I smile at Dalton. "Must be the patrol."

He nods. There's another path just north of us, and it's used for militia patrols. When I peer into the trees, I catch a glimpse of green clothing. Yes, it's not easy to see green clothing in a forest, but this particular shade is familiar. It's the emerald of Anders's windbreaker, which I may have bought him after a tipsy female resident waxed eloquent on a green shirt he'd been wearing, how it brought out the green in his eyes. His eyes are brown. Just brown. So I bought the jacket and never fail to tell him it brings out the green in his eyes. He'd stop wearing it if it wasn't actually a very nice coat, just the right weight for this weather.

Seeing it, I grin at Dalton and mouth *Will.* He nods, and when I motion that I'm going to sneak up on him, he only rolls his eyes and leans against a tree. I gesture for Storm to lie down, and she does not appreciate that, but she does so, with an accusatory huff.

Before I leave, Dalton touches my arm and murmurs, "Make sure."

I nod. Obviously, I plan to be sure it's Anders. I'm not taking the chance of play-pouncing on a dangerous stranger because he's wearing the same color as Anders's jacket.

I creep into the forest. For a moment, I don't see Anders, but then he rounds a corner and I can make out his back. I continue on, walking as quietly as I can. He's going in the opposite direction. He isn't alone, and I think the other person is Kendra, but again, I want to be sure.

I step out onto the path. They're about a hundred feet ahead of me and about to round another corner, but it's definitely them. I take one long stride, prepared to break into a jog. Then something rustles behind me.

I spin just as a figure darts into the forest.

For a moment, I stand there, as if hitting Pause and Replay on the mental footage. What exactly did I just see? A person, yes. Definitely a human, not an animal. They'd been on the path behind me, and when I turned, they were already ducking into the woods.

A human figure.

Not noticeably short or tall. Wearing dark trousers and a dark coat with the hood pulled up.

I take out my gun and glance over my shoulder. Anders and Kendra have vanished around that corner. I could call them back, but if I do, I'll alert whoever I just saw, and I have a feeling that the person I just saw was . . .

I let the thought trail off as I creep to where the person disappeared into the forest. I don't see anyone there, which either means they're long gone or they're right on the other side of that wide tree ten feet away.

I adjust the hold on my gun. Then, slowly, I make a show as if putting it away, but only lower it, hidden by my side.

Then I take a chance. "Gretchen?" I say softly. "It's me. We met the other day."

Silence.

"I know something happened to Blake. I know you must be scared. I want to help you."

Of course I'm at least fifty percent sure that what happened to Blake was at Gretchen's hands. And I'm also only fifty percent sure that this is actually Gretchen. But if she killed Blake, I want her to think that I'm the sort of person who could never imagine such a thing. A man murdered in the forest? His wife on the run? Clearly she's fleeing from whoever killed him, and so I'm coming to her rescue.

"Gretchen," I say again.

Silence.

I start forward. The only place she could hide is behind that tree. As I walk, I keep softly talking to her, as if she's a timid woodland creature.

Everything is okay. It's safe to come out. I won't hurt you. If you saw me with a gun, that's just because I didn't know it was you.

I reach that big tree and stop on my side. When I listen, I don't hear anything.

"Gretchen?" I say. "I'm right here. If you would like me to go away, I can do that. Just tell me what you want."

Lies. I'm sure as hell not walking away. But I'll say whatever it takes to convince her.

"We can talk from here if that helps," I say. "I won't come any closer."

Silence.

I try for a laugh. "Or maybe I'm talking to myself and you're not right there. Okay, I'm going to come around the tree. I need to know you're okay. Then I'll do whatever you want."

I lift my right hand to tuck the gun under my coat as I circle the tree from the left, that empty hand raised. "If you don't want me coming closer, say something."

I get around the tree to find . . . Yep. I'm talking to myself.

I exhale and raise my voice. "Okay, Gretchen. If you can hear me, I really want to be sure you're okay. Just—"

The softest crunch behind me. I wheel just in time to see Gretchen swinging a tree limb at my head. I dodge, but it catches my shoulder and spins me off balance. My hand is still under my jacket with the gun, and the moment it takes me to debate pulling it out is a moment too long.

She swings the branch at my legs, and it hits hard. If she'd struck my good one, I'd have been fine. But she hits my bad leg right where old muscle damage has weakened it. I start to fall, and I could still stop myself, but I decide against it, instead dropping onto my butt, gun raised.

"Don't move," I say, my voice going hard, every trace of helpful Casey evaporating.

She tenses her muscles, ready to run, and I shift my finger onto the trigger. Outrage floods her face, and then undiluted rage.

"Going to help me, huh?" she says. "Did you really think I'd fall for that?"

"I meant it," I say. "Right up to the point where you attacked me."

"I attacked you because you murdered my husband."

"What?"

She rocks forward, as if she wants to stomp me. "Don't play dumb. You said you know he's dead. You killed him. You and that guy you were with."

"If you mean my husband—"

"I don't give a shit who he is. He *murdered* my husband." Tears glisten in her eyes. "Blake wanted to leave that day. He didn't trust you. A couple with a baby out here? A seemingly *normal* couple? That doesn't happen. He said if you were really living out here, there was something wrong with your so-called husband. That he's one of those crazy mountain men, and you're his mail-order bride."

I could comment on the racism of that remark, but I only say, "A mail-order bride with a Canadian accent? You met my husband. Did he seem like a crazy mountain man to you?"

She ignores that. "Blake wanted to go. I insisted he rest, but he was up before dawn, and I agreed to leave early as long as he soaked his ankle first." The tears well, her voice rising. "That's where you killed him. While he was soaking his foot."

"No, we didn't," I say. "We found Blake's body, and we've been looking for you ever since."

"You've been *hunting* me," she spits. "That man of yours. Hunting me and—"

"Step away from her." Dalton's voice comes from the trees to our right.

She spins, and while I can't see Dalton, she must, because her eyes go wide with terror. Rage flashes, and she feints his way. Then she turns and runs.

CHAPTER TWENTY

I scramble to my feet and give chase, with Dalton and Storm behind me. We barrel through the thick forest, heading northeast until we reach a foothill, where Gretchen scrambles up and whips rocks back down. When one hits me in the leg—my bad one again—I yelp and lose my footing. Dalton catches me. I start going after her again, but he holds me back.

"What are we doing when we catch her?" he says.

"Finding out what the hell is going on."

I try to wrench away, but he tightens his grip and lowers his voice. "We can't take her to Haven's Rock."

"We'll find another solution."

"What? Leave her in the forest with a tent and tell her to make camp? Presume she won't follow us?"

"She thinks we killed Blake."

"Which doesn't mean she *isn't* the killer."

I open my mouth to argue, when the truth of his words hits, and my cheeks heat. I should be the one making that observation. I should be the one holding back, thinking this through, even as I feel like a terrible person for not rushing to her aid.

"Right," I mumble. "Hormones."

He pulls me into a hug and kisses the top of my head. "You don't need to have an excuse for wanting to help someone, Casey."

"Still blaming hormones." I give myself a shake. "Yes, I hate seeing her run off when she might be in danger. I also hate seeing her run off when she might *be* the danger. Blaming us for killing him sets up her story, if she needs it."

"But she might also be telling the truth."

I exhale a long breath. "That whoever killed him is now hunting her. Yes. But we can't run her down and forcibly confine her for her own good." I lower my voice. "She got close to Haven's Rock. Too close. I think she saw Will and Kendra."

"Which doesn't mesh with her crazy-mountain-man and mail-order-bride rant." He tilts his head. "Do they still do that? I've heard of it in Old West histories."

I make a face. "It does still happen, in a much more modern way, usually online. One of the best-known origins for the women is the Philippines."

"Ah." He nods his understanding. My mother was half Chinese, and half Filipino. "So clearly an average white guy with a hot Asian wife bought her online."

"Did you just call me a 'hot Asian wife'?"

"Never."

I shake my head. "But yes, if she saw Will and Kendra—which I really think she did—then clearly we're not what she expected."

He lifts a finger. "Kendra is Indigenous. Didn't one of our new residents mistake her for April? He heard that your sister was the doctor and presumed it was Kendra."

"Ugh. Yes. So clearly we're running a whole town of crazy mountain men and their mail-order brides." I rub my face. "Okay, so we let Gretchen keep running."

"For now. We can't have her hanging around until she stumbles into town. We'll stay in lockdown and increase patrols for the night. Skip sending Will and Kendra to Lilith's place. Tomorrow, we'll track Gretchen and see if another night out there convinces her to talk to us."

We declare our day at an end. By the time we're back to Haven's Rock, it's late afternoon and we're exhausted. Our workday started early and was so jam-packed that it feels like it should be midnight. We need to give Gretchen time to decide she's safe. Or, after another night out there, decide she's *not* safe and agree to talk to us.

First order of business is getting Lilith settled. Well, no, before that comes a combined late meal and baby time. Then Dalton stays with Lilith and Rory while I head into town to tell people we have a guest. I'm getting better at delegating this sort of thing, so I corner a few people and have them pass on the word. We say that Lilith is local to the area. We've known her since before the town opened. She's safe—as is her, um, Siberian husky. She needs a place to stay temporarily, and so she'll be in the family residence.

I'll give it some time for word to spread before I bring Lilith and Nero into town. While I wait, I want to talk to a couple of people. I find them just as they're coming in from patrol.

During a lockdown, I can't set a bad example by hailing anyone loudly in the streets, so I jog over as Anders and Kendra head to the gun locker, where Kenny and Yolanda wait to take the next patrol shift.

I wait for the shift exchange. Then I ask Kenny and Yolanda to hold on before heading out.

"We had a run-in with Gretchen," I say. "The wife of our dead man."

They're all staff, so they know the details.

"She's still out there?" Anders says.

"Actually, I was trying to sneak up on you and Kendra when I heard her behind me. I think she might have been following you."

"Us?" Kendra says. "Where was this?"

I tell her.

"Shit," Anders says. "I didn't hear anything."

"Me neither," Kendra says. "Lousy guards we are."

"She was a hundred feet behind and being quiet. Also, I can't say for sure she was following you and not me. Anyway, she bolted and we had a run-in and a . . . Well, I'd hesitate to call it a conversation. Apparently, Eric's a crazy mountain man and I'm his mail-order bride, and we killed her husband."

"That's . . ." Anders trails off. "You aren't kidding."

Yolanda snorts. "She saw a bearded white guy and his Asian wife and baby. What else could it be?"

"In her defense, that's what her husband thought, though he only saw me. She says we made him nervous, and he wanted to get out of here. That's why they left so early. He went to soak his foot, where he was murdered. Since then, someone has been hunting her."

"Hunting her?" Kenny says. "So we actually do have a killer out there?"

"Or she's setting up a story," Yolanda says. "Help, my husband was murdered by a crazed mountain man, living in the wilderness with his poor mail-order bride."

"Either way, she bolted," I say. "We've decided to let her run and track her down tomorrow. That means be extra cautious out there. She doesn't seem to be armed, but she does wield a wicked tree branch. If you see her, you can try to talk her down, but don't pursue."

"And if we do talk her down?" Kenny asks. "You don't want her back here."

"If that happens, radio it in. Lilith is letting us use her cabin."

Kenny nods. "Good idea. Since she's in town for a while."

"Lilith's in town?" Anders says.

"I'll explain on the way," I say.

I pick up both Rory and Lilith after that, letting Dalton get in a bit of work. I take Lilith on a tour of town. People gawk, but it's mostly friendly interest, with a few hellos. Sebastian is walking Raoul, so I take the opportunity to introduce Nero to our own resident wolf—half wolf, at least. Raoul isn't having any of it. Not only is there another male canine in his town, but he's hanging out with Storm, which is absolutely unacceptable.

There's a bit of a row. It's settled easily enough, because this isn't Nero's territory, and he seems to feel no need to get defensive about it. While Raoul barks and growls and snarls, Nero stands calmly beside Lilith as if this dog is clearly upset about something unrelated to him.

The meeting between Lilith and Sebastian goes better. In her wandering, she's seen the First Settlement—and steers clear of it. I explain that Sebastian spends part of his year there, with his girlfriend, and that gives them something to chat about as we walk . . . and Raoul sulks.

We round a corner to see someone bearing down on us, cleaver in hand.

"What are you doing to my dog?" Mathias says. "I thought we were on lockdown, and you have him barking . . ." He trails off as he sees Nero. Then he sees Lilith.

His gaze goes to me and he says, in French, "This is not your stranger with the dead husband."

"I hope not," Lilith replies in perfect French. "Since I don't have a husband. Though, if I did, I *might* kill him, so . . ." She shrugs.

"This is Lilith," I say as I switch Rory to my other arm. "She's a photographer who's been living backcountry with her dog."

Mathias looks down at Nero. "That is a wolf."

Lilith laughs. "Everyone says that. Nope, he's just a very big husky."

He meets her gaze. "One hundred percent *Canis lupus*."

She squints at Nero. "Are you sure? The guy swore he was a husky." She sighs. "You can't trust any itinerant dog breeders you meet in the wilderness."

Mathias snorts a laugh. "Wolf, as I am sure you know. I would be curious as to how he is so well-behaved." He hooks at thumb at Raoul. "That one is impossible, and he is only half wolf."

"It's the dog part that's the problem. Like werewolves. It isn't the wolf blood you need to worry about: it's the human blood."

"Unless your pet *is* a werewolf," Mathias says, "and so he knows how to behave."

"Could be," Lilith says. "See, I didn't murder my husband after all. He's just currently in wolf form."

That makes Mathias laugh. When he reaches a hand down for Nero to sniff, Raoul growls and Mathias turns to Sebastian. "Take him home before he barks again."

Sebastian salutes. "Yes, sir."

As they leave, Mathias says, "As Casey is apparently not performing introductions, I am Mathias. The local psychiatrist."

She gestures at the cleaver. "Specializing in lobotomies, I presume."

He looks down at it. "Ha! No. That is for my other job. I am the butcher. Everyone here wears many hats. You should come by the shop, and I will find a bone for your not-wolf."

"He would appreciate that. Thank you."

I finish the tour and then show her the apartment where she'll be staying. We built a family residence for families and couples, but we only have one of each right now—Dana and the boys, plus a recently arrived couple. That means Lilith can have a decent-sized apartment for her and Nero. Afterward, we're standing on the porch, Rory dozing in my arms, when Max comes around the corner, and stops short, seeing Nero.

"Hey, Max," I say. "I'd like you to introduce you to Lilith. She'll be staying here for a while with her dog."

"That's a wolf."

"Why does everyone keep saying that?" Lilith says. She sighs. "Next time, I'm asking for pedigree papers."

Max doesn't crack a smile. "That's a wolf. Even before I came here, I could tell when they used sled dogs instead of wolves on TV. And I knew it the last time I saw him . . . at your cabin."

Lilith goes still, and I curse under my breath.

"I forgot that," I say as I lower my voice. "Yes, he's a wolf, and he's the one you saw. It slipped my mind, or I would have warned you."

Max shrugs. "He seems fine now. He just really didn't want me going near your cabin."

"I'm so sorry, Max," Lilith says. "I was inside that night, and when I heard him growling, I came out. I should have gone looking. I just thought he was scaring off an animal."

"I heard you. I could have gotten closer, but I didn't know you." He rocks back on his heels. "So you'll be staying with us?"

"If you'd rather not have Nero around, he can stay with Casey and Storm."

"His name's Nero?" Max tilts his head, looking at the wolf. "Can he be touched? Or is he not that kind of pet?"

"You can pet him. Just let him see your hand first."

Max puts out his hand, and Nero sniffs it. Then he tentatively pets the wolf. "Is he going to be outside your apartment? Like at the cabin? He might not be used to people walking past."

"Good point. I was planning to keep him inside with me. He needs more exposure to people if I plan to take him back to civilization."

Max nods. "He does. Being here will help. Get him used to different people walking past your apartment and all that."

"Excellent idea." She looks at me. "I think I'm in good hands here. I'll take that invitation for dinner, though. You said seven?"

"Come by anytime after six. Dinner will be at seven."

CHAPTER TWENTY-ONE

I've invited Lilith to more than just dinner. It's games night. This alternates between D&D and board games, to accommodate both those who won't play D&D and those who won't play anything else. Tonight, it's board games, and we decided to proceed by making it a curfew-appropriate silent games night. April usually won't play the non-D&D games, but I brought home something special to entice her—a whodunit game.

Dalton makes dinner—that's his forte. While it's cooking, I'm jotting notes as he plays with Rory, and I pause to watch them. He's on his stomach on the floor, piling blocks for her to knock down. They're blocks made by Kenny and painted by Max—and Gunnar, I think—with letters, numbers, and Yukon flora and fauna. As Dalton lifts each, he points out the animals.

Musk ox. Wolf. Mountain goat. Fox. Arctic hare. Ground squirrel.

Someone else might skip that part, reasoning Rory is too young to understand. And she is. But it's not about teaching her the animals or the alphabet yet. It's about hearing her father's voice, his patience and his care and his own interest in what he's sharing. She listens so intently you'd almost think she did understand, but her eyes aren't on the blocks; they're on him, basking in his full attention.

Dalton worried he wouldn't be a good father. While most new dads have concerns about that, he grew up in Rockton, where he was the only child. But I knew this is exactly what he'd be like as a father, because it's what he is—patient and kind and loving and endlessly fascinated by the world around him and eager to share it.

Movement flashes outside the window. Our guests arriving. I rise and walk over to see Kenny and April. She's talking, and she's obviously irritated by something, needing to vent about it to someone, and Kenny is that someone. Maybe the *only* one she really feels she can talk to that way, who will let her vent without belittling her concerns or offering advice. He walks beside her, nodding and occasionally replying with a word or two, which is all anyone needs for a good vent.

I look from Dalton, still playing with Rory, to Kenny, engrossed in what is almost certainly a very minor issue of April's and treating it with all the serious concern she needs. We're lucky, both of us, to have someone who so perfectly fits what we need.

"That April?" Dalton says, obviously hearing her voice.

I walk over, bending to hug him from the back and kiss his head.

"What's that for?" he says.

I smile and say, "Nothing," and then I go to answer the door.

It's the middle of the night, and I'm on patrol. Actually, Dalton and I are both on duty. We've felt bad about opting out so far.

Of course, no one really expects us to take our turns when we have a baby *and* an active investigation, but we feel the weight of that responsibility.

We head out at four, after feeding Rory and delivering her to Dana. It's still dark. Pitch-dark. We're on the path with Storm, circling the town on first one path and then another, with only a faint light to guide us.

I'm usually up at this hour anyway. The only difference is I'd be cuddled in a chair, sipping tea before a roaring fire, waiting for the sun to rise. Okay, it's a big difference, compared to freezing my ass off in the predawn hours, walking in circles while trying to pay attention to the slightest noise or movement around us.

We can't talk either. That's even more important now, when the darkness seems to add a layer of silence. Even our footsteps whisper on the hard path.

I'm struggling to focus. It's dark, and I'm cold and bored, and my mind wants to help out by taking me someplace else. Think about the case. About Blake. About Gretchen. About the mining camp. So much to consider, and yet the moment I even idly process a thought, my brain deep-dives into it, yanking all my focus along for the ride.

So I am stuck walking and trying to just enjoy that while paying attention to my surroundings. Then, when we're on the outermost path, Dalton puts up a hand to stop me, and the moment I halt, I hear a voice.

A woman's voice?

That's what it sounds like. It's low, as if whispered. Another voice responds, this one sounding male.

Dalton looks at me. Considering the options. I gesture for him to take this one, while I hang back with Storm. He still pauses, but ultimately, he nods. It might just be residents, up early and not realizing their voices are carrying, even in whispers. But someone needs to sneak up for a look, and that should be him.

As he goes, I back up against a tree and take out my gun. Storm sits in front of me. And we wait.

Any other time, I'd marvel at how silently Dalton moves, but when it's this quiet, I can hear him. The scuff of his boot against the ground. The swish of his sleeve against his jacket. Soon that fades, and I'm alone in the dark and the silence. Even Storm leans against me, as if she doesn't like this any more than I do.

The voices are sporadic, and I can't tell whether that's disjointed conversation or only part of it is reaching me. There's no chance that I'd recognize either with the whisper rasping through both. I still try, hoping to decipher a word or two, but it reminds me of a horror movie, where you decipher what sounds like voices, but you can't be sure you aren't just hypersensitive.

Then the voices stop. I tense and strain to listen.

Did they hear Dalton? But then a few more words come, this time from the man, and his tone is even. A word from the woman. Then the crackling of undergrowth loud enough that it sounds like gunfire, though it's just the normal rustle of fall foliage underfoot.

Someone is leaving the conversation, heading away from us, their footfalls fading into silence. A second person comes this way, more quietly. I adjust my gun, but the trajectory is sending that person to my right, heading northwest. Still, I ease into the forest and motion for Storm to follow. She does, and while her passage makes a bit of noise, the footfalls don't stop. Whoever is out here isn't paying attention—or dismisses the sound as an animal.

I track the person's passage until the steps seem to hit the trail we've been on. Then the crackling of undergrowth stops, replaced by the dull thump of boots on hard ground. I hold my breath until I'm sure they're going in the other direction. Then I gesture for Storm to stay where she is, and I step onto the path.

I can grumble about the dark, but the half-moon shines enough light for me to see shapes, and I can make out one farther down the path. It's a person walking in the other direction. By the shoulders-to-hip ratio and the gait, I'd guess male. I note a branch as the figure passes under it so I can estimate height later. For now, I only watch.

"Behind you," a voice whispers, and I jump, only to hear Dalton's soft sigh. He'd tried to warn me, but that never really helps in a dark forest.

I whirl back toward the retreating figure, who doesn't seem to have heard anything. I motion to it. Dalton nods. He already knew.

The question is: Does one of us go after them? We can't both follow with Storm, but nor can we just let someone walk away.

Do we follow quietly? Or do we confront?

Confronting would be more dangerous but also more efficient. Still, it's not quite dawn, and we have no way of being sure this person is alone—they definitely weren't a few minutes ago.

Dalton bends to my ear. "I'm going to swing around. Try to get closer through the forest. Follow with Storm, but stay as far back as you can."

I nod. It's the best solution when we can't see who we're following or whether they're armed.

I ease back toward the forest as Dalton sets out. Then I wait in the shadows, until the figure vanishes from view, before I set out.

After a few steps, I pause and remove my boots. Then I take another couple of steps. That's better. Without boots, my steps make no sound on the hard path. Of course, this also means that I am in stockinged feet, and I'd better hope I don't need to run. If Dalton sees me, he'll either be impressed or amused. But it makes me feel better. I can walk in silence if I stick to the middle of the well-groomed trail. Storm isn't completely quiet, but her padded paws don't make nearly as much noise as my boots had.

I can't see the figure ahead. They've rounded a corner, and as I approach that, I slow to a near stop and peer around it to see an empty path.

Damn it.

As often as I've walked this route, I'm not entirely sure where I am along it. Does the trail bend again just up ahead? Does it branch off?

Or is the person I'm following poised in the forest, having heard someone behind them?

I holster my gun and take out my bear spray instead. I won't hesitate to use that, and my open jacket means I can easily grab the gun if needed. Then I continue walking. I've gone maybe fifty paces when I see the adjoining trail. It's a faint one, another started by game but now also used by us. That tells me where we are. It does not, however, help me know where my target is. Or where my husband is.

Do I continue on the main trail and presume my target is just too far ahead for me to see? Or do I veer onto this one?

I glance at Storm, but I haven't given her any command to track. Not that she could, when the path must be laden with scents.

This one is up to me.

I think the path ahead is straight enough that I should have been able to see my target if they didn't veer onto this one. So I make the turn.

As I walk, I listen, but the only sounds are those of the forest waking up. Light streaks the sky. No sun yet, but it's coming. I take another step. Then I realize I'm walking on softer ground—not the hard-packed trail from before. I pause to put on my boots.

Yesterday, Gretchen hit my bad leg, and while I've been trying to ignore it, it's definitely bruised and swollen, and I can't get my boot on as easily as I got it off. I need to lean against a tree and tug it on with my leg screaming at me for forcing it up. That pain distracts me for a second too long, and when Storm's head shoots up, I freeze, laces in hand.

She's looking into the forest behind me.

I ease away from the tree. There's enough light for me to see up and down the trail, but not into the forest where Storm is staring.

Could it be Dalton?

As if hearing my thoughts, Storm growls, and I have my answer.

Not Dalton.

I make sure my jacket is open, the gun easily accessible. Then I step to one side, with my gaze laser focused in the direction Storm is looking.

A rustle in the forest followed by silence. I take one slow sideways step. Then I see it. A figure among the trees. A figure that is definitely human, and almost definitely male. He's at least six inches taller than me. I think he has dark hair, but then the smoothness of his scalp suggests it could be a hood or balaclava.

I can't make out a face. He's too far away and too shadowed for that.

We stare at each other in a standoff. I don't dare raise my bear spray for fear of scaring him off. Or of having him fire a gun at me, because I can't see his hands.

Should I say something? He's sure as hell not going to answer.

But he's not running either.

Not running because he isn't sure I see him? Or not running because he isn't frightened? Because he's holding a damn gun on me and, between the distance and the shadows, I can't see it.

Damn it, I don't know what's the right call here. I feel as if I'm in a face-off with a predator, not knowing which side of the divide I'm on: dinner or danger.

Finally, I break the impasse with improv.

I bend and pat Storm's head. "What's the matter, girl? It better not be another moose, not after the last one you chased."

I swear I get side-eye from Storm for that. But I also swear the figure relaxes. Clearly, I can't see him. Also, in case he was wondering, I'm not alone. I have a dog.

"It's getting close to breakfast time," I say. "And I could really use a coffee. What do you say we wrap this up?"

A sudden explosion of sound in the forest has me jumping, bear spray raised, expecting to see the man charging my way. Instead, he's running north . . . and someone's following.

Dalton. He heard my voice and zeroed in on his target. Which is totally why I was talking. Well, it would have been, if I'd thought of it.

He must have tried sneaking up on the man, and if I'd realized that, I'd have chattered more to distract the guy, but there was no way for Dalton and me to communicate. Now Dalton is running after him, and I'm racing down the path parallel to them, with Storm behind me.

The man Dalton is chasing must be just as fast as he is,

because he doesn't seem to gain on him. And as they run, I fall back. Not intentionally. My leg just can't keep up at the best of times, and definitely not when it was whacked with a tree branch yesterday.

I try to go faster. After all, I'm on a clear path and they're in the forest, dodging obstacles in the dawn light. But soon the noise of their chase heads farther west, and my path continues due north.

"Goddamn it!" I curse as I finally slow.

Storm nudges my hand, and I pat her head as I peer into the forest. I need to let Dalton take this one. Even if I run into the woods, they have too much of a head—

A woman's scream cuts through the forest. I spin, tracking the sound. It's to the south, in the direction we came.

Another shriek, and then a sound that stops me cold.

The roar of a grizzly bear.

CHAPTER TWENTY-TWO

The sound comes from the direction of Haven's Rock, which means I don't pause to consider. A woman is screaming. A grizzly is roaring. And both sounds come from the south, where we have a town full of people.

I take off with Storm. Dalton will need to figure out what has happened. I cannot imagine he'd miss that roar.

As I run, I reach for my sat phone to notify Anders . . . only to realize Dalton didn't give me the backpack before he went to investigate the voices.

At least I have my gun and bear spray. Also my dog, but when it comes to bears, that can go either way. I've met people who swear no bear will come near people with dogs, and I've met those who swear you aren't in danger *unless* you have a dog. The truth, I'm sure, lies somewhere in the middle.

The forest has gone silent, giving me no cues, and leaving me running in the general direction while sticking to the paths. I'm not barreling through the forest and risking barreling into a grizzly.

When I do hear the crash of something in the trees, I wheel

just as Dalton bursts onto the path behind me. He quickly catches up.

"You lost him?" I say.

Dalton shakes his head. "Made an executive decision. I wasn't getting any closer, and I knew you'd go after the bear."

"It's the screaming woman I'm going after."

He nods grimly. "I know."

"It's near town."

He shakes his head. "East."

When I frown, he only runs into the lead. We hit the cross trail, and he turns left. Heading east. To him, the voice must have sounded as if it came from that direction. Which means it's also the same general direction where we'd heard a man and a woman talking.

When Dalton slows, I catch a woman's voice again, a quiet—almost whispered—babble of desperation. I can't pick up words, but I have a damn good feeling the "person" she's pleading with is seven feet tall and covered in brown fur.

Dalton pauses, silencing our footfalls as he listens and pinpoints the voice. Then he sets out again at a lope.

We're on the outer perimeter path we'd been patrolling earlier. It loops around the town, and when it turns south, the woman's voice comes from the east. Away from town, like Dalton said.

He pauses again to zero in. Then he sets out, sticking to the trail until the sporadic voice comes again from our left, due east. From there, he motions for me to stay close behind him and starts into the forest.

It's thick woods here, and with the early dawn, shadow quickly envelops us. I still have my bear spray in hand and my jacket open for the gun. Dalton has the rifle out—he saw that I'm armed with bear spray so he opted for the secondary weapon. The last thing we want is to both be holding bear spray, come upon the grizzly, and realize it's upwind, where spray will only blind us.

"Please, please, please," the woman whispers. Her tone is strained, and there's no hope of recognizing it.

The answer is a grunt and the sound of very large claws scraping the ground.

"Oh God. Please. Go away. Please."

More scratching, harder now, and stifled whimpers from the woman.

Dalton motions for me to fall farther behind. I roll my shoulders in irritation, but I do as he asks, and Storm slows behind me.

I understand what Dalton means. He can't see what's going on ahead, and we can't bust in like a train, all in a row. He needs space to back up fast if required. I just don't like letting him go on ahead without me right there to protect his back. Yes, the threat comes from the front, but I'm not taking chances. If a bear charges him, I want to be right there.

He continues on, and I follow at exactly three paces. When he stops, I do, too. Then he eases to the side, maybe for a better look or maybe to let me look.

At first, all I can see is a bear. There's no mistaking that massive brown bulk on all fours. When I ease to the right—away from Dalton—it comes into view. A thin and aging grizzly with a white scar running down its back haunch.

The grizzly we dealt with earlier. The one we stole Blake's body from.

What I don't see? The woman whose voice we've been hearing.

First, I make sure we're downwind of the bear, which we are. There's not much of a breeze, but it's definitely coming our way.

Then I glance at Dalton, but his gaze is forward, watching.

I scan the small clearing. There's no sign of anyone. Just that grizzly, intent on scratching grubs from a fallen tree.

The tree is massive. I actually recognize it as one we'd marked last month for removal. It was one of a few that toppled during a windstorm. Massive conifers ripped out by their roots. Fallen trees are the first we harvest for wood, and this one is on the list, but it's so big it'll take a while to carve up.

The bear stops scratching and snuffles, and a half-stifled whimper echoes through the clearing.

Okay, yes, the woman is here. But where—?

My gaze flies to the tree. The grizzly is snuffling near the ripped-out roots. There's a hollow between the tree trunk, the roots, and upturned ground. That's where the woman is hiding. When I sidestep, I can make out what looks like a boot.

The bear scratches hard again, and the woman whimpers. Then the bear backs up to assess. I try to see how she's wedged in, but I can't.

The bear pushes experimentally on the tree. It must shift, because the woman yelps, but the trunk is a good five feet in diameter. It doesn't move enough for the bear to get at her.

I glance at Dalton again. He has the rifle raised to his shoulder. The obvious solution is to shoot the bear. The problem is that Dalton must not be able to see how the woman is positioned either. If he shoots, and the bear moves, that bullet could kill whoever we're trying to rescue.

The bear scratches again. Then it walks the length of the trunk. Dalton's hands move on the rifle. He's waiting for a shot that definitely won't hit the woman. But the grizzly only walks a few feet and then paces back, never getting far enough away.

Our best bet might be to wound it. We're almost certainly going to need to do more than that, but a wounding shot will get it away from the trunk, and then Dalton can fire properly.

It still won't be easy. Killing something this large and deadly never is.

Killing it, though, is what we'll need to do, and we take responsibility for that. We chose to steal Blake's body from the bear. Maybe that corpse would have been enough for it to survive hibernation. Or, worse, maybe in fleeing the bear, we'd pissed it off enough that it's been stalking the woods, and now it has found a human, and it's damn well not letting her go.

Whatever the answer, the bear has crossed the line into a clear threat, and there will be no scaring it away.

When I look again, Dalton is shifting the rifle, testing out other shots. He can wound the grizzly or he can spook it by firing past. The latter is safer, but with a bear this desperate, it could turn on him, and Dalton will rather have fired a shot that might incapacitate—

The bear rises on its back legs, and I exhale as that head shoots into the sky, well above the fallen tree where the woman hides. Dalton takes aim. His finger moves on the trigger—

The bear drops.

It falls so fast that I think Dalton fired, and I somehow haven't heard the shot. Then the woman screams, and I realize the bear dropped onto the trunk. If it can't lift the tree out, maybe it can crush it. All eight hundred pounds of the bruin crash down on that tree, and the woman's scream fills the clearing.

The bear rears up to try again, and Dalton fires. He hasn't had time to properly aim—the bear is in motion—and he miscalculates. The bullet sears the top of the bear's skull.

The grizzly roars and drops to all fours beside the tree. It looks our way, snorting, its shaggy head swinging from side to side as it tries to pick up a scent. Blood trickles into one eye, and it roars in fresh rage. Then it sees something, and it charges, and I realize it's coming straight at me.

I raise the bear spray, and in that second, it feels as ridiculous as putting up my empty hand. A grizzly bear is charging me, and I'm holding a little can of spray. I can't even pull my gun at the same time. I need both hands on the can and—

Dalton fires again. This one strikes the bear in the haunch, right by that old scar, and its roar fills the air as it careens to one side.

The bear is less than ten feet from me. I press the trigger. The pepper spray hits the bear full in the face. It roars again, and backs off, shaking its head, blinded and in agony. Dalton's in the clearing now, rifle raised, but before he can fire, the bear charges. It can't see. It doesn't care. It charges at me, and I easily swing to the side, but Storm must only see a grizzly charging at me. She runs full out and launches herself at it.

"No!" I shout, but it's too late.

Storm grabs the grizzly behind the front haunch. The bear swings around, and its jaws click shut, missing Storm by inches. She's still clinging, jaws ripping, blood flying. The grizzly roars and rears up, and Storm, as big as she is, dangles in midair for a moment. Then the hide she's holding rips free and she starts to fall just as the bear's massive paw strikes. It catches her, and she goes flying.

Storm hits the ground. The bear falls onto all fours, still blinded but smelling dog, dropping onto her so hard that I scream. I have my gun out now, the spray can discarded.

"Casey!" Dalton shouts. "Get back!"

I barely hear him over the pounding in my skull. All I see is Storm's black fur under that grizzly. All I hear is her yowl of pain and terror. All I smell is bear and blood. Its head swings back to bite, but Storm grabs it, her jaws clamping down near its throat. It bellows. I raise my gun, sights locked on its open jaws.

A rifle retort. Before I can pull the trigger, the bear falls back, blood and flesh spraying from inside its mouth. I still fire as soon as it hits the ground, putting another bullet into its skull.

When I start to run for Storm, Dalton shouts, "Casey! No!"

I know he's saying we need to be sure the bear is dead, but I don't care. Right now, what matters is that it is on top of Storm.

I press my gun to the bear's closed eye and put my fingers under its jaw. When I don't feel a pulse, I dart to its side to start heaving its body off my dog. By then, Dalton is there, and in his intake of breath, I hear imminent heart attack, seeing me shoving at a grizzly that might not be dead. It is dead, though, and then both of us are pushing with everything we have as Storm scrabbles to get free, whining in a way that sets the blood pounding in my ears again.

When she's almost out, I help, digging her from under that mound of fur. She tries to rise but can't, and her breath comes labored and shallow, her brown eyes rolling in agony.

"I've got you," I say as tears stream down my face. "I've got you, baby." I pet her with one hand as my other runs down her side. She whimpers, and her breath makes a horrible sucking sound that I know means a punctured lung.

There's a sound to my side. The scramble of boots on dirt. I don't look up. I know it's the woman coming out from her hiding spot, and know I should run to help, but all I care about is my dog.

"Stop!" Dalton snaps. "Stop right there, or I swear I will put the next bullet in *you*."

I glance over just long enough to be sure Dalton isn't talking to me. A woman stands, poised to run.

Gretchen.

Of course it's Gretchen.

I return all my attention to Storm. The momentary distraction gave my heart a moment to slow, and I focus on my own breath. In and out. Do not panic. Just assess.

Storm is breathing. The sound is labored and shallow, and her eyes roll in panic, but she's breathing.

"Backpack!" I say.

Dalton throws it to me as Gretchen says something that I don't bother to process. Storm's still struggling to stand, and I press her down gently.

"Shh, shh. I've got you."

My hand comes back covered in blood, and the panic surges again. There's raw flesh on her side, a chunk ripped open, and blood streams from it. When I try to check, she convulses in pain, and I take more deep breaths and fumble with a syringe, pulling sedative from a bottle.

"You are under arrest for the murder of your husband," Dalton says to Gretchen.

"What?"

I don't hear the rest. I give Storm the needle, all the while praying it's the right choice. Not enough to knock her out, but enough to relax her.

Dalton starts talking on the sat phone. When I glance up, his handgun is trained on Gretchen as he tells someone—Anders, probably—to bring the ATV and bring it now.

I block everything again and turn my attention to Storm. She's quieting, the sedative pulling her down, and I gently prod the chunk of flesh back and—

My heart seizes. Bone juts through just below the bitten chunk. It'd been covered in bloody fur and I hadn't seen it. Her rib has broken and jabbed through, and her breathing is still labored, still raspy, even with the sedative.

Is it worse? Did I *make* things worse? She's punctured a lung and a second rib has punctured her side, and I don't know what other internal injuries she has.

A grizzly crushed her. All that weight falling on top of her, and I don't know how badly she's injured, and maybe I just made things worse by sedating her. What if she can't breathe? What if—

I take deep, ragged breaths myself. I'm ready for that. If she stops breathing, I am ready.

"Casey?" Dalton says, his voice low. "Will's on his way. What can I do?"

"Just make sure that woman doesn't fucking run away again. Because if anything happens to our dog because we had to rescue her, *after* she ran away yesterday . . ."

I don't finish that. It's probably not in my best interests to threaten someone with bodily harm if they stick around and things go wrong. But Dalton only comes over and kneels beside Storm.

"Gretchen's not going anywhere," he says.

I look over to see he's tied her up. I don't know when that happened. I know I should feel sympathy for her ordeal, but Storm's hurt, and right now, I'm blaming Gretchen for that, justified or not.

"Make sure Storm's breathing," I say. "I gave her something to calm her, and now I'm afraid I shouldn't have and—"

"She's relaxed and breathing."

"But she punctured a lung. I can hear it."

"So can I." His voice is wonderfully calm, and as long as I don't look into his eyes and see the panic there, I can draw on that calm, believe in it, let it tell me everything is fine.

He continues, "I'm listening to her breathing, and I will tell you if it changes, okay?"

I nod.

"Then we're all set. I'm here. Focus on what you need to do."

He runs his hands down Storm's back, and if those hands seem to shake, I tell myself it's just because *I'm* shaking. He's not freaked out. He's calm because Storm is fine and I have this under control.

I don't have it under control.

She's bleeding, and her lung is punctured, and I have no idea what else is wrong.

I take more deep breaths and concentrate on that rib poking through. It looks horrible, but I need to leave it be. It's only trickling blood. Let April handle that. The same with the chunk of missing flesh. While blood keeps seeping, it's not gushing, and there's no major artery there. It's just ripped muscle and skin.

Look for more. What else—

The roar of the ATV cuts me short. Anders whips into the clearing. The first thing he sees is Gretchen, sitting with her hands bound behind her. His lips compress, and his eyes shoot daggers her way, but after that, he ignores her, running instead to us.

He drops down beside Storm. I quickly tell him what happened and what I can see.

"I don't know what else could be injured," I say. "I haven't had time to look."

"She's breathing," he says. "We just need to keep her that way while we get her back to town."

"Should we do that? Should we have called April out? Maybe we shouldn't move—"

"I'm here," a voice says through panting breaths.

My sister appears, still wearing a nightshirt and sweats. And she's not alone. Kenny is right behind her, with the cane he uses when he doesn't have his braces on, and he's still wearing sweats and a jersey pulled on backward, and there's a moment where my brain pauses to process that. Then I remember April saying last night that she wouldn't be able to watch Rory early this morning because she had an appointment.

No, apparently she had an overnight guest.

I should be cheering with joy, and instead, my heart plummets, this thing I wanted so much for her coming at the same time as this.

I vault to my feet and run to April, and then stop short before I hug her, knowing that isn't her thing. But she gives me a quick embrace.

"Thank you," I say, tears filling my eyes. "For coming."

"Of course."

That's all she says, along with a pat on my back, as if I'm a child needing reassurance. Then she's striding to Storm.

I start telling her what's wrong, but she lifts a hand to stop me. She'll make her own judgments. So I just say that the grizzly fell on her, and we had to pry her out.

"Punctured lung," she says, running her hands over Storm's chest. "Possibly the other part of that broken rib. No, two broken ribs. The rest seem intact."

She checks Storm's eyes, which are flagging but the dog isn't fully asleep.

"I gave her a bit of sedative," I say. "To keep her still."

"Good."

She continues her examination and pulls out a stethoscope for the breathing and heart rate. As she checks, she murmurs, "Good, good," and I finally start to relax. If there is one person in this world who will never give me false reassurances, it's my sister.

"We'll take her to the clinic," April says. "She's stable, and her vital signs are fine. There could be internal injuries besides that lung, but nothing that will get worse for transporting her. Now, let's get her into the ATV."

CHAPTER TWENTY-THREE

Anders, April, and I head back to town with Storm. Dalton and Kenny stay behind with Gretchen. I have no idea how Dalton intends to handle her, and I don't really care.

We get Storm to the clinic, and April sets to work, with both Anders and me assisting when we can and standing ready the rest of the time. While April has worked on Storm and Raoul before, she's obviously not a veterinarian, and when she snaps more than usual, I know that's anxiety. Fortunately, what she's seeing isn't much different than what she'd see in a human, the procedures the same.

The punctured lung isn't as grave as it seems. It just requires immediate attention, and after some examination, April declares that the attention it requires is surgery, because the rib is still poking into the lung. It's a relatively minor operation. The whole rib hasn't gone through. It's not even completely fractured. It's a splinter that's gone in, and once that's removed, April tests to see whether the lung will remain inflated on its own. It mostly will, which means a small repair, and the rest left to the body's ability to heal.

April uses ultrasound to check for internal bleeding. There is some, but Storm's blood pressure is strong enough that April will only continue to monitor it. An X-ray shows those two broken ribs, and nothing else. Her spine doesn't seem damaged, which is a huge relief. Now we just need to wait for her to wake up from surgery.

I don't leave Storm's side. Dana brings Rory for me, and I sit with her in April's exam room, where Storm sleeps with her heart rate and breathing monitored. I know things must be happening with Gretchen, and any other time, I'd be fretting about that, but I don't care. Dalton can handle this. He can always handle it. Anders goes to help him, and I stay with Storm.

It's a little over an hour before Storm starts to rouse. Rory is sleeping in her portable crib, and I'm right there at Storm's side, petting her and whispering to her and reassuring her.

I call Dalton to let him know she's awake. While I've been ignoring the situation with Gretchen, I have not been ignoring my husband. Technically Storm is my dog. He got her for me, as a gift. But any couple who have a dog know actual "ownership" is an absurd concept and insulting to the pet. This is our dog. Our pet. Our companion.

He's stepped away during this crisis only because one of us has to look after Gretchen, and he's acknowledging Storm's original "ownership" in that. It doesn't mean he won't be anxiously waiting to hear from me. Ten minutes after I call, he's at the back door, out of breath, coming to see her.

As she rouses, we continue petting and reassuring her. She's groggy and confused, but she's a patient and trusting dog who accepts that if she's waking up on a table feeling strange, we know what we're doing and everything's okay.

Once she's ready, we take her down so she can try standing. That's what I'm waiting for—making sure she can stand and move and seems aware, if woozy and disoriented. When she stands up, a little shaky, and licks my face, I burst into tears and Dalton's arms go around both of us, hugging us close.

Storm is sleeping again. We've brought her bed to the clinic. Any other time, April would grumble about a dog—with endlessly shedding fur—in her exam room, but now she's the one who insists we leave Storm there. Today's patients will need to accept a large dog sleeping—and snoring—during their appointments.

When I leave the clinic, I keep Rory with me. She's awake, but quiet, having already had an early-morning play session with Dana and Max. Soon she'll be too old to just sit and watch Mom work, but for now, if she's in the right mood, this is acceptable. I have her in my front carrier as I set off to talk to Dalton.

After April had checked out Storm, Dalton had needed to zip off again. Gretchen is still in that clearing where we found her, and Dalton has ignored her there as he worked with Mathias to skin and butcher the grizzly. It's not great meat, but up here, we use it all, and that will make dog food and sausage.

When I arrive with Rory, Dalton's gaze immediately swings over my shoulder. He spots Kendra and relaxes.

"No, I didn't come alone," I say.

Kendra helps Mathias with the bear. She doesn't say anything. They've turned Gretchen to face the other way, and it's a testament to my exhausted brain that at first I think they turned her away from the slaughtering. No, they turned her so she wouldn't see more people than she already has.

"Is she talking?" I ask Dalton. At the clinic, he hadn't mentioned Gretchen, knowing I didn't care until Storm was stable.

"Haven't bothered trying," he says. "I figured you'd want to do that, and I didn't feel like arguing with her."

I nod and leave him to his work as I walk around to Gretchen. She sits, hands still tied, glaring at me. Earlier, she'd been gagged, but someone has removed that.

"You can't hold me," she says. "If I'm under arrest, you need to charge me, and you can't tie me up."

"Not a lawyer, huh?" I say. "Police have twenty-four hours to charge you, and if you cannot immediately be transferred to a holding facility, you can be restrained in any way necessary without using excessive force, which we have done."

"You didn't identify yourself as law enforcement when we first met."

I shrug.

Her jaw sets. "There are no communities out here. At least, no permanent communities with RCMP detachments."

I shrug again. I've been very careful. I never claimed to be law enforcement. Never even used "I" or "we" when talking about arrest procedures. Yes, Dalton said she was under arrest for killing her husband, but I won't repeat that.

I have no idea how we'll handle this in the long term. She's seen several of us. She saw the ATV. She knows we aren't campers. This is where I thank our lucky stars for Émilie, because I don't need to handle that part. Émilie will, once we have what we need from Gretchen and send her back home.

"I didn't murder my husband," she says.

"Husband . . ." I draw the word out as I bounce Rory. "That was your story, right?"

"My *story*?" Her voice rises.

"You implied you'd been married for decades."

"Twenty years last spring."

"Yet his wedding band is new."

Her eyes snap. "Because he lost his a few years ago, and we just replaced it this spring." She tries to thrust out her hand, only to realize it's bound. "Look at mine. It matches. We had a jeweler make a duplicate."

I move around her and examine her ring. It has the same etched pattern on the gold. Hers is definitely worn.

"He's my husband," she says. "We're legally married. You can check."

"We'd need your ID for that, which it seems you dropped into a stream."

She lets out a long hiss of breath. "We dropped the pack that contained our ID, yes, along with our sat phone and GPS. But I can give you our names and you can check them. We have social media accounts. Gretchen and Blake Landry, from Whitehorse. You'll find us with our photos."

I make notes. While I can't check myself, Émilie can.

"Tell me what happened," I say. "You said he wanted to leave early . . ."

"I'm not telling you anything without a lawyer present."

I look left and then right. "Is your lawyer with us now?"

She scowls.

"Obviously there is no easy way of getting you a lawyer," I say. "And we have zero legal obligation to help you."

"What?"

"Moral obligation, yes, but not legal. We tried to help you yesterday. You attacked me and took off. Today, we saved your life—and our dog nearly lost hers in the process. Yet you still tried to run." I wave around us. "Run to what? Yesterday, you claimed you were being stalked. Hunted. That someone wanted to kill you, and you thought it was us. But we just saved you from a grizzly. We wouldn't do that if we wanted you dead. In fact, letting that grizzly kill you is better than killing you ourselves. Death by misadventure. Yet afterward you still ran."

Silence. Then her gaze slides to the side. "I didn't think it through."

"We had to tie you up to stop you from running because we don't want to keep risking lives saving you. Where the hell were you going, Gretchen? What was your grand plan? Just keep running in circles until *something* kills you?"

"I heard voices. I was trying to figure out whether there might be regular people out here, people who didn't murder my husband."

"You heard voices when? And where?"

She seems to relax a little. "First, on the day Blake died. He shouted, and I came running and saw someone dragging his body into the trees. He was obviously dead. I took off. Once I got away, I didn't know what to do, so I just . . . hovered. I should have fled, but our pick up was still six days away and I wanted to see who killed him. The next voices I heard came from near the mountain, followed by an ATV that sped off before I could see anyone. Then there were two men talking, and I crept up to see them leaving a clearing. I went into it, but it was empty."

"You said you saw someone dragging Blake away?"

"A man. That's all I know. I could tell Blake was dead and I . . ." She sucks in breath and looks away. "I panicked and ran."

"And the two men you heard talking? Can you describe them?"

She shakes her head. "I wasn't close enough. I heard voices, hurried in that direction to spy on them, and then saw them from the rear as they left the clearing. They looked and sounded male. That's all I know."

I'll return to that and press harder. I just don't want to get too far into the weeds yet.

"Go on," I say.

"After that, I rested, trying to figure out what to do. The obvious answer was to flee, hole up, and wait for our pick up. I'd tried playing detective, and I didn't get anything. So I went back to our camp. Someone had been there. When Blake went to soak his foot, he left his backpack behind. It was gone. My stuff had been rifled through, but left behind. Except for the food. They'd taken my share of the food."

"Your share?"

"We split it. Blake had more—he could carry a heavier pack. Mine was gone. I grabbed my backpack and set out. I didn't get far before I spotted someone up ahead, waiting, just off the path. I'm lucky I saw him."

"Him?"

"Him or her. I didn't get close enough to tell anything except that it was definitely a person."

I'll return later to asking her where this happened. "And then?"

"I backtracked, and they came after me. Through the trees. They were trying to be quiet. but I heard them. So I ran. I full-out ran. I turned onto any new trail I hit, and then started ducking through any opening. Finally, when I thought I'd gotten enough of a head start, I hid."

Again, I'll get details later. I nod for her to continue.

"I stayed there for a couple of hours, planning to head out at night, but then it got dark and I couldn't see where I was going. I found water and drank, and then just found another place to sleep. I couldn't sleep, of course. When I wasn't crying over Blake, I was afraid for my own life. I had no idea what was going on, why anyone would kill him. Then I heard something. I thought it was an animal, and I went very still, and it was so quiet, I heard breathing. Someone was out there, right near me."

She pauses to catch her breath, as if the memory set her heart racing. "I thought it must be a coincidence. They couldn't have found me. I didn't leave a trail. I was *so* careful. I went completely quiet, and I heard them getting closer until they were right there, and I knew they'd seen me. Somehow, they'd seen me. I pretended to be asleep. I had my knife in my hand, and I just wanted a look at them, and then I'd run. I heard someone lean over me, and I leapt up and stabbed at them."

She laughs, the sound hollow and ragged. "They grabbed the knife before it even made contact. I couldn't see anything. It was fucking *night*. How did I expect to see them? They didn't have any kind of flashlight, but they could obviously see me. All I could make out was a dark face with goggles."

"Dark face? You mean dark-skinned?"

"I think so, but I couldn't even see eyes behind the goggles. They—I'm sure it was a he—put their hands around my throat. I felt those hands, gloved hands, and I . . . I'm not even sure what I did. Kicked? Screamed? Bit? Punched? I did something, and they couldn't get a good grip. I ducked and kicked hard. I don't know where I kicked—the stomach, the nuts—but it made him yowl and fall back, and then I ran."

Dalton moves up beside me and reaches for Rory. "We're done with the bear," he says. "I'll take her."

"Thanks." I pass the baby over, and then turn to Gretchen. "So you ran."

"I did. Once I was up and going, I could see enough by the moonlight to tell the difference between an open passage and a tree, and that's all I needed. I kept running. I don't think he followed, though. Not for long anyway. Then I was alone, and I just kept going. When it was light out, I found a spot, and by then, I was so tired, I slept. It was nearly dark again when I woke, and that didn't do me any good, so I stayed there until dawn. That day—yesterday—I was stalked. I could tell someone was there, but they weren't trying to get to me, just following me, tracking me. And then I ran into you."

"And after that?"

"By that point, I didn't even know what was happening. Sometimes I'd hear voices, but before I could get close, they'd be gone. I started to think I was hallucinating. I haven't had anything but water in three days. I don't have my backpack—I left that behind when I escaped whoever tried to strangle me. I've just been wandering around, hoping that one of those voices is someone who can help me."

Does that make sense? She knows her husband's killer is out here. She suspects his killer is after her. Yet she hears other voices and believes *they* could help? After she attacked us for trying to help the day before?

Of course, she was actually right—there are two settlements of people out here who could have helped—but that's not what you expect to find in the middle of the Yukon wilderness. If someone killed your husband out here, and you hear voices, there's a good chance one of them is his killer.

If it were me, I might have gotten close enough to see them and make a judgment call. That's what she seemed to be doing, and I don't know how many options she had, lost in the forest, without any food.

"And then the bear found you?" I say.

"After I heard the voices. It was a man and a woman, but it didn't sound like you and your husband. Again, I started getting close, and again, the voices stopped. I heard someone walking. I even thought I saw a man walking away. I went to get closer, and I lost track of him, and stepped out in front of that bear. That must have been what I saw. I didn't have my spray, and I was trying to think of what to do when it charged. I remembered seeing that tree—thinking I could sleep under it—and I ran back and dove under just in time."

I walk over to where our own backpack has been abandoned. I take out two energy bars and a water canteen. When Dalton sees what I'm doing, he passes Rory to Kendra and comes over to undo Gretchen's bonds.

"If you run," he says, "I swear we aren't going after you. Whoever is trying to kill you will get another chance."

She only nods. I come around her front and hand her a bar and the canteen. She eats one bar in a few bites and reaches for the second. When I withhold it, she scowls.

"You will get it," I say. "Just not so fast. Give your stomach time to start working on that one and get some water down."

Once she's had the water, I hand her the second bar and warn her to eat it slowly. "There's plenty more where that came from. Just take your time, and don't get sick."

While she eats, I ask her more pointed questions. Without a compass, she can't pin down where all the events took place, but she gives me what she can. Same as for the voices she heard, which had no distinguishing accents or other features—not particularly low- or high-pitched.

When it comes to the figures she saw, I get whatever details I can. Then I need to talk to Dalton, but that's tricky. Mathias left after he finished butchering the bear, and I won't expose Kendra. So I quickly discuss plans with Dalton, speaking as obtusely as possible.

We decide to put Gretchen in Lilith's cabin, as we planned

earlier. She's seen Anders, so he'll guard her. I'll want a second guard, but I need to speak to people and find out who will do it. She's also seen April, but my sister isn't a proper backup guard. It might end up being Dalton. We need two people with Gretchen, both to keep her from running—if she's lying to us—and keep her safe—if she's telling the truth. We already know that someone has been staking out that cabin.

Dalton agrees. For now, he'll take her to Lilith's place with Anders. They won't use the ATV. If it comes to it, the ATV might be a way to lure in her supposed stalker, but for now, I have a laundry list of other things I need to do.

CHAPTER TWENTY-FOUR

Lilith offered to stay with Anders, since it's her cabin, but in the end, it'll be Yolanda. Not only does she have training—and her own handgun—but she considers herself bulletproof, at least against exposure threats. For Yolanda, Émilie would pull out all the stops.

Yolanda was also Anders's first choice, and I won't read too much into it.

I'm still wrapping my head around what I saw this morning, which certainly seems to indicate that Kenny came from my sister's bed. Given what she said about not being able to take Rory this morning, it wasn't a spontaneous event. Am I hurt that I didn't know things had changed? Yes, but I also can't imagine April telling me. It would require Kenny's gently prodding to persuade her to take the relationship public, and she'd want to be sure it was working first. Being someone who wouldn't read the obvious clues herself, April expects I won't either. So for now, I guess I'll just pretend I can't put two and two together.

I check on Storm and sit with her awhile, as I make arrangements to talk to Émilie about Gretchen and Blake. Then I feed and change Rory and play with her a bit before passing her off to my sister, who's done with her appointments for the day. I'd taken Rory to speak to Gretchen the first time, but only because it was close to town and we'd already made enough noise—screams, gunshots, the ATV—that I was hardly worried about a baby crying. The walk to Lilith's will be different.

Yolanda and I set out with backpacks of supplies. Anders took a bag, too, and now we add food and a deck of cards, along with Yolanda's overnight stuff and things I gathered from the store for Gretchen. I've added a couple of novels and small games, along with treats from the bakery, things I hope might be a comfort to her, as I begin to more strongly consider the possibility she's actually a traumatized new widow.

It's a quiet hike out. Now that I don't need to stay alert, I can sink into my thoughts. Oh, sure, I *should* stay alert, so I don't stumble over Gretchen's alleged stalker, but I can trust Yolanda to hear him as well as I do. I can also trust Yolanda to not take offense at my silence. If anything, she probably prefers it. Better that than awkward small talk.

As we get closer to Lilith's cabin, I do run a few things past her. Her reading is exactly what I expect—she doesn't trust Gretchen's story and sees too many holes in it.

"So someone randomly murdered her husband in the forest and started stalking her. Two hikers minding their own business? Why?"

"Why kill him or why stalk her?"

"Both. Well, no, her theory on why her husband was killed is that Eric is a crazed mountain man."

"Her husband thought it first—and he only saw me."

Yolanda shakes her head. "How the hell does someone

mistake you for a mail-order bride? No, don't answer that. I know how. For the same reason people used to assume I was Gran's foster granddaughter. Such a generous family, taking in a disadvantaged Black girl and giving her the chance of a lifetime."

"Those billionaires. Always doing good deeds."

She snorts. "Right? Anyway, if Gretchen's leaning into the mountain-man bullshit, she's probably barely stopped to consider why her husband was killed. Clearly, these woods are teeming with unstable killers."

"As opposed to stable killers?"

"Nah, it actually has those. But unstable ones will be her theory. Theory or excuse, depending on whether she murdered him herself."

"That also applies if she knows why he was murdered. She'd be redirecting our attention. Of course, we don't know what she'll say."

"Oh, we do. Trust me. *Crazed mountain man killed my husband.*"

Sadly, Yolanda is right. While those aren't Gretchen's exact words, the gist is there. She has no idea who would murder her husband. He taught earth sciences at the Yukon University campus in Whitehorse. No one is going to follow him up here to murder him. Clearly, he ran across one of those renowned murderous hermits of the north.

I know that's what people think about Alaska, but it bleeds over the border into the Yukon. Who is out in these woods? Hippies and killers. Well, not necessarily killers, but paranoid men who will murder you if you stumble on their territory.

Of everyone I've met up here, no one falls into that category. Even Brent, who *had* paranoid schizophrenia, was no danger to anyone. Sure, there's Tyrone Cypher, who actually *was* a hired killer, but he retired to Rockton—becoming sheriff, no less—to get away from killing. Okay, also probably to avoid being brought to justice for his crimes. The point is that we keep running into a stereotype that no one actually fits.

Is it impossible? Of course not. I'm sure that somewhere in the Yukon there are people living on their own who might shoot you if they see you, lost in the paranoia of their own muddled minds. But mostly, if someone kills you, they're going to have a reason.

Otherwise, Gretchen has no idea who killed Blake, and the more I push, the more upset she gets. Why am I ignoring the obvious answer? If *she* didn't kill him and *we* didn't kill him, then there's a madman in the forest who murdered her husband and has been stalking her.

I ask a few more questions, but if I keep pushing, I'll be leaving Anders and Yolanda to deal with the agitation I caused. So I calm Gretchen with meaningless questions that make it seem as if I believe her story. Then Dalton and I head back to town.

Once we're definitely out of earshot, I start talking, my voice low, filling in the parts that Dalton didn't hear in my earlier interview.

"There's a lot to unpack," I say, "and it all depends on how honest she's being. I've tried to start by taking her word for it, and seeing how that fits."

Dalton nods and waits for me to continue.

"Gretchen says she wasn't there when Blake died. We did find her footprints, but they could be from earlier—when they were getting water—or later, when she heard him shout and came to find him. Then she sees him being dragged off but can tell nothing about the person dragging him. She can't even confirm it was *one* person."

"Likelihood of that?"

I shrug. "I've met assault survivors who refuse to pick their assailant out of a lineup because they didn't get a good enough look. I've met witnesses who saw nothing of the perpetrator, either because they were focused on the victim or they were focused on getting out of there. Both are better than someone who claims they got a good look and accuses the wrong person. Things happen fast, and you rarely have time to stop and think."

"Then she went back trying to see the killer."

"Which is plausible. She flees. Realizes she missed an opportunity. Sneaks back."

"And finds her husband's backpack gone."

I nod. "Which fits what we discovered. Blake's buried backpack. No food in it."

"She says the food was also removed from hers."

"Which makes sense if you want to convince her to leave."

"Except she doesn't leave."

"Right. She's still hoping to ID the killer. Not the choice I'd make, even as a cop, but if this is all true, then she's in shock. Her husband has been murdered. All she can think about is finding out whodunit. She hears voices. Tracks them to a clearing as two people are leaving it. Which would explain Storm finding her trail in that clearing."

"Where a man had been buried. A man we still can't identify."

"Yes," I say. "Not that she'd know that. We saw no sign that the burial had been disturbed. But it would explain why she overheard two people talking there."

"They were burying him."

I rub my temples. "Two people murdered in two very different ways. Two victims who supposedly have no connection. That's not working for me."

"Not working for me either."

"We need to keep Gretchen's pick-up date in mind. Someone is coming for her, and if we haven't resolved this—at least enough to convince her to cancel it—we're in trouble."

"I know."

"So the next step is to talk to Émilie and hope we discover that Gretchen's 'innocent hiker' story is shit."

"She's counting on us not being able to verify her story. Or, at least, that it'll take us time to verify it, which gives her time to escape." He pauses to listen to something and then continues, "Now what about the voices we heard this morning?"

"Which Gretchen also claims to have heard? Either that's the truth . . . or she's covering her ass in case we heard them, too." I shake my head. "I need to talk to Émilie. Until then, I'm being pulled in a dozen directions by clues with a dozen explanations."

Back in Haven's Rock, we fetch our baby and visit our dog. I'd love to take Storm home, but April doesn't want her moved. For now, we'll just keep stopping in so she knows we're here.

Once we're home, I message Émilie that I'm ready. She's gets back to me right away, and Dalton takes over feeding while we talk.

I hold off on the complete explanation. I just tell Émilie we seem to have information on our dead man and his wife, and I need to verify it. Gretchen provided full names, addresses, dates of birth, and occupations.

Fifteen minutes later, Émilie says, "I have them. Or I have people matching that data, which I know is not necessarily the same thing."

"They could have borrowed identities."

"Yes, and while this is where I would love to be able to transmit images, we're going to need to do this the old-fashioned way. Tell me what they look like, in police-sketch detail."

I do that. When I finish, Émilie exhales. "I think this is them."

"You don't sound happy about that."

"I'm not, because it's much easier to prove a negative than a positive."

"It is," I say. "If I told you that our Gretchen has a snub nose, and the real one does not, then we know ours is an imposter. But a police-sketch ID is imperfect."

"Let me keep digging. I'd like more."

As I wait, Dalton hands me a bowl of stew. I take it with grateful thanks and eat most of it before Émilie calls back.

"All right," she says. "Either this is a very elaborate hoax or Gretchen is who she says she is. I found her social media, where she said last week that they were going hiking up north. Blake taught in the summer, and he has the fall term off. People on the post are warning them that it's late in the year—bears, snow, and such."

"Which is what Gretchen said."

"I can also confirm that Blake really does have this term off and did teach this past summer."

"So they are who they say they are . . . which doesn't necessarily prove they're *only* a couple of hikers."

"True," she murmurs.

"Gretchen says Blake teaches earth sciences. Can you get me something more specific?"

A pause.

I continue, "I'm asking because earth sciences sounds very middle school. He must specialize in something. Now, maybe

Gretchen is simplifying it. Or maybe she's deliberately avoiding mentioning one specific area that is definitely taught in the Yukon."

She's quiet, then she curses softly as she understands my meaning. Keys patter under her fingertips. Finally, she exhales a long, low breath.

"Yes?" I say.

"Yes. Blake's specialization is geology. Specifically geological mapping and field methods."

Mining.

CHAPTER TWENTY-FIVE

So we finally have our link. It still doesn't tell us what the hell is going on here, but it points us in a very viable direction.

Blake was a professor of geological sciences, specializing in an area associated with mining. And the gold claim that our neighbors are currently mining? It was discovered by Mark . . . who was a professor mining on his summer terms.

Is it possible that's a coincidence? Sure, but it's also possible that Blake was killed by a Sasquatch. Or aliens. Or that ever-present crazed mountain man.

No, this link is too obvious to ignore. There are hundreds of people with small placer mines in the Yukon. Most are here in the summer, like Mark.

But as paranoid and secretive as miners can be, I imagine that the more tech-savvy of them would be in online communities. Of course, they won't share where they're looking, but they have a very unusual hobby, and they'll want to talk to others, both for fellowship and tricks of the trade. Those most likely to be communicating online would be people like Mark and like Blake, well-educated and relatively young for prospectors.

Now, this doesn't mean Blake *was* a prospector. But if Mark was mining up here and went looking for resources, he might reach out to the university or the instructors there—especially when he was a professor himself. Even without that, prospectors might find themselves in the same online—or in-person—groups of those with an interest in the minerals that lie beneath our feet.

I can't speculate too much on the exact nature of that connection. Émilie will do more digging. She has never identified Mark. After he and his wife died, our biggest concern then had been someone realizing they'd disappeared and *where* they'd disappeared. Émilie had monitored for stories of a miner and his wife not returning from the Yukon, but no stories appeared. Miners are notoriously cagey, and we had to presume that no one knew where he'd been mining, maybe not even realizing it was in the Yukon. I'd never liked that story, but Émilie had promised she'd keep monitoring while trying to identify him.

Identifying him has proven tricky. All we have is that first name, which is probably fake. But we have some details of his past, and we know that both he and his wife vanished up here, which someone *must* have noticed, though nothing ever turned up. While this hasn't been critical, her investigator has found some more leads and now they'll go all-in on identifying Mark . . . and his connection to Blake.

That means our attention turns to the mining camp.

One thing we could do is question Gretchen about her husband's interest in mining. I'm going to hold off until I have more. You only get one chance to tackle a hostile witness from a fresh angle.

If I have smaller questions, I can ask through Anders, using the sat phone. Otherwise, I want to wait until I can see her reactions firsthand.

The other source of answers is the mining camp, and I'm sure Rogers will happily tell us everything we need to know. Yeah, he's not telling us jack shit. Anything we get from the camp needs to be learned on our own. The guards are heavily armed and, as we've seen, not afraid to use those weapons.

We need more before we even think of talking to them. And by "more" I mean leverage . . . and it can't be the sort they can fix with a few shallow graves.

Thinking of shallow graves takes me back to the body we found. There's no clear indication he's a miner, but *could* he be? While we didn't find a tracker, are there other identifying details we missed?

First thing tomorrow, I need to check the body again and talk to April.

A call in the night wakes us. It's the sat phone, and I pause for one bleary moment before remembering that Anders has one phone at Lilith's cottage and April has one at the clinic, and if either is calling in the middle of the night, that's bad. I lunge for the phone at the same time Dalton does. Fortunately for me, it's on my side of the bed, which means I get it first. Unfortunately for me, it's on my side of the bed, which means Dalton accidentally bashes into me when he leaps for it.

I blink to recover before quickly answering and putting the phone on speaker. When Yolanda says hello, my stomach flutters with relief. If it'd been April, that would mean something was wrong with Storm.

"Everything okay?" I say, which is a ridiculous thing to say during a 2 A.M. phone call, but I'm still fuzzy from sleep.

"Lilith's stalker is back," Yolanda whispers.

I sit upright and give my head a shake. "Someone's outside the cottage?"

"Yes. Will and Gretchen are sleeping, but I definitely heard someone out there." She pauses. "Could be an animal, I guess, but I'm sure as hell not peeking out to check."

"Good call."

"It *sounds* like a person. Twigs cracking underfoot. A scuff in the dirt. Also, I'm pretty sure I heard him take a leak."

"Uh . . ."

"Hey, it's really quiet. I could hear the proverbial pin drop. Right now, I have a blanket over my head to muffle any sound I'm making, and he still might be able to hear me. My question is whether I should wake Will."

"Yes."

"And then . . . ?"

I look to Dalton.

"Hold," he says. "Stay inside. Both of you. It's dark, and whoever's there will see you before you see him." Dalton pauses. "How long has he been there?"

"I heard the first noise maybe fifty minutes ago. I wasn't absolutely certain it was a person until I heard someone taking a whizz against a tree. That was five minutes ago."

"Okay. I'm going to come out there. He's intent on the cabin. It might be our best chance to ambush him. It'll take me about thirty minutes."

At a noise from me, he glances over. I shake my head. When he scowls, I say, "You're not going alone. You'll take me or someone else."

"She's right, Eric," Yolanda says. "Yes, that'll add a few minutes to your ETA, but you need backup. You guys work that out, and I'll expect you here in forty-five. In the meantime, I'll wake Will."

"Make some noise, too," I say. "Or turn on a flashlight. Something to be clear that the cabin is occupied. That should keep your intruder curious enough to hang around until we get there."

"We?" Dalton says.

"If you want someone else, say so, but Dana said we can drop Rory off at any time."

He grumbles, but I'm right. If this was a patrol mission, he'd have a list of people he could take. But it's an ambush, and that's police work, and the only people he'd trust with that are Anders and me.

I get up and wave for him to finish the conversation while I dress. "I'll take Rory and meet you out front."

CHAPTER TWENTY-SIX

It takes more than fifteen minutes to get a sleeping baby up and relocated, complete with diaper bag and bottles. But we make up the time by moving fast through the forest, and we're there within forty-five minutes. If someone's still around, they'll see our flashlight. We aren't concerned about drawing attention until we get close.

When we do approach, we douse the light and pause to let our eyes adjust. It's a quarter moon and a clear night. We can see well enough to stay on the path without light.

There's a rise to the east of the cabin, and we silently climb it, being careful not to scrape rock underfoot. Once we're in position, we can see the cabin and the open land in front of it. Open and empty land. We keep scanning until I spot a dark shape, hunkered in the woods. When I point it out to Dalton, he grimaces, as if I'm seeing a bush.

I take out the binoculars and look. Yes, I *am* seeing a bush, but it has a dark hood protruding over the top. I don't pass the binoculars to Dalton yet. I focus on the man's face. He's looking toward the cabin, which means I'm on an angle, but I should be able to make out the guy's profile. Instead, all I see is black.

Is he looking the other way? I don't think so. I can see a hood, but where there should be a face, there's a dark nothingness.

Gretchen said her stalker seemed dark-skinned. What I'm seeing is blackness—the kind that comes from fabric . . . like a balaclava. We certainly have plenty in town, and so would anyone up here in winter. I should see eyeholes, with surrounding skin or light eyes, but I don't. Dark skin and dark eyes?

No, there's an odd bulge where his eyes would be, the profile going out where it should dip in.

He's wearing goggles.

I hadn't really processed that part of Gretchen's story. She said she couldn't even see her attacker's eye color because he was wearing goggles. That's not *why* he wore them, though. It would be hard to see with goggles at night, where any impediment is a problem. Unless the goggles are the opposite of an impediment.

"Night vision," I murmur under my breath.

Dalton grunts in question, but I only pass him the binoculars. He takes them, and I wait until he focuses on the head peeking above the bush. Another grunt tells me Dalton sees him.

I lean in and whisper, "Balaclava and goggles, probably night-vision."

He nods and then returns the binoculars, takes out the phone, and motions that he's stepping away to call the cabin. He needs to let Anders know we're about to move in.

I keep my binoculars trained on the man. I'm going to presume it's a man. Gretchen thought so, and Yolanda's line about hearing someone peeing on a tree suggests Gretchen was right.

He stands there, just watching the cabin. There's a light on inside. Is that why he isn't making any moves? Is he waiting for that light to go out?

Lilith said her intruder tried the door and then seemed to be taunting her. If he couldn't get in, maybe he could lure her out.

A blip sounds as someone inside answers the phone. Then Anders's voice, low and steady. I can't hear what he's saying. It's just a low male voice. But at the sound, the stalker's head jerks up. He creeps toward the cabin, head tilted to listen.

Then he takes off.

"Eric!" I whisper-hiss as I start after the guy. Dalton catches up as I reach the cabin.

"He bolted," I whisper.

"I can hear him. Wait here."

I don't like that, but Dalton's already running. We can hear the rustle and thump of the man's flight, and I'm about to run faster when I then remember Anders. I bang on the door, saying, "It's me!"

He opens it.

"Guy took off," I say quickly. "Something you said sent him running."

Anders comes out after me, telling Yolanda to lock the door. As we run, he says, "I didn't say anything that would tip him off."

"Then I guess the sound of a male voice was enough."

"Damn it. Right. He thought there was a woman inside—Lilith or Gretchen. A lone woman."

"When he realized his mistake, he bolted."

We keep running, easily following the sound of Dalton and his target.

"Go ahead," I say to Anders. "You know I can't keep up."

"Yeah, and if he circles back?"

"Uh, armed law-enforcement professional here? But yes, good point. He may have been hoping to lure you out and circle back. I'll stand guard at the—"

A shot rings out. Then another in quick succession. My heart leaps into my throat, and I bear down, running full out, ignoring the screaming pain in my leg.

Dalton would not have fired unless he had to, which means that first shot wasn't his. Another shot comes, and I run faster even as Anders takes the lead. He's racing in the direction of the blast, me right behind him, my leg on fire, both of us ducking and dodging around trees until—

"Hold!" a voice calls ahead of us.

Dalton's voice.

We both stop and listen, and I can barely breathe, picturing Dalton in a standoff with an armed man. When a figure appears in the moonlight, my hand goes to my jacket, but it's only Dalton.

I run to him. "Are you okay?" I say, as my gaze sweeps over him.

"Yeah, he didn't hit me."

"That was his gunfire? All his?"

Dalton nods. "He shot my way once, and I hit the ground. He kept running and fired two more shots."

"Backing you off," Anders says, his own gun in hand.

"Yeah. I didn't see where the shots hit, which means they were wild. A ploy to stop me from chasing him, and I hate that it worked but . . ."

"You had an armed man shooting at you. In the forest. At night," I say. "Backing off was the right thing to do."

Dalton exhales. "Well, now we know he's armed. I don't think I would have caught up anyway. He was pulling away. Same as yesterday. He's faster than me."

"He's wearing night-vision goggles, which gives him the advantage."

"Yeah. He was dodging trees much faster than I could."

I look toward the cabin. "We should get back in case this was all about luring Will away."

Anders snorts. "I almost wish it was. I'd love to see his face if he opened the door and found Yolanda with her gun pointed at his crotch."

I shake my head, and we return to the cabin.

We will eventually try to track our escaped stalker. But we're giving him room—lots of room. Let him flee to wherever he feels safe. The problem is that we don't have Storm to follow him. Still, Dalton can give it a try. With the guy running full out, he wasn't exactly hiding his trail.

We poke around the bush where he was hiding. The only thing we find is footprints, which match the ones left by Lilith's stalker.

The mask and goggles also tell me this is the same guy who attacked Gretchen, the one she presumes killed Blake. If so, he could have thought it was Gretchen inside, having found an abandoned cabin to shelter in.

But why not just break in and kill her?

Because he wasn't sure it *was* her. Or that she was alone. He hoped to lure her into peeking out, so he could confirm his target and act. Then he returned tonight, only to hear Anders and know he's not getting his chance.

There are other theories, of course, but this is the one that best fits all the parameters. It also means that Gretchen's story seems to be correct. She *was* being stalked, which means she's almost certainly not Blake's killer.

After searching, I ask Anders to come out and walk with me. We need to plan our next move, and I don't want to talk too much in front of Gretchen. Dalton and I murmured ideas while we were searching, and now he's going inside to stand guard with Yolanda.

"Here's what I'm thinking," I say, once we're far enough from the cabin. Then I tell Anders my theory.

"Sounds reasonable. I *know* nothing I said on the phone would spook the guy, so hearing a male voice must have been enough."

"So next steps . . ." I say with a slow exhale. "We have two options here. Well, three, if you include taking Gretchen to Haven's Rock, but I'd rather not consider that."

"Agreed. If we need to bring her, she'd have to be blindfolded and confined to the guarded and windowless apartment, so she sees nothing, especially our residents. And we'd need her consent for that—we don't want residents thinking we'd kidnap someone."

"Yes, but that's a last resort. For now the options are to leave her here under guard or have Émilie come and pick her up. Personally, I'd rather postpone the Émilie option—I want access to Gretchen so I can continue questioning her. The problem is that I don't want to ask you and Yolanda to stay where it might be unsafe."

Anders shrugs. "If the guy ran after hearing my voice, I'm not too worried. I'd be more concerned about an ambush if we take Gretchen out of the cabin. We're going to need to stay inside, though, so we'll have to check with Yolanda. She'll tell me if she wants to leave."

"Thank you." I turn to look back at the distant glow of the cabin. "We have a forty-eight-hour maximum. If we haven't solved this by then, we need to rethink this. Someone is coming to pick her up, and we have to deal with that."

"Yep."

"We'll also move her out if there's any clear threat to her. She's not bait."

"Unless you want her to be," he says, with a knowing look.

"I'll think about it, but again, I'd want consent, and I'm not sure she can give it rationally."

He nods. "She might agree to anything to find her husband's killer."

"There's something else."

I tell him about the potential link between Blake and Mark.

"Shit," he says. "You going to confront her about that?"

"I don't know enough yet, and she can just make something up. I need to find out more."

"Then go in hard. Because she might not be her husband's killer but she may know why he was killed."

"Yep."

We start back toward the cabin. Then Anders says, "And hey, worst case, if she's confined to this cabin long enough, with someone stalking her, she may break down and tell us the truth about what they were doing up here."

I smile over at him. "That's my backup plan."

Yolanda wants to stay. She advises us to notify Émilie about the pick-up window, get her advice. If we can resolve this quickly and win Gretchen's confidence, she can cancel that and Émilie can have the plane ready to extract her ourselves.

Back in Haven's Rock, we retrieve our daughter. Once she's fed and cuddled, it's seven in the morning, which is late enough to call on my sister. We go to the front door and then stay in the waiting room after calling April. Five minutes later, I'm pretty sure we hear someone sneak out the back door.

April cracks open the door and pokes her head through. "Your dog is fine. I gave her something to help her sleep, and she is doing exactly that, while drooling all over my floor, I might add."

"It's not about Storm," I say. "Yes, we want to see her, but we're here early because I need to reexamine the man we found buried."

She checks her watch. "At seven in the morning?"

"You can go back to bed. I'm not asking you to help or to watch Rory. Eric and I have been out half the night dealing with a threat, and since we're up, I want to move on this. The sooner I can resolve it, the sooner Will and Yolanda can return."

"Where are they?"

"At Lilith's cabin. Guarding our dead hiker's wife. I think our other dead man is from the mining camp, and I need to examine him."

"We have already determined he is not."

"April," Dalton says behind me, "Casey doesn't need to explain why she requires access to a victim. We just need you to know that we're here, and if you have appointments this morning, we can work in the adjoining room."

April flushes. A mild rebuke from Dalton cuts deeper than the sharpest from her little sister.

She backs up. "Of course. Come in. I have nothing scheduled until eleven. You may use the main examination room, and I will assist."

CHAPTER TWENTY-SEVEN

We bring the man's body up from under the clinic. April puts out her sign for patients to knock and then locks both the front and back door. We don't want anyone bursting in for a bandage and seeing a dead stranger.

Dalton cares for Rory while April and I examine the man again. As we do, I tell my sister about the possible connection between Blake and Mark—the original mine owner. Yes, as Dalton said, I don't need a reason to reexamine the victim, but I don't want my sister thinking I'm being "silly."

Old wounds will always be sensitive, and part of me will always need her approval. She agrees that we seem to have a link. As for how it connects to *this* dead man, she's not convinced that it does. If Blake is here for the mine, then it's unlikely our dead guy is their companion. As Petra pointed out, a trio of spies doesn't make sense.

Whatever the connection, if Gretchen is telling the truth about hearing two men in the burial clearing, then I believe someone at the mining operation killed him.

After an hour of examining the body, I sit back, pull my

gloves off, and rub my hands over my face. "There's no chip, is there? Not an existing one. Not a removed one."

"Doesn't mean he couldn't be from the mining operation," Dalton says. He's on the floor with Rory, stacking blocks for her to knock over. "A new hire. Management. Visitor."

"I know. I just keep thinking the tracker *could* be there. It's like searching for a needle in a haystack. One tiny mark on a human body. But since we know the others were implanted in the shoulders, looking for it elsewhere feels like a wild-goose chase."

"The mark is not 'tiny,'" April says.

I clamp back a frustrated growl. "You know what I mean. It's small. Very small."

"But I still believe we'd see it."

Dalton scoops up Rory as she makes a mad scramble for Storm, sleeping on the floor. When he lifts her onto his shoulder, she immediately grabs for his hair . . . which works far better with me and she grunts in frustration when she can't get enough.

"Have you checked under his hair?" Dalton asks.

"We've searched his hairline," I say. "And the tops of his ears. We also shaved off his beard."

"I could shave his head," April says.

I sigh. "At this point, we'd just be making extra work for ourselves."

"Shave it," Dalton says. "Let's be sure."

I want to argue, but April already has the scissors. I shake my head and start looking for the clippers.

"Good job, Rory," Dalton says, patting the baby's back as she wriggles to get free. "You're going to be a fine detective."

"You're the one who suggested looking under his hair," April says, frowning.

"But it was Rory's idea. I just interpreted the clue."

I peer at the dead man's scalp. The quarter-inch cut we uncovered is exactly the right size for extracting a tiny chip.

At some point, the mining operation must have realized the danger of inserting them all in the shoulder—eventually one of the employees would notice.

There's also a reason this man's was implanted in his scalp. Because, when he'd come to work for them, he was likely bald.

In our initial examination, we'd noticed what seemed like an old scalp tattoo, as we'd searched for signs of a contusion. Now that his hair is gone, we can see the tattoo in full, along with two smaller and newer ones.

"I don't understand those," Dalton says. "I mean, I understand tattoos in general. Body art. If you're bald, you might put them on your scalp. Also easy to cover up if you don't like them later. But those are ugly as fuck."

He's right. One is a cross made from two simple lines. Another is three hatches. The largest is a very crudely drawn symbol that looks like a rune.

"These aren't meant to be art," I say. "Like Will's, they can be symbolic."

"Will's tattoo shows he was an American soldier," April says.

"Yes. I very strongly suspect this big one"—I point to the rune—"also signifies membership in a group. But definitely not the army."

"Do you recognize it?" April asks.

"No, but I recognize the very basic style. I also recognize the way they were all done." I glance over at Dalton. "They're prison tattoos."

"Which means we have a chance of identifying this guy," he says.

"We just might."

We have two more identifiers, as well. The fingers on the man's right hand show arthritis that an X-ray reveals as two poorly healed bone breaks. He's also had dental work that, again, was badly done.

We'd noted these things in our first postmortem exam, but since they hadn't been a cause of death, we'd only filed them away. On their own, they wouldn't identify our victim. Together with those tattoos, they might. He has several scars, too. We send all that information to Émilie.

"So he's from the mining camp," I say as I sit with Rory while Dalton helps April tidy up. "While he could be a guard, I'm going to guess he's a miner."

"Because of the prison tattoos," April says. "He would be unfit for law enforcement."

I make a face. "Being an ex-con doesn't make you unfit for security work. I believe in rehabilitation, even if our prison system doesn't always seem to. The rune tattoo suggests he was part of a prison gang, possibly white supremacy, which sadly doesn't rule out security work. But the mining operation is so security conscious that, yes, I don't think they're hiring ex-cons as guards."

"But they'd hire them as workers?"

"Good point. If I were running a mining operation up here, ex-cons wouldn't be my first choice. There's a security risk plus an increased risk of violence in an isolated community. But we're talking potentially hard physical labor in less than ideal conditions. Including ex-cons would widen your pool. I'd just be sure to not hire anyone convicted of violent offenses."

"Former prisoners might actually make good miners," Dalton says. "They're accustomed to harsh conditions and hard work, right?"

I nod. "Yes, some countries allow penal labor, and it can be hard work under harsh conditions with a regimented routine. Okay, forget what I said earlier. As long as they weren't convicted of violent crimes, I can see why they'd be hired. Ex-cons might be more likely to accept the conditions, and their employment options are limited. The mine could take advantage of that and underpay them."

"It'd also explain the extra guards," Dalton says. "And the chipping."

"Yes and yes. Okay, so our victim is likely a miner. Either they specifically hire ex-cons or they just don't mind hiring them. That would actually fit our former experience with the camp."

"The pedophile."

I scoop up Rory. "Rogers knew the guy's background. He understandably thought it didn't matter in an area without children. He also warned us about his workers, said they could be a rough bunch, and he didn't like the idea of there being women and children nearby. That would fit with a camp of ex-cons. Let's—"

Someone bangs at the outside door. April takes off her apron and folds it. Then she slips out, shutting the door behind her. From the next room, I hear Arturo's voice.

"Someone watched her go in there this morning, and no one's seen her since, so she must still be in there."

"My sister is busy with a case," April says. "She is not on duty. Nor am I."

"So no one cares what's happening out here? The rest of us are stuck on lockdown, getting cabin fever but obeying the rules, and Muriel is allowed to do as she pleases."

I groan and rest my head against Dalton's shoulder.

Outside, Arturo continues, "She isn't just breaking curfew. She's in the forest, where she's not supposed to be at *any* time, but who cares about the rules? *She* wanted an early-morning walk."

Dalton shakes his head, but I go still. Then I pass Rory to him and open the door.

"You said Muriel was in the forest? Early this morning?"

"No, yesterday morning."

I murmur to April, "May I take him into your office?"

She nods, and I usher Arturo in.

Arturo and I talk in April's office, which also serves as a room for patients who need to sleep over. I've given Arturo the desk chair, while I lean against the bed.

"Muriel was out early yesterday," I say. "In the woods."

"That's what I said."

"You also said that no one cared. Who did you mention this to?"

He shifts, some of the belligerence leaving his voice. "I just found out this morning."

"So you didn't personally see her come out of the forest yesterday?"

"Someone else did, and I'm not giving you his name because he doesn't want to start trouble. We were talking about the lockdown, what a pain in the ass it is, and he said he saw Muriel come out of the forest around dawn. He was at his window, looking out, because, you know, we're all bored *shitless* and we can't leave our rooms until eight thirty. He felt like he should tell someone—for security reasons—but worried that it sounded like snitching. He asked my opinion. I said I'd pass it along."

"If I can't get the name of the person who witnessed it, I'm going to need all the details from you. Exactly what time it was. Where she was seen. Even what she was wearing or how she was acting. Can you get that from him?"

He reaches into his pocket and pulls out a notepad. "I have it all here."

Arturo reminds me of those nosy neighbors that everyone hates . . . everyone except cops. Well, no, cops *do* hate them when they're reporting nuisances, but when an actual crime happens in a residential neighborhood, that's who you want to talk to. The stereotypical little old lady with her binoculars and notebook. She's a pain in the ass . . . until her testimony catches the person who has been breaking into nearby homes.

Those nosy neighbors might tell themselves they're keeping the street safe, but most times, they're just looking to judge others. Likewise here, as useful as Arturo's information is, he isn't trying to help. He's only feeding a grudge. But he also just handed me a major clue, one that I hope I'd have figured out when my brain had time to rest and ruminate.

We knew Muriel had been going into the forest. She'd admitted it, and while she was breaking the rules, her explanation was plausible, and supported by evidence. She was an introvert who needed alone time, and her stowed backpack proved it. She'd readily agreed to not do it again, and so I'd dropped the matter, especially since we had far more pressing issues.

But yesterday morning, we heard a woman in the forest. A woman talking to a man. After we found Gretchen in the area, it seemed to have been her. Sure, she claimed she was nearby because she also heard the voices, but I hadn't been completely convinced of that.

Once I had time to rest, I would have come back to this and—I hope—put two and two together. Who did we hear? Maybe the woman who'd admitted to being in the forest alone before her early-morning shifts.

Except, if that was Muriel, she *wasn't* alone.

CHAPTER TWENTY-EIGHT

I'm in the town hall with Muriel. I've asked Kendra to join us. She's not there as an official witness—she's making coffee and then puttering about, as if putting in some work time. But whenever I conduct a potentially adversarial interview, I want a witness. Kendra is the right one for this job. She's not officially law enforcement, and she's so universally well liked that her presence should put Muriel at ease.

I lean into that impression. This is not an interrogation. Not a hostile interview. Just me chatting with a resident about an annoying little issue that doesn't seem to be resolving itself.

"I hate to call you in on this again," I say as I serve her coffee. "I thought it was wrapped up, and it's certainly the least of our concerns right now, but I need to address it."

She frowns. "Is it my schedule? I'm working my full hours. Even a bit extra."

"No, it's the curfew. We have an eyewitness who saw you coming out of the forest around dawn yesterday."

"Yesterday?" The frown deepens. "Are you sure it wasn't a few days ago? We already discussed that."

"Yes, but this was yesterday. After the curfew was in place."

"How did someone see me if everyone's supposed to be inside?" She leans my way, lowering her voice as if not wanting Kendra to overhear. "Is it Arturo? I don't know what's going on, but he really seems to have a problem with me lately."

"It's not Arturo. Someone had their shutters open at dawn and was looking out, waiting for the sunrise."

She goes quiet and sips her coffee.

"Muriel," I say. "I need you to answer this very carefully. Before I called you in today, Eric and I went to your old spot. There are fresh footprints that match your boots."

"I have standard-issue boots."

I take a deep breath, letting her see my growing frustration. "Muriel. They are your size, and the impression matches the others, the depth indicating someone with the same boots in the same size, with the same weight and gait."

I'm stretching the truth, but I can see that I've sold it, as she nibbles her lower lip.

"Muriel," I say. "We are dealing with a serious threat, and the last thing I want to spend my time doing is arguing about whether or not a resident was in the forest. But I can't drop this because we have a curfew, and you broke it. If you can admit to that, we can move forward."

"Yes." She exhales the word. "Okay, yes. I went out there. I'm sorry. I know it was wrong, but this lockdown . . ." She swallows hard. "It's too much for me."

I could point out that she'd been in lockdown for one day before she broke it. But I need this confession, so I nod as if in understanding.

"I made a mistake," she says, "and it won't happen again."

"Good. That's what I needed to hear. Now, I'm afraid we'll

need to discuss a penalty, but if you stick to your promise not to repeat it, we can go easy there."

She nods vigorously. "I won't repeat it, and I accept the penalty."

"Thank you. That makes this much easier. Now I just need one more thing."

"Sure."

"The name of the person you were with out there."

Her head snaps up. "What?"

"You were out there with a man. We found his boot prints."

"What? No. I was alone. If there are other prints, someone else must have been in the same spot. But not with me. I swear it."

I gentle my tone, still trying for sympathy. "I don't think you want to do that, Muriel."

Her chin rises. "Why not? It's the truth. I was alone."

I exhale, slowly and audibly. Then I take out my notebook and flip to the right page. "You were spotted exiting the forest at six thirty. You were seen coming from the northeast, in the direction of your clearing."

"I admitted that."

I lift a finger and keep reading. "At six fifteen, two witnesses heard a male and female voice coming from that direction. They went to get a closer look, but the pair parted before they could get close."

Her jaw works, eyes flashing. "This is Arturo, isn't it? Both your so-called witnesses. No one was supposed to be in the forest, but he obviously was, following me and making up stories—"

"I'm the one who heard you in the forest."

She goes still. "What?"

"Eric and I were on patrol with Storm. We heard a male and

female voice in conversation. We went for a closer look. You may have heard that Storm was injured in a bear encounter. That's when it happened. That's why we didn't get a look at either party."

"Then you can't prove it was me. Just because I have a spot where I like to go before dawn doesn't mean I'm the one you heard."

"I didn't consider you until the witness reported seeing you exit the forest about fifteen minutes after we heard voices. You just admitted you were there at that time."

"I was," she says quickly. "I heard them, too. A man and a woman. Then I heard the bear. That's why I went back to town."

Across the room, Kendra rolls her eyes.

"Yet you didn't report hearing people in the woods," I say.

"I thought it was you and Eric. I heard about the bear attack, and I was certain that's who I heard."

"So it's all a wild coincidence. We were all out there at once. You just happened to get back to town right after the voices stopped talking. There just happen to be a man's boot prints in your clearing."

"Coincidences happen."

"Okay." I nod slowly. "Okay. Well, I wish I had time to pursue this further with you, Muriel, but I'm afraid I don't."

"There's nothing to pursue. Like you said, you have important things to do."

"True, true." I heave a sigh and get to my feet. "Okay, well, I'm afraid I won't be able to continue this conversation today. Maybe tomorrow morning."

"No rush," she says, very obviously trying hard to look sincere.

"Kendra?" I say. "Could you please take Muriel to the solitary apartment? If you can stand guard awhile, I'd appreciate that. I know you have work to do as well, so I'll find someone to take over as soon as possible."

Kendra nods and walks to Muriel. "We'll swing by your apartment first, so you can pack an overnight bag."

"I . . . I don't understand."

I answer. "As I said, I won't be able to follow up on this until morning. Until then, you'll need to be held in the solitary apartment."

"The what?"

"It's an apartment with a guardroom. It's about the size of your usual quarters, and very comfortable. No windows, and obviously, you can't leave but . . ." I shrug.

"Am I charged with something? You can't just confine me for no reason."

"I have reason. You've broken curfew. That's cause for confinement if you check the papers you signed." I take out my tablet and start thumbing through to find the contract. "Now, usually, we wouldn't enforce that for a first offense. But you not only broke curfew—you were in the forest, which is a second offense. Still, even with all that, I'd rather not waste Kendra's time guarding you, and I wouldn't, if you'd just tell me who you were meeting."

"No one. I was meeting no one."

I hold her gaze long enough to see the lie clearly in her flush as she struggles to make eye contact.

"You're lying," I say.

She flinches, as if expecting something softer.

"We're dealing with a security issue," I say, "and you're breaking curfew to meet a man in the forest. Can you see where that would be a problem?"

She looks away.

"So this is how it's going to be?" I step into her line of sight. "I'm dealing with a security concern, a curfew, an injured dog . . . and now I have to deal with you, too. You're making us give up a militia member who should be on patrol but now needs to guard you."

"You don't need to do that. You're *choosing* to do that."

I lock gazes with her until she ducks out of it. Then I turn to Kendra. "Take her. I'm going to call a militia meeting. We have a man in the forest who may or may not be a resident. If he's seen, exercise extreme caution bringing him in."

"What?" Muriel says.

I'm already at the door. "Tell everyone to be armed and to consider him a threat."

"Wait!" Muriel says, but I shut the door before she can continue.

This one needs time to stew, and I don't have time to wait her out.

And . . . right after declaring I didn't have time for Muriel's bullshit, I find myself with little else to do. Émilie has our information on the miner, but she needs to get her investigator involved. Finding a guy who matches the parameters I've provided isn't something she can do with a simple internet search.

She also has the investigator looking for a connection between Blake and Mark, though that requires first identifying Mark.

When I realize I'll just be spinning my wheels, my impulse is to go back to Muriel. Dalton stops me, rightly. I just told her she's spending some time in solitary. If I break that thirty minutes later, she knows I'm not serious.

I do have things I *can* do, obviously. Shore up patrols, with Yolanda and Anders gone. Spend time with my baby. Or sleep. Sleep is always good, when I've had so little. As anyone who knows me might guess, I pick the first two instead. I patrol with Gunnar for an hour while Dalton is with Rory, and then we switch off. Once I've fed Rory, we have a "take your daughter to work day" outing.

I pop my head into the Roc. It's quiet within. The café closed early, to allow a short opening of the pub part before curfew. There's an hour between the two, and I've slid in during that. Devon and Brian have packed and left, and Isabel and Phil are setting up for cocktail hour.

"No one under nineteen allowed," Isabel calls from the back room, on hearing Rory babbling.

I ignore her and take a seat at the bar. She comes out and steals my child, putting Rory on one hip as she arranges the bar.

"Everything okay?" she asks me.

I sigh. "A case that suddenly has too many clues and not enough connections. But I wanted to check in on another case—the one I abandoned. Your break-in."

She snorts. "Bored, are you? Or, I should say, frustrated and stalled and making work for yourself."

"Maybe. But I still should check in. Any clues? Anything turn up missing?"

"Not a damn thing. I'm sticking with my original theory. They broke in hoping to grab booze and left when they realized we keep it all in the locked stockroom. Now, Phil thinks they wanted something else."

"What?"

She shrugs. "Pencils? Envelopes?" She looks back at the stockroom. "Phil?"

He comes out with a box of liquor and sets it on the back counter.

"Casey's asking about the break-in," she says. "Tell her your theory."

He sighs. "It's not a theory. Simply an observation."

She makes a hurry-up gesture.

He starts unloading liquor bottles for the bar stock. "There were footprints leading to my desk at the back. I checked with Brian, and he said they'd definitely swept the shavings before they left, so the prints were new. They weren't distinguishable. If they were, I would have called you. Simply marks showing that someone went over there."

"To your desk?"

He nods.

I walk deeper into the bar. Phil's "desk" is in the back corner, where he works at a table, sometimes when the coffee shop is open and sometimes when the bar is. What he calls his desk isn't that table but the small dresser of supplies beside it. That explains Isabel's quip about the thief looking for stationery.

"What's in there?" I say.

Phil keeps unloading the box. "Nothing of value. A calculator. Steno pads. Pens."

"Any files?"

He looks up, clearly affronted. "Certainly not."

"I don't mean anything confidential. Regular stuff, like inventory logs or supply lists."

"None of that. I consider *everything* to be confidential. The desk contains supplies I need to work. Any paper in there is blank. The files are kept locked in a secure location that only I have access to."

"I don't even know where it is," Isabel says.

"For safety, no one does, although I have left the location

with Émilie, in case I should be incapacitated. And, before you ask, no one has been near those files."

"He's right about the intruder leaving prints leading there," Isabel says as she bounces Rory. "But I think they were hoping the cabinet contained Phil's secret booze stash."

Again, that affronted look. "I do not have a secret booze stash. Why would I even need one, if I have the key to the stockroom?"

She squeezes his arm. "Teasing you. No, I think they were just hoping we were stashing booze in there in general. Or credits. Something of value. Nothing's missing from there either." She hands me back the baby and continues setting up the bar. "Now tell me about your real case."

I sigh. "It's just complicated, and it seems to be connected to the mine."

"What a shock."

"I know, I know. Émilie is investigating a few things, and until then, I'm stuck. Can I run another thing by you? One that probably isn't even connected."

"The doctor is in. Let me fix you a mocktail, and you can tell Dr. Iz all your troubles."

CHAPTER TWENTY-NINE

I tell Isabel about Muriel. When I finish—both the story and my mocktail—she says, "Well, she's lying, obviously."

I adjust Rory, who has drifted off. "I know, but I feel like I got angry and overreacted. Her story checks out. If she's meeting someone, he's almost certainly a resident, and they're having a fling. Her stonewalling and outright lying pissed me off, so I punished her."

"You really think that's why you did it? Because that doesn't seem like you."

I sigh. "I keep thinking that this could be the guy we're looking for in the forest. The guy who staked out Lilith's cabin. But why would he be meeting Muriel?"

"You said you found boot prints."

I nod. "We also have prints for the person hanging around Lilith's."

"Do they match?"

"They don't *not* match. The ones at Muriel's spot are partials, lacking a full tread. What we have is very roughly a match, which I think is why I'm going so hard on this. But, honestly, the partial print also matches our men's standard boots. It's not exactly unique."

"If her guy is a resident, they broke curfew for sex, but there's no reason for that. We aren't telling residents they need to sleep in their own bed. The walls are soundproofed for a reason. They deliberately ignored curfew without cause. I can see Muriel refusing to name him and taking the fall for both of them, but she's telling you there *is* no man. Blatantly lying. I'd have locked her up, too."

"For that? Or for actual cause?"

She takes my glass. "You have cause. If she won't admit to it and give his name, then he could be your killer." She studies my expression. "You don't think that's a possibility."

"I'm not sure how it would be. He kills two people, stalks the wife of one victim . . . and he's also sneaking around with Muriel?"

"Two people? I thought we had *one* dead body."

"Long story. The second seems to be a miner who was poisoned."

"*What?* How does that connect to your hiker?"

I throw up my hands. "This is the problem. We have one poisoned miner. One strangled hiker who may have known the original prospector. And an unidentified man secretly meeting with a seemingly unconnected resident."

"I'm very confused."

I exhale. "Join the club. I think, for now, I need to leave Muriel under guard and not feel guilty about it."

"Agreed."

"Give her time to stew, while I pursue my murder cases."

"And care for a baby, nurse your injured dog, and keep a town under curfew."

"At least I have help. With all that."

She reaches to squeeze my hand. "You do. I know Phil and I haven't been pulling our weight with the patrols and curfew enforcement. We're not militia material. But feel free to drop Rory off anytime."

Phil appears from the stockroom. "I could watch Muriel."

I smile. "Better than watching a six-month-old?"

"Er . . ."

"Yes, please. If you could take over Muriel duty, that would help a lot. Thank you."

As I take Rory to Dalton, I am very aware that I'm on a deadline. One more day to solve this, or at least get Gretchen to the point where she'll cancel her pick up. I can't help feeling that she holds the key. If she didn't kill her husband, then she knows more than she's telling.

I need to question her about a connection between Blake and Mark.

I cannot question her about that until I know who the hell Mark was.

An interview fishing expedition is a last resort. I need facts.

I can't rush Émilie. I can't push Gretchen. While I told Isabel that I was dropping the Muriel thing, that's really the only avenue I can pursue tonight. Not talking to her but doing exactly what I plan to do with Gretchen. Get more ammunition.

Time to search Muriel's apartment.

Muriel's apartment is clean. Ridiculously clean. I consider myself a tidy person. Or at least I was before I had a baby, which made me accept a whole other standard, one with dirty dishes in the sink, toys on the floor, baby blankets everywhere . . . But even at my best, my place never looked this immaculate.

Those in the single residences share bathrooms and common areas. It's like a midrange dorm, where you have a room to yourself, but it's little more than sleeping space. A twin bed, a dresser, a small desk, and a chair.

We don't offer many luxuries in Haven's Rock—it's as all-inclusive as possible. But for people who spent their lives in a capitalist society, if all their needs are covered, they see their labor as unpaid. So we still have the credit system for true extras. In furnishings, some remove the desk and chair and upgrade to a double bed. A more popular option is giving up the desk and ordering a more comfortable chair from Kenny. That was Muriel's choice, which fits with her claim of being an introvert. She has a gorgeous rocker-recliner, complete with cushions, which would have been purchased separately.

I spend a few minutes wondering what she does in that chair, when there's no sign of any leisure activities. Then I find her book stash—three in her dresser drawer, all library borrows from the past week.

So her introvert story checks out. She saved up for the best chair possible and is an ardent reader. She also must spend time cleaning her apartment, given the state of it. Or, maybe, if she's in this small space most of the time, she needs it this tidy. I get that.

What I don't get are any clues. There are absolutely no signs of a woman having a fling. I hate to stereotype, but usually, when someone goes from single to not, there's evidence. I remember shortly after I arrived in Rockton, Dalton started shaving his beard, and apparently, it was his way of sprucing up for me. Shave. Wear your most flattering clothes. Use more mouthwash. Manicure, pedicure, new underwear . . .

There's nothing of that here. No sign that she used credits to buy new clothing. Her underwear all comes from home, and it's well-worn, as are her bras.

Could I have been wrong?

No, but clearly I am stereotyping. There must be an affair; she just isn't changing anything for it.

I'd asked Isabel whether she'd seen Muriel in the Roc more often, and the answer was that she rarely showed up there at all, and when she did, she was with women. That was definitely a man's voice we'd heard.

I pace around the tiny room, every surface clear and dusted, the bed made, not even a sweater lying out. I open the drawers of her dresser again. Every piece of clothing is folded, right down to her underwear. Her toiletries are in a bag, which I already checked. Hell, even the books in a drawer are stacked by size.

Nothing to see here.

That's what the room screams, what it had screamed from the moment I walked in and screamed louder when I opened the drawers. It's easy to hide things in a mess. My first reaction had been that this might be the easiest search job ever. I only had to look under the bed, and flip through stacks of clothing.

Nothing to see here.

Is that intentional? Or am I projecting, unable to imagine this degree of cleanliness. Surely people leave *something* out when they live alone.

Fine, yes, I'm projecting. This seems suspicious because I don't know anyone who keeps their space this perfect before hurrying off to work. But still, it nags at me, that little voice whispering "nothing to see."

I take a deep breath, and then I start with the bed. I'd already checked under the coverlet. Now I dismantle it and shake out everything. I crawl under the bed with my flashlight, and

I don't even need to cringe or hold my breath—there's not a dust speck, let alone a dust bunny. I check the frame. I lift the mattress and look there.

I look under the chair and squeeze the cushions, all the while feeling like I'm being ridiculous. It's a single woman having a fling, not a murder suspect. Am I angry because she stonewalled me? Lied to me? Is my frustration over this case bleeding into an overreaction?

It hits then. A memory. Last week, going into the greenhouse for mint leaves. I've been drinking a lot of herbal tea, and I've started getting fresh herbs.

"Mint," Muriel said, scanning the rows. "Oh, yes. Down on the left. Bottom row. Don't mind the mess. That's mine. I'm getting to it."

I'd had to pick my way through a row littered with fertilizer and half-filled pots. I'd presumed she was in the middle of a planting, but when I came back two days later, it wasn't much better. Not a mess, per se, but certainly not the pristine condition of this apartment.

This tidiness is intentional.

Nothing to see here.

I dive into a full-on search, and I finally find my clue taped to the bottom of a drawer.

A key.

I'm in the clinic. Dalton was spending a few minutes with Storm, and I find him there with my sister. April wants to keep our dog for another night, and Dalton was halfheartedly objecting. Halfheartedly because he knows she's right. We're too busy with this case to give our injured dog the attention she needs. The objection, I know, is guilt, which I share.

"She should stay," I say. "One more night. I want Storm home tomorrow night, and if we're called out in the night again, only one of us responds."

I sit on a stool and take Rory from Dalton. "I searched Muriel's apartment, which was even tidier than April's."

"Impossible." April sounds offended.

I point at the counter, where she's left a pen and a mug.

Her hackles almost visibly rise. "Those are items of convenience, left there temporarily."

"Right. Everyone does that. Unless you're expecting guests, you leave things out. A sweater. A water glass. A pen. There was none of that, which I found suspicious."

April's snort clearly states that this is a "me" problem.

I continue, "So I searched and found this." I set the key on the counter as I bounce Rory on my knee. "I stopped by the town hall and opened the key locker. It doesn't match any in there. Staff are allowed to bring lockboxes, but residents aren't. This key's brand-new." I turn the shiny key over. "I know Mathias and Isabel have locked boxes for case files, Sebastian has them for his medication, April has them here for medication. Phil mentioned having one for his records. I ran this by all of them, and I know it's not for the med cabinet here."

"It is not," she says.

"So while it's possible Muriel stole the key to a staff member's personal lockbox, I don't think that's the answer. It's too new, and they'd have reported it missing. It does look like one for a box, though, or a cabinet."

"Small." April picks it up and turns it over. "Too small for a cabinet."

"So likely a locked box, which Muriel is not supposed to have. We must have missed it in her belongings."

Dalton grunts. It's always awkward searching a new resident's luggage. We have to, of course, to look for weapons or drugs, but if we'd found a box of mementos, we might not have looked closely enough to realize it had a lock.

"Whatever this opens, it's not in her apartment," I say. "I hate to suggest we head back to her clearing. We will, obviously, if we need to—tomorrow, in daylight—but I'm not convinced it's there."

"Buried if it is," Dalton says. "There was nothing lying around."

"On the topic of buried treasure, there is a place I consider more likely. I just wanted to be sure you didn't recognize the key, Eric, before I go digging much closer to home."

"The greenhouse," he says.

CHAPTER THIRTY

My mystery-loving sister approaches the puzzle logically. Presumably, Muriel needed to access the box, so it couldn't be under delicate plants. It *could* be under something easily pulled up and replaced. Or something with a high turnover and low value, which she could dig in without Arturo noticing or caring. While there are plenty of pots awaiting new plants, that was too risky—Arturo could easily grab the wrong one and plant something in it.

We start by narrowing our hunt to pots where the soil seems disturbed. The one where we find it appears to be the opposite—the soil is overly packed . . . which is what tips Dalton off.

The box we recover is small, maybe only three inches square. When Dalton hands it to me, it rattles enough to have Rory perking up in April's arms, where she'd been drifting to sleep.

"Sounds like money," Dalton says. "She's hiding a box full of dollar coins."

"Pffft. *Two*-dollar coins at least," I say, hefting it.

"Jewelry," April says.

"Coins," Dalton says. "Maybe pennies, before they went out of circulation. What are they worth now, one and a quarter cents each?"

I shake my head and open the box to reveal . . .

Dalton puts out his hand to April. "Pay up."

"I never laid a bet."

I kiss his cheek. "There. Your prize."

"What would I have gotten?" April asks.

"Acknowledgment that you were right, which is all you really need."

I shake the box's contents onto my hand. They are indeed coins. Not loonies or toonies. Not modern Canadian or American coins of any sort. I'm . . . not sure what they are. The dates make them very old, but the coins look new, and they're loose in the box, like spare change.

"So Muriel's secret treasure was a bunch of old coins?" Dalton says.

"Why do I feel like I'm in one of those escape rooms?" I mutter. "Here's a random clue—now figure out how it applies to the mystery."

"You need to decipher the language on the coins," April says. "And then arrange the numbers in the right order to open a combination lock located in another planter."

I snort. "Probably. And inside that will be a playing card that leads to the next clue." I hold out the coins. "Are these valuable? Or just mementos? Do we have any residents who might know? I really hate to add more work to Émilie's list."

"Kenny used to collect coins," April says. "It was a hobby when he was young. He might have some idea what we are looking at."

★ ★ ★

Kenny lifts one coin and stares at it. "This . . . this . . ." He looks at me. "You found these just tossed into a box? Where they could get scratched?" From his expression, you'd think we'd left Rory in the woods by herself.

We're just outside town. Kenny had been on patrol, and Dalton and I had waited along the path until he appeared with Brian. We ended their patrol early, so Brian could go, leaving us alone to explain things to Kenny.

"I take it that's a rare coin?" I say.

"It's a buffalo nickel. I wouldn't say it's extremely rare, but it's worth about five grand. The others are all foreign coins, and I don't recognize most, but I'd guess you're looking at anywhere from thirty to forty grand here."

I whistle. "Wow. Okay. That's . . . a lot. Thank you. Eric and I will finish up your patrol shift. My sister's at the clinic with Rory, but we'll come by right after and take her. Rory won't be spending the night with April."

"Uh . . . okay."

I shrug. "Just in case you were heading over there."

Kenny rocks back on his heels as Dalton shakes his head. "If that's a very clumsy way of asking me something, Casey, I'd rather you didn't."

"It wasn't. I just wanted to be clear that we are aware of a change in the situation and will accommodate it without saying anything to April."

A slow exhale. "Okay. Just . . . give your sister time. She needs that."

"I understand."

He catches my gaze. "And please don't take it personally, even if I know it stings."

Now I'm the one exhaling. "I know. She needs to tell me in her own time. I won't push, and I won't hint. That's why I was telling you that we'll be picking up Rory, and if we need someone to watch her at night, Dana's on call."

"If you need April, she's there. Just give her a minute to get to the door. And don't be offended if she doesn't invite you in."

I laugh softly. "Got it." I look at him. "I'm happy for you. Both of you."

"For what?" His eyes widen. "I have no idea what you're talking about."

I squeeze his arm, and then we say our goodbyes.

I sleep well that night. I shouldn't, with a case deadline looming and a headful of dangling threads. But a lack of sleep the night before must help, because I go to bed after Rory's last feeding, and don't wake until after seven, Dalton having risen for her first meal.

"I'm interviewing Muriel again this morning," I say as we eat breakfast, Rory on my lap. "I don't have nearly enough ammunition but . . ." I shrug. "I can only hope she's freaked out enough about the solitary confinement to talk, and even then, it'll just be wrapping up a thread almost certainly unrelated to my case."

"And the coins?" Dalton says as he gives Rory a piece of toast to gnaw on.

"From her story, we know she's supposedly broke. If she didn't have them insured, she could have hidden them when declaring bankruptcy."

Dalton nods. "It's her nest egg. She brought them and hid them, in case we searched her apartment. Helluva lot of money for coins, though."

"Maybe? It depends on how well-off she was before her

boyfriend fleeced her. They could also have been an inheritance. No offense to Kenny, but most coin collectors are older relatives." I sip my tea. "I'll get that done. Then—"

A buzz tells me we have a message on our sat phone. I check it and set down my mug. "And that's Émilie. She wants to talk to us as soon as we're up."

"Take it in the living room. I'll top up your tea and look after Rory."

"Thank you."

"I've found Mark the miner," Émilie says. "Mark wasn't his real name, but the other data he provided was correct. Widowed, remarried a few years ago, mines in the Yukon during his summers. Do you want his real name?"

"Only if I need to take it to Gretchen. Am I going to need to do that?"

"I believe so. Blake knew him. So did Gretchen. They're online friends. Or they were when Mark's first wife was alive. You mentioned that she'd join him on his mining expeditions."

"Yes. His first wife always came along. That's what he told us."

"It seems the women both attended UBC. Sorority sisters, in fact. When Mark and his wife would come up north, they'd spend a day or two in Whitehorse with their dear friends, Gretchen and Blake Landry."

"Damn. That is some fine detective work. Hats off to your investigator."

"The only hard part was identifying Mark. Once we had that, the rest was a simple matter of finding his Facebook profile. He's friends with both Blake and Gretchen. That could just mean online friends, but a bit of digging brought up pictures with the four of them, all tagged, and posts from both Gretchen and Mark's wife about their get-togethers."

"So it was the first wife they were friendly with. And the second?"

"Not so friendly, if I read between the lines. Neither Blake nor Gretchen was Facebook friends with the second wife, and there's only one post from a couple of years ago, where Mark evidently went out for dinner with Blake and Gretchen on his way north."

"So the bond was mostly between the women. Mark's first wife dies, and his second doesn't take her place in the friendship. But Blake and Gretchen still knew Mark."

"They did."

"Not much of a chance they coincidentally ran into trouble near his old mining spot, is there?"

Another low laugh. "There is not."

"Thank you." I relax into my chair. "That is the solid connection I needed. Whatever happened with Blake, it must be linked to the mining camp, considering it was originally owned by his old friend. And Blake himself works in a field related to mining. Is there anything more? Please tell me Blake and Gretchen worked on former claims alongside Mark and his first wife."

"They did."

I bolt upright. "What?"

"Sorry, I should qualify that. Before Mark's first wife died, Blake and Gretchen went hiking up around where Mark and his wife were mining. They joked about not being able to reveal their whereabouts."

"Because Mark wouldn't appreciate that when he had a nearby claim."

"Correct. They did, however, try their hand at panning.

They mentioned that later, after Mark and his wife would have returned home. It wasn't the same claim site, so it's not the solid connection you might hope for, but it's something."

I move onto the floor, where Dalton listens, lying on his back as Rory crawls over him. "So they knew Mark, and now they're in the area where he and his second wife both vanished. Mining might not be our answer. They could be searching for clues about their friend's disappearance."

Silence.

"Or not?" I say. "How did that play out? Obviously no one came searching here, and you never saw anything about a missing prospector and his wife."

"Mark and his wife died in a single-vehicle accident. Back at home, they crashed along a country road."

"I . . . What?"

"That's the story, according to the obituary I dug up."

"I . . ." I move back onto the chair, so I can better concentrate on the call. "Well, you obviously didn't do that, since you just identified Mark."

"Correct. I'd have told you if I quietly handled it. At the time, we decided it was best if I didn't dig into Mark's true identity, for fear of opening a suspicious trail. Instead, I monitored for any sign of a missing woman or a prospector who didn't reappear after the season ended. When that didn't come, I presumed those in charge of the mining operation handled it. They knew he was dead, and they essentially took over his claim—presumably without completing their transaction and paying his estate."

"Do you still think the mining company did this? Covered up his death?"

"Yes, but . . ."

When she trails off, I wait. Then I say, "Émilie?"

"That's the only logical explanation. The extent of the cover-up, though, is more elaborate than I would have expected. As you know, from being on the board in Rockton, I saw firsthand how such things were handled. I was prepared to make sure Mark and his wife's disappearance wasn't connected to your region. I had ideas and the contacts to pull it off."

"And this was more elaborate?"

"Faking an accident means buying off a lot of people, especially when you don't have bodies. That makes me wonder what sort of mining operation we're dealing with. How deep are their pockets? How much gold—or other valuable resources—are they expecting to be worth that level of cover-up? Granted, Mark's death meant they didn't need to pay him, but still . . ."

"We've always suspected the new camp isn't a simple mining operation."

"Yes, and then my investigator located your dead miner."

I pause, and it takes a moment for my brain to segue.

"The man we found buried," I say.

"Your description of the runelike tattoo helped immensely. It's specific to one maximum-security American prison. It signifies membership in an internal gang. Once we had that, we easily identified him."

"Good. I'm not sure how it ties into all this, but any added information on the mining operation helps. Did you track down the other guy? The one who kidnapped Max last year?"

"I did."

"Former prisoner?"

Again, she goes quiet.

"Not an ex-con?"

"That . . . would depend on your definition. If you mean someone who served his time and was released, then no. If you mean someone who was incarcerated before his death, then yes."

I frown at Dalton, who has sat up, leaving Rory chomping on a teething ring.

"Émilie?" he says. "I'm going to ask you to be a lot less enigmatic. It sounds as if you're saying the guy who took Max was still a convict at the time of his death."

"Yes."

I say, "An escaped convict? A paroled one?"

"No."

Dalton growls. "Émilie. This really isn't the time for puzzles."

"I'm not trying to give you one. I'm still wrapping my head around what my investigator has told me, because apparently, it applies to both your dead miners—Max's captor and this man you found buried."

"They were *both* convicts?" I say. "Not on parole. Not escaped."

"Yes. At the time of their deaths, both men were incarcerated."

I rub my temples. "So the men who died here are not who they seemed to be? They somehow match the identities of men currently in prison? Or . . ." My head slowly rises. "Are you telling me that the mining operation is a prison camp?"

"Apparently, yes."

CHAPTER THIRTY-ONE

"That's not possible," I say after I take a moment to digest Émilie's words. "No Canadian correction facility would be located— But it's *not* Canadian. You said the tattoo was from an American prison."

"Yes, though that's not the same prison that sent the man here. He was released, reoffended and put into a privately run institution—also American."

I shake my head. "I know the US has some private prisons, but they're not running camps in the Yukon. That isn't how the system works."

"You mean that's not how the system is *supposed* to work. I won't pretend that I understand what's going on here, Casey. My investigator hit a dead end very quickly, with signs that they should stop digging, for their own safety. No one is claiming that a gold-mining operation in Canada's Yukon is a *legitimate* American prison camp. But it also might explain how Mark and his wife's deaths were so easily covered up."

"In Canada?"

"Mark was from Vancouver, until he married an American. The accident occurred there."

I squeeze my eyes shut.

"Casey?" Émilie says gently. "You need to set aside the law-enforcement side of your brain that says this isn't possible. Pretend it is possible."

"I know." I take a deep breath. "Imagine a scenario where American prisoners could, somehow, be brought to Canada to work on a mine. We know the operation *is* American. That part fits. But why? What is the point? Cheap labor?"

"Maybe, if they found something valuable enough."

"Bringing prisoners, across the border, into a prison camp . . . How much would that cost? How many palms would need to be greased? How can cheap labor possibly justify that?"

"Once they're in Alaska, getting them here is easy enough. It's a vast wilderness. No need to officially cross a border. With prisoners, the labor is practically free. And didn't you say that your Mr. Rogers was very upset at the thought that a community of regular citizens lived nearby? He expected isolation. He warned you that some of their employees could be 'rough men.'"

"If this is what the camp seems to be, then that's what it is, and whatever questions I have remaining, I need to work through."

"It might explain one thing," Dalton says.

I glance over at him.

He shrugs. "Mark's former friend comes sniffing around, maybe looking for answers to a death that doesn't quite fit. What happens when he gets too close?"

"They kill him," I murmur. "And then realize he wasn't alone, and they have one more person to silence."

★ ★ ★

We're on our way to Lilith's cabin. I've barely said a word, my brain spinning. Finally, I look over at Dalton.

"That explanation works for you?" I say. "A prison work camp?"

"I don't know enough about gold and whatever else they might be looking for. I do know how much trouble everyone went through with Rockton, and those guys sure as hell would do all this, for the kind of money they pulled in. But that's different."

"They've gone through so much trouble. I can't imagine it'd be worth it." I keep walking. "I suppose hiring prisoners would help with the privacy aspect. Their employees aren't in a position to ask too many questions, and definitely aren't in a position to sell their secrets. But still . . ."

Dalton doesn't answer. He only grunts, which tells me he agrees.

"If it's not about gold, then what?" I say.

And he has no answer for that either.

At Lilith's cabin, we give Anders and Yolanda a much-deserved break. We've discussed having Dalton stay behind, while one of them returns with me, but they're prepared to finish this, and I appreciate that.

They head out for a walk, while Dalton settles in, making coffee. I begin the interview on an equally comfortable note. That's much easier now. Gretchen is almost certainly an innocent victim and deserves my sympathy. I ask how she's doing and promise we've made arrangements to fly her out in the morning, which is technically true. She's obviously irritated at being confined to this cottage, but I stress that we're going to make sure she's picked up safely, guarding her the whole way. That subtly reminds her that this is protective custody, and she relaxes.

"So," I say as I settle in with my half cup of coffee. "I only have a few more questions, I hope. We're making progress. Can you start by telling me about Matthew Gordon?"

Her head shoots up. That's the name of their miner friend, the one we knew as Mark. At her startle, grim satisfaction swirls in me. I've caught her off guard, as I expected. Yet her expression isn't furtive or worried. It isn't wary or even confused. There's a flash of surprise . . . and then she smiles.

"You knew Matt?" she asks.

I make a noise she can take as assent.

"I never even considered that. I should have. We knew he was mining up here." Her smile falters. "Oh. You . . . Do you know what happened to him?"

I keep my expression impassive and only say, "No." Then I wait for her to ask what I *do* know.

"He died in a car accident," she says softly. "Him and his wife. Driving home from up here actually."

"I'm sorry," I say. "No, I didn't hear that."

She lifts one shoulder. "It barely made the news even in their township. Single-car accident. We heard about it through a mutual friend."

"Oh?" I frown. "We were under the impression you two and Matt were close."

Her gaze shifts, uncomfortable. "I knew Matt's first wife. From university. We were the friends. Matt could be . . ." She trails off with a shrug. "Sometimes you get lucky, and your friend marries a great guy who just fits in, you know? You like him. Your husband likes him."

She flushes, her discomfort growing. "We didn't *dis*like Matt. But once Helen was gone, there wasn't any reason to keep in touch."

"I thought he was in a similar field to your husband? Both profs. Both interested in mining."

"Matt was the prospector. Blake's only interest is—" She swallows, grief flashing. "His only interest *was* academic. Sometimes, I think that's why Matt pursued the friendship, though. He mined in the Yukon. We were locals, and my husband had connections, through his job."

"When was the last time you spoke to Matt?"

"A few years ago." A grimace. "He needed something from Blake, as usual. Information about this area, actually. He'd been here the year before, scouting." She looks up sharply. "Remember I told you someone raved about this region? The natural beauty? That was Matt."

"Do you know whether he found anything up here?"

Confusion, and then a slow smile. "Oh, is that why you're asking? Got a bit of gold fever yourself?" She shrugs. "He never mentioned finding anything, but he wouldn't even if he did. He played fast and loose with the claim laws, too, so if he found anything, I doubt he claimed it officially. If you were hoping for tips, I don't have any."

I shake my head. "We're more worried about someone following up on his claim. We prefer to keep this area quiet."

"If he filed a claim, I think it would have been considered part of his estate. I don't know who that would have gone to. They didn't have kids. His parents? Siblings?" She shrugs. "If you're concerned about more people passing through, just check for a claim, but like I said, I doubt he made one, and he certainly wouldn't have left notes. I'd say you're safe."

"Thank you. We knew he'd been in the area a few years ago,

and the person running our background searches came up with a connection between you and him, which was concerning."

A wry twist of her lips. "Small world, huh? Nope, it isn't a coincidence. Just . . ." Her eyes glisten with tears, and she looks away. "When Blake wanted to come here, I resisted. I said it was too late in the season. I gave lots of excuses, some of them valid. But really, it just gave me a bad feeling, and I knew that was associated with Matt. I . . ." She swallows. "Never trusted him, and I knew that was a silly reason not to come here. It wasn't as if we'd run into him." A humorless laugh. "Wasn't as if he'd lured us here for some nefarious purpose. But it feels like that, because we came and . . ."

She turns fully away now, crying softly. I pass her a tissue and refill her coffee.

When she recovers, I ask gently, "I hate to keep poking, but we're really trying to figure this out, Gretchen. I knew Blake was the one who wanted to come. You say it was because Matt gushed about it. Is there any chance Blake was looking for Matt's claim?"

A short laugh. "Definitely not. He liked Matt more than I did, but he always said Matt was wasting his time out here. All this natural beauty, and Matt kept his head down, digging for gold when the real treasure was all around him."

When I go quiet, she stiffens. "You don't believe me. You think my husband came here to find gold, and that the hike was an excuse. It's the end of the season. Winter is right around the corner. We have no mining equipment. Laying a claim requires work, and we'd have no time to do that before weather forced us out. If we planned to just find it this year and mine it illegally next year, our very presence here could jeopardize a future claim. An illegal claim would cost Blake his job."

"Someone killed your husband," I say. "It wasn't us. But if

Matt found gold, that would explain how someone else could be here. Someone who might not appreciate Blake poking around."

"You think a prospector killed him?" She leans back. "God, that would be . . ." She shakes her head and makes a noise that is half laugh, half sob. "The cruelest of ironies. We come to see the landscape Matt raved about . . . and someone trying to find his claim kills my husband."

She meets my gaze. "Blake wasn't 'poking around.' He had no interest in prospecting. He never even jokingly mentioned finding Matt's claim."

"When he fell," I press, "he was trying to get a better look around."

"Because we were lost!" Her voice rises in exasperation. "He wasn't looking for . . ."

She trails off, and I try not to react. I try not to glance at Dalton, quietly sitting behind her.

"He saw something," she murmurs. "Or he thought he did."

"What?" I ask.

"A person. Out in the forest. That's actually why he fell. He was looking for landmarks, something to tell us which way to go, when he spotted movement. He figured it was a bear, but then the figure looked up, as if seeing him. Blake realized it was a person, and that startled him enough that he stumbled. Later, after we met you, he grumble-joked that you owed him those bandages, since you or your husband were probably responsible for him falling. Inadvertently, of course."

"Do you remember where he was when he fell?"

She nods. Dalton hands me a map of the region, and we figure out where they'd been.

"Do you know where he spotted the figure?" I ask.

"Roughly, yes." She looks at the map and points. "Southwest.

He was facing this way. He said the person looked to be a few hundred feet from the bottom. So maybe . . ." Her chin jerks up. "Oh. Is this . . . ?" She looks at me. "Remember I told you I heard voices in a clearing? Where you found my footprints? That's about where Blake would have seen someone. Right around there."

She leans forward. "Blake saw someone in the same area where I later heard voices. Unless that was you guys, there's definitely someone else out there."

I look at the map, and then look at Dalton, who gives a grim nod. She's right—where Blake saw a figure is the same general area as the clearing where we found a dead man. A convict miner who could have been buried the day Blake saw someone in the forest.

Blake saw whoever buried that miner.

And they saw him.

CHAPTER THIRTY-TWO

We manage to convince Gretchen to delay her pick up, using our sat phone. That's a start, but we aren't out of the woods yet. She isn't ready to cancel altogether and let us take her home . . . with Émilie making sure she doesn't expose Haven's Rock.

We've headed back to town, quietly talking on the way.

Was Blake killed for what he saw? From that distance, he wouldn't have been able to identify anyone. They could have just not wanted to take chances. Eliminate all witnesses. After all, Blake and Gretchen *had* lingered in the area afterward.

But circle back to *who* they were burying. A convict laboring in a mining camp. A guy who didn't die of natural causes, who hadn't perished in an accident. He'd been poisoned.

I hate to think a prison camp would murder one of their charges, but they did execute one of their guards in front of us. They may also—as we speculated at the time—have killed the man who kidnapped Max. It's not a huge leap to killing a miner, maybe one who was causing trouble.

But would they kill Blake—and try to kill Gretchen—for potentially witnessing the burial?

Although it's not *im*possible, I think there's more to it. We know they're security paranoid. Now we know why. What if they spotted Blake on that rock, surveying the land around their secret and highly illegal mining camp?

They track him and notice he's with a woman, and they appear to be outsiders, not residents of our settlement. The next morning, still watching Blake and Gretchen, they follow Blake to the creek. Maybe he sees them. Maybe they confront him. Something is said that makes them decide he's come for them, for their prison camp or their mining operation.

Wrong place, wrong time.

Is that the answer here? As Gretchen said, just the cruelest bad luck? I'm starting to think it is.

Blake and Gretchen weren't here by accident, but they *were* what they claimed to be. Hikers . . . who happened to be in the area because they knew the prospector who started all of this.

I know there are other answers, but everything fits, and Gretchen's reactions had seemed genuine. They weren't even here because they thought Mark/Matt's death seemed suspicious. They literally only came because he said it was a beautiful area.

If all that is true, then it seems someone from the mining camp must have killed Blake. There's no third party running around murdering hikers. We never really thought that was the answer. We just needed our link, and we thought we had it in Blake and Gretchen's connection to Mark, but the reality is that Blake probably died because he stepped onto the side of a mountain. He was spotted, and that sealed his fate.

So what do we do next? We know what we *want* to do, obviously.

"Confront the bastards," Dalton says as we near town. "Tell them we know what they are, and we know they poisoned their own employee. They could argue about Blake, insist they didn't do it, but that doesn't matter. We have enough."

"Enough to send them packing?" I say. "Or enough to have them decide we need to be handled the same way they handled Blake?"

Dalton mutters under his breath.

"That's the problem, isn't it," I say. "This only confirms how dangerous they are. We can't just confront them and tell them to leave." I take his hand and squeeze it. "But it's a start. We send Gretchen home and then we have a long talk with Émilie."

Dalton opens his mouth, but we're on the outskirts of town, and it's still daytime, with people milling about.

"We'll get Rory and keep talking," I murmur.

"Casey," a voice says behind us.

We turn as Phil strides from the direction of the town hall. "May I speak to you?"

Dalton says, "I'll grab Rory and check on Storm. Meet you at the clinic."

I agree, and he leaves.

"May we speak in private?" Phil says, nodding toward the town hall.

I follow him in and shut the door. He locks it, making me raise my brows, but he only heads to his desk and begins tidying papers.

"I have something to confess," he says.

"You're *not* leaving Haven's Rock? Yes, we know."

He only gives a faint eye roll and pops the cap onto a pen. "It's about the break-in. Something I failed to mention because I didn't want to cause friction with Isabel."

I settle into a chair. "Is something missing? Something you don't want her to know you had?"

He frowns, as if he can't fathom what such a thing might

be. "Of course not. The problem . . ." He sighs. "Isabel and I disagree about locking our cabin door. I am uncomfortable leaving it unsecured. She teases me about being a city boy who hasn't adjusted to small-town life. About a week ago, I thought someone had entered our home. I didn't mention it to Isabel because we'd only recently had another point of friction about the door—I locked it, and she didn't take the key, so she was locked out."

"All right . . ."

He stacks papers. "If I said I believe someone entered our home, she might think I was . . ." He shrugs.

"Lying to bolster your argument? I can't imagine that."

"Perhaps, but since nothing was missing and I wasn't sure someone *had* entered, I decided not to mention it. I forgot it until yesterday, when I said I believe the intruder at the Roc tried to access my desk. Afterwards, I remember the potential break-in at our home. The reason I believe someone entered there was that several things on my desk were out of place."

"Your desk at home? How many desks do you need?"

"I don't know, Casey. How many pairs of hiking boots do *you* need?" He looks pointedly down at my latest pair. "You like having a choice of footwear. I like having a workstation in each place where I work."

"Okay, okay. So you think someone entered your home and checked your desk there. Then they did the same at the Roc."

"I believe it is a possibility. Now, while I was here working, I checked for signs that anyone tampered with *this* desk or filing cabinet, but given that it's a communal workspace and not everyone keeps it tidy, it's impossible to tell."

There's clear condemnation in his voice, but I ignore it. His idea of a messy workstation means a crooked stack of papers and one uncapped pen. Instead, I say, "Also, the town hall is one of the few buildings we do lock. Even when it's open, anyone can see you enter. Unlike the Roc, where there's a back door."

"That was my thought as well."

"Someone checked two of your desks. Looking for more than a stapler. You mentioned your files."

"Yes, as I said, I keep them secured and hidden. There is no sign that anyone has tampered with that storage unit. I wouldn't expect that anyway, as only you and Isabel know I keep them in a separate place and neither of you knows where."

I lean back in my chair. "My first thought would be that they're looking for resident files, but we're very clear we don't keep those on-site."

"And if they suspected that was a lie, they'd presume you and Eric have them. I am very clear about the scope of my position."

"You aren't the people person. You're the thing person. Inventory, schedules, supplies. Everything about the town infrastructure and operation, excluding the residents. So what would someone want with that?"

He hesitates.

I peer at him. "Phil?"

"I don't know," he says a little too quickly.

"But you have a suspicion."

"Let me continue to think and dig. Even if I'm right, it's not an immediate threat."

"Do I get a hint?"

He shakes his head. "You have murders to investigate. I only wanted to mention it, in case you see a connection between the murders and the break-ins, though I cannot imagine what it would be."

★ ★ ★

I don't push Phil. There's no point. He's a corporate guy, and this is corporate ass-covering. He realized he may have neglected to tell me about a break-in, so he remedied that.

Why would someone want town-manager files? Even though I consciously dismiss it for now, it nags at the back of my subconscious as I head off to the next bit of business, partly because this is yet another item on my to-do list that seems unconnected to the much bigger issues.

Earlier, I'd planned to speak to Muriel, before I was derailed by Émilie's new information. Now it's time to get her to give me the name of who she's been seeing. And while I chafe at that waste of effort, there's also a possibility it might lead to something useful. And maybe that's why, when I settle into that interview, I push a specific theory harder than I should.

"Fine," she says, sitting primly on the edge of her bed. "I've been meeting someone. No, I won't tell you who it is. Whatever the punishment is for breaking curfew, I accept it for both of us. Double the punishment to maintain his privacy."

"Is it Eric you're meeting?"

Her head shoots up. "What?"

"Maybe Phil?"

"Of course not." She bristles. "You're mocking me, and I do not appreciate it, Detective."

"How am I mocking you?"

Her glare intensifies. "By mentioning two men who are very happily in relationships. Men who are younger than me, attractive, and taken. Out of my reach."

"No, I'm only referencing the first part of that equation—the two men who are taken. Well, so are Devon and Brian, but if you said it was one of them, I might be even more certain you were lying. My point, Muriel, is that the only reason you'd protect your lover's identity is if he were off the market. That takes it down to a very small number of men."

Her mouth hardens. "My lover is in a relationship. Just not with anyone in town. Back home."

"Cut the shit, Muriel. I know your lover isn't from Haven's Rock. I have evidence of that."

Here's where I bluff. Where I push a theory I have zero evidence for because it suits my own needs. If her lover isn't from Haven's Rock, that means he's from the mining camp, and I would *love* to have that extra bit of leverage with Rogers.

Hey, so, one of your guys has been regularly trespassing to visit one of our residents.

"Not from town?" Muriel gives a high, nervous laugh. "Where else would he be from? There's no one else out there. You really are reaching, Detective. Maybe you should take some time off. I can't imagine how tough it is, working out here with a new baby, hormones still running wild."

I bite back a response. She's panicking and swinging wildly.

"There actually is another settlement," I say. "A distant one. That's where your lover is from, and I have proof. I just need you to admit it so we can move on."

She squirms. She denies. I stand firm until finally, she blurts, "Yes, okay? Yes. He's from another settlement. I wasn't lying about needing time to myself, though. That's how we met. I would go for walks, and one day, I bumped into him. Scared me half to death, but it was obvious he wasn't some recluse living in the forest. He was well-dressed—in expensive outdoor clothing—and he had perfect manners. He said he lost track of time and walked too far from his camp. We got talking and then . . ." She shrugs. "One thing led to another."

"You said he was well-dressed, well-mannered . . . Can I get a little more?"

She hesitates and glances down, murmuring, "I don't want to get him into any trouble."

"You aren't. I just need to confirm he really is from that settlement."

She frowns. "Where else would he be from?"

"Well, we run a town for people in hiding, where we promise privacy. In some cases, like yours, they're in hiding because people are after them. People who want to hurt them."

"Oh!" Her eyes widen. "No, he's definitely from the other place. He has no idea what our town is. He asked. He was very curious but—" She stops short and swallows. "You don't think . . . Oh God. What if . . . ?" She squeezes her eyes shut. "What have I done?"

"Muriel," I say, keeping my voice soft even as a bell clangs in my skull. "Did he ask you to find information on Haven's Rock?"

Her head whips up. "Wh-what?" The terror on her face tells me everything I need to know.

"He asked you to get information, right? On the town?"

"N-not about the residents. I wouldn't do that. He just . . . He was very curious about how our town runs, because he runs the other one, and they're having trouble. He wanted to know how we get supplies and so on. It—it seemed harmless enough."

"And how did you attempt to obtain that information?"

She glances away again. "I, uh, went to talk to Phil. I thought maybe I'd just, you know, express an interest in the town's operation. I figured he'd be at the Roc, so I went inside. He wasn't there."

"Did you look for that information?" I catch her gaze. "Answer very carefully, remembering that I would not be pressing if I didn't have proof. Also remember that you're already on thin ice, having outright lied to me—yesterday and today—and implied today that my problem is hormonal."

She has the grace to color at that. "I—I didn't mean—"

"Where did you look for the information your friend asked you to get?"

"In Phil's desk," she blurts. "Quickly. I felt horrible afterward, and I didn't touch anything. But I swear, my—uh—friend only asked about town operations. Nothing on residents."

I won't push her to confess that she also went into Phil and Isabel's house. I have enough here. "Now are you going to describe your friend?"

She does . . . and it's exactly who I expect.

CHAPTER THIRTY-THREE

"Mr. Rogers is romancing Muriel?" Émilie says over the sat phone as Dalton settles in beside me with Rory and a bottle.

"Seems so," I say.

"Romancing her to get information on Haven's Rock."

"Mmm, yeah. She's very aware of the déjà vu there. She came here after she was screwed over by a boyfriend, and now she's been screwed over by her new boyfriend. She's humiliated, and I don't know what we're going to do with her, but she's definitely going to need some therapy."

"No doubt," Émilie murmurs. "So Mr. Rogers seduced her to gather intel on the town."

"I think he was trying to figure out what Haven's Rock is. Muriel swears she never told him. She says he didn't try too hard to figure it out. He only seemed interested in how we run, allegedly so he can apply it to his own settlement."

"Bullshit," Dalton mutters.

"Oh, I know," I say. "He knew better than to just ask her what we're doing here. He was trying to find out under the guise of asking for harmless operational data. Émilie? Does this give us leverage?"

I swear I hear the smile in her voice. "I believe it does."

I thought having one of the mining camp guards romancing Muriel would be valuable, but having it be the boss man himself? Priceless.

Rogers not only trespassed. He actively tried to uncover our secrets.

Sure, we did the same, but it's going to be a lot harder for him to cry foul when he was doing it, too, using much more invasive methods.

What this gives us is *personal* leverage—against Rogers himself. Will it be possible to cull him from the herd? Speak to him separately without overtly threatening his employer?

That's our plan. After getting the new information, Émilie's investigator has dug deeper and provided additional ammunition. What we want to do now is negotiate. She's instructed us on how to make it clear that we are protected by powerful forces. Okay, those forces are Émilie herself, but with her money and clout, it's not an idle threat. Rogers needs to know that killing us wouldn't eliminate his problem, any more than killing him would eliminate the danger of the mining operation.

Émilie wants Gretchen brought into Haven's Rock, and we agree. Not into the town itself, but to the hangar, where she can await a new pick up. If Gretchen agrees, she'll be flown to Émilie, who will debrief her, which I presume means a combination of subtle bribes and subtler pressure to convince her to go along with the story Émilie concocts.

The reason we want Gretchen here isn't just for her own good. It's for Anders and Yolanda. We need them here if things go south. We don't want them *isolated* if things go south.

We summon them back by sat phone and prepare sleeping quarters at the hangar. Once they've arrived safely, we head off to visit our friendly neighbor.

Visiting Mr. Rogers isn't as easy as knocking on his door. Technically, we shouldn't know where that door is. We're supposed to leave a message at a designated spot and wait for a response, but we're sure as hell not doing that.

It's late afternoon, which means his work crews should still be out. We skirt around the edge of the camp's turf until we hear voices. Then we call out and tell the guard that we have urgent business with their boss.

We wait, staying just off their territory. There's always the chance—a good one—that Rogers will blow us off, but relations have been smooth lately, and I suspect he won't want to upset that by being an ass.

Twenty minutes later, someone appears on the path. It isn't Rogers, though. It's the Brit—the man we aren't supposed to know about.

"Hello," he says, extending a hand. "Paul Rutherford. I work with . . ." His lips twitch. "Mr. Rogers, you call him?" He rolls his brown eyes. "My colleague does love his cloak-and-dagger. I'll grant him anonymity, though, and we'll keep referring to him by that moniker."

"I . . ." I try to look confused. "I'm sorry. We haven't met you."

The man—Rutherford—makes a face. "Corporate sent me.

I'm one of those types—flown in to check out their operations. Rogers is still here. Or at least he's supposed to be." Irritation flutters over his face, quickly masked. "It seems he has stepped out. I was told this meeting was urgent, so I came in his place."

"Ah," I say. "Okay. Well, no offense, but it really is something we'd like to discuss with him. It's not immediately urgent. Just cause for concern on a matter we've already been discussing with him."

"The hikers?" He frowns. "Are they still around? Rogers told me about that."

"It's related. Do you know when he'll be back?"

That annoyance again, though it doesn't seem directed at us. "I wish I knew. He's been MIA a few times since I arrived, though it's usually early in the morning." He sighs. "I shouldn't get snippy. I know it isn't easy, having someone from head office visiting and peering over your shoulder, checking that all the i's are dotted and t's are crossed."

I glance at Dalton, who only shrugs. Then I say to Rutherford, "Can we make an appointment to see him?" I check my watch. "Maybe seven tonight? Here?"

"Certainly. I will convey the message. In the meantime, it was lovely to meet you both."

Dalton and I don't talk after we leave Rutherford. We walk in silence until I murmur, "I'd like to check out that clearing again. Where the miner was buried."

Dalton looks at me.

"I want to see what we can spot from the area. Would they have seen Blake? How well would they have seen him? That sort of thing."

"Good idea."

We veer in that direction, and as we draw close, we hear the tramp of footsteps. We stop short, hands dropping to our guns just as Rogers rounds the corner. He's obviously distracted, so much so that he doesn't even notice us until Dalton clears his throat. Then his head jerks up, and he blinks before he pulls on his cloak of authority.

"Yes?" he says. "May I help you?"

I look around. "We're allowed to be here. It's neutral territory."

"Of course." He nods. "Good day then."

"We actually just left your colleague, Mr. Rutherford."

The faintest reaction. Almost a flinch. I suspect Rutherford has arrived at a very bad time, while Rogers is busy putting out fires.

Fires Rutherford isn't supposed to know about?

Spying on our settlement.

Murdering an employee.

Killing a so-called hiker and hunting down his wife.

No wonder Rogers looks as if he's missed a few nights' sleep.

As I think that, I realize it's the first time I've seen his eyes. He always wears sunglasses, no matter how overcast the day.

Now, as if he's reading my thoughts, he flips out his shades and snaps them on.

"Yes?" he says, with impatience, as if I'm keeping him from leaving.

"Mr. Rutherford had to come and speak to us because no one could find you."

"I said I was going for a walk. I checked in with the duty guard as I left." He pauses. "You were looking for me?"

"Yes." I meet his eyes—or the lenses of his sunglasses, at least. "It's recently come to our attention that your town employs some very unique workers, and that concerns us. As you know, we have civilians—including vulnerable ones—in our settlement, and now we discover that our neighbors are running a prison work camp."

"A what?"

"Your miners are convicts. American convicts."

He leans back. "You do realize we are in Canada, yes?"

"I do."

"I know people in your country can have a very distorted view of mine. Yes, we have private prisons. No, we cannot open a work camp in a foreign country. There are laws against that." His tone is dry, even sardonic. Mocking us.

"I know," I say. "Which means it would be illegal, and that's an even bigger concern." I lift my hands. "We don't care about the particulars. We just care about ensuring the safety of our residents. We already had a serious incident, resulting in a traumatized young boy, because your operation employed a convicted pedophile."

"That situation was resolved before anything happened, yes?"

I give him a hard look. "He was *kidnapped*."

I brace for him to argue that no assault took place, but he glances to the side, as if he realizes that's not the point.

"Yes, of course," he says. "I apologize. However, I did warn you."

"*After* the fact, you warned that you didn't screen for things like pedophilia because you're in an environment without children. You didn't warn me that you had actual pedophiles. *Incarcerated* pedophiles, as well as rapists, murderers—"

"Now you are letting your imagination run wild. As I said, we are not—"

"Owen Day," Dalton says.

Rogers jumps at his voice, telling me he's not nearly as calm as he seems. He looks over. "Excuse me."

"Owen Day. That's the name of the pedophile who kidnapped our boy. Neil Hansen. That's the name of a rapist and murderer you also employed. Both were currently incarcerated, with Hansen serving a life sentence."

Rogers goes quiet. He's thinking, and when his gaze slides to one of us, it's to Dalton.

"I believe we had a man by that name, though I don't know his particulars," Rogers says. "Like Mr. Day, he is no longer with us."

Dalton snorts at that.

"Mr. Hansen is not part of our current team," Rogers says, mistaking Dalton's snort for disbelief.

"As I said," I continue, "our interest is in securing our town and residents. The reason we wanted to speak to you alone is that you personally broke our agreement." I look up at him again. "You've been spying on our town. Trespassing on our territory, to the point of being close enough to see our settlement."

His brow furrows. Then it smooths. "If you are telling me that one of our men has been on your land, then I can categorically say that is untrue."

"Because you're tracking them with GPS chips?"

His mouth opens. Shuts. And he decides to say nothing.

"There's a loophole, though," I say. "One person that I presume isn't being tracked. You."

That brow furrows again, more, and he says, carefully, "I don't understand."

"You have been personally spying on our town. You persuaded one of our residents to break into our town manager's office for information. Or maybe for blackmail fodder."

"I did what?"

"You had an affair with one of our women. An ongoing affair, it seems."

He laughs. The sound is so unexpected, I startle before finding my glare.

"If you're going to pretend you'd never sneak around the forest to gain information—" I begin.

"Of course I would, if that were part of my mandate. What I would *not* do is seduce a woman for it. A man maybe, but a woman?" He tips the glasses up, letting me look into his eyes. "Even I have limits."

"The woman described you to a *tee*." I take out my notepad and read Muriel's words aloud. Then I look at him. "Are you telling me you have someone else in town who matches that description? Someone else whose movements aren't tracked?"

"No, which means I am being framed, and I believe I know by whom."

The answer hits before he speaks. Who *else* wouldn't be chipped? Rutherford. The same man who just grumbled to us about Rogers disappearing all the time, especially in the early mornings . . . when someone was meeting with Muriel.

There's just one problem with that scenario.

"We heard the spy talking," I say. "We didn't get to him on time, but that voice didn't have an English accent."

His brows lift, as if he's shocked that I figured out he was referring to Rutherford.

"*Is* Rutherford English?" I press. "And when did he arrive at your camp? He talked as if he'd just gotten in."

"He has been here for several weeks. As for the accent, it seems legitimate. However, shortly after he arrived, we caught a couple of the guards imitating him. Goofing around. He did the same back, imitating *their* accent, and said that if they were going to mock his, they'd best get better at it. His American accent was perfect."

"And the English one would be a dead giveaway to our resident."

"Yes." Rogers straightens. "I do appreciate you bringing this to my attention. I apologize for the trespass, and I assure you, it will be dealt with. Now, if you'll excuse me—"

"You really think that's going to work?" Dalton says. "We don't trust you to do shit."

"I can assure you—"

"Fuck your assurances. We've had enough of them. You know you have us over a barrel here. We can't just pick up and leave. So you keep giving 'assurances' and when you break them, it was all a terrible mistake, and you will do better."

"We *have* done better. We instituted boundaries. We improved employee tracking. Yes, I will admit to the implants, as it proves we are doing our due diligence. Our guards know their movements are being monitored."

"And the employees don't, but that doesn't matter because they gave up those rights when they were incarcerated."

His lips press into a thin line. "I do not know the specifics of our employees' backgrounds."

"Yeah, you're just the middleman. You have no idea what's happening here. You just do your job, and if that includes murdering your own employees . . ." Dalton shrugs. "They were criminals, right? Who cares."

"If you are referring to Mr. Day, we did not kill him. That was his partner-in-crime, the guard—"

"Yeah, yeah. We actually don't believe that story, but we don't care. We're talking about Mr. Hansen."

"Mr. Hansen is gone."

"We know. Dead and buried. Like you said, 'he's no longer with us.'"

Rogers shakes his head. "Mr. Hansen left on a recent exchange. Two employees departed and two arrived."

"We didn't hear a plane."

"Because you never do. Unlike you, we don't fly in this far."

"So Mr. Hansen is alive?"

"Presumably."

"Huh. Well, then who's the guy we dug up? The corpse in cold storage."

Silence. It stretches far too long.

"You have Mr. Hansen's body?"

"That's what I said."

I clear my throat. "One adult male with three tattoos under his hair, along with the chip. I can describe him and the tattoos."

"That won't be necessary," Rogers says. "You say you found his *buried* body?"

He's not telling us we made a mistake. Not saying that if we found Hansen, it had nothing to do with him. Not bluffing or blustering in his usual condescending way. Nor does he seem shocked.

"Right around here, as a matter of fact," Dalton says. "Where you seem to be just taking a late-day stroll."

He turns around. "Show me the spot."

"To prove it?" Dalton says. "If you want that, we've got his fucking *corpse*."

"I would like to see where he was buried."

We take him to the place and roll back the sod. He says nothing. Only examines it and then pokes around the clearing.

"Looking for more?" I ask.

The question seems to genuinely startle him. Then he finds his composure and decides not to answer.

"You didn't see Hansen get on the plane, did you," I say.

"Mr. Rutherford is in charge of employee exchange."

"So he shows up, makes the exchange, and then leaves. Only this time, he didn't leave."

"He has been here for a few weeks. I was notified." He looks at me. "Whatever happened to Mr. Hansen, it was, as they say, above my pay grade. I presumed everyone who leaves departs safely."

"But you're discouraged from witnessing their departure. And you've begun to find that suspicious. That's why you were out here. You heard—or overheard—something."

He doesn't answer.

"Did Hansen cause trouble at camp?" I ask.

"No."

"So the problem is that he raped and murdered a senator's daughter," I say.

Rogers looks up sharply.

"I'm sure most miners go home," I continue. "It'd be too suspicious otherwise. That allows this to operate as a seemingly legitimate operation. Well, not *legitimate*. But most go home. Yet, every now and then, they bring someone who won't be missed. Someone who can disappear quietly. Someone that people with very deep pockets will pay to see disappear."

"As I said, I know nothing of specifics."

"Generalizations, then?"

His lips compress. "Not about murder."

"But the operation in general? Executions for hire can't be the sole purpose of your camp. Nor is gold. Oh, I'm sure you're digging up actual gold and probably other minerals. That's what makes it seem legit to the convicts, keeps them believing they're mining up north."

"I do not know the specif—" He stops himself before I can ask for generalizations. "I know there are multiple levels of investment in the project. It's very complicated."

"I'm sure it is. Probably kickbacks for employing convicts. Investors who think there's gold-rush-level profits to be had. Plus the executions for hire. What you're taking from the ground is just gravy, enough to cover supplies, maybe pay your convicts a very small salary to keep them happy. The real money comes from everything else."

"I am not at liberty—"

"Yeah, yeah," Dalton cuts in. "We don't need you to confirm it. But if you care about *your* liberty, you might want to cooperate. You have your investors. We have ours. Ours can get your ass out of this mess. Yours . . ." He shrugs. "Well, I think we all know how *yours* would get your ass out of it."

"Remember those hikers?" I say.

He blinks at the change of subject. "Yes, of course."

"One's dead," I say. "Strangled. The other has been on the run from someone who seems to consider her a loose end."

He frowns. "That would have nothing to do with us. We were concerned, of course. But whatever you might think of our operation, we are not murdering hikers."

"*You're* not," I say.

"Were they more than hikers?" he asks.

"Actually, no. But our dead man happened to be looking in this direction from up on that mountainside." I point. "Someone spotted him. Someone who was likely burying Hansen's body at the time. Did they think he saw too much? Or did they think he was a spy?" I shrug. "He's dead. That's all I know."

"Leave this with me—"

"Back to your colleague. What did Rutherford say when you first told him about us?"

"Nothing. He already knew there was a settlement in the area. I had reported that to our employer."

"And how did *they* react when you first told them about us?"

"It did not come as a surprise. Clearly their initial visits—when they were surveying the future site—told them you were here."

"So they weren't surprised. Were they concerned?"

"No." The word comes clipped with annoyance. "They completely failed to understand the significance and the danger of being so close to another settlement."

"Oh?"

He straightens. "I told them I thought it was a serious concern, and they told me it was not."

"Did they ask you to find out what we were doing out here?"

"No. They said they already knew."

CHAPTER THIRTY-FOUR

A theory is forming, one so far-fetched that I don't even dare voice it to Dalton . . . until he says the same thing as we walk back. I don't want to imagine what Yolanda would say. It's outrageous enough that she wouldn't even scoff or tease us about our paranoia. She'd probably gently suggest that it's time for us to start seeing Isabel professionally, to work through our past trauma. And she might not be wrong.

I pick up Rory while Dalton gets my interview subject. I'm in the town hall playing with my daughter when Dalton arrives with Muriel. He takes the baby to play with her across the room. Muriel seems to relax at that, which means she didn't learn a damn thing from her first interview, when Kendra was in the background.

I'm sitting at the desk. When Muriel approaches, I empty the coins onto the desk. She sucks in a breath.

"Yours?" I say.

"What? No. I—"

"The key was concealed in your dresser. The box it opened

was buried in one of the planters. Before you say you were framed, I've lifted fingerprints and I have yours on file."

She crosses her arms. "Those are my private property."

"They wouldn't have been allowed into town. No valuables, for your own safety. You received the box and the coins while you were here. Nontraceable payment for a job. That job being the crime you've already admitted to. Espionage."

"Espionage?" She huffs the word. "I checked Phil's desk for operational records."

"And you did the same in his home. You entered illegally and attempted to steal information from an institution. That is espionage." I lean back in the chair. "Though it was a nice touch, crying about how you'd been tricked by another man. Poor Muriel just never learns. You weren't tricked either time, were you? You were in on the first crime. Before your partner double-crossed you and fled with the money."

"What? Absolutely not." She stands. "I won't stand here and take this victim-blaming—"

"We don't care about that incident. We care about this one. You sold out Haven's Rock—and the people who helped you get here."

Her eyes blaze. "Helping me would have been finding that bastard and getting my money back. Or giving me money to start over. Not dumping me in the middle of nowhere."

"You weren't *dumped* anywhere, Muriel. You were offered this option, and you accepted it. No one forced your hand. No one conned you. Now you're complaining because it wasn't what you wanted? That's like eating a free burger and then blaming the diner because you actually wanted sushi."

"My bastard of an ex-boyfriend stole everything from me. Do you get that? I spent my life working and saving to be financially independent and stable. He stole that. All of it. Then I meet someone who offers me a lot of money to get a few papers? Of course I'm going to do it. You would, too."

If she *wasn't* in on the original theft, then I feel for her situation. I really do. I also worked and skimped and saved to be comfortable on my own. If someone stole that security, would I have stolen from others to get it back? Of course not, but I won't sneer at her choice.

As for her anger at us, I'm disappointed, as anyone is when they think they've given someone a gift, only to have them spit on it. But that happens here, just as it happened in Rockton. Desperate people make desperate choices, and sometimes, when the stress disappears, they look around and decide this wasn't what they wanted. Of course, we're the *reason* their stress disappeared. But we can't and don't expect everyone to appreciate it.

I won't harp on the theft or the betrayal. I only wanted to confront her with them both so she stops lying. I *won't* confront her about deliberately misleading us regarding Rutherford. He obviously told her to describe Rogers, and she did as she was instructed.

No, I want something else here.

"Back to what you were asked to get," I say. "You claim he wasn't curious about the purpose of Haven's Rock? I find that hard to believe."

She shrugs. "Suit yourself."

"He never pushed for answers? Even clues? About what's happening here?"

"In your top-secret little sanctuary? That's what you sold me. What you sell all of us. Only you don't even provide that. He didn't ask what's happening here because he already knew. He'd figured out exactly what Haven's Rock is."

I frown, as if confused. "He knew what we do here? Don't tell me he only wanted information on our supply chain and operations. That's not worth what he was paying you."

"He wanted dirt," she says smugly. "He knew there must be problems, and he wanted details. He asked how things were running, whether you and Eric were having trouble juggling it all with the baby—he even knew about the baby. I told him everything seemed to be running smoothly. He asked about discontent, angry residents. I told him I wasn't happy—this place is hardly the Ritz—and I said people do complain about this and that, but he said that was all petty stuff. He wanted real dirt, and he thought I could find it with Phil's files. He knew all about Phil—his name, what he did here, everything. He said Phil documents everything, and he wanted his records. Inventory, bookkeeping, journals. Everything."

"Looking for problems."

"Seems so." She smirks. "I get the feeling someone's planning a hostile takeover, and I'm here for it. Imagine how much better this place could be if you had some real money behind it."

Oh, we can imagine. Because we've been there before.

I find Phil working alongside Isabel in the Roc. It's open for another hour before curfew kicks in. I ask him to join me, and we head for the clinic to check on Storm. I enter to find April gone and Storm pacing.

"Ready to go home, huh, girl?" I pat her head. "Tonight, I think."

I settle her in—she's not supposed to be too mobile. Then I turn to Phil. "You said you had a theory about the would-be thefts, one you weren't ready to share. Because it made you feel paranoid, I bet. Who you think was ultimately behind it." I meet his gaze. "The same people who were behind Rockton."

His exhale tells me I'm right. I catch him up on everything we learned, from both Muriel and Rogers. When I finish, he slumps into a chair, and he's quiet for a few moments.

"Phil?" I say.

"I should have said something, but yes, I thought I was being paranoid. I was still working it through."

"Muriel said they were looking for dirt. Reasons to shut us down?"

His lips purse. "More like reasons to convince you to let them in."

I squeeze my eyes shut. "Muriel speculated on a hostile takeover."

"She has a background in corporate finance. She recognized what this was. I wouldn't call it a hostile takeover, though. If they did that, the staff would all leave. Émilie would pull out. They'd only have the buildings, which they could construct themselves. What they want is . . ." He shrugs. "My guess is that they're homing in on Eric."

"That's what I told Émilie. In Rockton, they harassed him endlessly, implied he wasn't doing a good enough job. Now they know better."

"Yes. Émilie says their new venture is failing. They likely believe Eric is the key. They can be very simplistic that way. They may recognize what the rest of you bring to the table, but Eric is the Pied Piper. Lure him to their side, and everyone else follows, possibly even Émilie."

"So they're trying to see whether we've bitten off more than we can chew, especially now that we have a baby. New parents who've embarked on a massive undertaking might be ripe for a *friendly* takeover."

Phil nods. "As you recall, initially, they hoped to recruit Eric for their new venture. But now that Haven's Rock is established—and their lodge is failing—they'll offer their assistance here, in return for allowing their residents in, while assuring you that their residents are nothing worse than white-collar criminals, and you can certainly continue offering free spots to those in need. From there, it will escalate."

"Like it did before. From a sanctuary to a for-profit operation. Except, I would presume, that escalation won't take decades this time." I scratch behind Storm's ears. "But what I can't figure out is the link to the mining camp. Whoever is in charge of that knew about Haven's Rock before they moved in. Knew exactly what we are. Someone working for them who also works for the old Rockton board?"

Phil is quiet for a moment. Then he says, "A corporation's interests often extend beyond a single product or line of products. In some cases, they are somewhere between a hydra and a nesting doll."

"Many arms, the main body deeply hidden in shell companies."

"Yes. Rockton brought in money. A great deal of it, from residents with the means and the need to disappear. But Rockton was one project. It wouldn't have been worth the required corporate structure all by itself."

"There were other Rocktons?"

He considers. "Likely not in North America. Otherwise, their new version would be running much smoother. I suspect what they have are other variations on the theme."

"Such as an illegal prison camp?"

He frowns, and I tell him about the mining operation.

"Oh." He goes into deep-thought mode while I pet Storm. Finally, he says, "I don't wish to complain, Casey, but how long have you known what that camp truly is?"

"Less than twenty-four hours."

He exhales. "Thank you. I'd hate to think you had been sitting on this, when I would have immediately seen a potential connection."

"Well, maybe if *we* knew that Rockton wasn't a single project, we'd have seen it sooner ourselves. But if Émilie saw the connection, she didn't tell us. That's a problem."

"Émilie didn't know. Rockton didn't pass to the corporate entity until after Émilie and her husband had stepped back. The corporation's business interests deal largely with illegal enterprises, so each arm is thoroughly boxed."

"Each arm doesn't know about the others . . . or about the company in charge."

"Even I wasn't supposed to know, but the trail was there and of course I followed it. Information is knowledge, and knowledge is power. Which came in handy when they attempted to shut down Rockton and leave all the staff without compensation."

I remember that Phil took over that conversation—a private one—and then we were all paid. I'd thought that whatever he used for blackmail was about Rockton itself and its past misdeeds. Apparently not.

Dalton skipped the chat with Phil in favor of looking after Rory, knowing that the baby's presence wouldn't help the conversation. Some people are distracted by the siren call of tiny humans. Others are distracted by the urge to flee the vicinity before someone asks them to change a diaper.

After talking to Phil, I head straight for our chalet. I message Émilie, saying it's urgent. Then I tell Dalton everything. Fortunately, the baby is asleep at that point, or she'd hear Daddy say a whole lotta very bad words.

"So this Rutherford guy works for—" Dalton has begun when a banging at the door cuts him short.

I hurry over, expecting trouble, only to find Arturo on our front steps.

"This is it," he says. "I have had enough, and I want to speak to whoever is in charge of this place."

"That would be us," Dalton says, his voice a low growl as he walks over, holding Rory.

"I mean the people *you* work for. *Your* bosses."

"That would be us."

"For fuck's sake. Really? No wonder you can't handle one simple issue. The people in charge are younger than me and busy looking after a baby. You need to start disclosing that, because if I had any idea what kind of amateur hour—"

"If you have another human-resources problem," I say, "take it up with Phil. We're busy."

"Playing house. I can see that. While Muriel just keeps breaking the rules, and no one gives a shit."

"Muriel will be leaving soon."

"Oh, she already left. Traipsed off into the forest a few minutes ago."

"Into the forest?" I turn to Dalton, who's already cursing under his breath. I look back at Arturo. "We'll handle this."

"You better!" he shouts as I start to close the door. Then I stop. “Wait right there. You need to show us where you last saw her.”

Dalton will go with Arturo while I take Rory and speak to the person who was supposed to be escorting Muriel back to her solitary-confinement apartment.

“You asked April?” I whisper to Dalton as I pull on my boots.

Dalton throws up his hands. “We’re a little short-handed. Will and Yolanda are getting some sleep. Kenny is guarding Gretchen. Kendra and Gunnar are on patrol. I was figuring out who I could put on Muriel-duty when I ran into April coming back from taking dinner to Kenny and Gretchen, and she volunteered.”

We encounter April before we even reach town. She’s marching toward our chalet, her mouth set in a firm line, her shoulders tense. I murmur to Dalton, and he takes Arturo down another path while I catch up with April.

“Muriel evaded me,” she says, her eyes brimming with humiliation.

“Are you okay?” I say. “Did she hurt you?”

“Did she club me on the head and flee? That would be less embarrassing.”

“What happened?” I bounce Rory, the baby fussing from being woken mid-nap.

“I was guarding the apartment when she asked to retrieve herbs from the greenhouse. She’d grown lemongrass at the restaurant’s request, and Arturo wouldn’t know where to find it. She'd promised it to the restaurant by tomorrow. I followed her to the greenhouse, where she found the herbs, which were—as she said—not with the others. I watched her harvest them and then, like a gullible fool, I escorted her to the kitchen."

"That wasn't gullible or foolish. It sounds like a legitimate request."

Another tightening of April's lips. "A legitimate *excuse.* She asked me to wait at the kitchen door. Being escorted in there would seem odd, and she didn't want everyone gossiping. I decided to allow it."

"Ah. She ducked out the other door."

"I was not aware there *was* another door. Which isn't a defense. Only last month I read a mystery where the suspect escapes through the bathroom window, and I rolled my eyes at the thought that any police officer wouldn't have checked for a window."

"You're not the police officer in the family," I say gently.

"But I agreed to guard Muriel, and I should not have done so if I could not do it correctly."

I want to hug her. I know better, so I only pat her arm. "It's fine. Everyone's exhausted and being pulled twenty different ways. This is a minor hiccup. There's no place for Muriel to go."

"If you need Storm to track her, a very brief walk would be acceptable but not ideal."

"We'll be fine without her help. The only thing I need you to do is take this one." I bounce Rory.

"You may not wish me to do that, as I have proven myself a poor guardian."

"Nah. You're fine. But if she makes some excuse for popping into the Roc, don't let her get away with it. She only wants to sneak a little coffee liqueur for her milk."

She stares at me and then shakes her head. "You have a very strange sense of humor, Casey."

"It runs in the family."

I hand over Rory, and then take off. I've only gone about twenty steps when I spot Arturo and Dalton at the edge of the forest. The northeast edge. In the exact direction of Muriel's little clearing. Seriously? At least that'll make this easy.

"Casey!" a voice calls.

I look to see Tish, Kendra's girlfriend, who works in the kitchen. She runs over, her long curls bouncing, her full cheeks red from the exertion.

"Something happened," she says. "I don't want to get anyone in trouble, but I thought you should know."

"Were you working in the kitchen?"

She nods.

"And Muriel came in?" I say.

"Yes. Your sister followed afterwards, asking where she was. She was alarmed. Dr. Butler, I mean, and that seemed odd. Nothing ruffles her feathers. I figured there's a medical reason—and that's why she was urgently looking for Muriel—so I was concerned. I said Muriel had hurried out the back door."

I open my mouth, about to say it's fine, we know what's going on, but before I can, Tish continues, "I figured it was none of my business, so I went back to work. I was deboning fish, and I'd left my knife right there on the butcher's block. It was gone. Then someone said they thought Muriel took it."

"They thought Muriel took the boning knife?"

She nods. "I didn't like the sounds of that. So I came to find you."

I don't like the sounds of it either. Not at all.

CHAPTER THIRTY-FIVE

"Muriel has a knife?" Dalton says. We're striding into the forest, having left Arturo and Haven's Rock behind.

"A boning knife. So maybe six inches long. Sharp." I hurry after him as his strides lengthen. "She might have just spotted it and thought it could come in handy, both as a weapon and a tool. But that might also be why she used the kitchen as her escape spot in the first place."

"To get a weapon."

After a moment, I say, "Are you following her trail or just heading for her clearing?"

"Trail," he grunts, and points to the foliage, where he must see something I don't. "Which seems to be heading for her clearing."

"She might have something still stashed there."

Another grunt. Then he says, "We've got our sidearms. If she wants to bring a knife to a gunfight, let her. I'm just glad we got a heads-up that she's armed."

He stops short, and I narrowly avoid bashing into him. When he looks north, I resist the urge to ask what he hears. He keeps looking, and then shakes his head and continues walking.

"The patrol," he murmurs, voice lowered.

"Kendra and Gunnar? You thought you heard them?"

"Maybe. Either way, they need to be warned. They have a radio?"

"They should."

I pause to call, and Kendra answers.

"Hey," I whisper. "We may have a situation in the woods. Whereabouts are you guys?"

"By the lake."

"Good. Stay over there. Get into the open if you can. Muriel's bolted, and she has a knife, but we think she's on the north side."

"Got it. We'll hang tight."

"Whoever you heard?" I murmur to Dalton. "It's not them."

"Probably an animal," he says. "It was just a twig crack."

He continues on, but his gaze is pulled north often enough that I tap his arm.

"You don't think it's an animal," I say. "Let's change direction. It could be Muriel, if she got enough of a head start that she's already collected whatever she left and is moving on."

He nods and pauses to peer around, mentally marking this spot in case we need to resume tracking. Then we head north.

I fall in behind Dalton and don't try to keep up. While I need to be aware of our surroundings, he's doing the same, now that he doesn't need to focus on her trail, and I can back off and give him space while I cover his back.

This time I'm the one who notices something. I'd like to think it's a sudden growth spurt in my wilderness skills, but I suspect it's because I fell behind a few paces. Something moves to our right, passing by after Dalton has gone past that spot.

I jog forward and tug his jacket, motioning to the east. He squints, and then he must see what I did—a dark shape moving maybe thirty feet from us, heading along one of the smaller trails. Dalton clocks the trajectory and then frowns. The figure is moving toward Muriel's clearing.

Dalton eases out his gun. I do the same, and we make our way silently to that narrow path. He stays in front, moving carefully, sticking to the shadows.

I look up at the sky. The sun is dropping, and it's darker in here than it was in town. At least the shadows hide Dalton, letting him move quickly. He lopes about fifty feet and then stops with one hand raised.

I reach him and peer around as he steps aside. Someone is up ahead. A male figure, dressed in black, the hood of his jacket pulled tight.

We aren't absolutely fixed on Rutherford as our culprit. Muriel did give us a description that matched Rogers, and while we believe she'd been fed that, in case she was caught, there's still the chance Rogers really is her contact. His defense was that he's gay, which is easy to claim. Also, we have no evidence that Muriel was actually having an affair with her spymaster. It might have been a purely monetary transaction.

The size of the figure matches both Rogers and Rutherford, the two mining employees who don't have GPS chips. What I *do* know is that whoever we see is heading for the clearing, where Muriel presumably waits—

Where Muriel waits with a knife.

Before I can speak, Muriel's voice rings out. "*There* you are. I told you I was in trouble, and it took you—"

"Shh!" the man says. "They're patrolling."

While the speaker doesn't have an English accent, the timbre seems to match Rutherford's voice.

"You need to get me out of here," she whispers. "We had a deal."

The man mutters something and then says, "Come on then. They seem to have vacated that cabin. You can stay there while I make arrangements."

"I need to get my bag. I hid it in our clearing."

He sighs. While it makes sense that she only grabbed the knife in case anyone tried to stop her, I still grip my gun tight, every muscle tense.

"I think it's a setup," I whisper to Dalton.

His frown tells me his mind hasn't gone in that direction, and I resist the urge to back down.

"Just follow me," I whisper. "In case she tries—"

A scuffle up ahead, and the man saying "What the—?" before he lets out a hiss and stops short.

"You fucked me over," Muriel says.

The man's voice comes tight and angry. "How? You were paid. You were caught. Now I'm taking you someplace safe, exactly as I promised. Lower that knife or you will find yourself facing your mess alone."

"My mess?" Her voice rises as we jog silently toward them. "You told me they'd never catch on. They know *everything.*"

Silence. Then, his voice even tighter. "What?"

"They know I broke into the Roc and Phil's house. They found the coins, and they know I was being paid by someone in the mining camp."

"What did you tell them, Muriel?"

"I gave them the description you fed me, which saves your ass, but it doesn't help me, does it? You promised me a hundred grand, and you've given me a fraction of that."

"I promised a hundred if you got what I needed." His American accent begins to slip. "You didn't. I'm not paying you for making a hash out—" A sharp intake of breath.

We've reached a spot where the path turns. Muriel and

Rutherford are just up ahead, and we can't barrel out and risk spooking Muriel into attacking Rutherford with that knife.

Dalton eases into the forest, placing one foot down after another, as carefully as he can. I wait until they start talking again, in hopes it'll cover any sound of my own approach.

"What do you want me to say, Muriel?" The American accent is gone completely now. "You have me at knifepoint. Arguing with you isn't going to help me."

I move up alongside Dalton, and he points. It takes a moment to see Muriel and Rutherford through the thick tree cover, but then I make out their figures. Muriel has him pinned to a tree, knife at his back. He'd been wearing a balaclava, but it's rolled onto his forehead.

"I want fifty grand," she says. "I accept that I didn't get what you wanted, but that wasn't my fault. I gave you all the information I could get."

"Which was useless. I needed to know how things were going wrong in town, and you gave me a list of penny-ante concerns. The bedrooms are small. The bathrooms are communal. The food options are limited. You're expected to work. You sound like a bloody tourist complaining that your three-star resort doesn't have a spa."

He cuts himself short, as if realizing this won't help. "I needed ways to know how things are going *wrong*, Muriel. At the very least, I need evidence that Eric and Casey are overwhelmed, between their new town and their new baby. The fact that they caught you and figured out *everything* suggests even that isn't a problem."

"People have complaints. I gave you those."

"People will always have—" He stops short again. "I presume you cannot get access to your coins?"

"Yes."

"That is your problem, and I will count them against the fifty thousand you earned. You will get twenty-five."

"Forty."

A long hiss of breath. "Thirty-five."

He's faking the negotiations. Muriel hasn't thought this through. Rutherford is at knifepoint. He could promise her the whole hundred grand. He doesn't because that would be suspicious. He's going to play this out until he has Muriel in Lilith's cabin. Then he can ship her off without paying a cent. We need to rescue her, and we will—as soon as we can safely intervene.

"Forty thousand," she says.

A low growl, as if she's a shrewd negotiator driving a hard bargain. "Fine. Now will you lower the knife please?"

She backs up, and Dalton relaxes. I rock on my toes, tension thrumming through me. Do we grab her now? No, they're relaxing. Just wait for an opening.

Muriel steps back, knife raised. "Walk. And I want to be flown out *tomorrow*."

He sighs, as if he's dealing with a difficult teenager. "I can't promise tomorrow because it'll be late when I get back. But I will place the call and say it's a priority."

"I want to be flown to Seattle. No dropping me off in the middle of nowhere."

"I will see what I can do. At worst, I'll provide you with options, possibly Vancouver or Anchorage."

"Vancouver."

"We will *see*. Now, I don't suppose you have a tissue? The back of my neck is bleeding."

"I barely nicked you."

"I believe I have a tissue. May I tend to it, please?"

He doesn't wait for an answer. He reaches into his jacket, and my mouth opens as I lunge, ready to shout a warning.

The *pfft* of a silenced shot stops me short. Muriel falls back against a tree, her mouth opening and closing.

Dalton rocks forward, but I stop him, and he stares, wide-eyed, at Muriel, slumped backward but still upright, hand over her heart, blood pumping out.

I take one slow and careful step, braced for the slightest rustle underfoot. Rutherford faces Muriel, his gun still raised, but held casually, knowing that if his shot isn't fatal, he has plenty of time to fire one that is.

Muriel has dropped the knife—forgotten about it altogether—and she's slumped against the tree.

"You shot me," she says finally.

He doesn't even answer that. Just shakes his head at her naiveté.

Tears glisten in Muriel's eyes. "I did what you asked. *Everything* you asked."

Silence. He's not even going to give her the respect of an answer. To him, she's already dead; he's just waiting for her body to hurry up and finish the process.

This is the man who killed Blake and stalked Gretchen. Any lingering doubt evaporates as he stands there, cold-blooded and patient while a dying woman begs for an explanation.

He could say he killed her because she threatened his life and he can't take another chance. But I can see that he was always going to kill her in the end. Now he doesn't even need to worry about us searching for a missing innocent resident. Given her betrayal, we'll presume he flew her out.

Muriel is gasping, beyond speech, dying, and I know I'll pay for this later, regretting that I didn't move faster. I'd refrained for fear of her escalating the conflict, but I still made a mistake. Whatever Muriel has done, she did not deserve this.

I'm creeping up behind Rutherford, Dalton at my rear, our

guns raised. When we round that corner, Muriel spots us, and I tense, finger moving to the trigger.

She blinks, as if we're a mirage. And then, with her final breath, she laughs. The sound turns to a gasping snicker as her feet slide out from under her. Rutherford doesn't even twitch. He can't see us and he must presume her laugh is a final pathetic attempt at bravado.

Muriel hits the ground, still braced against the tree, head lolling, eyes shut. I wait for Rutherford to holster his gun, but he only lowers it and walks over to kick Muriel's boot, making sure she's dead.

Then he starts to turn.

"Stop," I say.

His gun barrel swings up. I fire. He's wheeling fast, and my bullet hits his arm, Dalton's shot slamming into his shoulder. Rutherford fires, too, but he's staggering back, his bullet going wild.

Rutherford tries to recover, but I'm there, kicking him hard, the gun flying from his hand. Dalton's fist plows into Rutherford's jaw. He reels, stumbles, falls, grabs for Dalton's leg, yanking to bring Dalton down, get his gun, but Dalton jerks free and backpedals. Then both of us aim our weapons at point-blank range.

Rutherford's gaze lifts to ours, grinding out pure hate. He knows why he's still alive.

"I'm not telling you anything," he rasps, wincing as he grips his bleeding arm. "You can shoot me or you can leave me here."

"Okay," I say . . . and I shoot him in the kneecap.

He screams, head flying back.

"Other one, too?" I say.

A string of profanity and pain.

"I'll take that as a no," I say.

He manages a short, agonized laugh. "If you think that's going to make me talk—"

"Nope," I say as I holster my gun and scoop up his. "But I think a few hours in the forest with three bullet wounds might."

I collect Muriel's knife. "Those wounds aren't fatal, but that blood's going to attract predators."

"Then I guess that's how I'll die. Without telling you a thing."

I shrug. "You don't have to. We know you work for the company behind our former town. We know they also run the mining operation, which is actually an illegal prison camp. Right now we have two goals. Shut down the mine, and get your employer out of our lives—permanently. Neither has anything to do with your continued survival. We just don't like to kill people if we don't need to."

I start to walk away, Dalton falling in beside me. Then I turn back to Rutherford. "If you hadn't fucked up and killed an innocent hiker, we'd never have known what was going on." I salute him. "Thank you for your service."

"Innocent hiker?" He spits the words before gasps. "Is that what that woman told you? He was spying on us. I saw him on the ridge. Unlike you, I know how to deal with threats."

I glance meaningfully toward Muriel. "No, you just don't mind killing anyone who *could* be a threat. Maybe that's why the company hired you, but I suspect it was just an unexpected bonus . . . that turned into a major liability. We'll be back in a while to collect Muriel and give her a proper burial. You can make your own choice."

CHAPTER THIRTY-SIX

When we return, Rutherford is delirious with pain, but what finally convinces him to open up is the morphine we give him for that pain. Sometimes there really is an advantage to never needing to worry about how you obtain a confession. At least not when the guy is a murdering scumbag.

I'm sure it's not entirely the morphine either. It's the giddy relief of having his pain disappear, and the exhaustion of running on adrenaline for hours, racked by agony while lying helpless in a forest as night falls.

It's also the fact that we already knew the connection between Rockton and the mining camp. No point in holding out . . . especially when you're flying high on opiates.

Turns out, to Rutherford, Rockton is just a name, the backstory of his current job. That could be his employers giving him the bare minimum of what he needed to know, but it also seems he just didn't care. It was a job. Specifics weren't important.

His primary position had been with the mining operation, escorting new convicts in and old ones out . . . some of them leaving and others buried in shallow graves. Shot. Strangled. Poisoned. Whatever worked best under the circumstances. His skills were flexible.

His main contact at the camp isn't Rogers. It's the older guard we've seen from the start, an army vet turned mercenary. He poses as a guard while also keeping a watch on Rogers and helping Rutherford.

How did Rutherford hire Muriel? Pure chance. On his trips to the camp, he was also expected to conduct surveillance of Haven's Rock. He spotted Muriel, who really had been out knitting and reading before her shift. He took some photos and later identified her through facial recognition. His employers instructed him to stage an accidental meeting and test her viability as a spy—her financial situation suggested money might be the way to her heart.

While the purpose of his latest visit was a prisoner exchange—and to execute Hansen—he'd lingered because of the Blake incident. When Rutherford is under the influence of morphine, he candidly admits he didn't have any solid evidence that Blake was a spy. He only knew that Blake *might* have been a threat. So he killed him. He'd always planned to kill Gretchen, too—no loose ends left untied. She'd just made it so damned difficult and then we got involved and everything went sideways.

He hadn't been ordered to kill Blake and Gretchen. That was his initiative. If you consult the higher-ups, they start weighing in with their opinions. Things are just easier handled quietly and efficiently.

Rutherford talks openly, any vestige of a conscience melted by the morphine, and after he's given us everything he knows, we kill him.

No, we don't kill him. That's the solution for guys like Rutherford. It's efficient but also shortsighted. We have enough to know who to hand him over to, and now he'll be our ticket to a much-needed conversation with his employers.

Three days later, we're in Whitehorse. Gretchen and Rutherford left the day after we took Rutherford into custody. Was it awkward, putting her on a plane with her husband's killer? We certainly didn't tell her that's who he was, but I still felt the discomfort of having her make that trip with him. She was safe—Rutherford was sedated and Émilie sent along a guard. It still felt cruel, but Gretchen wanted to leave, and Rutherford needed to, so they disappeared into Émilie's care.

Émilie will treat Gretchen well. She is a victim, after all. A new widow who has been traumatized for nothing she or her husband did. Gretchen understands that we didn't do anything either, and that helps.

A few days after they left, Émilie asked us to come to Whitehorse for a video conference. Phil needs to join us and has come along with Isabel.

Émilie meets us at the airport. Then it's off to a rented house, with an hour to settle in. When it's time for our meeting, we leave Rory with Isabel and follow Émilie into the living room, where Phil waits. The big-screen TV is hooked up to the video chat, and Émilie makes the call.

I don't know the person who appears. Our original liaison with Rockton's governing body had been Phil. He'd been a pain in the ass. Condescending, officious, and fussy, in a way that always had me imagining a middle-aged management type. His replacement had been so much worse. While Phil had been patronizing, he'd been coolly efficient and businesslike. Tamara had delighted in delivering bad news, and after the final fiasco, I suspect she got her own early-retirement package.

Those old meetings had always been audio-only, and it's clear that this new liaison is uncomfortable being on-screen. He's in his thirties, dressed in a three-piece suit, his face sheened with sweat that I don't think comes from the lighting. He sits at a table, facing us, and while the others could be videoconferenced in, I get the sense they're actually seated at the other side of that table. The liaison has his finger on the mute button, hitting it when others speak and then relaying their words.

Dalton and I are there because this affects us most of all. For now, though, we only listen. Like the board members, Dalton and I stay off-screen, and Émilie doesn't say we're there. It's just her and Phil.

Émilie has already told them what we figured out and what she's learned. They've come to this meeting with all that information in hand.

Of course they start by denying everything. Not that we're wrong about our facts—Émilie provided the data to back us up. We've just misinterpreted.

"Naturally the corporation is curious about Haven's Rock," the liaison says, "and yes, they'd love to woo Eric and Casey away, but if they're doing well, the corporation is happy for them."

"Curiosity means sending spies," Émilie says. "Possibly even trying to sneak in a resident for insider information. It does not mean setting up a prison-labor camp a few miles away."

"That was a coincidence."

She snorts. "It was luck. The luck of finding a man who had discovered gold nearby and was willing to sell his claim."

"Convenience then," the liaison says. "A happy collision of

circumstances. We do understand there was a negative interaction with a child, which we could not have foreseen, as Rockton did not allow children."

"But it allowed women," Émilie counters. "And your camp has convicted rapists."

"A mistake, which we will rectify, and it is our hope that we can continue coexisting peacefully—"

"No," Émilie says. "You will be shutting down that operation."

"I'm afraid that's nonnegotiable. We have invested—"

"It's a camp, not a town. You have thirty days to dismantle it." She shuffles papers. "Or I have the testimony of a man who executed felons on your orders, along with the location of every buried body and their identities."

"If Mr. Rutherford took a side job executing—"

"How was it a 'side job' when your records would indicate that those convicts never returned? You would have investigated. We can keep dancing, but you know what I have, and you know what I want. Shut down the camp. Leave Haven's Rock—and everyone in it—alone."

"We never bothered anyone in it. We were simply amassing data—"

"In the hopes of discovering a problem, and when you didn't, you would have caused one. You aren't getting Haven's Rock. You aren't getting Eric and Casey."

Phil clears his throat, speaking for the first time. "Eric and Casey are not a magic key. They are very important components in a system. What you need is to duplicate that system with staff who share their idealism."

The liaison hits mute and listens to what must be a conversation on the other side. When he comes back on, he says,

"The corporation would like to hire you, Phil. In a temporary position, lasting until spring. You could bring Isabel if you like. They want you to manage the new lodge and implement your system."

Phil nods, as if he expected this. "For the right price, I would do that. But you would need to follow Haven Rock's strategy. You cannot cherry-pick from it. You must promise to follow it exactly."

"Of course."

"Good. The first order of business would be to stop charging residents for their stay."

The liaison blinks. "I . . . don't understand."

"No one pays," Phil says, slowly. "Everyone's stay is covered. Oh, and the staff draws a modest salary."

"From where? Who pays for this?"

"The benefactors."

"I . . . don't understand."

Phil taps his pen, looking impatient. "It's very simple. Exchange the current investors for benefactors. Find people with money who want to make a difference and don't care about tax deductions."

"Don't . . . care about . . . tax deductions?" The liaison stares.

"Yes. Didn't your spy tell you this? His contact didn't pay for her stay in Haven's Rock."

"We thought she was a special case. We certainly would allow the occasional nonpaying resident, with fees to be covered by white-collar residents—"

"No fees. For anyone. Salaries for staff. These things are nonnegotiable."

"That's not . . . that's not . . ."

Phil leans back. "Not how you do business? Yes, I know. But

that is how Haven's Rock runs. It is how it will continue to run and how anyone who works there will expect other towns to run, should you headhunt them away."

"We will . . . We will discuss this," the liaison says, in a weak voice that says they will discuss nothing.

"You do that," Phil says. "I am still available, temporarily, for the right price. I believe six figures per month would suffice. But you must agree to exactly the sort of sanctuary we already have. Free of charge. Paid staff. Benefactors instead of investors." He pauses dramatically. "No charitable tax deductions."

"That is between you and Phil," Émilie says, as if there's a hope in hell they'd go for it. "For our part, you will have that mining camp dismantled in a month. You will never contact anyone from Haven's Rock or spy on it. You will, in short, leave them alone."

The microphone is muted again. When the liaison returns, he seems to have found some of his spine, sitting straight. "We would like to negotiate for the continued existence of the camp."

"No."

"You forget that we know all about Haven's Rock, which is an illegal settlement. You are squatting in the Yukon territory—"

"And you know as well as anyone that there are contingency plans for that. However, I don't think we need them." She waves the folder again. "Mutually assured destruction. Somehow, I think the authorities—Canadian and American—would be much more concerned about an illegal prison camp that takes payments to execute prisoners."

Muted again. Ten minutes pass.

"Sixty days," the liaison says.

"Forty-five."

He glances at the others, and then nods abruptly. "Forty-five."

"Then we have a deal," Émilie says. "Forty-five days to clear the camp, and you will never interfere with Haven's Rock again."

"Agreed," he says.

Dalton leans over, appearing on camera. "Now fuck the hell off."

It's been forty-two days since that meeting, and the mining camp is gone. Dalton and I are walking where it had been, nothing but an empty clearing remaining. It's early November, and we're tramping through snow, Rory bundled up in the sled, Storm pulling it. I remember last March, when they'd pulled me in a sled, how I'd dreamed of this winter, my pregnancy ending successfully, Storm pulling our baby in a sled.

I got that, and how I have something more. I have peace of mind. The wolves circling just outside our town are gone, and I don't need to keep lying to myself and saying it's fine, they won't attack.

Lilith is staying in Haven's Rock for the winter. Come spring, she'll be gone. As much as I'll miss her, I must quietly admit that I will be happier when these woods are home to no one outside our little town. While Lilith was never a threat, we felt terrible about invading her privacy, and we constantly worried about our residents realizing there was a stranger living out there.

So is this it? The moment when we can say Haven's Rock is a success and relax?

I wish it were. We can't relax yet. Maybe that really is our trauma speaking, but I think it's just common sense. So much has gone wrong in our first two years. Murders. Kidnappings. Betrayals. The looming threat of our former overlords, who've now stepped from the shadows, confirming that we weren't paranoid—they really were out to get us . . . and might still be.

Dalton picks up Rory from the sled as I unhook Storm. She's doing fine. A full recovery, which is a relief, given her age. Rory's fine, too. Oh, and last week, April "confessed" that she's seeing Kenny. She made it clear that we shouldn't read too much into this. They're exploring a romantic relationship, nothing more. Whatever she says. I'm just happy that we no longer need to pretend we don't see it.

Dalton circles the site of the encampment, looking for anything left behind. Storm and I wander, doing the same. We meet up near the creek, still running under a layer of ice.

"Eighty percent?" I say.

He glances over, squinting against the winter sun.

"We're eighty percent of the way to declaring Haven's Rock a success?" I say.

The corner of his mouth quirks. "I was thinking seventy-five."

"Wow. *I'm* the optimist? That's a first."

He walks over, cradling Rory under one arm, and hugs me with the other. "Sure, let's go with eighty."

Rory squirms, and he lowers her into the snow, where she promptly falls forward, gets a face full of snow, and squeals, not in distress but delight, her arms and legs working until she's on all fours and crawling over the thin layer of white stuff.

"Good thing she doesn't mind the cold," Dalton says.

I laugh. "Wait until she's a teenager, sitting in the chalet, grumbling all winter."

He looks out over the clearing, to the snow-covered trees and mountains behind, and when he smiles, I know he's thinking of it, dreaming of it the way I dreamed of that sled ride, a future where this truly is our forever home and he'll get to live that scene, our teen daughter grumbling, but only halfheartedly, because this will be her home, as it was his.

We're getting close. We've fixed so much and I think it's time I dare put out a hope to the universe. A hope that all the worst struggles are behind us . . . and I can hang up my homicide-detective cap for good.

Watch for Casey and Eric's final Haven's Rock adventure, coming in early 2027.

ABOUT THE AUTHOR

Kelley Armstrong is the author of more than fifty novels in mystery, fantasy, and horror. She believes experience is the best teacher, though she's been told this shouldn't apply to writing her murder scenes. To craft her books, she has studied aikido, archery, and fencing. She sucks at all of them. She has also crawled through very shallow cave systems and climbed half a mountain before chickening out. She is, however, an expert coffee drinker and a true connoisseur of chocolate-chip cookies.